RAVE R[illegible]
EMM[illegible]

A GEN[illegible]

"*A Gentle Magic* is a sweet [illegible] Ms. Craig's tale provides good entertainment."

—*Romantic Times*

"This is an enchanting romance with wonderfully written characters that seem to come to life and leap off the page at you. I applaud Ms. Craig on her creation of this magical series and I personally look forward to reading more of these stories."

—*Under the Covers Book Reviews*

"This one will bring tears to your eyes, laughter to your lips, and love to warm your heart!"

—*Huntress Book Reviews*

ENCHANTED CHRISTMAS

"A beautifully written satisfying book . . . *Enchanted Christmas* is just the book to get readers in the Christmas spirit."

—Robin Peek

"*Enchanted Christmas* is a delightful, uplifting read for the holiday season or any other time of the year. Her story will touch your emotions, and the magical happily-ever-after ending will leave you with a warm, contented feeling."

—*Bookbug on the Web*

"A sweet, enchanting and inspirational story full of the magic of Christmas and the wonder of love."

—*Romantic Times*

ROSAMUNDA'S REVENGE

"Ms. Craig displays a canny, or should I say canine-y, insight into the mind of a Yorkshire terrier."

—*Romantic Times*

"Ms. Craig will capture your attention, make you laugh and sigh as this lighthearted tale of adventure unfolds."

—*Under the Covers Book Reviews*

OUT OF THE FRYING PAN

"I'll do all the cooking for a month, Miss Heather. It won't cost you much at all, and by that time, you'll probably have the hang of it."

She squinted at him. "Why?"

He pressed a hand over his heart and blinked up at her as if her suspicion was painful. "Is it strange to want to help one's fellow man? I thought that sort of thing was expected out here on the wild western frontier."

She got a funny feeling he was teasing her, and she didn't appreciate it. "All right, Mr. D. A. Bologh, or whoever you are, what's your game? There's something very odd about this." She thought of something else. "Anyway, I'm sure Mrs. Van der Linden won't want a strange man in the house. She'll tell Mr. St. Pierre, he'll find out I've been getting help, and I'll get fired. I probably shouldn't have even let you in in the first place."

"Nobody has to know about our deal except you," D. A. Bologh said softly. "I'll see to it that not a single soul knows. I'm very good at that sort of thing."

"I'll just bet you are." She thought of something unsettling. "Are you a crook?"

He laughed. "A crook? Me? No. You might say I'm something of a gambler, though. I like to make deals with folks."

"Deals. What do you mean?"

"Like the one I'm going to make with you."

Oh, he was going to make a deal with her, was he? Well . . . Heather huffed, thinking about how terrible she was at cooking and how much she wanted Philippe St. Pierre's good opinion. Maybe he was.

Other *Leisure* and *Love Spell* books by Emma Craig:
CHRISTMAS PIE
ROSAMUNDA'S REVENGE

The *Land of Enchantment* series:
ENCHANTED CHRISTMAS
A GENTLE MAGIC
A GAMBLER'S MAGIC

Cooking Up Trouble

Emma Craig

EMMA CRAIG

LOVE SPELL BOOKS NEW YORK CITY

To the Lollies, with love

A LOVE SPELL BOOK®

October 2000

Published by

Dorchester Publishing Co., Inc.
276 Fifth Avenue
New York, NY 10001

ISBN 0-505-52398-1

Printed in the United States of America.

Cooking Up Trouble

Chapter One

Forever afterward, Heather Mahaffey blamed it on the wind. If the winds hadn't been particularly fierce that spring of 1895, she'd never have lost her head and done what she did.

But that spring the wind blew all day, every day. And it blew hard.

Folks woke up with their bedclothes sprinkled with fine, powdery dust that seeped in through cracks in their walls. Dust colored their hair and got into their food.

Children walked to school and arrived with their bare ankles red and raw, sanded by windborne grit. Clothes that were hung on lines had to be shaken out before they were folded. Even then, women despaired of ever seeing a white sheet again. Everyone's clothes took on a grayish cast—the color of the wind.

Farm wives and merchants wiped dust from

their furniture and wares every morning only to repeat the process in the evening.

Birds flapped forward and flew backward.

Mrs. Trujillo's cat, while attempting a leap from the fence onto Mr. Maynard's bald pate, got swept away by a gust of wind and ended up in Mr. Pollard's yard, frightening his dog under the house.

When cowboys on outlying ranches drove their herds down Main Street, the dust didn't hang in the air as it did during the summertime. Rather, the huge clouds of dust churned up by the cattle's hooves were blown by the wind into buildings and scraped the paint from the walls. Businessmen even stopped sweeping the boardwalks in front of their stores after a while; the gesture was so futile as to be downright depressing.

Therefore, Heather wasn't the only one who blamed the wind. Lots of folks went a little crazy during that blustery springtime in southeastern New Mexico Territory. The wind shrieked day and night, blowing to perdition everything that wasn't nailed down—and sometimes even things that were.

The steeple on Fort Summers's Southern Methodist Episcopal Church, erected by the congregation only the prior June, tumbled down, impaling one of Mr. Ojeda's hay bales and scaring his aging mother into a fitful string of prayers against the Methodists, from which it took her five days to recover. Mr. Ojeda wasn't a churchgoing man of any denomination, though, and so to him, his mother's prayers were almost more disturbing than the ruined hay bale itself. He didn't blame the Methodists; he blamed the wind. Heather, although a staunch Methodist herself, understood both points of view.

Mr. Custer's windmill blew over, too. The roof of the Packards' barn got blown into Mr. Gonzales's pasture and scared his cows out of a month's worth of milk.

More than one front door got ripped from its hinges when a child carelessly shoved it open; people learned that one had to hold onto doors if one expected to keep them attached to one's house.

It was not surprising, then, that Heather was sure it was the wind making her reckless that tempestuous April day. She knew it was the wind that propelled her into accepting the job Philippe St. Pierre had offered her as cook on his ranch.

If it wasn't the wind's fault, then Heather was in deep trouble, because she couldn't cook a lick. Her whole family knew it, so perhaps the wind had addled her father's brain, too, when he'd told Philippe how handy Heather was in the kitchen.

It had all started at the spring dance, held at the Fort Summers Civic Hall. Everyone who lived in the area went to the dance on that wind-whipped spring evening, because it had been rumored that Mr. St. Pierre would be there. He'd lived in the area for more than a year, but had until now been rather reclusive. Everybody wanted to snag this opportunity to meet him. After all, none of the folks who lived in Fort Summers or on the farms and ranches in the vicinity had ever met a wealthy man before. Life was a hardscrabble affair on the high plains, and it didn't afford men much in the way of riches. Except for a lucky few, like Philippe St. Pierre.

"He's from Louisiana," Geraldine Swift,

Heather's best friend, told Heather at the dance. "That's how come he has a French name." Her pale blue eyes, masked slightly behind her spectacles, glittered with curiosity.

Heather eyed Geraldine over her fan—even though the wind was raging outside, the Civic Hall itself was warm and stuffy, mainly because nobody dared open a window for fear the guests would be blown out the windows on the other side. "What does Louisiana have to do with it?"

Geraldine, who read a lot, looked superior. Heather didn't mind. As far as she was concerned, Geraldine *was* superior. She was also a great source of information. "Lots of Frenchmen live in Louisiana. The French used to own it, after all."

"Oh." That made sense to Heather. Sort of like the Spanish used to own New Mexico Territory. That's why there were a lot of Spanish-speaking folks living here.

"Anyhow, I don't know why he decided to move here to this out-of-the-way place, but he's established the biggest cattle ranch since John Chisum's day. Now he's rich as Croesus."

"Who's Croesus?"

Geraldine looked at Heather with pity, and Heather guessed she shouldn't have asked.

"Croesus was like Midas."

"Oh." Heather remembered Midas.

"Anyway," Geraldine continued, "everything the man touches turns to gold, and he's awfully rich."

"Mercy." Heather guessed Mr. St. Pierre must be rich if his operation rivaled Chisum's—she presumed in the days before Chisum went bust. Chisum's was an impressive act to follow. "I hope he's got more morals and higher standards than Chisum had."

Heather's foot began tapping when the fiddles started. She loved music and adored dancing. She hoped she'd get to dance with Mr. St. Pierre. A body could tell a lot about a person by the way he danced.

Geraldine giggled. "How you talk, Heather! I'm sure Mr. St. Pierre has morals and standards. And he's as handsome as the devil, too, isn't he?"

Heather glanced at her best friend again, and Geraldine blushed. Geraldine, a fine, upstanding young Christian woman, didn't often use words like *devil* in everyday conversation. Unlike Heather, Geraldine was extremely proper and well behaved.

However, Heather had to agree that Philippe St. Pierre was a very handsome man. And—good heavens! He was talking to her father.

Heather's heart hitched. She hoped Pa wasn't telling tales to Mr. St. Pierre. As much as she loved and honored her father, she'd lived with him for too many years not to understand his failings, one of which was a tendency to embellish his family's virtues and downplay their failings.

The men turned, and Philippe St. Pierre cast a bored-looking glance at Heather and Geraldine. The young women gasped in unison. Heather plied her fan wildly and whispered out of the corner of her mouth, "Oh, no! They're headed this way!"

Geraldine's own fan had been hanging on a ribbon at her side. She lifted it quickly, flicked it open, and hid behind it. Remembering her spectacles, she yanked them off and stuffed them into her skirt pocket. "Do you think they're coming to meet us?"

Her voice shook with half-terrified excitement.

"I imagine so." Heather, in contrast to her friend, was beginning to feel pretty gloomy. "I wonder what Pa's been telling him about me."

Shoot, she hoped he hadn't said anything too awfully outrageous. The last time Pa got carried away, he'd managed to convince a visiting lawyer that Jimmy, one of Heather's younger brothers, was a circuit judge. Since Jimmy was, at the time, only eight years old—a precocious eight, to be sure, but still and all—his term in office, if any, lay far in his future.

"I hope he hasn't said anything about me," Geraldine muttered.

Heather shook her head. "He won't. He only brags on his children. I wish he'd stop." She said it wistfully, knowing the wish to be idle. Patricia, Heather's older sister, had once thrown a king-sized temper tantrum at her father. The man had looked sad, apologized, and then gone out the next day to tell folks that his darling Patricia was going to be the finest actress the world had ever seen.

Most of the folks in town accepted Mr. Mahaffey's foibles as they accepted those of the rest of their neighbors. Fort Summers, sitting as it did in the southeasternmost part of the territory, smack up against the Texas border and hundreds of miles away from a city of any size, was too small and isolated for feuds to blossom successfully. People needed each other and, therefore, the citizens had become a far more tolerant lot than those of many other communities. Heather often had reason to bless them for their forbearance.

Of course, Mrs. Mahaffey was a saint, and that helped the family's standing in the community considerably. Heather believed her mother's overall wonderfulness did much to soften the effects of her father's tall tales. At least nobody called him a flat-out liar, a degree of restraint that the whole family appreciated.

He claimed he couldn't help it because he was Irish. Heather, never having met any Irishmen other than those in her family, all of whom shared her father's dramatic tendencies, had thus far discovered no reason to doubt him. She hoped this didn't bode ill for her own personal future. She'd hate to fall victim to some Irish curse that doomed folks in her family to a life of counter-veracity.

She breathed a relieved sigh when she saw that Pa and Mr. St. Pierre had been stalled in their forward progress by Mrs. Van der Linden. Heather believed Mrs. Van der Linden could stop a train if she took it in her head to do so. Stout and determined, the large woman didn't scruple to force herself and her opinions on others. She was happy to tell everyone that, unlike Heather's father, she believed in plain speaking, and that she always called a spade a spade.

Personally, Heather thought Mrs. Van der Linden sometimes jumped to conclusions, and that she'd called a shovel a spade on more than one occasion, but she'd never say so to Mrs. Van der Linden's face.

"Let's move," she suggested under her voice to Geraldine. "I don't want them to catch us." She took her friend's arm.

Geraldine resisted. "No. I want to meet him. I wonder if he's married."

"Lord, Geraldine, what difference does that make?"

"You never know. He might favor one of the local girls." She smiled musingly.

Heather wanted to smack her.

Geraldine sighed. "I've never seen such a handsome man."

"You can't see him now, either, unless you put your cheaters back on," grumbled Heather.

"Oh, I can't do that!" Geraldine cried, appalled. "What would he think of me?"

"He'd think you're a sensible young woman who isn't vain about her appearance." Heather wouldn't say so, but she didn't think Geraldine's specs detracted from her overall looks any, seeing as they weren't that great to begin with.

Heather, on the other hand, was acknowledged to be the loveliest girl in the village. Heather herself didn't put much stock in other people's opinions of her looks. She'd learned from the cradle that they counted for little in a rough-and-tumble world like the one in which she lived. Besides, she knew herself to possess many detrimental qualities that would negate her attractiveness to any sensible person. Indeed, she'd overheard Mrs. Van der Linden tell a neighbor, "Heather Mahaffey's beauty is a mockery. If there was any justice in the world, she'd be as ugly as her sins."

Still, Heather—while acknowledging that the woman had reason to be distressed at that particular time, since Heather had accidentally dyed Sissy, Mrs. Van der Linden's white cat, green—she didn't account one tiny accident as a sin. And that other time, if she'd been reading and allowed Bessy, the Mahaffey milk cow, to roam into Mrs. Van der Linden's onion patch, she was sorry about it. And she'd paid for the onions. Indeed, the entire

Mahaffey family had paid for that particular error by having to drink onion-tainted milk for three days. And she had to admit, the butter made from the same source had been rather interesting when spread on ears of hot, sweet corn.

But that was nothing to the point. "Please come with me, Geraldine. I don't think I want to know what Pa's said to that man about me."

"I do." Geraldine dug in her heels and didn't budge.

Heather sighed despairingly. Usually her bookish friend did as Heather asked, since Heather had the more forceful personality of the two, but every now and then she got a stubborn spell. From the expression on her face, Geraldine was in the thrall of one of those spells now.

"I'm going to get myself some lemonade." Heather, who could be pretty stubborn herself when circumstances called for it, dodged away and headed to the lemonade bowl. Her gratitude was unfeigned when Gil McGill offered her an arm.

"Let's dance, Heather."

"Happy to." She was extremely glad to be bounced off in Gil's arms, almost in time to the music. Gil wasn't much of a dancer, but he'd spared her what she feared might be an embarrassing encounter.

Her happiness in reprieve was short-lived. As Gil yanked her this way and that, Heather caught the occasional glimpse of her father and Mr. St. Pierre. "Fudge," she muttered. Mr. St. Pierre was looking directly at her, and her father was still talking. He was also making huge, sweeping gestures with his hands. Heather knew what that meant.

"Beg pardon?" Gil panted.

She gave him a smile that she knew to be stunning. She'd practiced, after all, and used it on certain boys when she wanted them to leave her alone. It usually stunned them into immobility, and she made her escape while they were still gawking. This time her smile made Gil stumble, but that was all right, because his stumble propelled them out of the line of Mr. St. Pierre's hot, French gaze.

"Oops. Sorry." Gil's face flamed red.

"Think nothing of it." Heather gave him another smile. This one evidently struck him dumb, for he didn't speak. He didn't stumble again, either, however, and Heather considered that an improvement. She managed to sneak discreet peeks at Philippe St. Pierre as she bounded around the dance floor with her partner.

She gulped. Mercy, but Mr. St. Pierre had dark eyes, and they were framed by the sootiest lashes she'd ever seen. He also appeared to have lots of dark hair; it shone in the lantern light and looked thick and wavy and fell almost to his collar. That was a lot longer than most men in Fort Summers wore their hair. Heather suspected Mr. St. Pierre would find it practical to keep his own hair short after the cattle season progressed toward summer, what with the heat and dust and all.

He also had darkish skin. Were all Frenchmen so dark? Heather's heart had begun to palpitate alarmingly. She chalked it up to the energetic dance and her partner's awkward steps.

The fiddles had been playing a lively tune and were building to a climax. The end arrived at last, and Heather and Gil came to a huffing stop. Gil snatched a bandanna out of his back pocket and wiped his brow. He grinned at Heather. "Thanks. That was fun."

"Thank you, Gil. I enjoyed it."

Heather turned and saw her father and Philippe St. Pierre. Blast! They'd found her again, and now they were heading for her like a couple of thirsty longhorns would charge a river. She knew she couldn't postpone the meeting any longer. It was probably better this way. The longer Mr. St. Pierre spent in Pa's company, the further Heather would fall in the Frenchman's esteem if he ever learned the truth. The good Lord only knew what sterling—and erroneous—attributes Pa had crowned her with this time.

Steeling herself, she smiled at the two men. Not her stunning smile, this expression was one meant only to welcome Mr. St. Pierre to the community. It was friendly. Pleasant. Not necessarily inviting. Neutral. Yes indeed. It was the most neutral smile Heather had in her repertoire.

He, on the other hand, had about the coldest expression on his face that Heather had ever seen. She swallowed. He looked intimidating, actually. She caught a glimpse of Geraldine in the crowd behind her father, and wished she hadn't tried to avoid the introduction before. Now she'd have to meet the man all by herself, without her friend for support.

Bother! What was wrong with her? She'd met men before. She cranked her friendly smile up a notch. "Hello, Pa. Nice dance, isn't it?"

"Aye, me girl, 'tis a lovely dance. And I have a new fella here who wants to meet you. I've told him all about you."

Mr. Mahaffey winked, and Heather's heart sank

to her dancing slippers. It was as she feared: Her father had been filling Mr. St. Pierre's head with exaggerated claims.

"Heather Mahaffey," her father went on. " 'Tis a pleasure to introduce you to the newest addition to our little community here in Fort Summers, Mr. Philippe St. Pierre."

Heather gulped and extended her hand. She even managed a small but creditable curtsy. Mr. St. Pierre bowed slightly, took her hand in his much larger, darker one, lifted it to his lips, and brushed a surprisingly potent kiss across her knuckles. She almost fainted dead away from the thrill that shot through her at the touch of his lips on her flesh.

"Charmed," he said, in a voice as thick and sweet as molasses.

"How do you do?" Heather was proud that her voice didn't tremble. She even managed to maintain a friendly smile.

She heard a muffled buzzing in the room—unless it was her ears ringing—and glanced around to see folks staring. Well, and why shouldn't they stare? Men didn't, as a rule, kiss women's hands in Fort Summers. She saw Geraldine gaping with her mouth open, and Heather lifted her fan to hide her mouth as she grimaced at her. She didn't want Mr. St. Pierre to see the grimace. It did its work, though. Geraldine understood immediately, shut her mouth, and stopped gaping.

Because she was worried, Heather said, "I, ah, hope my father hasn't been filling your head with fanciful tales about his children, Mr. St. Pierre. He, ah, tends to extol us to an unwarranted degree."

"He's been telling me tantalizing tales about your many talents, Miss Mahaffey."

Blast. Exactly as she'd feared. She refused to allow her smile to waver.

"Please be aware that my father always fails to see his children's flaws, Mr. St. Pierre. Whatever he's told you, I'm sure he's exaggerated."

"Pisht!" cried her father, slamming a hand over his heart as if Heather's words had cut him to the quick. Heather rolled her eyes. "The lass is the brightest thing on these plains, Mr. St. Pierre. I'm sure you can assess her charms for yourself, but she's got amazing talents, too. Amazing."

Mercy sakes, how was she ever going to live this down? Another glance around confirmed Heather's worries. Every single person who was close enough to hear Pa was snickering behind their hands or fans and eyeing one another. They were going to be talking about this for the rest of her life; she knew it. Nothing good for gossip ever died here in Fort Summers, because there were so few tasty stories available.

"That's not true, Pa, and you know it," she muttered. "You just love us too much, is all."

Philippe St. Pierre smiled, and again Heather feared for her consciousness. Lord above, the man's smile ought to be outlawed.

"Can a father love his daughter too much?" His voice was like silk. Very dark, very expensive silk.

She swallowed. "Er, no, I suppose not."

"And surely you don't mean to cast doubt on your father's integrity."

Did he have a faint trace of some kind of accent? There was a southern drawl, of course, but Heather thought she detected something else.

Something foreign. Maybe French? Cajun? She had no idea what a Cajun was. She'd have to ask Geraldine if she survived the evening.

"My father is a marvelous man, Mr. St. Pierre," Heather said a little stiffly. "But he can never be brought to admit that his children have faults."

"Not a terrible failing in a father," Philippe said dryly.

"No, I guess not."

"Ach, Heather, you're only bein' modest." Her father shook his head and smiled sadly.

"I wish that were so," she said, with absolute honesty.

Mr. St. Pierre chuckled. His chuckle was deep and rich, like his voice, and it warmed Heather like melted chocolate. Gads, she had to get her imagination under control.

"I'm sure your father is right, Miss Mahaffey," he said. "I believe it's traditional for young ladies to disparage their own accomplishments in hopes that others will laud them."

Huh? Heather squinted up at him. That's another thing: The man was tall. And broad-shouldered. And built like a mountain. An elegant, suave, sophisticated, muscular mountain. She wished she hadn't noticed. "I fear that's not the case here, Mr. St. Pierre."

"Nonsense," her father said heartily. "I've only told the truth."

I just bet. "Good. I'm glad."

"And since Mr. St. Pierre's established himself and has built that spanking new house east of town, he's lookin' for a household staff to work in it as well as men to keep the ranch and grounds in shape."

"Oh." Heather's interest perked up. That actually might put a different light on things. If the man needed maids and such, Heather might be able to land herself a job. The good Lord knew her family could use the money. Her father, as delightful a raconteur as ever lived, was relatively dismal in the money-making department. All of the boys worked here and there, and Patricia helped Mrs. Wade with her sewing and served at the local chop house during busy times. Their mother took in laundry.

Heather, the most useless of the lot, would be willing to do almost anything, but folks tended to avoid asking her. Her heart pinged painfully, and she wished for at least the thousandth time that she'd been given grace and skill along with her beauty.

But even she, useless Heather, could dust and mop floors. And she could probably even help with the domestic animals, although men tended to doubt women's abilities when it came to outdoor activities. The unhappy truth was, however, that Heather could cowboy with the best of them. It was the female talents she lacked. She couldn't sew a straight seam to save her life, and the last time she tried to cook, the family had to vacate the house until the smoke cleared.

She'd lost track of the conversation between her father and Mr. St. Pierre until she caught her father's last several words and her eyes nearly started from their sockets. Her mouth fell open, and she shrieked, *"What?"*

The room went still, and Heather felt heat creep into her cheeks. She cleared her throat. "I, ah, beg your pardon, I don't believe I caught your last few words, Pa." Because she didn't trust him, she lowered her eyebrows and glared at him, hoping in that way to make him behave.

She ought to have known better. Nothing could keep her father's tall tales in check once he got started. He winked at her, a sure sign that bad things were to come.

"Ah, and I know you're a modest girl, Heather Mary Mahaffey, but you should learn to accept these little compliments you get paid." He turned to Mr. St. Pierre. "It's as I was tellin' you, Mr. St. Pierre, my Heather's not only the loveliest creature in this world, but she's also the best cook in the territory."

A gasp went up in the room.

Oh, no. Heather closed her eyes and prayed for help from above. Or even below. Any kind of help at all would be welcome at the moment.

"Is that so?" Philippe St. Pierre eyed Heather with more interest than he'd formerly exhibited.

"Aye—"

"No, it's not true. Not one tiny little bit." Heather tromped over her father's words almost desperately. "I'm probably the worst cook in the territory, not the best. Not anywhere near the top. No, sirree, Bob. I'm about the lousiest cook you've ever seen, Mr. St. Pierre. I nearly poisoned the whole family the last time I cooked supper."

It might have been her imagination that made her hear a townful of breath exhalations, but Heather didn't think so.

There went his smile again. Heather's heart was thumping too hard for her to experience the full effect of those gleaming white teeth against his dark skin. She wanted to scalp her father, even loving him as she did.

Why me, Lord? The Lord didn't answer, but Mr. St. Pierre did.

"I'm in need of a cook, Miss Mahaffey."

She goggled at him. "But I just told you I can't cook."

He chuckled again, sending her emotions rioting. This wasn't fair. Not only was her father out-and-out lying about her, but this wretched French Louisianan's presence was so overwhelming that it muddled her thought processes so that she couldn't rebut anything properly.

"Your modesty is most becoming, especially in such a lovely young woman—"

"But—"

Philippe held up a hand, stopping Heather's protest before it had even had a chance to form. "No more of this, please, Miss Mahaffey. I trust your father to know you and your skills. If you're interested in cooking for me, I should be happy to hire you. There aren't, after all, cooks waiting on every street corner, begging for work."

This was true. For one thing, there were perilously few street corners in Fort Summers. For another thing, most of the folks who lived here already had enough to do keeping body and soul together. They couldn't afford the time to cook for other people.

Heather decided it was futile to argue further. She smiled up at him. "Thank you, Mr. St. Pierre. I think I'll have to decline your generous job offer. I—ah—am already employed."

His eyebrows went up. "Oh? Your father had given me to understand that you might be interested in employment."

Blast. Heather shot her father a look she hoped

would curdle his liver. Fat chance. Her father was impervious to most things and extremely so to Heather's killing looks. "He, um, didn't know."

"Ah. I see."

All Heather wanted to do then was crawl away and die. Fortunately she didn't, and, as the party progressed and the moment of her humiliation receded into the unhappy past, her spirits rose. She ended up dancing her feet off and having a wonderful time.

Mr. St. Pierre claimed her for the last waltz. He was as wonderful to dance with as he was to look at, and she went home in a dreamy mood. She might be the world's worst cook, and she might have an embarrassing father, but she could dance like one of those Irish fairies her father was always talking about. And she'd finally met a man whose skill on the dance floor equaled her own. She wished she'd been able to dance with him all night. If she had, her feet probably wouldn't be aching so much.

She went to sleep and dreamed about Philippe St. Pierre, and awoke the next morning wishing she could dance with him for the rest of her life in a castle far, far away, in a land of green grass, tall trees, and lush meadows. Dotted with wildflowers. Fragrant with honeysuckle and roses and stuff like that. And with a resident cook who was so good, Heather never, ever had to set foot in a kitchen again.

As the days passed and the winds continued and Heather sneezed out dust and grit every few hours, those pleasant fantasies of her after-dance dreams faded from her mind.

Four days after the dance, the wind blew the

laundry line down, flinging all of the clean sheets into the dirt.

The young peach tree in the back yard, the one Heather had been pampering like a baby, finally gave up its fight against the wind and cracked right in half.

The hinges holding the door to the Mahaffey barn, stressed beyond endurance with the dry weather and relentless wind, tore away from their moorings and the door sailed into the pasture fence, knocking it flat. The cows would have escaped but for their reluctance to walk into the wind.

The bucket of milk Heather carried from Bessy in the barn to the kitchen door got full of grit when the cloth with which she'd been attempting to protect it blew away.

Patricia's dress caught a gust and flew over her head, causing her to trip over the stile and fall flat on her face, squashing the tomatoes she'd been bringing home for supper.

Heather's older brother, Jerry, while accepting a shipment of hardware from Santa Fe, got conked on the head with the sign that he'd planned to hang over his shop. He had a lump the size of a goose's egg, and his poor pregnant wife had to clerk in the store for a week while he recovered.

Jimmy's homework paper got carried by the wind into Sissy Furbush's yard. Sissy found the paper and gave it to her brother Sammy. Sammy erased Jimmy's name, turned the paper in, and received Jimmy's A from the schoolmarm. Poor Jimmy got an F for failing to do his homework, even though everybody in town knew that Sammy couldn't string two coherent English sentences together if he tried for a year.

Little Henry Mahaffey, making his way home from school, was blinded by blowing dirt and walked smack into Mr. Lopez's mule, Tom, who resented it and kicked poor Henry. Mr. Lopez, smiling apologetically, carried Henry home in his wagon, but the boy's arm was broken and there was no denying it.

Of course, the family had very little money with which to pay Doc Grady, who was kind enough to say he'd wait and take eggs in exchange for his services. Since the hens were as upset by the horrible weather as the humans in the community, their egg-laying had slowed almost to a complete stop.

That was when Heather decided she didn't care if she was the worst cook in the territory. Or even the whole wide world. Her family needed money, and she needed to do *something* to help them out.

It was no surprise, therefore, that she ever afterwards blamed the wind for forcing her to walk—heading directly into the wind and nearly losing her way in the blowing dust—to Philippe St. Pierre's huge ranch house a few miles east of town, and ask if the job of cook was still available.

Chapter Two

Mrs. Van der Linden answered Heather's knock at Philippe St. Pierre's door. Heather gaped at her for a moment before she recollected the rumor that the women was now working as Mr. St. Pierre's housekeeper.

Blast. One more hurdle to overcome.

Mrs. Van der Linden looked her up and down, leaving Heather in no doubt, if she'd harbored any, that the stout and fussy matron didn't want Heather there.

"What do *you* want?" Mrs. Van der Linden asked uncivilly.

Heather cleared her throat and clasped her hands together. If this had been any other time or any other house, she might have told Mrs. Van der Linden exactly what she thought of ungracious people who answered other people's doors and then rudely barked at the knockees. She was too nervous to be indignant on this occasion, though.

"Um, I'd like to talk to Mr. St. Pierre about a job he said was available, actually."

Mrs. Van der Linden sneered. "And what kind of job do you think you're fitted for, Heather Mahaffey?"

"Um, actually, I think he needs a cook." Her voice went so low on the last word, she couldn't even hear herself.

"I couldn't hear you," Mrs. Van der Linden said, raising her voice to counter Heather's lowered one. "What did you say? Spit it out, child."

Heather would have liked to spit at Mrs. Van der Linden. She didn't, of course. Instead, she sucked in a deep breath and said, "I came to apply for the position of cook."

Mrs. Van der Linden's eyes opened so wide, Heather got nervous. She added hastily, "Or any other job that's available. Henry got his arm broken, and we need money to pay Doc Grady, and even though he said he'd take eggs, the hens aren't laying, and I thought I'd try to earn some money if—"

"A job as the *cook*?" The woman's voice cracked. "Are you out of your mind, child? You can't boil water, and the whole town knows it."

"What's going on out here?"

Mrs. Van der Linden's face flushed. Heather would have felt a grim sense of satisfaction about that if Philippe St. Pierre's deep and smoky voice hadn't frozen her in her tracks. She tried to swallow again, but discovered a boulder had lodged in her throat and she couldn't.

Mrs. Van der Linden recovered first, which Heather resented. The old coot pointed at Heather as if she were a pile of rags that had blown in. "This person had the audacity to come to the front door to apply for a position as your cook, Mr. St. Pierre. I was about to tell her that people of her stamp should use the back door."

Philippe squinted at Mrs. Van der Linden as if she were a rare and not especially welcome species of animal come to plague him. Heather might have been amused if she hadn't been so frightened.

"Nonsense," he said, making Heather jump a little. "Miss Mahaffey is a neighbor, Mrs. Van der Linden. Neighbors don't need to use the back door, even when they're applying for work." He smiled at Heather, who had to grab the door frame or fall over. "In fact, I believe that in the egalitarian West, no one should be obliged to use the back door. Otherwise, what's the point? Won't you step inside, Miss Mahaffey?"

Heather blessed Geraldine, who had explained to her what *egalitarian* meant for a vocabulary test once, and followed Philippe into the house. She didn't even smirk at Mrs. Van der Linden as she passed the older woman, mainly because she was too nervous. Philippe led her into a wood-paneled room that was loaded to the ceiling with books. It also contained a huge, beautifully polished mahogany desk. There were papers stacked on the desk, at which Heather presumed he'd been working before she'd knocked at his door.

He waved Heather to a big leather sofa before he took the big leather chair behind the desk. "Please be seated, Miss Mahaffey, and tell me to what happy circumstance I owe the pleasure of your visit today."

A pleasure, was it? Heather wondered how long

that would last. Not past the first meal, or she missed her guess. She cleared her throat. "Um, I wondered if the position you spoke to me about was still available. Sir." She added the *sir* because he suddenly seemed so imposing.

He shut his eyes and tipped his head back, as if he were trying to see the ceiling without using his eyesight. Heather watched him, fascinated. Suddenly his head righted, his eyes opened, and he stared straight at her. Again she jumped, then told herself to stop acting like an idiot. A tiny part of her mind told her it was too late for that.

"I'm afraid I don't recall—oh! Of course, you're the cook, aren't you?"

"No," Heather said honestly, then gritted her teeth. "I mean, I've never cooked professionally, but I'm willing to, um, try." Oh, sweet mercy, what was she doing?

She was helping her family, is what she was doing. She told herself that firmly and commanded her nerves to calm down. They didn't.

"Ah, yes."

His smile was a work of art. He was, hands down, the most spectacular male Heather had ever seen in her life. The fact that he was so different from any other man she'd ever met only augmented the impression of foreignness. Or something. It didn't seem quite fair of God to have given this man so many gifts. Anyone who had his face, for instance, shouldn't have that incredibly well-muscled body. He should be skinny and pale, like one of those sickly—but handsome—poets she'd read about.

Not Philippe St. Pierre. Philippe St. Pierre looked like Heather's notion of Hercules.

She attempted a little smile when he didn't go on, but wasn't sure if it was effective or not. "Um, yes. That's the one, all right. Cook."

"I see. I believe the position is still open, Miss Mahaffey. Mrs. Van der Linden has been serving in that capacity as well as that of my housekeeper, but if you'd like the job, it's yours. I'm sure Mrs. Van der Linden will be pleased. I don't think she likes cooking much."

"I'm sure." Heather wished it were so. Even if Heather were the most accomplished cook in the territory, Mrs. Van der Linden wouldn't be happy. In truth, Heather knew the woman would love nothing better than to see Heather fail miserably. She feared she was going to make the housekeeper happy all too soon.

"I am pleased to have you as part of my household, Miss Mahaffey."

"You are?" Heather mentally kicked herself. "That is to say, yes, I'm glad too. Thank you." Lord, she was doing this all wrong.

"When will you be available to start?"

Heather gazed at him blankly. "When? Um, anytime, actually." Now, in fact.

"Fine."

Philippe stood, and Heather was reminded once more that he was a very tall man. She blinked up at him, wishing this wasn't her real life, but some sort of fairy tale in which she was Cinderella and he the handsome prince. He could fill the role, hands down, no matter how ill she filled hers.

"Why don't you pack up your belongings and begin working for me the day after tomorrow, then. Will that be enough time for you to gather everything together?"

"Er, yes. Certainly." Heather, feeling uncomfortable with him towering over her, stood too. He still towered over her, but she felt better about it. "Um, you want me to live here?"

He cocked his head. She wished he wouldn't do that. Every time he tilted his head that way, she had a mad impulse to run her fingers over his cheeks and lips. Shoot, she'd better get herself under control soon.

"Most of the household staff sleep here, Miss Mahaffey, since my ranch is so far removed from the town. It seems to work out well that way. Otherwise, I fear you'd never get any rest at all." He smiled kindly, and Heather felt silly. "After all, you'll have to be up early to prepare breakfast and stay up late putting food away and cleaning up after supper."

"Of course." She managed a fairly commendable laugh. "I hadn't thought, is all."

He smiled at her, and she got light-headed. This was terrible.

"Fine, then," he said. "I'm looking forward to your tenure as my cook, Miss Mahaffey."

"Thank you."

He pulled a red velvet rope beside his desk. Heather had never seen a real bell pull before. She'd read about them in novels. She heard Mrs. Van der Linden stomping to the door before the door opened and the older woman entered the library.

"Yes, sir," the housekeeper said. Disapproval dripped from the two words, and Heather was surprised. She hadn't believed even Mrs. Van der Linden was bold enough to so clearly express disapproval of an employer's activities.

"Mrs. Van der Linden, I believe you're acquainted with Miss Heather Mahaffey," Philippe said, his voice sounding benign and reasonable.

"Humph," said Mrs. Van der Linden.

Heather smiled and gave the woman a little finger wave. The only thing her gesture produced was another grunt from her enemy.

"Miss Mahaffey has agreed to come to my ranch and cook for me."

This time Mrs. Van der Linden sneered. "Oh, she has, has she?"

"Yes. She has. And I'm very pleased about it." The glitter in Philippe St. Pierre's eyes would have stopped Heather in her tracks had it been directed at her.

Even Mrs. Van der Linden was affected by it. She stiffened, bobbed a curtsy, and said, "Yes, sir."

"Indeed." The word was said with icy clarity. "And I expect you to extend every courtesy to her."

Heather almost protested. After all, Mrs. Van der Linden already hated her guts. If she had to be courteous as well, Heather feared the woman would explode.

"Of course," Mrs. Van der Linden said, sounding not quite as sour as she might have. Heather took heart.

"Please see her to the door, Mrs. Van der Linden. She will begin her employment two days hence."

"Certainly, sir."

Mrs. Van der Linden shot a hot, mean scowl at Heather, who turned, said, "Thank you, Mr. St. Pierre," to Philippe, and fled.

Mrs. Van der Linden sped her on her way with a few well-chosen and not-very-nice admonitions, to which Heather paid no heed. Her head was spinning too sickeningly for her to pay attention to Mrs. Van der Linden, who everyone in town knew was a mean old biddy.

Mrs. Van der Linden's being a mean old biddy did not, unfortunately, negate the certain fact that Heather Mahaffey couldn't cook worth squat. She tried, in the two days left to her, to learn. Her mother tried to help her. Her sister Patricia tried to help her.

Heather managed to avoid learning a thing from either one.

"I don't know what's wrong with me." She was almost in tears as she stared at the chicken she'd failed to fry. It was lying in the pot, naked, looking soggy and sad. Heather knew just how it felt.

Patricia glanced unhappily at another burned pot—the one that had held the first chicken—and sighed. "It's because you don't really want to, Heather."

Heather rounded on her sister, shocked. "But I *do* want to! I'm supposed to be the man's cook, for heaven's sake! How can I be a cook if I can't cook?"

Patricia shrugged. On her, shrugs looked ladylike and delicate. Heather didn't understand it. "No you don't. Not really." She gave Heather one of her sweet smiles, and Heather nearly burst into tears. "You can do anything you really want to do, Heather. We all know it. If you *really* wanted to cook, you'd be the best cook in the world. You'd rather ride horses and round up cows and do things like that."

Heather hung her head, feeling that perhaps her sister spoke the truth. "But I need to be able to cook," she said feebly.

Patricia patted her on the shoulder. "I'm sure

you'll do fine, Heather. You're the smartest one of us all."

Heather gawked at her older sister, her astonishment unfeigned. "What?"

Patricia's musical laugh tinkled out, soft and pretty. "It's true, sweetheart. Everybody but you knows it."

Heather could only shake her head. Patricia was wrong. Heather knew it, but her sister's wrongness surprised her; Patricia was wrong about very few things.

Nevertheless, she didn't back down from her commitment to Philippe St. Pierre. Two days after she'd been hired by him to do a job for which she was unqualified, she stuck her few belongings in a pillowcase—the family owned no luggage—slung the pillowcase over her shoulder, and trudged the five miles to the ranch. The wind tried to blow her off her feet but, stubborn in the true Mahaffey tradition, she didn't let it.

Mrs. Van der Linden opened the door to Heather's knock, and Heather's heart sank even further than it had already.

"I hope you know what you're doing, Heather Mahaffey."

Heather smiled at the ogress—that is to say, she smiled at the woman. This was one of her sweet, good-girl smiles. She said, "So do I, Mrs. Van der Linden." From the sniff the older woman gave, Heather knew Mrs. Van der Linden had her own opinions, both about Heather and about her attempt to put herself across as a good and useful young woman.

"I've made his breakfast, and he's going to take

his noon meal in town because he has some business there. So you won't have to serve him a meal until dinnertime." Mrs. Van der Linden looked her up and down in a way that told Heather the housekeeper didn't expect her to be around for many meals after that.

When she was at last left alone in the kitchen, Heather glanced around with dismay. Good Lord, what had she done?

"You've gone crazy, is what you've done," she said to herself, not bothering to mince words. But she still held the job, at least until Philippe St. Pierre ate supper that night, so Heather decided she'd better begin making the most of the opportunity.

How in God's name could one make the most of a kitchen? Heather took a deep breath and refused to panic.

All right, the first thing she had to do was take stock. She took two more deep breaths to calm herself and then walked slowly through her new domain, pulling out drawers, peering into cupboards, and assessing things.

The icebox was a daunting appliance. It was as cold as winter in there, and it was full of things Heather didn't know what to do with. Foodstuffs. Meat. *Raw* meat. Eggs. Uncooked vegetables. Milk. Milk? Did grown men drink milk?

"I'm probably supposed to cook something with it," she muttered, wishing she knew what that something was and how to make it.

Sighing soulfully, she shut the icebox door and walked to the pie safe. It was empty, which probably meant she was supposed to fill it. Blast.

And there was the sink. It was a nice sink. Enameled. Nicer than the wooden tub Heather's family had to use. *Must be nice to have money*, she thought uncharitably.

Oh, and look there. Mr. St. Pierre was so rich, he even had a water faucet. Heather had seen pictures of water faucets. She turned this one on gingerly, and leapt back when water spurted out into the sink.

"Mercy." She heard the awe in her own voice, and told herself to get used to it.

Or maybe she shouldn't. As soon as Mr. St. Pierre ate his first meal prepared by Heather, she'd probably be tossed out on her ear. How humiliating.

Mercy sakes, look at the stove! Heather gaped at the gleaming range, one of the newfangled variety that had a variable temperature gauge and a hole in the top where you could set pots to keep soup warm. The range was big, too. The stove in her parents' house was tiny by comparison, and her mother had to feed six people. Mr. St. Pierre's cook only had to feed him. And perhaps one or two indoor servants. There weren't a battalion of flatirons set out on this stove, either, probably because nobody wanted to mar the surface of the shiny new appliance. Mrs. Van der Linden must keep her flatirons heating somewhere else.

My goodness, what a fabulous place this was.

Her heart ached when she turned to peruse the rest of the kitchen. There were two bins underneath the sink, one holding flour, and one holding sugar. Of course. Her mother had bins like that. That's because flour and sugar were used so much in the average kitchen. There was probably cornmeal somewhere, too. Heather thought she could probably make up a batch of cornmeal mush in a pinch because all that entailed was mixing water with the meal and adding a little pinch of salt.

Maybe not.

And look at all those pots and pans. Gleaming brass and cast-iron black, they hung on neat little hooks, only waiting for someone who knew what she was doing to take them down and cook in them. That cut Heather out.

Oh, and there were sacks of potatoes and onions and things, too. There was probably a kitchen garden that she'd be expected to care for. She opened the back door and looked outside. Yup. There it was.

"That's one thing I can do, at least," she said in order to bolster her self-esteem. "I'm good at gardening." For whatever that was worth.

As soon as she backed into the kitchen again and glanced around, what little dignity she'd just gained departed in a rush.

Gad, she'd never make it here. Feeling a good deal disheartened, Heather made her way to the pantry. There were tins of things and jars of things and boxes of things—baking soda, cornstarch, yeast, salt, pepper, coffee, tea. There was some oatmeal up there. The last time Heather had prepared oatmeal for her siblings, it hadn't turned out too badly. Of course, she'd had to throw a bunch of raisins in to disguise the lumps. Perhaps Mr. St. Pierre had some raisins in here somewhere. Oh, yes, there they were.

"Now, if only I can convince him to eat oatmeal for every meal, maybe I'll last for a week or so."

Right.

Well, there was no getting out of it now. Heather

had possessed the foresight to bring along an apron and one of her mother's cookbooks. Straightening her shoulders and telling herself to buck up, she put on the apron. Frantically she went over Patricia's kind words about her native ability. They didn't help a whole lot, but she wouldn't give up. Not yet.

She plopped the cookbook on the table that sat in the middle of the kitchen. Then, armed with her apron and a whole lot of grit, she plunked herself down on a chair and thumbed through the book, hoping to find something to prepare for dinner that was so easy even she couldn't ruin it.

"Fricasseed chicken and dumplings," she read. "I can probably boil a chicken, but I wonder if I can make a dumpling."

An incident from her checkered cooking past slithered into her memory, and she vetoed the dumplings. Maybe she could serve something else with the fricasseed chicken. Bread? But then she'd have to make the bread, wouldn't she? The last time she'd helped her mother with the bread-making, the whole batch had gone flat because she'd killed the yeast with too-hot water. Fudge.

She was sitting at the table, staring at the cook-book in black despair and praying for help from somewhere—anywhere—when a knock came at the back door, startling her. Heather looked up from the book and stared. Who could that be? Only one way to find out.

With a heavy heart, she heaved herself up and walked to it. She sighed with despair as she opened the door—and discovered herself standing face to face with a man who was, in his own way, as hand-some as Philippe St. Pierre. He had icy blue eyes, dark hair, and a droopy black mustache. He was a complete stranger, which was odd, considering Fort Summers was a small place and people generally knew each other—and, when a stranger did come to town, it was big news.

She stared at him, puzzled. "Yes? May I help you?"

He removed his hat and smiled. He had a lovely smile. Only it seemed a tiny bit sly. His smile made Heather's nerves skip. On the other hand, she was already a nervous wreck, so she was probably exaggerating the effect of his smile.

"How-do, ma'am. My name's D. A., and I understand you might need a little help with your new job. It would be my great pleasure to help you."

She blinked, sure she'd heard him wrong. "I, ah, beg your pardon?"

He chuckled low in his throat, and Heather's skipping nerves took to racing like frightened mice.

"I understand from friends that you might have taken on a job you're not quite sure of, ma'am. I'd be happy to help you."

Heather frowned at him. "I don't understand. How did you hear about my new job?"

"Word gets around, ma'am."

That might be true, but word of this guy hadn't gotten around to Heather, and that was a very unusual circumstance. Any time a personable young male stranger came to town, Geraldine and Heather were among the first to hear about it. Geraldine's parents, in particular, wanted to get Geraldine hooked up with a gent, married, and out of their hair—which didn't seem quite fair in Heather's estimation, as Geraldine was a credit to her family. Unlike herself. Heather shut the door on that unprofitable track.

She had less luck shutting the door on the stranger. Without her being aware of what he was doing, the man had maneuvered her backwards until he was inside the kitchen. How'd he done that? Heather glared at him, but he was no longer looking at her. Instead, he was surveying the kitchen as if he owned it.

"I still don't understand," she said, trying to reestablish her place of authority as Mr. St. Pierre's duly-hired cook, standing in her duly-assigned kitchen. So what if she was a fraud? This man couldn't possibly know that. Could he? Maybe the local gossip mill was even better than she'd believed it to be. Trouble was, she'd still never seen this man before. "Who are you?"

He winked at her and tossed his hat onto the table. Heather did not approve. "I told you. Name's D. A. D. A. Bologh."

"D. A. Below?" Odd name.

He laughed again. "Bologh. B-o-l-o-g-h."

"Oh." It was still an odd name, and he was an odd duck, even if he was handsome in a creepy sort of way. "What do the D. and the A. stand for?"

"My first and middle names."

Big help. She intensified her frown for his benefit, but it seemed to have no effect. She ought to have practiced frowns along with smiles, but she hadn't bothered. The more fool she. "You're new around here, aren't you?"

"New?" He threw back his head and laughed.

Heather didn't understand that, either. She didn't think she'd said anything even remotely funny.

"No, sweetheart, I'm not new here. Except, maybe, to you." He winked at her again.

Sweetheart? Heather stiffened. "I don't appreciate your attitude, Mr. Bologh, and I don't like strangers calling me sweetheart. If you haven't any business here, please leave." It suddenly occurred to her that perhaps he did have business here. She backpedaled quickly. "Er, are you a tradesmen? Do you have a delivery for Mr. St. Pierre?" Maybe it was part of the cook's duties to receive tradesmen. She knew nothing about running a big, elaborate house belonging to a rich man. For all she knew Mr. St. Pierre received shipments of merchandise from faraway places every day.

Ignoring her first suggestion, that he leave, D. A. Bologh sat in the chair lately vacated by Heather herself. "You might say I'm a tradesman. In a way."

What was that supposed to mean? Heather, already nervous and upset, bristled. "Listen, Mr. Bologh, I have a lot of work to do, and I want to get at it. If you have business here, please tell me what it is, so I can get on with my job."

"Your job?" He lifted an ironic eyebrow. "From everything I've heard, you're in over your head, Miss Heather."

Lord, wasn't that the truth? Still, Heather didn't relish his smirking way of expressing it. Actually, she didn't relish his knowing about her at all. Her nervousness burned up in a fit of wrath.

"Now you listen here, you." She poked her finger emphatically on the table in front of him. "I don't know who you are, don't care who you are, don't have any idea why you think you know anything about me, but I want you to leave now. I have work to do."

"Yeah?" He smiled up at her, not at all benignly. "And how do you expect to set about it? From everything I've ever heard, you're more apt to burn the place down than fix a meal."

"Who *are* you! I've never seen you before! How do you know anything about me?"

"Word gets around," he repeated.

"Well, you can take your word and everybody else's, and go away right this minute, if you please."

"Wait a minute, sweetheart—"

"I'm not your sweetheart!"

He laughed again. "Maybe not, but I can help you."

"I doubt it."

"Ah, but I can. You see, I'm willing to do the cooking for you. For a whole month. And it won't cost you much at all."

She gaped at him. "What? What did you say?"

He held his hands up. "I'm serious, Heather—"

"And I didn't give you leave to call me Heather, either."

This bit of defiance earned her another laugh. She huffed indignantly. "Yes, Miss Heather." His tone was mildly sarcastic. "But, if you'll only listen to me, I think we can strike a bargain here."

"I doubt it." Although she had been told by friends all her life that most men weren't to be trusted, Heather had never really run up against one who she feared wanted to take advantage of her. Until now. She didn't trust this handsome devil an inch.

"Honest Injun," D. A. said, grinning. "A little bargain, is all I'm suggesting. I'll do the cooking for you in exchange for something really, really small."

She was back to frowning. "How do I know you can cook?"

"How do you know I can't?"

Bother. She hated this word-bandying. "If you were to cook for me, what would you want in return?"

"Oh, an exchange of some sort."

"An exchange of what sort, exactly?"

He shrugged. "Haven't decided yet. Nothing much."

"What kind of 'nothing much'?" For all she knew, he wanted her to kiss him. Or more. She blushed, thinking about how much more than a kiss he might require of her in payment. Most of the men who lived out here were gentlemen, but she'd heard stories.

Obviously, he suspected what she was thinking, because he grinned again. "Heather, Heather, Heather, get your mind out of the dirt."

"It's not in the dirt!"

He laughed again, outright. "I promise you that I won't require much in exchange for the services I aim to perform for you." He adopted a wide-eyed, innocent expression that looked remarkably out of place on his sly, handsome face. "And you can watch me and see how I do it. That way you can learn your way around a kitchen. On-the-job training, is what they'll call it one of these days." He buffed the well-manicured nails of his right hand on his shirtfront.

Heather stared at his hands, which were too clean for anybody living rough out here in the territory. And what did he mean about that on-the-job training nonsense? She almost asked him who he was again, but she knew he'd only tell her his name was D. A. Bologh. Trying a different tack, she asked, "Where are you from, Mr. Bologh?"

He shrugged. "Here and there. Mostly down south, but I get around."

Big help. "How do you know about cooking?"

"Like I said, I get around."

She had a feeling she was making a big mistake, but his offer tempted her. "Um, how do I know you won't ask for more than I'm willing to give in exchange for your help?"

"I never ask more than a person's willing to give, Miss Heather." His expression turned guileless again. "I'm here to help. You need help. I've heard stories about how you get on in a kitchen, sweetheart, and believe me, you need help."

Shoot, wasn't that the truth? Heather frowned down at him for several moments. He gazed up at her, a half smile on his face, his icy blue eyes wide. She couldn't read any expression at all on his countenance at the moment. The slyness had faded. Even the guilelessness was gone. He was just looking at her—a blank.

Blast. What could she do? "You promise you won't ask me for much in return?"

"Absolutely," he said.

Why didn't she believe him?

"Let me think for a minute."

He waved a hand. "Think away. You've got about an hour or so. After that, one of us will have to get busy fixing dinner."

Dinner. Oh, Lord. Heather nearly lost what was left of her self-control and wailed in anguish. She turned and walked to the kitchen window. When she peered outside, she caught sight of Philippe St. Pierre, standing out by a nearby corral, talking to Gil McGill, who worked as wrangler on the St. Pierre spread. Seeing Gil made her feel better—more normal, or something. The young man was solid, a man of the earth. She understood Gil and others like him.

Mr. St. Pierre, on the other hand, made her break out in shivers. Hot shivers. She didn't understand it, but she rubbed her hands over her arms, trying to get her gooseflesh to settle.

Then there was Mr. Bologh, sitting like a lump in the middle of the kitchen, peering around as if he hadn't a care in the world, drumming his fingers lightly on the table. He began whistling softly, a plaintive old tune popular several years before, during the War Between the States. It always gave Heather the tingles when she heard it.

His offer was awfully tempting. If he meant what he said and could cook, her job was safe for a day, at least. But what then? She decided to ask.

"What about after dinner?"

He glanced up and smiled at her. "Beg pardon?"

"What about other meals? If you cook tonight, that still leaves me to struggle with breakfast, lunch, and dinner tomorrow. And the next day, and the next, and the next."

He held up a hand to forestall further protests. "I already told you a month. I'll do the cooking for a month, Miss Heather. It won't cost you much at all, and by that time, you'll probably have the hang of it."

She squinted at him. "Why are you doing this, Mr. Bologh? I still don't understand."

He shrugged. "Little things like this amuse me."

"You're a very strange man," she muttered, realizing as she did so that she was being mighty uncivil. But she was unnerved, both by his presence and by his offer. Not to mention her own inadequacy to deal with the job she'd been hired to do.

He pressed a hand over his heart and blinked up at her as if her words hurt his feelings. "Is it so strange to want to help one's fellow man? Or, in this case, woman? I thought that sort of thing was expected out here on the wild western frontier."

She got a funny feeling that he was teasing her, and she didn't appreciate it. Crossing her arms over her breasts, she spoke sharply. "All right, Mr. Bologh, or whoever you are, what's your game?"

"My game?" He stared at her as if he couldn't imagine what she was talking about. "I have no game. I'm offering to help you."

"There's something very odd about this," Heather murmured. She thought of something else. "Anyway, I'm sure Mrs. Van der Linden won't want a strange man in the house. She'll tell Mr. St. Pierre, he'll find out I've been getting help, and I'll get fired. I probably shouldn't have let you in in the first place."

"Nobody ever has to know about our deal but you and me," D. A. Bologh said softly. "I'll see to it that not a single soul knows."

"How are you going to do that?"

"Oh, I'm very good at that sort of thing."

"I'll just bet you are." She thought of something that completely unsettled her. "Say, you're wanted by the law, aren't you? Outlaws are always running out here to escape their misdeeds in the States. Is that why you don't want anyone to know about—"

He cut her off. "I'm not the one who doesn't want anyone to know about this deal, Miss Heather. You're the one. I don't care if the whole world knows I'm helping you."

"Oh." She frowned at him for another minute or two. "You mean you're not a crook?"

He laughed. "A crook? *Me?* No."

"Oh."

"You might say I'm something of a gambler, though. And I like to make deals with folks."

"Deals. What do you mean?"

"Like the one I'm going to make with you."

Oh, he was going to make a deal with her, was he? Well . . . Heather huffed. Maybe he was.

"Better think fast, Miss Heather," he suggested. "Time's running out."

"I know." She turned, walked to the window and looked outside again, turned back, glared at D. A. Bologh, and said, "Very well. I'll do it."

D. A. Bologh got up from the chair and walked over to her, his hand held out to shake on the bargain. It was all she could do to keep from shrinking back from him. She'd never had this reaction to a person before, and it troubled her. Was it that she didn't trust him?

Maybe. But there was something else, too, and she couldn't put her finger on it. He gave her an uncomfortable feeling that something bad was going to happen.

Stop it, Heather Mahaffey! she scolded herself. *Something bad has already happened: You took a job you're unfit to fill.*

When she looked at it in that light, she wasn't as

reluctant to take the hand D. A. Bologh held out to her and shake it.

"Deal?" he said.

"Deal," she said.

She had the oddest sensation that her fate had just been sealed.

Chapter Three

Heather had to admit that Mr. D. A. Bologh, the man from nowhere, was as efficient as anything she'd ever seen in the kitchen. He didn't even put on an apron, but as soon as the bargain was struck, he got to work.

He didn't ask Heather where anything was, but went here and there, picking out potatoes and onions, carrots and green beans, flour and milk and chickens. He worked so fast, Heather sometimes had the sensation that her vision was blurring. She even rubbed her eyes once or twice.

"What can I do to help?" she asked as he filled a pot with water and set it on the stove to boil.

"Not a thing. Just watch." He winked at her.

Heather watched, but she didn't believe what she saw. She could have sworn she saw a spatula fly across the room and into D. A. Bologh's hand, but when she mentioned it, he only laughed at her.

"That's an old trick amongst us cooks, Miss Heather. I'm surprised you fell for it."

"Oh." She puzzled that one over for a minute. "Ah, have you ever worked in a circus or anything? As a magician, maybe?"

"I've done my share of this and that."

That told her a whole lot. His lack of candor grated on her nerves. She watched him some more, frowning. He caught her at it and grinned some more.

As if he knew her nerves were shaky, he said, "I've worked at all sorts of odd jobs, Miss Heather. I've done lots of entertaining. You might say my whole life's been a circus of one sort or another."

"Really? My brother Henry would like to be a clown."

"Ah, yes. Kids love the clowns."

He tossed an onion in the air, slashed at it with a knife, and it fell to the counter, split into four neat sections. Heather was absolutely certain she'd never seen anyone do that before. Even her mother didn't have this man's facility with a knife, although she was a pretty good cook.

"How did you do that?"

"What?" He glanced at her over his shoulder. "Oh, the onion. It's an old trick. Learned it in the army."

"In the army?"

"Yeah. You can learn a lot about how to use knives in the army, if you keep your eyes open."

Ick. The only uses she could think of for a knife in the army were ones that involved human flesh, unless—"Oh, were you a cook in the army?"

"As I said, I've done all sorts of work in my life, Miss Heather. Lots of it with armies here and there. There's a lot of work for a man of my talents in the military."

"I see." She didn't see anything at all. She also didn't much like the gleam in his eyes. "Er, exactly what are your talents?"

"I'm demonstrating them to you as we speak."

As he spoke, he threw a potato in the air. As it spiraled down to the counter, D. A. held up his knife, and the potato was peeled before it landed. Heather rubbed her eyes again. "Did you really peel that potato by tossing it in the air?"

Yet another laugh. "I've got lots more tricks up my sleeve, Miss Heather. You just watch me."

"I'm trying to watch and to learn from you, but I think it might be easier if you were to go more slowly."

"Can't."

"You can't go more slowly?"

"Not if you expect me to get all this done in time to feed the master of the house."

"Oh."

"Pull up a chair and take a squint at how I work. You can learn a lot by watching."

She hadn't learned a blessed thing so far except that D. A. Bologh was some kind of an actor-type person, and immensely talented. Maybe he'd been a performer in the theater. Every now and then a traveling acting troupe would pass through town. The whole family had piled into their wagon and ridden to Roswell to see the circus once.

Since watching D. A. work didn't seem to be doing her a whole lot of good, she decided to ask some more questions. "What are you preparing?"

"Thought I'd whip up a tasty French dish. It's sort of a stew with beef and carrots and onions. A little garlic." He shrugged negligently. "Beef Bourguignonne is what they called it in the old days." He tapped his chin. "Maybe I'll do a sort of Wellingtonnish crust." He shrugged. "Maybe not."

Heather didn't care about the crust, Wellingtonnish or otherwise. "What old days?"

"Oh, around Louis XIV's time or so."

Heather felt her eyes open wide. "Louis XIV? What are you, some kind of cooking scholar? Have you studied the history of cooking? Do you look up old recipes in libraries or do research in foreign countries or something like that?"

"Ha! No, I don't have to do that, Miss Heather. They're all right here." He tapped his head. "No need to look anything up. I've been around long enough that I can cook any kind of dish from any time period you can possibly mention."

"You haven't been around since Louis XIV's time," Heather grumbled, wishing he were a more open and forthcoming person. He evidently knew cooking and what he was doing, and she'd like to learn from him. If he'd only go slower. She couldn't keep up with him.

He laughed again. "Sweetheart—whoops, sorry. I remember you don't want to be my sweetheart—"

"You got that right," she muttered.

"But I can cook up a dinner that the Pharaoh of Egypt might have eaten in 3000 B.C., if you want me to. Hard to get some of those ingredients anymore, but I can do it."

"Good heavens. You must have studied cooking for a long time."

"A very long time."

He had the wickedest grin on his face. Heather got the feeling she was missing some hidden meaning in his words, but she was becoming too fascinated watching him to concentrate much on anything else. She stood up suddenly, and squinted hard at a bottle that seemed to have materialized from nowhere, straight into his hand. He was pouring a big dash of reddish-purple liquid into the pot where he'd thrown some onions, carrots, and meat cubes. "What's that?"

"Burgundy wine."

"Burgundy wine? What's that?"

"Burgundy wine is wine."

Of course, Heather knew what wine was—but this was the New Mexico Territory. Folks didn't cook with wine here. If they used spirits at all, they took whiskey for snakebite or beer at the saloon in town. Cowboys were notorious for drinking too much whiskey and shooting off their guns on Main Street during cattle drives. Heather had never heard of anybody *cooking* with the stuff.

"Where'd it come from?" She hadn't seen any wine in any of the cupboards she'd looked in—and she'd looked in them all. Now there was suddenly a whole bottle of it in D. A. Bologh's hand. If this was another of his conjuring tricks, it was a very disconcerting one. Heather had opinions about folks who drank strong spirits, and they weren't good.

D. A. turned and gave her a pitying smile. "The man's from Louisiana, Miss Heather. He's used to fine dining. He keeps a stock of wine."

"But this isn't Louisiana," she said, feeling a little desperate. How could she ever learn to cook fancy like this? She couldn't even fry a chicken.

"I'm sure the man still wants to dine well."

She sighed. "I suppose so."

"Absolutely. Besides, he's of French heritage, and you know how the French are about their food."

Actually, she didn't know anything of the sort, but she wouldn't admit it. In the meantime, while D. A. Bologh fixed up a meal fit for a Louisiana king, Heather was still no farther along on her road to learning the fine arts of kitchen craft. His hands were a blur, and watching him work was making her dizzy. "Um, I don't suppose you can move a little slower now that you've got the pot on the stove, can you?" she asked without much hope.

"Nope. I do what I do, Miss Heather, and that's what you've bargained for." He tossed her another wink. "But keep watching. You're sure to pick something up if you only keep watching."

"Maybe."

The door opened at her back, and Heather whirled around, her heart in her throat. She gasped.

Philippe St. Pierre stood in the door of the kitchen, smiling at her. He sniffed the air appreciatively. "Smells good in here."

Unable to speak, Heather turned, trying frantically to think of some way to explain the presence of D. A. Bologh in this man's kitchen.

D. A. Bologh was gone.

"I do believe you've been hiding your light, Miss Mahaffey."

Heather tried to speak, but couldn't get her tongue around the words.

Philippe walked to the stove and lifted the lid on the pot. "It smells like something fit for a king."

Heather's mouth shut, opened, and she managed to blurt out, "Louis XIV."

He chuckled. Now when *he* chuckled, Heather wanted to curl up and purr. His chuckle didn't give her chills like D. A. Bologh's did. She figured both reactions on her part were bad.

Philippe turned, leaned against a counter, crossed his arms over his chest, and watched her. His lips were turned up a very little bit, giving him a little half smile that sent the blood galloping through Heather's veins like stampeding beeves. "Beauty and talent in one fine package. I'm impressed."

And then there was his voice. It caressed her. It petted her. It made her want to do unspeakable things with him. Good God, she was bad.

"Thank you." Remembering how many hours of smiles she'd practiced, Heather managed to paste one to her lips, but it didn't want to stay there.

"Thank *you*."

Mercy, mercy, look at those arms. Heather swallowed when she saw the way the fabric pulled over his biceps. It was unfair of him to be so gorgeous in every detail. God shouldn't expend all of his efforts on one human being because that wasn't fair to the rest of His creations. He ought to spread the masculinity out some. Gil McGill, for instance, could use a little of Mr. St. Pierre's suavity to counteract his gangliness.

"Um," she said. "You're welcome."

He'd crossed one leg carelessly over the other. Heather saw that his boots, while obviously good ones, were well-worn, and that his clothes had put in a full day's work. He evidently didn't let the ranch run itself, but got in there and worked with his men. Heather would have approved if she hadn't been so rattled. His trousers pulled over massive thighs the way his shirt pulled over his biceps, and gave Heather an idea of what was underneath the clothes. She wished they didn't. She was a red-blooded, full-grown female, and she didn't need to see sights like that. Or like the bulge between his legs.

She turned, suddenly embarrassed to death, and walked blindly to the sink, where she turned on the tap and pretended to wash her hands. She heard him walk up behind her, and smothered a whimper with difficulty.

"I meant to stop in to see you this morning, Miss Mahaffey, but I had to go to town. I wanted to make sure there was nothing you needed in the way of supplies."

Arming herself with a prayer and a deep breath, she turned again, and found him surveying the kitchen. His smile had gone. In its place was a small frown. He looked every bit as handsome frowning as he did smiling. That wasn't fair.

"Um, no. No, everything's fine, thanks." But what if it wasn't and she'd just lied to him? For all she knew, D. A. Bologh needed all sorts of things and had only been making do. "But—but I'll think about it, if that's all right, and get back to you."

"Fine. That's fine. I appreciate it."

"Oh, no. I appreciate your giving me this job."

"I'm sure you'll do very well."

He touched her cheek, and Heather sucked in a breath to keep from fainting.

"You're quite a surprise to me, Miss Mahaffey," he said in his deep, liquid voice that held faint traces of Louisiana and fire and smoke and all sorts of things Heather would give anything to learn about firsthand.

She knew not what to say to that, and so her employer walked to the door, opened it, and prepared to exit the room in silence. At the door he gave her a small salute, smiled, and left.

Heather sank back against the sink and fanned herself with her hand, sure she'd never recover.

Philippe St. Pierre sighed and sat back in his chair. Truth to tell, he hadn't, at first, held out much hope for Heather Mahaffey's working in his kitchen. Since meeting her at the barn dance, Philippe's ears had been assaulted by people's opinions of Heather's culinary abilities. According to town repute, Heather was nowhere near her father's claims.

Mrs. Van der Linden had been particularly blunt. "The man's a liar, Mr. St. Pierre, and the whole town knows it. He's always bragging about his children, embarrassing them no end. The girl's pretty enough, but she's a disaster in the kitchen. You'll see if you hire her, but you might have to call in Doc Grady if you ever expect to eat again."

Philippe had laughed at the woman's dire prophecies, but he'd stopped laughing after several others had given him similar opinions. Even people who liked and admired Heather weren't optimistic about her ability to put pots and pans to good use.

Gil McGill, who worked as a wrangler and who was clearly sweet on the girl, had even ventured to say dubiously, "If she don't work out in the kitchen, I reckon she can clean house or rope steers or something. She's good with cows."

His expression was eager, from which Philippe deduced Gil would welcome Heather's presence at the ranch. Not that he blamed the young man.

Heather Mahaffey was an eyeful, with her thick blond hair and sky-blue eyes. However, he had begun to doubt his wisdom in hiring her as his cook.

The problems that had started a week ago on his spread, however, had distracted him, and he hadn't given his new cook much thought. And when he did think about her, his thoughts ran to things other than cooking. She was quite an eyeful, Heather was, and she looked like she'd be quite an armful, too. Philippe was disgusted with himself for those thoughts.

He was now, however, ecstatic to learn that everybody had been wrong and that Mr. Mahaffey hadn't lied to him after all. Mrs. Van der Linden, looking stern and disapproving—she always looked stern and disapproving—entered the dining room to pour him some more coffee and set dessert in front of him. Philippe glanced at the dessert with interest.

"I didn't think I had room for anything else, Mrs. Van der Linden, but that looks too good to pass up. What is it?"

Mrs. Van der Linden sniffed. "Miss Mahaffey calls it an apple torte, although it looks like a skinny apple pie to me."

With another disparaging sniff, she plunked a pitcher of cream down beside Philippe. "She says you're supposed to pour some of this cream over it. *She* pronounced it *krem*. And it's thick as the dickens. Don't look like no cream I've ever seen." She mistrusted it; that much was plain.

Philippe chuckled and eyed the torte with renewed interest. "Ah, yes, a French dish, I perceive. The burgundy beef was superb. That was French, too, I daresay. I suppose she's trying to make me feel at home." His heart twisted, and he ruthlessly ignored it.

"Is she?" From the expression on Mrs. Van der Linden's face and the tone of her voice, Philippe deduced that she didn't approve of Heather's attempt at foreign cooking. She probably didn't trust that, either. Some of these territorials were ridiculously provincial and narrow-minded. "Hmm. I think she's doing an admirable job so far, and I hope she continues to do so."

Mrs. Van der Linden left in something of a huff. Ignoring the old cow's pique, Philippe poured a little cream on his torte and took a bite. It all but melted in his mouth, and he had to shut his eyes and savor it for a few moments before he allowed his natural cynicism to surface.

He took another bite and chewed thoughtfully. If little Miss Mahaffey was trying to make him feel at home, she was going about it all wrong. In order to do that, she'd have to feed him leftover tidbits from her lover's meals.

But that part of his life was over now. He'd made a successful new start, and had prospered. He was now reaping the rewards from all of his hard work, and he assuredly didn't mind adding fine dining to his list of attainments. He'd have preferred a style other than French, but if that's what Heather knew, that's what he'd get, he reckoned. He wasn't going to let her go simply for not knowing how to fix an Italian sauce. She was obviously too precious a find.

A glance around his new dining room gave him a slight pang, however. The blessed thing was so empty. This table, for instance, which could seat ten without a leaf being added, gleamed in lonely mahogany perfection. It seemed to mock Philippe and his achievements in life. What he needed was people seated at his table. Or something.

"Hell," he muttered. Dammit, he *had* achieved a lot. He'd pulled himself up by his own bootstraps, conquered poverty, misery, his own dismal origins, and fear, and made himself a fortune. If he'd done it alone, and if he had no one with whom to share it now, so much the better. He didn't want anyone, at least on a permanent basis. Philippe knew good and well that a family only drained a fellow. His own family had all but killed him before he'd broken away from it; and there had been only one other person in it besides himself.

His black musings were interrupted by Mrs. Van der Linden, who entered the room bearing the coffeepot. "Would you care for more coffee, Mr. St. Pierre?" She eyed his empty dessert plate bitterly, as if she resented Heather Mahaffey's having created so superb a meal.

"Thank you, Mrs. Van der Linden." On an impulse, he added, "Would you please ask Miss Mahaffey to come to the dining room? I'd like to tell her how much I enjoyed her first meal as my cook."

Her eyebrows rose in overt disapproval. She had bushy gray eyebrows, and they reminded Philippe of a couple of caterpillars crawling over her forehead. He stifled a grin.

"Yes, sir," she said coldly.

Philippe sighed as Mrs. Van der Linden waddled out of the room. He wasn't sure if it was a good thing that his housekeeper and his cook didn't get along. At least the housekeeper didn't get along with the cook. He had no idea what Miss Mahaffey's views were on Mrs. Van der Linden.

A few moments later, he barely heard a soft knock at the dining room door. Lifting his coffee cup, he said, "Enter," before taking a sip. He had to shut his eyes to properly savor the drink. Even the coffee was delicious.

Heather Mahaffey, looking absurdly frightened, her hands folded under her apron, tiptoed into the room, glancing around as if she expected something to jump out from behind the door and murder her. Philippe rose from his chair and smiled. She was certainly a pretty girl. Amazing that she could cook so well, too.

"Miss Mahaffey."

She jumped. "Yes, sir." Her voice cracked.

"Please, take a seat." He waved at one of the never-before-used dining room chairs.

"Oh, that's all right, sir. I don't need to sit." Then she swallowed convulsively. She was clearly afraid of him. How odd. Philippe wasn't accustomed to comely females being afraid of him. They were more apt to try to get him to seduce them so he'd have to marry them. Little did they know.

He cocked his head to one side and smiled quizzically. "There's no need to fear me, Miss Mahaffey. I won't bite." Although the notion was a tempting one.

"No, sir." She offered a strained laugh. "Of course not."

He shook his head. Obviously, she wasn't going to calm down anytime soon. He might as well take the bull by the horns and get it over with. "I wanted to tell you how very satisfying I found my first meal cooked by you, Miss Mahaffey. Your father didn't exaggerate about your skills in the kitchen at all."

"Thank you, sir. I'm, ah, glad you enjoyed it."

He waved a hand toward a chair. "Please, Miss Mahaffey, I insist that you sit. I enjoyed the meal very much."

Philippe didn't understand why a spasm of what looked to him like agony passed over Heather's face before she stumbled over to the chair he'd indicated and sat on its edge. She took several deep breaths, as if she were trying to prepare herself to endure some ghastly ritual.

This was extremely peculiar behavior on her part, by Philippe's way of thinking. He wondered if she'd taken all the local gossip about her poor cooking skills so much to heart that she no longer believed in her own immense talents. That would be a pity if it were true, and Philippe aimed to see that she understood how wrong her neighbors were.

"Please, Miss Mahaffey, try to relax."

"Yes, sir." She sat up straight and looked like she might break in half from tension.

Philippe sighed again. He took out one of the thin cigars he'd become accustomed to smoking when he lived in New Orleans, clipped the end, lit it, and sat back. He was so full of good food and contentment that he guessed he'd just have to relax for the both of them. "I'm curious, however, about a couple of things."

Although he'd have believed it to be impossible before it happened, her back got straighter. "What things?" The question came out in an agitated bark.

He eyed her without much appreciation. He didn't understand why she was in such a dither. Of course, he knew women found him attractive, and that they were sometimes nervous in his presence.

He'd been fending off females most of his life.

If that was Miss Mahaffey's problem, however, it surprised him, because she was so lovely in her own right. He'd have expected her to be an expert at manipulating men by this time in her life. Granted, there wasn't much scope for a vamp's talents in this out-of-the-way place. Or perhaps her family was more strict than Philippe had come to believe. He'd taken her father for a happy-go-lucky sort who would sooner take a nip than discipline his children.

He told himself to stick to the subject. "For one thing, I didn't know we had a supply of wine in the ranch house. I'm very happy to have discovered my mistake."

"You didn't know?" She sat forward on her chair and sucked in a deep breath. "Oh, dear."

He waved a hand in the air in a careless gesture. "It's not anything to worry about, Miss Mahaffey. It must have been sent with some other shipment, and I'd forgotten about it. Actually, I'm happy to find that we have some wine available. You put it to excellent use."

"Oh. Good." She didn't relax a whit.

"And the beef dish contained mushrooms. I was surprised to find them there."

"You were?" Her voice was a little squeaky.

"Yes. Now where did you find the noble mushroom in this sunny territory?"

"Um, they were growing in the garden?" She sounded not at all sure of herself.

Philippe frowned. "In the garden? I was under the impression that mushrooms had to grow under trees in moist climates. In France, I believe people find them in deep forests. In New Orleans, folks grow them in their cellars."

She began kneading her hands together in her lap. "Um, yes, that's it, all right. They grew in a cellar."

"Oh?" He lifted an eyebrow. "Whose cellar?"

She closed her eyes momentarily and opened them again. "My mother's!" It came out in a blurt, and Philippe got the impression she'd just made it up. "My mother grows things like that—mushrooms and so forth—in her cellar."

"And so forth? What and so forth?"

"Um, well . . ." Heather waved her hand in the air. It appeared a rather hopeless gesture to Philippe. "Um, other kinds of mushrooms, I meant to say."

"My, my." Now why, he wondered, was the girl lying to him? Or was she lying? This conversation was very odd. "I didn't know folks had cellars out here. I thought they had dugouts or soddies."

She flipped a hand in the air again, this time banging the back of it on the table. She started, jerked it back to her lap, and rubbed it with the fingers of her other hand.

Philippe experienced an almost overwhelming impulse to take her hand and kiss it better. He didn't understand it at all.

Heather babbled again. "Oh, well, yes. She grows them in the dugout. Behind the house. Where she keeps the roots and potatoes and onions and so forth."

"I see." He nodded, not seeing at all. "I don't want to use up your mother's supply of foodstuffs, Miss Mahaffey. I'm happy to purchase what we need for my table. And if a recipe calls for mushrooms and they aren't locally available, perhaps you can omit them. I can't imagine why a mushroom or the lack thereof would ruin a dish."

"All right." She popped up from her chair. "Thank you, sir. I'll do that. Omit them. That sort of thing."

Philippe eyed her keenly. "There's no need to rush off, Miss Mahaffey. Please, sit again. I'm very curious about you."

"Oh, Lord, you are?" She sank into her chair and looked like she might cry.

Her attitude was beginning to irk Philippe. "Miss Mahaffey," he said severely, "I don't know what people have been saying to you about me, but I'm not an evil man. I'm ruthless in business and intend to achieve my goals no matter what that entails, but I don't trample young women underfoot or pursue illegal avenues of income. I don't see any reason for you to be so jittery in my presence. I asked you to come in here so that I could thank you for providing me with the best and tastiest meal I've had in years. I shouldn't think that's anything to be afraid of."

"Oh. Oh, no, sir. That's not it. I—ah—I was only worried that you wouldn't like your food, sir."

"Then you can cease worrying immediately. I liked it very well, ma'am, and I thank you. I think you're a wonderful addition to the household staff."

"Thank you."

"And I don't much like the notion that members of my household staff believe they need to defer to me. Of course, I expect everyone on my staff to work for their keep, but I don't see any reason we can't be comfortable with each other. Even friendly." He tried to produce a friendly smile. "After all, this is the West, where everyone is equal to everyone else."

"Right. You're absolutely right. Sir."

Philippe sighed. He was far from satisfied. Not only did she persist in calling him "sir," but her voice was so tense, it nearly squeaked. She looked like a spring that had been wound too tightly and was on the verge of snapping and bouncing all around the room. Her attitude made no sense to him. He also didn't have a clue as to why he leaned over and put his hand over hers. She jerked like a frightened rabbit.

"Please, Miss Mahaffey, relax. I don't mean to alarm you. Truly, I don't."

She stared at his hand, which looked very dark resting on her pale one, as if she expected it to slap her. Not much chance of that. He might think of many things to do with his hands in relation to Heather Mahaffey, but none of them were of a violent nature. Far from it.

Damn, he wished he hadn't thought about Heather with respect to the things he'd like to do to her involving his hands.

"I—I'm not scared," she lied. Her eyes, big and as blue as cornflowers, plainly showed how terrified she was.

Philippe sighed yet again. Although he enjoyed her company and her looks and would like to become better acquainted with her, he began to think he might as well end this torture. She unquestionably wasn't going to calm down any time soon. "I'm sorry, Miss Mahaffey, that you should find me such an ogre—"

"No! No, not at all. Not an ogre. No, sir."

Since she'd all but shrieked her disclaimer, Philippe didn't believe it. "At any rate, I hope that in time you'll come to understand I mean you no harm. And I truly appreciate your efforts on my behalf. I haven't eaten such a tasty meal since I moved to the territory."

"Really? I mean, good. That's good. I'm, ah, glad you enjoyed it."

"Yes." He withdrew his hand from hers and noticed that she breathed a sigh of relief. This wasn't very flattering behavior on her part. Philippe, while far from vain, knew he was a good-looking man, and a very rich one. For the latter reason alone, women generally found him attractive.

But that was nothing to the purpose. "I'd like my breakfast served at eight o'clock, please, Miss Mahaffey. I'm up long before then, of course, but I don't need more than coffee earlier. I'll be out doing my morning chores, and when I get back to the house at eight, I'm usually quite hungry. Will that be satisfactory?"

"Satisfactory? Oh, of course. You're the boss." She licked her lips. She had very pretty lips.

Damn. Philippe wished he hadn't noticed her lips. "And dinner can be at one o'clock in the afternoon on a regular basis, if that's also satisfactory."

"Dinner. One o'clock. All right." She looked like she might faint if she had to remain in the room with him for very much longer.

His decision to end the interview wavered. He was curious as to why she feared him so much, and discovered within himself a desire to know her better. If he held her here a little longer, trying all the while to lull her into relaxing, maybe she'd crack and tell him what was wrong. "Mind you, these hours are relatively uncivilized." He gave her one of his more continental smiles. She only blinked at him, as if she were in too anxious a state to distinguish between various smiles and their relative seductiveness. He shook his head. "However, since we live in the Wild West, I suppose it's as well to conform to custom."

She didn't even nod, and he wondered if she was simpleminded or merely so scared she couldn't respond. But why in the name of God was she scared? Settling back in his chair, he surveyed her through slitted eyes. "And the custom of taking one's largest meal around noontime prevails for a reason. After all, when one works hard at physical outdoor labor all day long, one needs the energy provided by a large midday meal."

Looking at him as if she suspected he was a lunatic, Heather said, "Ah, yes. I guess so. Right. Of course."

Maybe he was a lunatic. He couldn't seem to let this poor frightened young woman go. She was too pretty, and her worry was too palpable, and there seemed so little reason for it. After all, if this meal was a foretaste of meals to come, she could cook for him forever.

He cleared his throat. "So, Miss Mahaffey, would you care to go over menus for the upcoming day or two with me?"

"M-m-menus?"

"Certainly. I believe it is customary for the cook to consult with the mistress of the house in order to determine what she's expected to prepare by way of meals. In this case, of course, there is no mistress." He gave her another wolfish smile and was interested to note that her demeanor didn't visibly alter. She was evidently already too unnerved to allow so small a thing as a wolfish smile to further unsettle her. "So you'll have to consult with me."

"Oh."

Lord, if she got any more pale, she might just faint. Philippe shook his head and said gently, "I'm not a harsh taskmaster, Miss Mahaffey. I'm not fussy. I'm sure you know all about preparing meals. Perhaps we can just talk about them a little."

"Talk about them?" Her voice had gone high and thin, and she licked her lips once more. "All right. Um, what do you like to eat?"

He tilted his head and considered her for a moment. She had absolutely no idea how to be a household servant; that much was obvious. Perhaps that's why she was so daunted by this interview. Yet she'd seemed perfectly at ease at the dance. He hadn't expected her to be shy just because she was in the presence of her new employer. Her reputation indicated she wasn't at all shy, in fact. He'd have expected her to take over the house, not hide away in a corner.

Ah, well, who knew what inanities swirled around in the heads of pretty females? Or even ugly ones. Philippe, who'd thus far in life not found many reasons to respect women, asked kindly, "Would you care to take notes, Miss Mahaffey? I'm sure your memory is excellent, but—"

"Notes?" she squeaked. "Notes? Oh, shoot, I don't have—" She rooted frantically in her apron pocket, and produced nothing more useful than a piece of lint, which she stared at with enormous, worried eyes.

Philippe cleared his throat, and she jumped in her chair. "Allow me," he said, and stood. He could feel her gaze following him as he walked to the sideboard, pulled out a drawer, and withdrew a pencil and a small sheet of paper. When he returned to her, she was staring at him as if she expected him to sprout horns and a forked tail and begin spitting fire. Interesting. He couldn't recall ever having had this effect on a personable young woman before. Perhaps he was getting old and losing his skill.

"Here, perhaps you can jot down a couple of suggestions on this."

Her hands shook when she took the paper and pencil. "All right. Thank you."

This situation was nonsensical. Philippe had to hide a smile behind his hand. He lifted his small cigar to his lips, took another puff, and decided to give the girl a break. He rose and went back to the sideboard, where he fiddled with a pair of silver candlesticks he'd ordered from New York City. "So, Miss Mahaffey, what delights do you have in store for me tomorrow? I'm sure that these first few meals will have to be planned around supplies already on hand."

He heard her suck in a huge breath and expel it in a long sigh.

Chapter Four

If this interview lasted much longer, Heather feared her nerves would split right in half and she'd run screaming from the room. In an effort to calm herself—she knew she was being enormously foolish to show Mr. St. Pierre how nervous she was—she took another deep breath and blurted out, "Delights?" in a voice that was much too loud.

Thunder and lightning. Heather shut her eyes, took a third breath, and mentally slapped herself silly. She *had* to get a grip on her nerves. Her first meal had gone well. And if she hadn't prepared it, Mr. St. Pierre didn't know that. Yet.

Of course, he'd know tomorrow morning first thing, unless D. A. Bologh kept his end of their bargain.

Which reminded Heather that she didn't yet know what her own end of said bargain entailed.

She told herself to stop thinking immediately

and concentrate on food. "Um—well—"

He turned around. He had the most magnificent eyes Heather had ever seen. They were dark as pitch and his lashes framed them and made them appear sultry and dreamy. And they looked hot, as if they might sear her if she got too close. Actually, his whole large body seemed to radiate heat. Unless that was her present state of hysteria making her flush. Then he smiled again, and Heather went light-headed.

This was stupid. She had to get hold of herself.

"Yes, Miss Mahaffey, what foodstuffs do we have in the kitchen for your further culinary experimentations?"

Experimentations? Oh, Lord in heaven, he didn't already know about her, did he?

But no. Of course he didn't. Heather mentally screamed at herself to calm down. She opened her mouth, but nothing emerged. This was terrible.

He sighed. "That is to say, do you have sufficient ingredients for tomorrow's meals? Do I need to send someone to town for supplies? Please let me know, because I intend to keep the larder well-stocked with whatever provisions you require. Obviously, you're a wizard in the kitchen. I don't want to stifle your creativity."

Stifle her creativity? Fat chance of that ever happening. She said, "Oh, I see. Well, I—I'm not sure. I'll have to check on everything and let you know."

Not that *she'd* know what a kitchen should be stocked with. Up until she'd accepted this position as cook in Philippe St. Pierre's big fancy ranch house, Heather had figured an average meal consisted of corn cakes and molasses. With maybe some side meat like bacon fried up for special occasions.

"Fine." He came back to the dining room table, his booted feet making thunder on the polished wooden floor.

She sucked in a breath when he sat beside her again. Mercy, she wished he'd stayed across the room.

"But you must have some idea what you intend to serve tomorrow."

He smiled. This smile didn't look as intimidating as his earlier ones had. This was a friendly, easygoing smile. Good heavens, he hadn't been practicing his smiles, too, had he? Until this minute, Heather hadn't considered the possibility that men practiced the art of flirtation as women did. She said, "Um . . ." and ran out of inspiration.

Actually, if she were to answer his question, she'd have to say no. She had absolutely no idea in the world what she intended to serve tomorrow. She sensed it would be unwise to admit it. "I'm not sure yet." There. If he didn't accept that, she'd just have to run away from home. She couldn't possibly remain in Fort Summers after she'd been exposed as a fraud by Philippe St. Pierre.

"I see. Well, perhaps after you've surveyed your kingdom further, you'll be able to give me an idea."

"Right. I mean, surely, I can do that."

"Fine." He stood over her for fully long enough for Heather to begin to sweat. She knew ladies weren't supposed to sweat, but she also knew she was about as far from being a lady as any female on earth. So far, in the course of a single day, she'd lied, made a vile deal with a stranger—and didn't even know to what she'd agreed—assumed a false position, and made a complete fool of herself in front of her employer, who was the most handsome man in the entire universe. Might as well sweat, too.

He held out a hand, and Heather shrank back before she caught herself doing it and stopped. She wasn't surprised when his smile vanished and he looked peeved. She was peeved at herself, too.

"Please, Miss Mahaffey, if you would condescend to shake hands with me? I truly do appreciate the fine meal you prepared for me this evening."

She rose from her chair. Because she felt like an idiot, and because he didn't deserve such brainless behavior from her as she'd demonstrated so far, she said quickly, "I'm so sorry, Mr. St. Pierre. I—I guess I'm not used to being employed." That sounded stupid. She worked all the time when there was anybody in town willing to hire her. "In such fine surroundings and all, I mean," she amended. "I guess I'm a—a little nervous about my ability to do the job." She took Philippe's offered hand.

"Of course." He bowed over her hand.

Heather had never seen a man bow over a female's hand before. The gesture thrilled her almost as much as his kissing her hand at the dance.

"Until tomorrow, then," he said in a voice that seeped into Heather's pores and trickled into her nerve endings and made her nipples pucker.

On that unseemly note, she escaped. As if all the demons in hell were after her. She scooted past Mrs. Van der Linden, who scowled at her as if she knew what was on her mind. Which, of course, she couldn't, because Mrs. Van der Linden was a proper gentlewoman if ever God had crafted one, and Heather's thoughts were decidedly improper.

When she'd shoved through the kitchen door and fallen, panting, onto a chair, she crossed her arms on the table, laid her head on them, and tried to catch her breath. Her chest ached from being scared.

What have I done? What have I done? sounded relentlessly in her head. What she feared she'd done was court disaster, and that it would not only affect her, but her family and their standing in the very small, close-knit community of Fort Summers, as well. She'd never forgive herself if she brought shame to her mother and father.

No matter how much her father deserved it.

She groaned aloud when she caught herself mulling over that mean-spirited thought. This was her fault and no one else's. She should have asked if Mr. St. Pierre had another position available and taken that. She knew better than to think she'd suddenly be able to cook a decent meal.

Shoot, he was part French, and Geraldine said the French were an eccentric lot. Maybe he'd have let her work with his cattle for a while. Or tend the gardens. She could do both of those things better than most folks. But cooking? She shuddered.

The door opened at her back. She jerked her head up and whirled around. When she beheld Mrs. Van der Linden in the doorway, she breathed a sigh of relief.

Not that Mrs. Van der Linden's expression was friendly. Far from it. In fact, the housekeeper took one comprehensive look at Heather and offered one of her offended—and offensive—sniffs and a fierce scowl. "Well, you got past that one, Heather Mahaffey."

Although Heather could usually hold her own in about any battle of wits and words, she was too worried at the moment to take exception to Mrs. Van der Linden's tone or disparaging comment. Instead, she said merely, "Yes. It's a wonder, too, isn't it?"

Mrs. Van der Linden stared at her as if she'd just blasphemed God and the twelve apostles. "I'm astonished that you dare to admit it."

Heather shrugged. "Why should you be astonished? It's the truth." And she wasn't sure what she was going to do about it, either.

"Well," said Mrs. Van der Linden, and said no more, probably because she'd entered the kitchen spoiling for a fight and Heather wasn't obliging her.

Heather glanced at the pots, pans, cooking utensils, and dishes stacked next to the sink. "I suppose it's part of my job to wash dishes." She was only asking. She didn't mind. Actually, washing dishes was one of the few things she could do without making a muddle. It would be sort of pleasant to do something at which she was adept for a change.

Mrs. Van der Linden sniffed again. "I think it should be your job," she said sourly. "But that man is thinking about hiring a girl to wash up."

"Oh. I didn't know that." It was nice of him. That meant Heather would only have to cook.

Good heavens! What was nice about that? She wanted to lower her head to her arms again and weep.

"But until he does there's nobody else to do it, so it's up to you to get this mess cleaned up." Mrs.

Van der Linden glanced around the kitchen with a supercilious frown. "You certainly dirtied enough equipment while you were fixing your fancy dinner, young lady. I'm surprised your mother allows you to cook things like that, quite frankly."

"Yes. Me, too." Actually, Heather's mother would fall into a faint if she heard that Heather had managed to cook any kind of a meal at all without burning the house down. That anyone, least of all her mother, would believe she'd created a fabulous French meal was beyond comprehension.

"I don't hold with fancy cooking myself," Mrs. Van der Linden continued. "This isn't Paris, France, after all. Folks generally have better things to do with their hard-earned money than throw it away on fancy cooking."

"Mr. St. Pierre has lots of money, I guess."

"Humph." Mrs. Van der Linden gave Heather one of her meaner sneers. "Of course he has lots of money. And you already know it. You're sly, Heather Mahaffey. I always said you were sly."

Heather let it slide. She had no energy left to disabuse Mrs. Van der Linden of her false assumptions. She shrugged. "I suppose a rich man can afford to buy interesting things to eat."

"I still don't hold with it. It's wasteful, and waste is unchristian. Waste not, want not, the Good Book says."

Again Heather offered no response. She felt herself to be on fairly shaky ground regarding the Good Book this evening.

Mrs. Van der Linden turned from her survey of the dirty dishes and glowered at Heather. "That man asked me to help you clean up this jumble tonight, so I'll do it. But it's not my job, and I want you to know it. And I still don't hold with dirtying all these dishes for one silly meal. A pot is all my mother needed, and a pot's all any decent, God-fearing woman needs to fix a meal in."

"Oh." For a second, Heather contemplated accepting Mrs. Van der Linden's help with the dishes. It took no more than that for her to realize she'd sooner be drenched in oil and set afire than remain in the older woman's company for any longer than was absolutely necessary. "Please, Mrs. Van der Linden, don't bother. I can wash these up in a minute."

Liar. Well, what was one more little lie? She'd lied about everything else today. If it took her three hours to do the dishes, Heather could look upon the experience in the light of atonement. Or something.

Mrs. Van der Linden didn't like to be deprived of an opportunity to martyr herself, and actually argued with Heather for a minute or two. Heather prevailed at last, however, and the older woman left in a snit.

"Nothing pleases that old coot," Heather muttered under her breath as she surveyed the mess of dirty dishes and cooking utensils piled before her.

Before she could tackle them, a knock came at the back door. With a heavy sigh, she went to the door and opened it. And there stood D. A. Bologh, smiling at her as if he hadn't performed a miracle mere hours earlier.

"You're back!" Heather didn't know whether to be happy or miserable. She guessed she was happy when he walked past her into the kitchen, took one look at the pots and pans, and said, "I'll clean these up in a jiffy."

"You will?" She goggled at him.

"Sure will. Part of the deal." And, with a wink, D. A. Bologh set about tidying up the kitchen belonging to Philippe St. Pierre in about a tenth of the time it would have taken Heather to do it.

As she'd done earlier in the day, she watched him. And, as had happened earlier in the day, she got dizzy doing it. He moved too fast. And inexplicable things happened. She could have sworn pots and pans flew through the air. He tossed dishes up into the air and they whirled wildly.

"That's going to become known as the spin dry cycle someday," he said with a laugh, and winked at her over his shoulder.

Whatever that meant. In the end, Heather had no more idea how he'd cleaned the kitchen than how he'd cooked the dinner.

She went to the bath house to wash up, thinking the entire time about D. A. Bologh and Philippe St. Pierre, and trying to make sense of either one of them. She couldn't do it.

It was all very unsettling, but she was so exhausted by the time she went to bed that she sank into her feather mattress, provided for her in the pleasant little room next to the kitchen, and slept the sleep of the innocent. Which was a big, fat lie, and she knew it.

Philippe stood at the window of his library and scowled out into the pitchy night. He was annoyed when he lifted his cigar to his lips and discovered it had gone out.

"What I don't understand is how a hundred head

of beeves could have vanished, as if off the face of the earth."

Gil McGill, who was sitting on the big leather sofa, looked up at him helplessly. "I swear to God, Mr. St. Pierre, I don't understand it either." He reached for the glass at his elbow and took a sip, as if he needed to wet his lips in order to talk.

Philippe turned and tried to soften his scowl. None of this was poor Gil's fault. Still, a hundred head was almost a fifth of his herd. This was bad. "Could it be rustlers?"

"I reckon it must be, but I haven't heard about any gangs working the area. Generally, we know about that sort of thing pretty quick, because of the fort and the sheriff."

Philippe nodded and offered another suggestion. "Indians?"

Gil thought for a minute and then shook his head. "I doubt it. The army rounded the Apaches up in 1864 and sent 'em to the Bosque Redondo along with the Navajos they herded from Arizona. There's hardly any loose Indians left around here anymore."

"Good God." Philippe knew the United States hadn't treated its native sons and daughters any too kindly, but that sounded like atrocious behavior to him. "I had no idea."

"Not many folks do, I reckon. From what I understand, they rounded up the Navajos in the wintertime, too, and drove them like a herd of cattle to the Bosque. A whole bunch of them died."

"I'm not surprised." Philippe eyed Gil, whom he knew to be a decent man. He certainly sounded unconcerned about the fate of the Indians, however. Philippe guessed most white men were. He sighed. He was long past wondering why decent human beings could harbor such blind spots in their minds and hearts. After all, he reminded himself with a wry grin, he was the product of mixed heritage himself. If he hadn't been so damned good looking, he'd still be paying for it, too, and he knew it.

"I'm not at all surprised," Philippe repeated. He decided to forgo any further questions about Indians. The subject was too depressing, Manifest Destiny be hanged. "So if it's not the Apaches, who do you think it is?"

"I've thought and thought, Mr. St. Pierre, and I just don't know. There have been gangs around here, of course, but not so much these days. Those old days of the Regulators and that crazy fellow folks call Billy the Kid are long gone. Twenty years gone, in fact, and we're pretty civilized out here now."

Philippe smiled. He really liked Gil. So did Heather. His brain conjured a vision of Heather and Gil in a passionate embrace, and his smile vanished without his consent. He mentally chided himself. Miss Mahaffey and Mr. McGill were perfectly suited to each other, for the love of God, and his reaction to the notion of them joined in carnal embrace was nonsensical.

"Civilization aside, I'm losing cattle, and we'd better find out why and who's doing it, or I'm liable to lose everything else as well."

Gil nodded and sighed. "I know. I've set the men to riding fences and keeping watch at night. We thought about bonfires, but the wind's been so bad lately, fires are too dangerous."

"Yes. I see your point." Philippe had never been

anyplace where the wind was such a constant accompaniment to life.

Gil took another sip of his drink and set the glass down with a clunk. "It's almost as if something's spiriting them cows away. It's almost like, well—" Gil broke off, and his face turned brick red.

Philippe lifted an eyebrow with interest. "It's almost like what, Gil? I promise I won't scoff."

"Well, if you do, I reckon I wouldn't blame you." He sat up straight and blurted it out. "It's almost like it's an old curse or something. I hear tell that the Indians laid a lot of curses on the whites who took over their land and run the buffalo off and started raising cattle instead."

"I see." Philippe took a long sulfur match from the mantel, scratched it on the rough stones of the fireplace, and relit his cigar. He took a deep pull, blew the smoke out in rings, and contemplated the nature of curses. "You'll probably be surprised to know that I'm not about to scoff at the suggestion of a curse, Gil."

"No?"

"No. I've had some experience with curses."

Gil looked up, interested. "Yeah? I didn't know that."

"Nobody knows that." Philippe guessed he looked a little grim, because Gil didn't ask any questions. Which was a good thing, because Philippe didn't have any answers. He shook his head. "I suppose there's nothing we can do other than be extra vigilant."

"I guess not."

"Are any of the other ranchers in the area having these problems?"

Gil looked uncomfortable. "I don't think so."

"Hmm." Philippe scowled into the night. Was someone in the area trying to put him out of business? He couldn't imagine who it could be.

Gil got up from the leather sofa and stood there, fiddling nervously with his hat. "I wish I could think of something, but I honestly don't know why it's happened or what else we can do, sir."

Philippe asked irritably, "Why does everyone call me sir?"

Gil opened his mouth, but nothing came out of it, and Philippe regretted his momentary lapse. Lapses in deportment were rare for him, and Gil didn't deserve a show of temper from him. "I'm sorry, Gil. Didn't mean to bark at you. I guess I'm worried about the cattle."

Accepting the apology with good grace, Gil said, "Yeah, I reckon we all are. I—it's—oh, hell, I don't know." Gil blushed again. "Sorry, Mr. St. Pierre."

Philippe waved it away. "Think nothing of it. I swear like a drunken sailor sometimes when I'm angry."

That made his wrangler grin, and Philippe forgave himself for having snapped earlier.

"What I was going to say was that I can't figure out where so many beeves could have got off to without anybody seeing it or without leaving a pretty clear trail, but we couldn't find any trace at all. And I know damned well that all the men are worried, because they like working here better than anywhere else. They'd be unhappy if anything happened to your operation."

"Really?" Philippe was surprised.

"Oh, yes, sir. This is a great ranch, and you've got more sense than most of the other ranchers around." The man had embarrassed himself, so he cleared his throat and hurried on. "As for the cattle, well, since the winds have been so bad and the weather so dry, we've tried to keep them pretty much together so's we can feed them the grain you got. That was a good idea, by the way."

"Thank you." Philippe appreciated Gil's praise, although he knew good and well any man with enough money could afford to supplement his cattle's food supply when the going got rough. He, Philippe St. Pierre, was a lucky man when it came to money. If a curse did hover over his life, it affected him in other ways.

"Anyway, since we've kept them pretty much together and close to the bunkhouse and all, we can't figure out how somebody's been able to sneak so many off."

"We'll have to keep watching."

"Yes, sir. There are men watching all the time. I'm sure some of 'em are better than others, but they all need their jobs, so I'm pretty sure nobody's bluffing me."

"I'm glad to know they're loyal."

Gil evidently either didn't catch or chose to ignore Philippe's sarcasm. "Oh, yes, sir. They are."

He meant it; Philippe could tell by the sincerity of his tone. Lord, had he ever been so young and innocent?

That was a stupid question. Of course he hadn't. What chance had he ever had to be innocent? He'd had a lot less to do with innocence in his life than with curses.

"Thanks for the report, Gil. Do you think it would help to offer a reward if the rustler's ever caught?"

Gil shifted his feet uncomfortably. "Hell, sir—

sorry—you don't need to bribe the men to do their jobs."

Another damned sir. Philippe didn't understand this notion people had that he was some sort of person to be kowtowed to. Nevertheless, he quirked an eyebrow and smiled. "I hadn't intended the offer as a bribe."

"Oh. I guess not, then." Gil shrugged. "I reckon nobody'd mind getting a little extra money for a job if they do something special."

"Right. Well, that's fine then. I'll not announce any kind of reward yet, but I'll keep it in mind."

Gil seemed relieved. Philippe felt his lips tighten and made an effort to relax. It irked him that the men who were in his employ seemed damned near as insecure around him as his pretty little cook. He could almost understand Heather's skittishness. For all she knew, he was a black-hearted satyr who wanted nothing more than to ravish her, after all. But Gil? It made no sense that Gil should fear him. Unless he'd created in himself something more than merely a wealthy businessman.

When he looked at the situation from another angle, though, it sort of tickled him to think folks were afraid of him. Him. Philippe St. Pierre. God, it was too funny.

He did not, however, laugh. Instead he walked over to his wrangler and held out his hand. "I appreciate all your good work, Gil."

The man's pleasure was obvious when he shook his employer's hand, and Philippe was glad. At least he seemed to have done this one thing right.

"Thank you, sir. It's a pleasure to work for someone who knows what he's doing."

Philippe laughed, Gil's choice of words having

tickled him. "Thanks. Don't most folks around here know what they're doing?"

"Not always. You'd be surprised at the people who settle out here with big ideas about making themselves rich. Most of 'em end up dirt poor, along with the rest of us. Even the ones with sense have a hard time of it. This isn't an easy country."

"No. It isn't."

After Gil left, Philippe contemplated the nature of the land he'd moved from his wretched origins to conquer. Gil was right. It was hard and unfriendly.

Even the rivers that gave the land and cattle life were hard. The Pecos, which flowed right through Fort Summers, had been honored as "the graveyard of the cowman's hopes" by none other than Mr. Charles Goodnight himself. And the man had been right.

The Pecos was as full of minerals as a river could be, there was quicksand on her banks, and the fact that herds had to walk hundreds of miles to get to her was a mean trick on Nature's part. By the time the cattle smelled water, they were dying of thirst, and stampedes were commonplace. It was difficult to persuade a herd of panicked cows that they needed to wait a while longer to slake their thirst, especially when the men trying to do the persuading were damned near as thirsty as the cows.

Philippe sighed. He knew why he was here. But why would anyone else settle out here? The indomitability of the human spirit astonished him occasionally—in those rare moments when he wasn't deploring man's fallen nature.

Ha. As if he were fit to offer any sort of opinion on the matter.

A movement outside caught his attention, and he pulled the curtain aside. Was it the rustler, come to pry around the house? He squinted into the dark for a moment, and then relaxed. He did not, however, lower the curtain or cease watching.

Heather Mahaffey, a towel thrown over her shoulder, and clad in some voluminous thing that was as sexless as it was ugly, was making her way from the kitchen to the bath house. The image the knowledge provoked in his mind was an entertaining one.

Wondering if he actually was, at heart, some kind of perverted satyr, Philippe found himself dropping the curtain, tossing his cigar into the fire, and heading out of his library. He'd never been a voyeur before and didn't intend to begin now, but he could at least make sure none of the other men on the ranch were looking. After all, Heather was his responsibility now.

Oddly enough, the notion didn't make his blood run cold.

Chapter Five

Damn. Philippe eyed the bath house with disfavor. There were curtains over the two windows, but they weren't very good curtains. He saw Heather's hands as they tried to draw the fabric together, but the curtains still gaped in the middle. He'd have to get new ones put up. Immediately. He'd be hanged if he'd allow Heather to be the object of salacious attention from his employees.

His own attention, however, was another matter. He told himself he was only checking to be sure none of his men were out and about. He told himself this is what came of employing females on a ranch. He told himself it was his duty to see that Heather wasn't molested—he didn't even think about Mrs. Van der Linden's safety, since any man who attempted to molest her would probably come out the loser, not to mention being the possessor of deplorably bad taste. He told himself he aimed to stand guard at the bath house to ensure Heather's privacy while she undertook her evening's ablutions.

As much as he tried to be honest with himself, however, he couldn't quite persuade himself that he was being merely responsible when he stepped to the window to determine if a man could actually see anything through the crack in the curtain.

A man could. Philippe swallowed hard and goggled. Lord almighty, the female had taken off that ugly wrapper and was standing before the wash basin, humming to herself, as naked as the day she was born. Only there was a whole lot more of her than the day she was born. Philippe was sure of it.

God in heaven, she had skin like cream. From behind she was ravishing. She reminded Philippe of a painting by one of those famous old masters, of a woman about to step into her bath. Succulent. She was succulent. Her hips taunted him. Philippe wished she'd turn around so he could see her from the front. The curve of her back when she lifted her arms to pin up her hair made him swallow again and utter an involuntary, inarticulate sound.

She must have heard him because she turned her head suddenly, still holding her hair up. She frowned at the curtain, and Philippe had a sudden, violent urge to crash through the window, stalk over to her, haul her into his arms, throw her onto his saddle, and carry her off like some ancient knight conquering a castle. He'd ravish her there, in private. He jumped back from the window, although there was no way in heaven she could see him. She was the one standing in the light, God save him.

Lord, what that lantern light did to her body

ought to be outlawed. Her breasts were perfect, high and medium-sized, and deliciously rounded. Not a sag in sight. Philippe had seen enough breasts in his life that he was mildly surprised Heather's had the power to make him salivate. But they did. The light played on them, making shadows on their curves and creating an aura of mystery. The air in the bath house must be chilly, because her dusky nipples were pebbled up tight and pointing straight at him.

He gaped when she stopped frowning, slipped the last pin into her hair, brought her arms down, put her hands on her hips, and contemplated the window curtains, as if trying to ascertain how she could make them more secure. The fluff of curls between her thighs was a little darker than her hair. Her thighs were enough to make the pope in Rome give up his vows. As a whole, she was enough to tempt a saint, and Philippe was no saint.

Then she walked to the window, her every step making her breasts bounce slightly and making Philippe wonder if she didn't know he was there, and wasn't deliberately tempting him. Stifling a groan, he forced himself to step aside. He was so aroused, he could barely make his legs work.

He also prayed that she wouldn't have any pins with her with which to secure the curtains, because he didn't want to stop watching her.

Good God, what did that make him?

A man. That's what it made him.

He waited until he was pretty sure she wasn't looking out of the window any longer, and took up his position again—and found himself staring straight into Heather Mahaffey's gorgeous blue eyes. He saw them go wide, and then she screamed.

His first impulse was to turn tail and skedaddle back to the house, and pretend it hadn't been *he*, Philippe St. Pierre, who had been peeping at the naked Heather through a gap in the curtain.

His second impulse overrode his first one, thank God, or he'd have been forever humiliated by this experience. Philippe was a big boy. He knew what he'd done was wrong. He knew he had to own up to his culpability. He also knew he was the boss, and that he could probably bluff his way through this one.

The bath house door flew open and crashed against the side of the wall. Heather's panicky voice cried out, "Who's there? Who are you? Why are you peeking in the window?"

Philippe knew he had to do some fast thinking. Unfortunately, all of his resources were occupied below his belt at the moment. Making a supreme effort, he said, in a questioning sort of voice, "Miss Mahaffey? Is that you?"

A pause. A gasp. Then a small voice asking, "Mr. St. Pierre? Is that you?"

This was it. He had to do something to redeem his position regarding Miss Mahaffey or be considered by her as a low-down skunk forever. Which he might be, although he'd never been one before.

Squaring his shoulders like the responsible adult male human being he was supposed to be, Philippe stepped around to the door of the bath house. He deliberately pasted a frown on his face, and hoped to heaven that Heather would be so intimidated by his frown that she wouldn't notice the gigantic bulge in his britches.

She still had her hair up, and was clutching the neck of her ugly wrapper in one hand and her hairbrush in the other. She held the brush like a club, as if she aimed to light into the peeper with it. Fat lot of good a hairbrush would do her. Philippe scowled at the brush, thinking he ought to arm his employees better.

When she saw him, she took a startled step back. "Mr. St. Pierre!"

"Miss Mahaffey." He made his voice stern.

She blinked in astonishment. "Were—were you the one peeking in the window?"

It didn't sound to him as if she could credit the idea of Philippe as a Peeping Tom. Thank God for small favors. "I saw a light in the bath house and noticed that the curtain didn't meet in the middle. I didn't know who was in there."

"Oh." She tilted her head, looking as if she didn't know whether to get mad or apologize. "Am I supposed to tell you when I go to the bath house? Is that one of the rules?"

"Of course not." Since he was in a state, it was no problem for him to sound exasperated and slightly huffy. "But we've had some trouble on the ranch lately, and I wanted to make sure no objectionable visitors were poking around."

Her expression cleared. "Trouble? What kind of trouble?"

He shook his head. "You needn't be concerned. We've lost some cattle."

"Lost some? You mean they were stolen?"

"It looks like it."

"Oh, my, I'm sorry to hear it."

"So was I."

"I—" she swallowed. The fact that cattle had

gone missing was no reason for him to be peeking at her as she bathed. Philippe hoped she wouldn't point that out to him. She didn't. "I see. And you were just curious about who was walking around outside?"

What a wonderful woman she was, to offer him such a delightful lie to hold on to. "Indeed. I'm sorry I startled you. I didn't expect to find you in the bath house." A brilliant thought occurred to him. "In fact, I really think you ought to draw the curtains together more tightly when you bathe, Miss Mahaffey. A woman must protect her modesty." Lord, had he really said that?

"I tried."

"Oh?" In an effort to appear the honorable employer, he said, "You mean they don't meet?"

"No, they don't. I should have brought some pins to pin them, but I didn't."

"I see. You shouldn't have to pin them. I'll see that new ones are put up as soon as possible." Then he'd never be tempted again, dammit. He made himself smile. "Please forgive me, Miss Mahaffey. We're not accustomed to having women on the ranch, I fear, and it never occurred to me that my investigation might precipitate an embarrassing situation." Liar. God, he could hardly believe this of himself. "Er, none of the men ever had occasion to worry about the curtains."

"I'm sure that's so. But it's all right. I'm sure you didn't see much, and it's all right now."

If she only knew. But Philippe said, "Of course."

They stood there, looking at each other, for a couple of silent moments. Philippe didn't know what else to say. Heather didn't either, apparently.

It was an odd thing, though, that now that he

knew how easy it was to spy on the gorgeous, succulent Miss Heather Mahaffey as she bathed, Philippe began entertaining the odd notion that all the men on his ranch already knew about that damned curtain. He had visions of the men gathering outside the bath house and ogling Heather, and his blood ran cold. "Please finish your bath, Miss Mahaffey."

He frowned, not liking the idea of returning to the house and leaving her out here. Alone. Except for all the men, lurking in the bunkhouse and waiting for him to depart, who might delight in spying on her feminine beauty. "I'll just wait outside the door here and walk you back to the house when you're through."

"I'm sure there's no need for that, Mr. St. Pierre."

Although it was dark as the tomb outside, the faint light from the lantern burning inside the bath house was enough for Philippe to see Heather blush. He managed a wry smile. "I shan't peek. I promise." And, however much he rued the fact, he wasn't going to break that promise.

Her blush deepened. "Of course not. I never thought you would."

Which went to show how little she knew him. Philippe sighed, wishing he hadn't discovered this aspect of his personality.

"But really," she went on. "You don't need to wait for me. I've walked outside at night many times."

His hands curled into fists at the thought of other men watching her do so. He said stiffly, "That was before you came to work here. Before the trouble started."

That got to her. She appeared startled for a moment and then said, "Oh. Of course. Very well. I'll try not to take very much time."

He waved her demur away. "Don't be silly. Take all the time you need. I'll wait here and smoke a cigar."

"All right. Thank you." Before she turned and reentered the bath house, Heather shot him a smile that almost leveled him.

He'd endured too much excitement for one evening, Philippe decided. Any time the smile of a little country lass could knock him around, it was time for rest.

He jumped when the door burst open again, and Heather's head poked out. "And I'll be sure to draw the curtains tight. I suppose I can use hairpins."

Philippe was too startled to reply. By the time he got his wits together, she'd shut the door again.

Good God. This was ridiculous. Heather Mahaffey was nothing to him but a pretty good cook. And an exceptionally pretty woman.

Yet when he leaned against the bath house, took a cigar out of his pocket, struck a sulfur match against his boot heel, and lit up, he couldn't stop thinking about what he'd seen. And when he made a tour of the bath house, searching in the shadows for possible lurking voyeurs, he remembered how her breasts had looked in the faint light of the lantern. And when he checked to make sure the curtains were tightly drawn—they were, dammit—the recollection of her creamy skin and the shadows playing over her back and buttocks made his palms itch.

He was on the other side of the bath house when he heard the door open. He walked around the corner and saw her standing there, looking tentative in her huge, shapeless wrapper, holding the kerosene lantern, peering around, presumably looking for him, and his heart skipped and skidded. This was absurd. He'd had females by the score. For God's sake, he'd grown up in a whorehouse. This quaint, independent frontier girl shouldn't be stirring him this much.

However, there was no use fooling himself. She *did* stir him, for whatever reason. And Philippe was sure the reason was an illogical one, because a man's libido—and his heart—never waited for reason, but dashed on ahead, forever keeping him upset. Damn.

She must have hurried with her ablutions, because Philippe hadn't calmed down much by the time Heather peeked about, looking as if she weren't sure she should be doing this. Philippe wasn't either. He wanted her so badly, his whole body ached.

She turned, saw him, and smiled. "Oh, there you are."

Philippe had to clear his throat. "Yes. All through in there?"

"I am. Thank you for waiting. I have to admit I got a little skittish, thinking about people peering through the curtains. And stealing cattle." She frowned. "I'm very sorry to hear about that, Mr. St. Pierre. We haven't had much trouble with rustlers in recent years."

He barely heard her when she started talking about his cattle. He was too busy thinking about people peering through the windows. And there was no lock on the door, either. He threw his cigar down and squashed it with his boot heel. "I'll do that tomorrow," he muttered distractedly.

"I beg your pardon?"

When he glanced down and saw Heather looking up at him, her eyes dark in the night, he almost lost control of himself. Sweet Jesus, this had never happened to him before.

"I'll get a lock for the bath house door," he said, ruthlessly suppressing his impulses. "I don't like to think of you—or Mrs. Van der Linden—" Thank God he'd thought about injecting Mrs. Van der Linden into the conversation. She could dampen any man's ardor. "—being bothered by people bursting in on you."

"Good idea. Thank you. I'll feel much better then."

"Good."

Philippe wouldn't. Dammit all to hell and back again.

Chapter Six

The next day's breakfast menu included shirred eggs, breakfast sausages that looked like somebody had spent the better part of a lifetime making them and which D. A. called saucisse Bavarienne, potatoes galette, and some rolls D. A. called brioches. Heather had never heard of any of them before, but she guessed it didn't matter much.

The whole meal looked and smelled good, especially when D. A. conjured—she'd begun to think of him as some sort of magician—a jar of green-tomato jam to serve with the brioches. She knew it was green-tomato jam because D. A. told her so, although he'd called it something else she couldn't pronounce.

She tried very hard to concentrate on watching him work. When her mind wandered, it invariably wandered back to what had happened last night.

Had Mr. St. Pierre seen her naked? The notion made her go hot, inside and out.

She hoped he had.

No, no, no. What kind of thinking was that? Of course she hoped he hadn't.

Bother, she did not. She hoped he'd seen her buck naked and had been stirred to lust by the sight of her.

Merciful heavens, she'd better get her notions under control, or she'd be a fallen woman in no time at all.

But the thought of being kissed—and more—by Philippe St. Pierre was certainly an exciting one.

"There. That should make him happy."

Heather jumped when D. A.'s voice interrupted her lurid thoughts.

D. A. had a satisfied expression on his face as he surveyed the breakfast tray Heather was about to carry into the dining room. She peered at the tray and said truthfully, "It would make me happy."

The most exciting breakfast she'd ever eaten was fried scrapple. Which was tasty, but it sure couldn't hold a candle to any of this stuff. "Don't forget to stick around so you can tell me what we're—I mean you're—going to cook for the rest of today's meals. And I've got to give him a list of supplies to get in town, too."

D. A. chuckled in his all-too-knowing way, which gave Heather shivers down her spine. She wished he wouldn't do that.

"I'll be right here, cleaning up, after you deliver the big man his breakfast."

"Thank you."

Feeling extremely humble and not at all happy, Heather carried the tray to the dining room. She had to brace herself to face Philippe this morning. Salacious images of him and her, together, in intimate detail, kept intruding themselves into her consciousness.

"Stop it this minute, Heather Mahaffey."

Her stern command had its effect. She squared her shoulders and pushed open the door. Philippe was there, looking as if he'd already done a full day's work. She knew he got up very early. He had to; he was a rancher.

"Allow me, Miss Mahaffey," he murmured, coming over and relieving Heather of the tray and carrying it to the table, where he set it down with care.

In spite of herself, she knew she was blushing. She said, "Thank you," and with no little relief was about to turn tail and flee the room, when he spoke once more, stopping her. Blast.

"My goodness, you've outdone yourself again, I see."

"Have I?" She turned, found him smiling at her, and experienced a brief moment of panic. Her nipples tightened, which told her something she already knew and embarrassed her, and she wanted to retreat back to the kitchen. But he'd stopped her. Tucking her hands under her apron, since that was the only way she could wring them without him seeing her, she nodded to Philippe.

"This looks wonderful."

"Thank you."

"Looks good enough to eat, even." He grinned at her.

Heather's heart stumbled and started racing. She wished he wouldn't smile at her; she always got light-headed when he smiled. His smile, combined with the outrageous things she'd been thinking ever since last night, was enough to turn her into a babbling idiot.

He had removed the covers from the plates and now gazed down at his breakfast. He looked mighty happy, which made Heather sort of happy, but not very. She'd be ecstatic, of course, if he were pleased by something she'd done. But he was pleased by a lie, and she felt not merely guilty but ashamed of herself. Not to mention the fact that she was, to put it in vulgar parlance, in heat. Like a stray dog or something. Mercy, this was terrible.

"My, my. Sausages. And they look and smell delicious. I'm surprised you had time to make sausages since you haven't been here very long."

Heather mumbled something that sounded like "Mmph." She didn't know what it was supposed to mean.

"And where did this lovely jam come from? Don't tell me you've had time to make jam already, too?"

"Er, no. I, ah, brought that from home."

He frowned slightly. "Really, Miss Mahaffey, there's no need for that. I'm sure I can survive quite nicely on the fare provided by my own larder until we can restock it with the items you need. I don't like to think I'm putting your family to any inconvenience."

"Good Lord, no!" Heather caught her breath and felt her cheeks heat up again. "That is, it's not an inconvenience, Mr. St. Pierre. My family needs the money I'm earning here. That's surely worth a jar of jam. And, well, it's only made from green tomatoes, and there are a million of those growing in the garden. You have to use them for something or they'll rot." That's what her mother always said, at any rate.

And it was true, too, even if it was one more elaboration of the already painfully large hoax she was perpetrating.

"Nevertheless, I should appreciate it if you wouldn't trouble your mother and father for provisions for my table." He sounded severe.

Heather swallowed. "Certainly, sir. I mean, no, sir, I won't."

Then he smiled again, wiping out the severe expression so suddenly that Heather felt her heart hitch, and had to take a quick step backwards to keep from falling into a faint.

"Have you made a list for me yet? I plan to send a man to town today to get supplies."

"I'll have it as soon as you're through eating breakfast," she promised.

"Fine." He took another look at the really quite lovely repast spread before him. "This looks magnificent. Thank you, Miss Mahaffey. You're a jewel."

Heather took that as her dismissal, and scrammed out of the dining room. A jewel, was she? If she was a jewel, she was a badly flawed one.

When she got to the kitchen, D. A. Bologh had cleaned it so thoroughly it sparkled. Heather stopped dead in the doorway and stared. "How did you do that?"

D. A., seated at the table in the middle of the room, idly buffing his nails on his shirt, glanced up at her. He was wearing his ingenuous expression, which she didn't believe. "Do what?"

"Clean up so fast." She knew she shouldn't have asked as soon as his smile appeared. She was beginning to loathe that smile. While Philippe St. Pierre's smile made Heather want him to take her into his arms and ravish her, Mr. Bologh's smile made her want to turn tail and run away.

Or fall on her knees and pray for deliverance. She considered that a very bad thing.

"Oh, it was nothing." He waved a hand in the air in a nonchalant gesture.

"Right." She disliked this man. She didn't trust him. She stomped over to a cupboard to make sure he hadn't put any dishes away dirty. He hadn't. She sighed and turned around.

On the other hand, she'd better not let on how much she didn't like him, because she needed him. With a sinking feeling that she was embroiling herself more and more deeply into some kind of deadly—or at least very unhealthy—quicksand, Heather took a chair across the table from him and withdrew a paper and pencil from her pocket. "If you wouldn't mind, I have to make a list now of the things we need to get in town today."

"Glad to help." D. A. took the paper from her hand, snatched the pencil and, with a swirl of both, handed her back a neatly printed list.

Heather stared at the list for a second or two before she swallowed. She didn't take the paper. "How'd you do that? And don't say it's nothing, because it's not nothing. It's something."

He laughed, and she felt a chilling in her bones. "You must have gathered by this time that I'm a very talented fellow, Miss Heather."

"I think you're a witch." Could men be witches? Heather didn't know, but she also couldn't think of another explanation for D. A. Bologh's incredible agility and speed. Even if she didn't believe in witches.

This time his laugh raised the short hairs on the back of her neck. "Nonsense. I just like my little amusements, is all. They're very effective on the right audience." He winked at her. Of course.

"Right." Heather heaved a huge sigh. "Well, will you please tell me what the rest of today's menu will consist of? Mr. St. Pierre wants to know that as well."

"He does, does he?"

"Yes. Please don't say you won't do it, Mr. Bologh. I mean, if you're going to help me, you have to really *help* me."

"Ah, I see." He eyed her strangely. "You mean, you're beginning to value my connivance in keeping the man in the dark."

"You don't have to put it that way." She knew she had no reason to feel so indignant. Blast it.

"No? But you do want to continue this deceit."

Heather's mouth fell open. Put that way, it sounded quite dastardly. Which, she guessed, it was. She sighed deeply and turned away to stare at the kitchen. It was a very nice kitchen. She wished she knew what to do in it.

D. A. rose from the chair. "Which, of course, I'm more than willing to do." He gave her another of his evil winks. "For a price."

She swallowed and glanced at him again. "I thought we'd already struck a bargain." Wonderful. Her voice was shaking. Mercy, mercy, how could she have sunk so low so fast?

"Indeed we did. For a month. And I'll be glad to help you, Miss Heather." He snapped his fingers and a paper appeared between the two of them.

Heather blinked at him. "Did—did you have that up your sleeve?" She'd heard one of her older brothers grouse about cardsharps coming to town and hiding cards up their sleeves. Maybe this man was an itinerant gambler.

Magician, gambler, outlaw, cook. Witch. Heather felt a headache coming on and wished she could go back to bed and sleep for a hundred years. Like Rip Van Winkle or one of those other old-time storybook fellows.

"I never use such cheap tricks as hiding things up my sleeve, Miss Heather. What do you take me for, anyway?"

She didn't think she'd better say. Besides, she didn't know yet. "Um, well, may I please see the menu? I guess I ought to know what I'm supposed to be cooking for him, since he doesn't know I'm not." Did that make any sense? Well, no matter. She took the list out of D. A.'s hand and scanned it.

What in the name of all that's holy *was* this stuff? She looked from the list to D. A. Bologh and back again. "Um, do you have a duck tucked away somewhere?"

"Of course I have a duck, Miss Heather." He grinned. "If I didn't have a duck, would I have offered to cook one?"

"I don't know," she muttered.

Roasted duckling with Flemish olive sauce, truffles, and shallots sounded all right to her, although she did have a qualm or two. "What's a shallot? For that matter, what's a truffle?"

"A shallot is akin to an onion. Sort of."

She glanced at him again. "Um, you don't think we can just use an onion, do you? I mean, I know where there are onions. I've never even heard of a shallot."

"My dear young child," D. A. said in a condescending tone. "If you expect my help, you're going to have to rid yourself of your provincial leanings. People who consume my cooking don't merely *eat*. They *dine*."

"Oh." She thought about asking what the difference was, but opted not to. Obviously, the difference was that if you ate, you used onions. If you dined, you used shallots, whatever they were. "Um, where are we supposed to get shallots?"

"Not a problem, dearie. I have everything right at hand."

"I see. And the truffles? What are they?"

"Truffles are a type of mushroom."

Mushrooms again. Fiddlesticks. Heather scratched off the truffles. "We won't be using the truffles, Mr. Bologh."

"And why not?" He sounded offended.

Why not? "Because Mr. St. Pierre questioned the use of mushrooms before as being too exotic for this neck of the woods. If a plain old mushroom's too exotic for us, I can just imagine what he'd say to a truffle."

"Provincial swine," D. A. muttered under his breath.

"We might have to scratch the shallots, too."

"Never." He turned and marched to the window and looked out.

Heather pretended not to hear him, but she had her own idea about the shallots. "Um, I guess there's celery in the garden, so that part is all right, but what's a celery root rémoulade?"

"A rémoulade is a sauce, sweetie pie, and I'm

going to finely slice the celery root, cook it, and serve it with the sauce. You'll learn."

Heather doubted it. "And what's this thing? A mer-ring-guh?"

"Meringue. It's made with egg whites and sugar. Great Caesar's ghost, child, didn't your mother teach you anything?"

"Yes, she did! And I don't want to hear you say anything like that again!" Heather could take a lot from this man, because he was doing her an immense service, but she'd be diced and fried before she'd let him abuse her family.

D. A. held up a hand. "I'm sorry. Of course, your mother is a saint. It's the circumstances that are hellish."

Whatever. Heather didn't respond, but continued to glare at him.

"And you'll notice that for supper, I'll be preparing a thin sorrel soup made with broth from boiling up the duckling bones, since I know you who live in this vile frontier have to use everything or people will talk."

"People are going to talk anyway," she grumbled under her breath. "They probably already are." She could almost hear them, actually, and they weren't saying anything nice. Not that she blamed them.

D. A. paused, evidently having been struck by an idea. "Or perhaps I'll fix a French onion soup. Sorrel's a little out of the way for this place. And that way we can use some of those onions you're so fond of and still have an edible meal."

"It's not so much that I'm *fond* of them, it's just that—that—" It's just that she knew what they were. As opposed to shallots. Or truffles. Or Flemish olives. Or celery root rémoulade. And she'd always thought a sorrel was a horse. She decided she'd only look stupid if she said so. Not that she didn't already.

She was holding the list, worrying, when the kitchen door opened. She turned abruptly to find Philippe St. Pierre standing there, smiling his wonderful smile at her. At once, her mind returned to the night before, and the list fluttered from her suddenly nerveless fingers. It had drifted to the floor before Heather could get her wits together. A panic-stricken glance around the kitchen revealed that D. A. Bologh seemed to have vanished.

How in the name of heaven did he do these things? She was beginning to think she probably didn't want to know.

"Please pardon me for bursting into your kingdom unannounced like this, Miss Mahaffey." Philippe stooped and picked up the menu. "I understand great chefs are often temperamental about things like that."

Great chefs? That counted her out. She murmured, "Oh, no, it's quite all right." She wanted to jump on his body, rip his clothes off, and beg him to teach her the pleasures of the flesh. He knew them. She'd bet anything that he knew every single, solitary one of them. She'd also bet he'd be a superior teacher.

She was losing her mind. Heather pressed a hand to her forehead to check for fever. None. Drat. That meant she was merely experiencing lust. She'd never experienced lust before, and she wasn't sure what to do to get over it.

He glanced at the paper in his hand and then back at Heather. "Roasted duckling?"

"I'm leaving out the truffles," she said quickly,

hoping to forestall him before he could ask.

"No truffles." He glanced again at the menu and shook his head. "Good Lord, girl, you're feeding me like a king."

She shrugged because she didn't know what else to do. "It's—it's no bother, really." And that, at least, was the truth, even if nothing else about her life lately was.

"I don't think it's nothing. I think it's a miracle." He handed the list back to Heather. It vibrated because her hand shook, and she slapped it onto the kitchen table, praying he hadn't noticed.

Philippe walked past her and sat in one of the other chairs, stretched his long legs out in front of him, crossed them at the ankles, and grinned up at her. "Do you mind if I stay a moment so that we can chat for a little bit, Miss Mahaffey? I have to admit I'm very curious about you."

Oh, no! Exactly as she'd feared.

Unless he *had* peeked last night and was now going to ask her to do something unsavory. Unfortunately, that sounded fine to her. But no. It must be something else. Something bad. Something to do with her job.

She sank into a chair and stared straight at Philippe St. Pierre, ready to face her doom. He'd found her out. And it hadn't taken long, either.

"Please try to relax, Miss Mahaffey. I know I make you nervous, but I'm not a bad man. Truly."

"Oh, I'm sure of it," said Heather, who was sure of no such thing.

"Didn't I prove my good intentions last night?"

Last night. Suddenly Heather's throat sprouted a lump the size of Gibraltar.

"I plan to fetch new curtains today in town."

She forced herself to swallow the lump. "Oh. Good. Thank you."

"So, you see, I'm trying to be a good employer. I'm not sure what rumors have been going around town about me, but I'm not bad."

"Of course not. And I've never heard any rumors." Except that he was a handsome man, and that was the truth, so it couldn't be a rumor. Could it? Heather would have to consult with Geraldine, who served as her moral guide in matters too ticklish for Heather to take up with her mother.

"I'm glad of that."

His dark eyes seemed somehow warm to Heather. Actually, they seemed hot. Unless that was her own internal temperature playing hob with her perception. "It's only that I—that I—" She ran out of steam. It was only what? That she wasn't accustomed to being a faker and a cheat, not to mention wildly in lust? True, but she thought she'd better let him bring up those particular subjects on his own.

"That this is your first job. I understand."

Heather wished she did. She did, however, nod, as if Philippe had hit the nail on the head.

"And you're nervous about it, I'm sure."

She nodded again.

"But you're a superb cook, Miss Mahaffey. In fact, I'm astonished to find anyone with your skills living out here on the high plains."

"Um, yes. I'm kind of astonished, too." And that was putting it mildly.

"A person would think you'd been to cooking school in Paris."

Cooking school? In Paris? There were actually schools where they taught a person how to prepare these fancy dishes? Good heavens, maybe that's where Mr. Bologh had learned his craft. Heather felt a little better about life. Not a whole lot better; only a little. She said, "Oh." Then she said, "Thank you," because it seemed polite to do so.

"Not at all. I thank *you*. I never supposed I'd be eating fine food out here. I thought I'd left that sort of thing behind when I departed from New Orleans."

"Oh."

"The two meals I've eaten that you've prepared have taken me back to my boyhood, in fact. We used to eat well, whatever else we did."

Heather didn't understand why he'd put it that way, but she was too nervous to ask. Besides, it wasn't her place to ask about her employer. Which wasn't *quite* fair, since employers could and did pry into the private lives of their employees. She told herself not to get sidetracked by notions of western frontier independence and liberty and so forth.

"Did your mother teach you to cook?" Philippe asked, confirming Heather's opinion that the world wasn't fair.

She mentally kicked herself and said, "Er, yes. She tried." Over and over and over, she'd tried, poor dear. Heather loved her mother very much, and had always felt both sorry and dreadfully guilty that she wasn't a better daughter to such a paragon of housewifely virtues.

"She more than tried, if she's the one who introduced you to the art of cooking."

Heather said, "Mmph" again, and added another, "Thank you."

"You're entirely welcome. Is your mother of French extraction, by any chance?"

"Er, no. Both my mother and father came from Ireland. I—I don't think any of her family is French."

"I see. I only wondered." Philippe glanced at the menu again and noticed the neatly printed list lying next to it on the table. He picked it up. "Ah, I see you had a chance to think about supplies, too."

"Yes." Blast. She wished she'd had more time to peruse the list. She couldn't remember what was on it.

"Corn meal. Potatoes. Onions. Shallots." He glanced up from the list. "Shallots?"

"If I can find any," Heather broke in quickly. "Otherwise, I'll use onions. In the soup. With the duckling bones." *Oh, dear Lord, please help me*. She wanted to put her head in her arms and scream for an hour or two.

"I see." Philippe peered at her, his dark, hot eyes seeming to pierce her darkest, most secret places. It was all she could do to hold his gaze.

She was about to give up the effort and run shrieking from the room when he spoke again. "Miss Mahaffey, perhaps I should go to town today. And you should accompany me. That way we can pick up all the supplies we need, and I can have a better idea how you intend to work in the kitchen."

"But—but—there's dinner to prepare." Not that she'd be doing the preparing, but she had a feeling D. A. Bologh, as quickly as he worked, couldn't roast a duck in time for dinner. Or, if he did, Mr. St. Pierre would know for sure that something funny was going on. Although, truth to tell, it didn't seem very funny to Heather at the moment.

He thought for a second or two. "Er, perhaps you can postpone cooking the duckling until tomorrow, and we can have a more simple repast at noon today."

That didn't sound right to Heather, but she was in such emotional turmoil, she didn't dare say so. He was probably being reasonable, and she was insane. She must be insane, otherwise how could she, a sensible, ordinary girl, have gotten embroiled in such a dreadful pickle? She cleared her throat. "Certainly, Mr. St. Pierre, if you'd like."

"I should like, Miss Mahaffey."

There went his smile again. Out of nowhere, it materialized in a flash of white teeth against a darkly tanned face. His smile made the flesh around his eyes crinkle slightly, and turned the heat in his eyes into dancing flame.

"And I should also like it if you'd help me pick out fabric for curtains in the bath house."

"Of course." Her voice sounded hoarse, and she cleared her throat and tried again. "I should be happy to."

She *was* losing her mind; that much was becoming painfully obvious. She'd heard the wind sometimes drove people mad. And, while she knew the wind had driven her to do a reckless and probably stupid thing by accepting this job, she hadn't until now realized exactly how far it had driven her. She was sorry to have been the Mahaffey singled out to be afflicted with wind-borne insanity.

"Are you ready now?" he asked after Heather had almost managed to get herself under control. "If you don't have to prepare that big meal at noon, perhaps we can leave soon."

"Now? I—ah—I—yes. Of course."

He rose from his chair and glanced around the kitchen. "You're truly a wonder, Miss Mahaffey. I can't imagine how you could have managed to cook breakfast, serve it, and clean up the kitchen so fast."

"It—I—um—I had help." There. That wasn't even a lie. Much.

"Really?" His eyebrows dipped over his gorgeous eyes, making Heather wish she'd kept her fat mouth shut. "And exactly who helped you, if you don't mind my asking?"

"Oh, no. I don't mind." She smiled, praying he'd forget there had been more to his question.

No such luck. His left eyebrow went up in an ironic question mark. His right eyebrow stayed down, which made him look angry. Heather had to swallow.

"Um, my friend Geraldine came over to help." Shoot, she wished that were true. She could use some of Geraldine's sensible advice right about now. "I, ah, hope you don't mind."

"Geraldine." The angry look faded from his face and was replaced by one of puzzlement. "Geraldine . . ."

"Geraldine Swift. My friend. The one with the spectacles. You met her at the dance?"

"Oh, yes. I remember her now." His expression eased. "I see. Well, I should think that would be all right. I'm not altogether sure I want strangers running free in my house without my knowledge, however, so please don't invite too many of your friends over, if you don't mind. Or at least ask me first, if you will. We've had trouble with the cattle and so forth."

Heather forgot to be frightened for a moment. "Good Lord, Geraldine wouldn't know how to rustle cattle, Mr. St. Pierre!"

He chuckled and her knees went weak again. Blast. "Of course not. I wasn't singling out Miss Swift, but only asking that you check with me before you invite friends to the house."

"Of course. Right. I'm sorry." If he objected to Geraldine Swift, how would he react to D. A. Bologh? Heather decided she'd sooner go out behind the barn and shoot herself than find out.

"No need to apologize, Miss Mahaffey."

If he only knew.

Chapter Seven

Philippe asked Heather to fetch a bonnet and shawl and to be ready to go in a half hour. She agreed, and he went out to hitch the horses to the wagon. His mood was unsettled, and he had a feeling it had more than a little bit to do with his new cook.

It wasn't so much that he was attracted to her. Hell, any man would be attracted to her—especially if he'd seen her naked, as Philippe had. She'd have made a spectacular courtesan.

However, he'd never felt the urge to spill his guts to another human being before. He'd learned even before he could talk that it was unwise to trust his innermost self with other people.

There was a quality about Heather Mahaffey, however, that made him impatient with his usual reserve. It wasn't only that she was a remarkably pretty girl and that he'd seen her nude. Hell, Philippe had been resisting—or not resisting, depending on his mood—pretty girls for more years than he could count. Granted, few of them had aroused him as Heather had done last night, but that was probably only because it had been a long time since he'd last lain with a woman. At least, that's what he'd been telling himself since tossing and turning in his bed for hours last night.

It was something else in her that he discovered himself responding to. She seemed so open, so honest, so much a lady of the West and a child of the soil out here in the pitiless frontier of the United States. She was independent. Forthright. Amusing. Solid. Uncomplaining. She was unlike any other female in his considerable experience, and she made him want to smile and tell her things. After they made mad, passionate love for several hours. Which was probably a very bad idea.

For the love of God, she'd brought a stranger into his house to wash dishes. Without asking. While cattle were disappearing in droves.

He frowned as he went upstairs to change his boots for more comfortable shoes. He'd been up since before dawn had cracked, and he'd worked like a slave before partaking of the magnificent breakfast Heather had fixed for him.

Perhaps she could be forgiven that one tiny lapse in judgment. Hell, anyone who could cook like she did could be forgiven almost anything. Almost.

And Philippe knew beyond the shadow of a doubt that neither Heather nor her bespectacled friend had anything at all to do with cattle rustling. For God's sake, the very idea was nonsensical.

Perhaps he was merely reacting to something else. Something dragged out of a past he'd believed he'd left behind, dead and buried, never to reappear to blight his life.

He hadn't been fooling when he'd told her the meals had taken him back to his youth. Philippe scowled as he tugged off one muddy boot and set it on the oilskin set out for the purpose beside the door. His youth. In the whorehouse where his mother worked on her back, giving pleasure to rich men so as to support herself and her son.

He'd learned pretty much everything there was to know about men and women and what they did together—barring rearing children and creating happy homes—before he'd left New Orleans at last and forever, in his sixteenth year. That had been seventeen years ago, and he hadn't been back since. He wondered if his mother was still alive.

Not that he cared, naturally, but he did wonder. Occasionally. Or he did now, anyway—now that Heather had dug up the past and flung it before him in the guise of her delicious cooking.

"Stop it, St. Pierre. You'll be getting maudlin next."

His lecture worked. He put on his shoes, brushed his hair, grabbed his hat, and descended the beautifully polished staircase that was carpeted with a beautifully woven Persian rug. When he got to the kitchen, Heather was ready. She'd been prompt last night in the bath house, too. Thank God, she didn't seem to be a dilatory female.

He was, however, sorry to have remembered the bath house episode. Ruthlessly, he drove the image of the nude Heather from his mind.

As usually happened when he caught sight of her, though, he smiled. The smiles that sprang from Philippe when he saw Heather were different from his run-of-the-mill smiles. Those he had to work to produce, and they came from his head. His smiles for Heather started from inside himself, somewhere in the middle of his chest, and all by themselves. It was very odd. He imagined he'd get over it soon. A woman had never yet roused anything deeper than temporary lust in him. He doubted that Heather Mahaffey, in her provincial loveliness, could do more, even though his case of lust in this instance was severe.

"Thank you for being ready, Miss Mahaffey."

"Of course, Mr. St. Pierre."

My, my, weren't we formal? And after that scene last night. Of course, she didn't know he'd been watching her, thank God. Nevertheless, her ladylike manners tickled Philippe—again a novelty. He didn't usually have much to say to proper ladies, not even ones he'd seen nude.

The wind was, as usual, blowing a regular gale. They both had to shield their faces from flying grit as they walked out to the wagon. Philippe would be glad when the trees he'd planted as a windbreak got tall enough to do some good. This was strange country. He loved it, but it was as hard as his own heart, and as tricky, besides. Maybe that's why he got along so well here.

With a grin, he wondered if Mr. Mahaffey, who was an Irish rogue if ever God had crafted one, liked the trickiness of life hereabouts as well as Philippe did. Philippe wouldn't be surprised. Men like Mr. Mahaffey didn't do too well in regular society, but they seemed to thrive in less regulated arenas. Philippe did, too, but for different reasons.

He helped Heather into the wagon and climbed up beside her. She looked quite at home there in the rustic seat. Philippe thought she was really quite charming. Among other things. He started to click to the horses to get them going but, recalling how scatterbrained women generally were, he thought he'd better settle something first.

"Do you have your list?"

"Yes. It's right here." She patted a small embroidered reticule clutched in her right hand.

"Good." Philippe urged the horses forward. He was pleased to see Heather clutch the wagon seat without dropping the reticule, anticipating the jerk when the wagon set out. She was matter-of-fact about so many things. There seemed to be no false airs and graces or coy gestures about her. Curious, he asked, "Did you make that bag, Miss Mahaffey?"

She glanced up at him quickly, as if she suspected a trick to the question. "Good heavens, no."

His lifted eyebrow must have embarrassed her, because she rushed on. "I mean, no, I didn't do this. My sister, Patricia, made it for me for my last birthday. I'm—not very good at sewing."

"I see. Your talents are reserved for the kitchen, are they?"

She sighed. It sounded like a soulful sigh, and Philippe didn't know why that should be.

"I guess so." Her voice came out sounding disheartened, too. Strange, that.

"Do your other siblings have special talents?" Not that he cared, but he sensed Heather would have to be drawn out carefully if he ever expected to know her better. He experienced a strong urge to do so. That was even more strange than Heather's being disheartened, actually. He seldom bothered to draw out a woman's inner thoughts, mainly because he didn't give a rap. As far as he was concerned, women were good for one thing and one thing only. Hell, his mother had taught him that, if she'd taught him nothing else.

"Well, my brother Pete likes to play cards and gamble. I guess he's pretty good at it."

Startled by the candor of her revelation, Philippe let go of a bark of laughter before he could stop himself. Then he was sorry, because he could tell his amusement had irked Heather. "I beg your pardon, Miss Mahaffey. I hadn't—until now—considered card-playing in the light of a talent. I can see now, however, that I was wrong not to do so. Obviously, playing cards well requires a good deal of skill."

She pinched her lips together. Philippe got the feeling she was trying to hold back an outburst of temper. He'd kind of like to see her in a tantrum. He'd wager—if he were a gambler like her brother Pete—that she had a passionate soul tucked away inside her lush and lovely body.

Damn. He had to stop thinking about her body, or this would be a very uncomfortable ride.

"No, you're probably not wrong to do so," she said at last.

Philippe wondered if she was trying to mimic his stilted way of speaking. If she was, that amused him, too. He'd practiced proper speech patterns for so many years now, he doubted he could use improper grammar if he tried. For years he'd done everything he could think of to disguise his origins. Now such affectations were normal for him.

She went on, "I'm sure most folks consider playing cards and gambling a no-account way to pass one's time. Pete's awfully good, though, and he makes fair money at it. And since he gives most of the money he wins to Ma and Pa, I reckon what he's doing isn't bad."

"I should say not. He sounds very talented, actually." In Philippe's experience, gamblers played because they had some kind of madness or addiction. They were rather akin to opium smokers and dipsomaniacs in that regard. Evidently Mr. Pete Mahaffey wasn't one of that breed, and Philippe admired him for the control he exercised over his impulses. Philippe himself was a master of that kind of control. He expected he and Pete would get along quite well together.

"Oh, I know," Heather said, sounding both defiant and resentful. "You think it's stupid to play cards and gamble. You think a man ought to be doing something worthwhile with his time. Working in a store, clerking, or herding cattle or something. But my family's poor, Mr. St. Pierre. We don't have lots of money and fancy houses and herds of cattle and piles of belongings. Pete's doing his best to help out, and I think he's good to do so."

"I don't recall saying that I think it's stupid of your brother to be a good card-player, Miss Mahaffey," he said gently. "In fact, I admire him." Particularly since his experience with gamblers contrasted violently with the estimable Pete.

She squinted at him as if she didn't believe it. Smart girl. Philippe didn't believe people, either, as a rule, although in this case, he was telling the truth.

"Well," she said, deflating like a pricked balloon, "the minister doesn't like it. He says gambling is sinful and that people who gamble are sinners. He says Pete is taking food out of the mouths of the children of the men he wins from." She looked as if she might agree with the minister if anyone but her brother were the recipient of such a reproach.

Never having experienced anything in the way of family feeling, Philippe was impressed. "I see."

"Oh, I know, he's probably right. The minister, I mean. But it's not Pete's fault he's good at cards. And it's not Pete's fault if Mr. Johnson gambles away his family's food money, either. I should think Mr. Harvey—he's the minister—should be lecturing Mr. Johnson, not Pete. Pete *helps* his family."

"Put that way, I absolutely agree with you," Philippe averred firmly. He adored her logic. It was so—logical. And she was so charming in her defense of a brother she loved. Although he'd never experienced family unity, Philippe could almost—almost—appreciate it as spoken about by Heather Mahaffey. "Er, do you have a large family, Miss Mahaffey?"

"I have four brothers and a sister. That's not as big as some of the families around here, but it's plenty big for the house we live in. Too big."

Philippe chuckled until he realized she was squinting at him, perplexed. "I beg your pardon, Miss Mahaffey. You express yourself in such businesslike terms. I'm not accustomed to young ladies exhibiting such practicality."

"Oh."

She sat like a lump for a minute, seeming to mull over his statement. Philippe watched her out of the corner of his eye, wondering what she was going to say next. He didn't have long to wait.

"I expect most folks out here in the territory are practical, Mr. St. Pierre. If you're not practical, you don't last long."

"A sensible observation," he said dryly. "That's one of the things I like about the territory." He didn't elaborate, because he didn't think Heather would understand how refreshing he found life lived amongst people who didn't play games with each other.

Except cards, which was a time-honored masculine pursuit. He grinned, thinking of Heather's brother Pete. Out here, you were practical, or you were dead. He liked that. It was simple and to the point and left no room for whining, arguing, pussy-footing, or bluffing.

"I guess it's kind of rough in the territory," Heather said, as if admitting to a grievous shortcoming. "My mother says she'll be glad when civilization arrives. I've never been anywhere else myself, so I don't know what she means exactly, although I read a lot, and I guess lots of other places have more—fanciness."

"Yes, I suppose they do. Of course, not everyone admires, ah, fanciness."

She sighed. "I wouldn't mind experiencing a little bit of it myself. Like your house, I mean. It's so pretty, and well-appointed. I mean, you even have running water indoors."

"I see what you mean." He glanced at her, fascinated. He hadn't before considered how life must appear to a young woman who'd never lived anywhere but this demanding territory. It was relatively uncivilized out here, he supposed, although there were plenty of churches and schoolhouses in it these days. Too many, if you asked him.

But the land was still as hard as it had ever been. Philippe scanned the countryside, and a feeling of contentment settled on his soul. "So you've learned about the world through books, have you?"

"Yes."

Her color was high, and Philippe hoped he hadn't embarrassed her. He'd learned about life in a whorehouse, which was much less appealing than learning through books. He didn't tell her so because he imagined she wouldn't appreciate it. "But you say your mother is from Ireland?"

She nodded. "Both of my parents are." She sighed again, wistfully. "Of course, they've told me about Ireland. It sounds like heaven to me. I can't imagine a place where everything's always green."

Heather glanced at the countryside, as Philippe had just done, and from her expression he judged her soul didn't appreciate it as his did. That was undoubtedly because she had nothing to compare it with except her parents' stories—and books. He imagined their stories got more colorful with the passing years. Books, of course, were always exaggerating things.

Actually, he had to admit this landscape appeared relatively bleak, at least when one first moved here. As Philippe glanced around, he saw not a speck of Heather's beloved green. And it was April, for the love of God. Yet he knew, because this was his second year in the area, that when summertime came, and the nightly thunderstorms drenched the land—and often covered it with deadly flood waters—the land would turn green. And the desert would bloom. The territory was a magical place in some respects. Harsh and hard, yet it harbored pretty little flowers in its bosom.

And then there was the sky. The huge, eternal sky that looked bigger than any other sky Philippe had ever seen. And it was generally decorated with clouds, from bouncy little puff-ball clouds to looming, threatening thunderheads.

He was going to make himself sick if he went on in that vein any longer.

"Um," Heather said, interrupting his cynical thoughts, "You're from New Orleans?"

"Indeed, I am." He hated talking about New Orleans. Yet again, however, he felt within himself an impulse to tell this girl things. He checked it ruthlessly. He might answer questions if she asked them, because he liked her, but he wouldn't volunteer anything.

"I see. I've read about New Orleans."

Philippe said, "Mmm."

"And about the big celebration there in the spring."

"Mardi Gras," Philippe muttered.

"Yes. It sounds like fun."

"Hmm."

She cleared her throat and gave up on Mardi Gras. "And, um, did you live in New Orleans until you moved to the territory?"

"No, ma'am."

"Oh."

When he glanced at her this time, she looked as if his short answers had quelled her, and he was ashamed of himself. Feeling ashamed of himself was almost as astounding as wanting to tell her things. He relented.

"No, indeed, Miss Mahaffey, I've visited pretty much everywhere in the United States."

"Really?" There was a note of wonder in her voice, and her eyes went as big and blue as Texas bluebonnets. "Oh, I'd love to travel someday."

"Perhaps you will," he murmured.

She heaved a sigh that was almost as big as she was. "I doubt it. It takes money to travel, and I doubt that I'll ever have any."

"Now, now, Miss Mahaffey, what kind of attitude is that?"

"A practical one," she said, and laughed.

Her laugh was lovely. She didn't titter and she didn't giggle, but she laughed exuberantly, as she seemed to do everything. Except talk to him. He made her nervous and he wished he didn't.

"Have you been to California? I've heard a lot about San Francisco. I'd love to see it someday."

"Yes, I've been there. It's an interesting city. Booming, I guess you could call it. Lively. Unrestrained. Full of itself, but with reason. It's much less stuffy than cities back East." He grinned, remembering. "I made a lot of money there."

"Really? Lucky you."

"Luck had something to do with it," he admitted. "I suspect luck has more to do with one's circumstances than people like to admit."

He realized she'd turned to gape at him, and he said, "What? Did I just utter a blasphemy?"

"No, it's only that I've never heard anybody but my father say that. Most folks claim luck has nothing to do with anything, and that people make their own luck."

"I suppose that's partly true. I've been lucky, though, and I don't mind admitting it."

"My brother says the only thing luck doesn't have anything to do with is cards."

"Ha! The philosophical Pete, I presume."

She smiled. "Yes. He says anyone who relies on luck when he plays poker is doomed from the start."

He laughed. "I suspect he's right."

Good God, every member of the family was a philosopher. Must be the Irish in them. Philippe was charmed.

"Pete works on Mr. Custer's ranch. I mean, that's his real job. He doesn't *only* play cards."

"I see." Philippe suspected Heather was trying to paint her brother in a more socially acceptable light. Little did she know. Philippe had liked Pete better when he thought he only played cards for a living. "And you say you have three other brothers?"

"Yes. Poor Henry is six. He's the baby, and he just broke his arm. But he's very good at school. He already wants to be a schoolteacher."

"A noble ambition," Philippe murmured, although he didn't necessarily believe it.

"And then there's Jimmy. He's eight."

"I see. And does he have any discernible talents? Eight is rather young, I suppose."

"Actually, he does."

Philippe heard the pride in her voice, and was moved. How wonderful, he thought, to come from a large and loving family, the members of which took pride in each other's accomplishments. He'd never know, although he enjoyed hearing about it. "And what talents does he display?"

"He's a wonderful horseman, and he's also the best tree climber in Fort Summers."

Philippe opened his mouth and shut it without saying anything. A tree climber? He didn't even know what to ask.

"It's very handy," Heather continued, "because he's small, and he can shinny up the pecan trees and shake the nuts down. He makes good money doing it. Lots of folks hereabouts have pecan orchards. They hire him at harvesting time."

"Ah. How enterprising of him." He meant it sincerely. He'd never lived anyplace where talents such as tree-climbing could be put to money-making pursuits. At least, not legally.

Heather seemed to have overcome her initial shyness. Evidently talking about her family made her expansive. "And my older brother, Jerry, is married to my best friend's sister, and he has a hardware and saddle shop in town."

"Ah, I see. I believe I've met him."

"Probably. It's the only hardware store there."

"Yes. Then I have met him, but I didn't know you were related." He might have. They both had the same blond, blue-eyed good looks. Jerry Mahaffey was a big, burly man, though, and Heather was small and very delicate. Feminine. Lush.

He cleared his throat. "And you say you also have a sister?"

"Yes. Patricia. She's very pretty, and awfully nice. She's a year older than I am and much nicer. She's sort of engaged to Will Armistead."

"Sort of?"

Heather shrugged. "They haven't made it official yet, but as soon as Will's saved a little more money, they will."

"Ah, I see. What is he going to use the money for?"

"Setting up his household," Heather said, as if he shouldn't have had to ask. "And improving his land. He's a farmer."

"I see. So Patricia will be a farmer's wife."

"Right. It's right up her alley. She loves farming, and she can do anything she sets her mind to."

Philippe turned to look at her. "You sound as if you wish you were more like her, Miss Mahaffey."

"Oh, I do," Heather said impulsively. "She's so good at everything. She can preserve fruits and vegetables, sew and cook and quilt and knit and do all of the things that I'm so dismal at."

"You're not at all dismal at cooking," Philippe said, his tone chiding. He hoped she wasn't one of those females who disparaged their own accomplishments in order to garner flattery. If she was, it was the first genuine flaw he'd discovered in her. He was startled when she flushed.

"Oh, well, I guess I'm all right in the kitchen," she muttered, as if she didn't mean it. "But I'm nowhere near as good as Patricia."

"That's difficult to believe."

"It's true." She sounded grumpy.

Philippe decided to skip it. They were approaching the village limits of Fort Summers, and traffic was beginning to pick up. Philippe grinned to himself, knowing he was being sarcastic. Traffic in this case consisted of a solitary rider heading their way.

Heather apparently recognized the rider, because she sat up and shaded her eyes. "Oh, look!" she cried, sounding happy. "There's Mike Mulligan."

Philippe's eyes narrowed of their own accord. "You sound as if you're rather fond of this Mike Mulligan." How had that peculiarly jealous tone crept into his voice? He had no idea.

"I am." She was all but bouncing on the wagon bench. "He and I went through school together, and except for Geraldine, he's been my best friend for years."

"I see." Philippe didn't approve, and he couldn't

figure out why. It was nothing to him if these two provincial young people were fond of each other. Hell, they could marry and produce a flock of little provincial brats, and it wouldn't affect Philippe St. Pierre to the slightest degree. Nothing affected Philippe St. Pierre unless he wanted it to.

But why was he suddenly furious? He wasn't sure he wanted to know.

Heather sat forward on the seat and began waving madly at the approaching horseman. Philippe was interested to note that the rider, who had been walking his horse along at a meandering pace, plainly not in a hurry, first lifted his head, then shaded his eyes, and then let out a whoop of joy and urged his mount toward the wagon at a gallop. These westerners. They were all remarkably spirited, he'd give them that.

When the rider, presumably Mike Mulligan, pulled his mount up in a cloud of dust next to the passenger's side of the wagon, Philippe perceived a gangly youth about the same age as Heather, with a bony, angular face, ruggedly handsome and suntanned, as were all the folks hereabouts. It was hard to avoid a brown skin out here, where the sun seemed closer to the earth than anywhere else Philippe had ever been.

Even ladies like his traveling companion, who assuredly had a mother hen seeing to it that she always wore a sunbonnet on her pretty hair, had a fair smattering of freckles across her nose. On her, freckles were charming.

Philippe himself had been given a head start in the brown-skin department, thanks to his origins.

"Heather!" Mike called, interrupting Philippe's thoughts, for which Philippe was grateful. The young man was grinning from ear to ear.

"Mike!" Heather called back.

Not an original lot, Philippe thought unkindly. Contemplating his origins always made him feel unkind. He had to admit, however, that, given the nature of society hereabouts, he didn't suppose they got much practice in clever repartee.

Heather, her cheeks pink with pleasure, sat up straight and put on her Sunday manners, which must have been difficult since she had to keep a hand pinned to her bonnet so that it wouldn't fly away on the wind. "Mike, please allow me to introduce you to Mr. Philippe St. Pierre."

Mike whipped off his hat and gave a fairly mannerly bow from his saddle. "How-do, Mr. St. Pierre. I'm Mike Mulligan. Pleased to meet you."

Philippe removed his own hat and nodded to the young man. "Likewise, I'm sure. And I'm well, thank you."

He felt Heather stiffen in her seat and realized he'd sounded bored and stony. Which was, of course, foolish. There was no reason to rebuff this boy. He mentally climbed down from his high horse far enough to add, "On your way out of town, I see." He smiled one of the smiles he'd practiced through his many years of trying to trick people into believing he was something he wasn't: an imperturbable and cosmopolitan man of substance and power in the world.

Mike brightened a bit with Philippe's shift in attitude. "Actually, sir, I was on my way out to your place. I understand you're hiring."

"Oh, Mike, wouldn't that be swell!" Heather cried, then slapped a hand over her mouth. "I mean—not swell—it would be grand, is what it would be."

Philippe smiled, with genuine amusement this time. Miss Heather Mahaffey used words like *swell,* did she? Little minx. He'd wager her mother tried her best to muzzle her use of such slang.

However, he wasn't sure about Mike Mulligan in connection with his spread. He didn't think he wanted too many handsome young male friends of Heather's working there and perhaps distracting his personal cook.

But that was nonsensical. Philippe didn't care if Heather married all of them. He smiled at Mike. "Do you know Gil McGill, my head wrangler?"

"Yes, sir. Known him forever."

"Talk to him. We are hiring and, depending on your skills, I'm sure we can use you."

Mike's grin was as bright as the sun beating overhead and trying to burn the wind away. "Thank you, sir!"

"Certainly. We've been having a little trouble with cattle disappearing on my spread. I'm sure we can use another good eye."

"Rustlers?" Mike appeared startled.

"Yes. At least, that's what we suspect."

"Golly. Sorry to hear it. Didn't know we were having those kinds of problems lately."

"I fear we are. At least I am." Philippe gave the boy a regal nod, regretted it because it made him feel old, and said, "Hope to see you again soon."

"Good luck, Mike," Heather added. She was beaming at her friend.

Philippe tried not to begrudge the easy way she communicated with her rustic acquaintances. After all, they'd grown up together. They would naturally be at ease with each other.

"Thanks, Heather. See you!" Mike tipped his hat to Philippe and spurred his mount on his way again.

Philippe realized Heather had turned his way and was gazing at him in a fairly worshipful way. He frowned back at her. "What?"

"Thank you, Mr. St. Pierre. That was very nice of you. Mike really needs a job now that his father is laid up."

Lord, if she made a hero out of him, Philippe didn't think he could stand it. "I'm sure I need good men to work my ranch, Miss Mahaffey." he said. "Especially now, with the troubles we've been having."

Although he despised himself for asking, he said. "You and Mr. Mulligan seem friendly. Are you interested in him, by any chance? Is he in love with you?"

She stared at him for a second before she burst out laughing. It took a while before she was able to answer. "G-good heavens, no!" She wiped her eyes, which had started streaming. "I'm sorry, sir."

"The *sir* is unnecessary." His repressive tone didn't noticeably dampen her amusement. Although her reaction to his question annoyed him, it also soothed his nerves, which had managed to frazzle themselves into an unaccountably ragged condition in the last several minutes.

"Oh, dear, I'm s-s-sorry," she stammered then.

"I guess that answers my question," he said, grumpy that he'd allowed himself to ask such a thing, even if her answer had pleased him. He was mortally glad when she stopped guffawing.

She heaved a happy sigh, and Philippe got the impression she didn't believe his haughty manner as much as he wanted her to. "Do all of your friends need work, Miss Mahaffey?" he asked in order to quell her.

"Probably." She sounded neither quelled nor concerned. "There's not a lot of money here in Fort Summers, and times have been hard since the depression of '93. Of course, most of the town is supported by the soldiers at the fort, but unless a fellow wants to clerk in a store or something, he has to work on a ranch. And until you moved out here, most of the ranchers didn't have steady work, especially as we've had a couple of hard winters and dry summers. Even in the best of times, ranching is mostly seasonal. You run a bigger operation than the rest of the ranchers and use more hands."

"I see." Philippe mulled that one over and decided to say what he was thinking. "I've been extremely fortunate in my business transactions."

"I guess so."

Heather sounded uninterested, which didn't square with what Philippe knew about women. All the females he'd ever known, from his mother on down—or up, depending on one's perspective—had been interested solely in money. The only reason they consorted with men at all was because men had money, and they wanted it.

He wondered if little Miss Mahaffey was playing a deep and dangerous game, trying to trick him into believing that she didn't care about his wealth, or if she really was as ingenuous as she appeared. She might, he supposed, be so much a product of the freedom of the West that she'd escaped developing the moneygrubbing tendencies so prevalent elsewhere. He withheld judgment, but he couldn't suppress a tiny flicker of hope in his bosom.

Which was insane. What did he, Philippe St. Pierre, who had created himself as a rich and successful entrepreneur out of whole cloth—in effect, making a silk purse out of a sow's ear—care about this unsophisticated young woman's basic character? Not a thing, that's what.

Still, he couldn't account for the faint quiver of optimism that took root inside him.

Chapter Eight

Heather took one look at Main Street, and her heart sank into her sensible, albeit hand-me-down, shoes. She considered pretending to slip off the seat and fall to the floor of the wagon, but rejected the notion immediately. That would only make her seem ridiculous, and she feared that was going to happen soon enough already. No need to rush things.

But how, oh how, was she going to explain to Geraldine, who was this minute walking toward them on the long wooden boardwalk, that she, Geraldine, was supposed to have gone all the way out to Philippe St. Pierre's ranch house this morning to help clean up the kitchen? She was about to start chattering to Philippe in an effort to distract him from Geraldine's presence, when she realized all hope was lost.

"Isn't that your friend?" asked Philippe. "The one

at the dance? The one who helped you with the dishes?"

Heather wasn't surprised to see that he looked faintly bewildered. "Er, yes. I do believe it is."

"She moves fast," Philippe muttered, and Heather knew he was trying to put two and two together.

She'd do anything to keep that from happening. Thinking fast, she blurted out, "It's her horse. Actually, it's her brother's horse. He's really fast."

Philippe looked at her strangely. Heather smiled and nodded, attempting to appear innocent.

"I see."

Any lingering hope she'd entertained that Geraldine wouldn't notice them was dashed by her friend's happy cry of greeting.

"Heather! Heather, what are you doing in town?" Waving vigorously with one hand, Geraldine picked up her skirts in the other and trotted over to the wagon, which Philippe obligingly pulled up next to the boardwalk.

"How do you do, Miss—Swift, is it?" Philippe politely tipped his hat to Geraldine, who blushed.

"I'm fine, thank you, Mr. St. Pierre. And you?"

A gust of wind almost lifted Geraldine's bonnet and she had to slap her hand on it.

Heather blessed the wind for the first time in ages because it distracted both Geraldine and Philippe for a moment. Drat. What was she supposed to do now? Fake it, she supposed. It wasn't as if she hadn't practiced dissimulation before. Shoot, she was always having to talk her way out of mischief and mistakes.

Putting on a brave front, Heather grinned down

at Geraldine. "Hello, Geraldine. We came to town to pick up some supplies."

"Oh, good! I'm so glad to see you. I miss you so much—you know, not being able to see you every day and all that."

Heather twisted in her seat so that her back was to Philippe and, using all the miming skills in her repertoire, mouthed a message to Geraldine. The girl looked completely blank. Blast. Geraldine, unlike Heather, was unpracticed in deception. Which probably came from having a smaller family and one with considerably more money and supervision than Heather's.

"Thank you for helping me this morning, Geraldine," she said, and winked wildly at her friend, hoping in that way to convey the message that Geraldine was supposed to play along with her.

Geraldine only looked confused. "Beg pardon?"

Heather made a terrible face, patently shocking Geraldine, who took a step backwards. "I said, thank you for coming out to Mr. St. Pierre's ranch this morning and helping me clean up the kitchen after breakfast."

"Oh!" Geraldine's gaze flicked between Heather and Philippe and came back to rest on Heather. "Oh, of course. Any time. Happy to help."

She still looked confused. Heather hoped Philippe, who didn't know Geraldine well, would accept the expression on her face as not being unusual for the generally competent and clear-thinking Geraldine.

Acting in desperation, Heather turned to Philippe. "May Geraldine accompany us, Mr. St. Pierre?"

He shrugged. "Of course. The more the merrier." He sounded bored.

That was all right with Heather. Let him be bored. Maybe he'd leave her and Geraldine alone for long enough that Heather could explain matters to her friend. Heather's conscience chided her for attempting to draw her best friend into subterfuge, but she told her conscience to shut up and mind its own business.

"Thank you," she said to Philippe. To Geraldine, she said, "Climb up, and you can ride with us to Mr. Trujillo's dry goods store." She turned quickly to Philippe. "That's all right, isn't it?"

"Of course."

Oh, dear. Heather didn't like the chill that had crept into Philippe's voice, and she feared she'd been overbold. Well, that was neither here nor there. She had to keep an eye on Geraldine until she could be sure the girl was in on her scheme. Good heavens, she sounded like a confidence trickster.

Perhaps she was. Perhaps this was the first step, and subsequent steps would lead her, Heather Mahaffey, on a long and winding descent into true evil.

She had to stop thinking things like that. She reached down to give Geraldine a hand, and Geraldine scrambled up into the wagon seat. In order for the three of them to fit, Heather had to scrunch up next to Philippe.

She hadn't thought ahead enough to realize she'd be sitting so close to him. Indeed, her thigh and his actually touched. Heather, who had never had qualms about a man in her life, having been sort of a tomboy in her youth, now felt her whole body heat in reaction to being pressed against her employer. Oh, dear, what had she done?

Last evening's debacle in the bath house came crashing into her head, and she had sudden, lurid visions of herself, naked, standing posed in front of Philippe St. Pierre like an artist's model. In her mental image, however, he wasn't going to paint her. He was going to do other, less banal and more thrilling things. Jehoshaphat, her mind was slipping.

Slanting a sideways glance up at him, she discovered his hot, dark eyes looking directly into hers. She got stuck there, staring into his eyes for a minute, fancying he could see every salacious thought in her head, before she managed to wrench her gaze away from his. Merciful heavens. She wished she could fan herself, but didn't dare let him know how much his nearness affected her. Anyway, the wind was doing a good enough job in fanning her face; she guessed she didn't need a fan.

Fortunately—or, perhaps, unfortunately—Geraldine spoke then, and Heather had to act fast or be discovered.

"Oh, Heather, this is so much fun. I was afraid I'd never see you anymore once you began working for Mr. St. Pierre. What did you mean when you said—Ow!"

Geraldine turned and frowned at Heather. "Why did you poke me in the ribs?"

"Oh, did I?" Heather tittered, which was so unlike herself that she ceased immediately and cleared her throat. "I beg your pardon, Geraldine. I didn't mean to. Poke you, I mean."

"All right. But why did you—Will you stop that?"

Heather turned so that her face was directly before Geraldine, and mouthed, *Don't ask. I'll tell you later.*

Geraldine, clearly confused, shrugged. "Very well, but I still don't understand."

Blast! For being such a smart girl, Geraldine could sometimes be very stupid. And sometimes Heather wished her friend wasn't so sweet and good. Any one of the members of Heather's own family would have realized that Heather was sending a message not to talk about whatever it was they'd been about to talk about. Not Geraldine. Geraldine, as upright and honest as the day was long, had no practice in trickery. Which undoubtedly made her a better person than Heather herself, but it also made her a dud as a conspirator.

Nevertheless, Philippe managed to drive the wagon to the dry goods store and hitch the horses to the rail without further incident. Heather wasn't sure she'd make it that far without having an apoplectic fit, brought on by extreme nervousness, and dying, but she did. She also wasn't sure she was glad of it.

"Here, ladies, allow me to help you down." Philippe's deep, low voice sent a creeping fire through Heather, who was still reeling from having to sit so close to him.

"Thank you, Mr. St. Pierre."

Heather was pleased to note that Geraldine, too, seemed to be affected by Philippe's presence. She flushed prettily and took his hand. Heather had to force herself not to frown at the two of them. There was no reason she should resent it that Philippe's attention was focused entirely on Geraldine. After all, he was being polite. And she'd noticed before that, when he spoke, it was as if there were no one else around but the person to whom he was speaking.

The trouble was, Heather wanted that person to be herself. Which was stupid. She was his cook, not his sweetheart. And actually, she wasn't even his cook. She was a cheat and a fraud, and she made herself sick.

She really, really had to get a handle on her nerves.

"Miss Mahaffey?"

Heather jumped slightly on the wagon bench. She'd been so caught up in her own black thoughts that she hadn't realized Philippe had turned from Geraldine to her.

"Oh, I beg your pardon. I guess I was woolgathering."

"Indeed." He smiled up at her, and Heather's heart tripped, fell, picked itself up, and started racing. She wished she didn't have this reaction to him. It was very uncomfortable. Not to mention unseemly.

It was all she could do to climb down from the wagon in an almost-dignified manner and alight on the boardwalk. It was impossible to be truly dignified while trying to hold one's skirts and hat and, at the same time, scramble over a dusty wheel and leap out of a wagon.

Add to that the fact that Heather experienced a mad desire to jump from the wagon into Philippe's arms, and she didn't know what to make of herself. Her mother would be shocked. Patricia would be shocked. Geraldine would be shocked.

Shoot, even Heather was shocked. She'd never had impulses of this improper nature before. Granted she wasn't the most ladylike specimen in the universe, but she was still a proper female. Or had been.

She had a sinking feeling that proper females didn't lie and perpetrate rank deceptions as she was doing, but she wouldn't dwell on it.

The three of them entered the dry goods store together. Heather managed to maneuver Geraldine over to the notions counter in a far corner after a few minutes, while Philippe talked to Mr. Trujillo. She told Geraldine to pretend she'd been out to the ranch that morning.

"But why? What's so important about me helping you clean up the kitchen?" Geraldine's eyes were large behind her spectacles.

Heather wished her best friend weren't so blasted innocent. Or so blasted curious. "Because I couldn't possibly have done it so fast by myself."

Geraldine, whose head had been tilted slightly to the left, now tilted it slightly to the right. "Heather, you're not making any sense. If you didn't clean it, who did?"

Blast! Heather remembered an old saw about tangled webs and deception, and sighed deeply. "I had help." She didn't think Geraldine would buy that one without further explanation. She was right.

"Who helped you?"

Oh, dear. Perceiving that Geraldine was going to be obstinate about this, Heather said, "A gentleman named D. A. Bologh. He's assisting me in the kitchen."

"Then why keep it a secret?"

"Because Mr. St. Pierre doesn't know about it, and he doesn't like strangers in his house."

"Then why do you want me to lie and say I, another stranger, am the one who helped you?"

"It's not a lie!" Which was, of course, a lie. Heather backed up and started again. "That is, it's not a lie that I have help. It's only a lie that the help is you."

Geraldine shook her head sadly. "I fear you're not making any sense, Heather. If you're ashamed of accepting this Mr. Bologh's assistance—"

"I'm not ashamed of it," Heather hissed, trying to keep her voice low for fear of being overheard. "That is, I am ashamed of needing help." She huffed impatiently. "Oh, Geraldine, you know how I am in the kitchen. I can't cook water. I tried to boil some eggs at home and they exploded all over the stove. The whole place stank like sulfur for a week." She hated admitting all of this, but Geraldine already knew most of it. "Anyhow, I'm a terrible cook. Mr. Bologh is helping me to learn, but Mr. St. Pierre doesn't know it."

"That's wrong, Heather. You know it's wrong. You're working there under false pretenses, and you're sure to be found out one of these days, and then what do you suppose will happen?"

"I'll get fired," Heather grumbled.

"That's right." Geraldine nodded sharply. "And what if this Mr. Bologh person is really a bad man and is only pretending to be helpful."

"That's folderol."

"You don't know that. He might well be weaseling his way into your confidence so he can rob poor Mr. St. Pierre blind."

"He's not poor." It was feeble, but Heather felt sort of feeble just then.

"You're waffling, Heather Mahaffey, and you know it." Geraldine looked very stern.

"Hmph."

"And one of these days you're sure to be found out. Then you'll bring shame on your family, too."

Geraldine sounded a little too self-righteous for Heather's peace of mind. Unfortunately, Heather couldn't fault her friend's logic. "I know it, but I needed a job. Besides, it was the wind."

Geraldine squinted at her. "What about the wind?"

"It drove me crazy. It must have, because I know good and well I can't cook."

"Yes, the entire town knows that."

"That's not very nice, Geraldine," Heather muttered. "Even if it is true."

Geraldine took Heather's arm. "I'm sorry, Heather. But you've got yourself in a terrible fix now, and I fear more lying won't help you much."

Heather stared at her friend, appalled. "Oh, Geraldine, you're not going to tell on me, are you? You can't do that!"

"Well . . ."

"Please, *please* don't tell anybody! I'm learning. Honest, I am. Mr. Bologh is teaching me. He's got to be the best cook in the world, and he's letting me watch and take notes and everything."

Geraldine frowned again. "I've never heard of a Mr. Bologh. Who is he?"

"I don't know. He just showed up."

"It sounds fishy to me."

It did to Heather, too. "What's fishy about it? I need help. He's helping."

"For free?"

Heather hesitated before she said slowly, "Not exactly."

"What do you mean, not exactly?"

Geraldine was beginning to sound serious again, and Heather didn't appreciate it. She had enough trouble without her best friend turning on her. "We made a deal. He'd help me, and I'd—" She'd what? She didn't know yet. Her insides gave a little spasm of dread. "I'd do something for him. Someday."

"What? Exactly what are you going to do for him?"

"I—ah—I don't know yet."

Geraldine slapped a hand to her forehead. "Heather! I can't believe—"

"Keep your voice down!"

Geraldine obliged. She whispered fiercely, "I can't believe you made a bargain with a total stranger and don't even know what payment he's going to exact from you. What if he wants you to—you know." Geraldine's cheeks caught fire.

"I'm sure he won't," muttered Heather, who was sure of no such thing.

"You really are crazy, Heather Mahaffey, do you know that? And the wind has nothing to do with it. Here you are, supposed to be a grown-up woman—you're twenty-two years old, for heaven's sake—and you're behaving like a naughty child. You ought to be ashamed of yourself."

"If I wanted a lecture, I'd go home and get a good one from my mother," Heather retorted hotly. "Now, are you going to tell on me, or not?"

"Well . . ."

"I thought we were friends." A lump had grown in Heather's throat and was now aching. This was all her fault, and she knew it, but she couldn't bear the notion of Geraldine turning against her. Even if she deserved it.

"Oh, Heather, of course I won't tell anybody." Geraldine gave her a quick hug, and Heather had to fight tears. "But you know as well as I do that this is a foolish thing you're doing. Perhaps even dangerous."

Heather had to yank a handkerchief out of her pocket and dab at her eyes before she could respond. "Thanks, Geraldine. You're my best friend and always will be."

"I know it. Nobody else would put up with you."

Heather's chuckle came out drowned.

Geraldine sighed heavily. "But I wish you'd reconsider this lunacy."

"I will," Heather said, not meaning it. "Truly, I will."

She took Geraldine's arm, and the two young ladies left the notions counter. She saw Philippe directing Joe, Mr. Trujillo's fourth son, to take some large sacks, presumably containing flour or sugar or something else she didn't know what to do with, out to the wagon.

When she glanced to her right, she stopped dead in her tracks.

"What is it?" Geraldine asked, startled by Heather's abrupt halt.

"That's him," Heather whispered.

D. A. Bologh stood leaning against the far wall, grinning his evil grin, and stroking his wicked black mustache. He winked at Heather, and her heart stood still for a moment. She was afraid of that man, and she couldn't understand why.

"That's who?" Geraldine blinked at Heather.

"That's Mr. Bologh. Mr. D. A. Bologh."

"It is? Where?"

Heather glanced at her friend and said, "Over

there." When she turned her head again, he was gone. She looked around the room, feeling something akin to hysteria growing in her. "At least—I know he was there. Against that wall. He's here somewhere. He's got to be."

But he wasn't. Everywhere Heather looked in the dry goods store, D. A. Bologh wasn't.

Geraldine shook her head sadly. "It's your guilty conscience playing tricks on you, Heather. You know what Mr. Harvey always says."

Yes, Heather knew. Mr. Harvey always said that a man's sins would find him out, and that the Lord would exact payment for every iniquitous deed.

"But I'm not wicked," she all but whimpered.

"Nobody starts out wicked," Geraldine lectured in her gentlest tone. "One's sins pile up so subtly that one isn't even aware of them. Then, one day, a body wakes up to find herself the possessor of a black heart and a soul that's headed straight to perdition."

"I'm not *that* bad."

"No." Geraldine sighed heavily. "Not yet you're not. But you soon will be. You're behaving in a reckless and misguided manner, and you know it."

"I know it."

Heather was utterly demoralized and completely miserable when she climbed back into the wagon, waved good-bye to Geraldine, and set out with Philippe to return to the ranch.

In a tall, elegant mansion with gingerbread trim and frothy wrought-iron balcony railings, D. A. Bologh stroked Yvonne St. Pierre's silky cheek.

"It's time to pay, sweetheart," he said.

The beautiful octoroon uttered a guttural, "Bah! I've been paying for decades."

D. A. chuckled softly. "Oh, but not enough, my sweet. The time's come for the final tally."

She jerked away from him as if his touch sickened her. Which, by this time, it did. At first, the bargain she'd struck had seemed merely sensible. She knew good and well that a woman like her only lasted as long as did her looks. And, thanks to the deal she'd struck with D. A. Bologh so many years ago, her looks were superb.

But she was sick of it all. That wretched bargain, which had done so well by her in the way of appearance and fortune, had cost her too much in the long run. It had, in fact, cost her everything she'd ever truly valued in her life. Knowing it, her heart ached.

"What in the world do you mean, the final tally?" she asked testily. "You've already got my body and soul and everything else of mine."

"Not quite everything." He twirled his mustache, grinning like the devil.

"I'd like to know what else I have that you don't have access to."

At first it seemed he wasn't going to answer her. He said softly, "I've been traveling a lot lately. You know, seeing the country and all that."

"So what?" She flung herself down onto a velvet love seat and drew her brilliant red—she looked particularly stunning in red—silk Chinese wrapper more tightly to her high, firm bosom. Yes indeed, not only was her face still beautiful, but she had the body of a woman a third her age.

D. A. shrugged. "You know how much I like to travel. I like to keep on the move."

"Right." She glared at him, not bothering to hide her loathing. Her open hostility only amused him, but she didn't care any longer. There was only one thing she'd ever cared about, and that had been denied her for so long she barely remembered any longer. "And you've been at it for a long time, too. I'm surprised there's anywhere you haven't been yet."

"There isn't, really, but things change with time. I never know what, say, Egypt is going to look like from one visit to the next. Or America. America's changed a lot."

"I'll bet."

"For instance, I've been interested in several of the western territories. It used to be there was nothing but cactus and creosote out there in, oh, for example, southern New Mexico Territory."

"And there's more there now?" She didn't believe it. She'd read tales about the Wild West and as far as she was concerned, the dime novelists could have it.

"Oh, much more." D. A. strolled over and sat next to her. Reaching out, he gently pushed the silk wrapper aside and gazed greedily at Yvonne's breasts.

She shut her eyes, wishing for at least the ten thousandth time that she didn't have to do this anymore.

"For instance, there are a lot of cattle ranches in that part of the territory now. Folks are moving there all the time for their health, as well. The dry air is alleged to be good for consumptives." He leaned closer and flicked her nipple with his tongue.

This was part of the bargain, and Yvonne knew

it—and hated it. As much as she abominated this fiend from hell, the minute he put his hands on her, she was aroused to the point of near insanity. She squirmed and tried to draw away, but he only chuckled.

"I don't care about cows," she said, close to tears. Youth and beauty and sexual allure seemed to her now to be pitifully petty things for which to barter one's soul.

"No? But you might care about a gentleman down there who has a whole flock of them. Or is that a herd? I forget the vernacular." D. A. pushed Yvonne's wrapper off and began feasting on her luscious body. It was his, after all.

"I don't care about cowboys, either," she said, writhing in spite of herself.

D. A. stood and stripped quickly. A moment later, he was buried inside of her and thrusting deeply as she met each thrust with a wild lift of her hips.

"But this particular gentleman's last name is St. Pierre."

Yvonne's eyes flew open, and she saw D. A. looming over her, grinning evilly—which was the only way he could grin. "What?" she panted, near her climax.

"Yes indeedy, sweetheart. A Mr. Philippe St. Pierre. Folks say he came originally from New Orleans."

Yvonne's release came along with a scream of anguish. She cried for hours after D. A. left her. Of course, not a speck of her distress showed the next morning when her latest protector, a northerner who'd opened a large tobacco processing plant nearby, joined her for breakfast.

She wished she could die. Unfortunately, even that pleasant option was now denied to her, thanks to the bargain she'd struck with D. A. Bologh when she was only a girl.

Heather knew something strange was afoot as soon as she stepped inside the house. The journey back to the ranch from town hadn't been as dismal as she'd feared. Philippe had seemed to be in a good mood, and she shortly managed to put Geraldine's dire warnings and predictions for Heather's future behind her.

By the time they entered the ranch yard, she'd almost convinced herself that everything would work out just fine in the end. She only had to pay close attention to D. A. Bologh and learn from him. If she was never as good a cook as he, she could probably become fairly competent if given enough time. And lots of luck.

But there shouldn't be the delicious fragrance of roasted duckling seeping through the house, because she hadn't been there to cook it. She hurried to the kitchen and threw the door open.

D. A. Bologh sat in his favorite chair, stroking his mustache and grinning at her.

"Why did you cook dinner?" she hissed as she stormed into the room. "Why, when you knew I wouldn't be here, did you do such a thing? You're supposed to be a secret. If Mr. St. Pierre finds out about you, I'll be out on my ear, and you will be, too. And I won't pay up if you don't keep your bargain!"

D. A. shrugged. "Everybody's got to eat, Miss Heather. I'm sure Mr. St. Pierre will welcome his dinner the same as any other man."

"But I wasn't *here*! How am I going to explain a full-fledged dinner to him?"

"I'm sure you'll think of something."

"What about Mrs.—" Heather pressed a hand to her head in sheer terror. "Oh, my heavens, what about Mrs. Van der Linden?"

"She'll probably just think you planned ahead." He slanted her a sly glance.

Heather gaped at him. "Mrs. Van der Linden? You're joking!"

He shrugged again. "What's she going to do? How can she refute you? There will be a delicious dinner being served up to the master of the house, and that will amply negate her words."

"When will it be ready?"

D. A. flipped his hand in the air. "Any time you're ready, my sweet."

"Oh, dear." Heather sank into a chair and sagged there for a minute before she realized she'd have to do some more lying, and quick. She jumped to her feet and ran to put on an apron. "You're not playing fair," she groused as she flung herself out of the room. D. A.'s laughter followed her down the hall.

She found Philippe in his library. The door wasn't shut, but she knocked softly anyway, feeling uncomfortable in such grand surroundings.

He turned and smiled at her, and her knees turned to water. "I smell something cooking," he said in his deep, rich voice that always sort of made Heather want to purr and stretch languidly, like a cat. "And I must say I'm surprised."

"Er, yes. I, ah, put the duckling on to roast—slowly, you know—before we left for town this morning."

One of his eyebrows lifted. "My, my, how enterprising of you."

"Um, yes. Thank you. Anyway, it's about ready, if you are."

"I'm more than ready for another of your succulent meals, Miss Mahaffey."

"I'll get it on the table then."

"Fine. Thank you."

"Um, all right. I'll just go set it out now," said Heather, and bolted.

Mrs. Van der Linden was in the hall, scowling at her, when she left the library. Heather gave the grouchy woman a wan smile, which wasn't returned.

"There's something fishy going on around here," Mrs. Van der Linden declared at Heather's back.

This was the second time today that Heather had been gifted with the something's-fishy line. Unfortunately, she couldn't very well deny it. There *was* something fishy going on around here. Heather feared it was D. A. Bologh, and the idea scared her.

Chapter Nine

On the sixth night of Heather Mahaffey's employment in his establishment, Philippe asked Mrs. Van der Linden to invite the young woman to join him in the library when she was finished washing up.

Heather stared at Mrs. Van der Linden, aghast, when the message reached her. "He wants to see me?" Her heart began hammering out a dirge of dread.

Mrs. Van der Linden sniffed. "So he says."

"What for?"

"I have no idea." Mrs. Van der Linden eyed the kitchen, which was, as usual, spotless. "I still say there's something fishy going on around here, Heather Mahaffey."

Heather lifted her chin. "You may say what you like, Mrs. Van der Linden."

"I will, believe me. And when I find out what it

is, you can rest assured that I shall inform Mr. St. Pierre."

"Fine. Do that." Heather knew she was being foolish to antagonize the woman, who didn't need any encouragement in that regard, as she was plenty antagonistic to begin with. She couldn't seem to help herself, though. "Mr. St. Pierre doesn't seem to share your doubts about my performance."

"That's because you've pulled the wool over his eyes, and you know it."

"And exactly how have I done that?" Heather asked hotly. She felt beleaguered and guilty, and wished this old witch would take herself off to her coven or to wherever she'd come from.

"I don't know how you've done it," declared the stout housekeeper, "but I aim to find out." And she stalked off with her nose in the air and her big rear end waddling up a disapproving storm.

Heather shut her eyes and breathed deeply, wishing she could just die and get it over with.

"Don't fret about that old biddy," came a voice from behind her.

She turned and wasn't surprised to see D. A. Bologh sitting in the kitchen chair—the kitchen chair that had been empty only moments earlier when Mrs. Van der Linden had been standing in the room. Heather almost forgot herself and asked how he managed to pop up here and there so effortlessly, but stopped herself in time. He'd never answered her before, and every time he didn't answer her, she got shivery feelings that she didn't enjoy.

"But she knows I'm a fraud," Heather said unhappily.

"So what? Nothing she can do about it. The man thinks you're a peach." He winked. "So do I."

Somehow that didn't thrill Heather. "I feel bad about deceiving everybody. It's wrong, and I shouldn't have started it. But now that I have, I don't know how to stop."

D. A.'s grin was purely wicked. "It's a shame how things like that happen, isn't it?" If he could sound more insincere, Heather hoped she'd never hear it.

"I'd better get this over with." She took off her apron and hung it on the hook beside the sink. She often wondered why she even bothered with the apron, since she didn't do anything but watch D. A. as he cooked, but she kept hoping she'd learn.

"Have fun," Bologh said as she walked to the door.

Before she left, she stopped and turned, having thought of something that might be important. "What was it I served for dinner tonight? I don't remember."

She absolutely *hated* D. A.'s knowing chuckle.

"Fresh river perch en Pipérade, sautéed vegetables, rice with saffron, and a cheesecake with a brandied apricot sauce. I won't bother giving you the French words for the latter several dishes."

"Thank you."

"You're quite welcome."

Heather squinted at him. "Did the perch come from the Pecos?" The Pecos River ran through the town of Fort Summers, and folks did a lot of fishing there.

D. A. shrugged. "Tell him it did, if it makes you feel better."

Tell him it did? What did that mean? Uneasy, Heather opened her mouth to ask another question, but decided not to. There was something not right about D. A. Bologh, and the more she let him work for her, the more edgy she became. She wished she had never let the wind drive her to this.

"Thanks," she said at last, and turned to go, telling herself as she did so that none of this was the wind's fault. Which didn't make her feel the least bit better.

She stopped in the hall to check her appearance in the small decorative mirror hanging above some sort of French table. She tucked a couple of loose strands of hair behind her ear, practiced one of her friendly smiles, gritted her teeth, and knocked at the door.

"Enter," came Philippe's deep velvety voice from behind it.

Every time Heather heard that voice, her insides tingled with pleasure and an anticipation she couldn't account for, although it had something to do with all the unladylike fantasies she'd been spinning around that wretched bath house incident. Philippe had already had Mrs. Van der Linden make new curtains. They now hung in the bath house, and in order for anybody to peek in now, he'd have to blow a hole in the wall. Heather sighed, partially with regret, and she knew she was falling fast.

It occurred to her that her life had become awfully uncomfortable lately, what with one man giving her shivers in the kitchen and another giving her tingles in the rest of the house. With another sigh, she did as Philippe had bidden.

He was standing by the fireplace, a book in his hand. He set it on the mantel when Heather entered. Because he made her nervous, she stopped just inside the room and folded her hands under her apron.

The library was a lovely room, all dark wood floors and beautiful Persian rugs. The furniture was new and, rumor had it, had been purchased from a catalog and shipped from a warehouse all the way in New York City. Mrs. Van der Linden called the stuff French Provincial, but Heather only knew it was gorgeous, and ever so much finer than anything her family had ever owned. Or ever would own, for that matter.

Philippe had built himself a sturdy house, and one with doors and windows that fitted impeccably. Very little dust dared to show itself in *his* house, and what little did manage to creep in was ruthlessly vanquished by Mrs. Van der Linden on a daily—or even shorter-than-daily—basis. This evening, the wood in Philippe's library exuded a dull gleam that fairly shouted wealth to Heather, who had been, until her tenure in Philippe's household, a total stranger to luxury.

A fire burned merrily in the grate, taking the chill out of the cool spring evening air. The heavy brocaded curtains had been drawn over the Battenburg lace sheers, and a rosy glow seemed to have invaded the whole room.

The impression of rosiness was probably augmented by the pretty rose-tinted etched glass globes on the two lanterns burning on side tables. They cast an almost magical aura on the room and on the room's owner. Philippe's dark complexion was imbued with a warm tint, making him seem softer and more approachable than usual.

Which was unfortunate, in Heather's way of thinking.

His very pose of casual elegance set her teeth on edge. She wanted to run into his arms and beg him to make mad, passionate love to her. And then to make everything right in her life. Which was nonsensical. Not only would she thus be abdicating her own responsibilities, but he'd be far more likely to toss her out on her rump than help her.

She was, really and truly, losing her mind. Poor Ma and Pa would be so sad when they learned of it.

"Please, Miss Mahaffey, come in and sit down."

He walked over to her, and it was all she could do to keep from shrinking away from him. This was idiotic behavior on her part. She knew it, and she also knew it sprang directly from her guilty conscience. She was reaping what she'd sown, blast it, just like Mr. Harvey always said people did. She'd never doubt the good preacher again. She took the chair at which Philippe gestured, sitting on the edge and feeling like a dry twig about to snap in two.

He took the chair opposite her and seemed to relax completely. Good for him. Heather wished she could do that. But he, unlike her, unquestionably had a clean conscience.

"You served another delicious dinner tonight, Miss Mahaffey. I must say I'm very impressed with your skill in the kitchen."

"Thank you. Um, it was perch en Pipérade, sauteed vegetables, rice with—" Oh, Lord, she forgot what the rice was with. Why had she started this? Hoping he wouldn't notice that she'd stopped in the middle, she said, "Glad you enjoyed it." She licked her lips, searching frantically for something else to say. "Um, the fish came from the Pecos."

He lifted his eyebrow. "Yes, I imagined it did."

Mercy, mercy, why hadn't she kept her mouth shut? She did so now; too late.

He continued, "So, I get the impression that you have adjusted to your employment in my house, Miss Mahaffey. I presume you noticed that there are new curtains in the bath house." He smiled engagingly.

"Yes. Thank you, I did notice." Of course, as soon as he mentioned the bath house, she felt her face catch fire. Jehoshaphat.

"Good. I wanted to take this opportunity to chat with you and see if there's anything that needs to be attended to."

Heather sat bolt upright, provocative thoughts forgotten. "No. What do you mean? Is something wrong?"

Again she wished she'd not spoken when that blasted eyebrow of his lifted. Why couldn't she calm down? This was so stupid. She sucked in a deep breath, hoping it would help. It didn't.

"That's what I'm asking you," Philippe said gently. "You seem awfully nervous. Is there anything I can do to make your job less nerve-wracking for you?"

Heather swallowed. "Oh." She thought for a second. "Um, no, I don't think so. Your kitchen is very well appointed." At least, that's what D. A. Bologh had told her. Heather wouldn't know a well-appointed kitchen from a barn. The truth made her nerves skip. Since they'd been racing, the skip almost made her faint. She sucked in more air, let it out slowly, and commanded herself to stop being so jittery.

Philippe sat back and observed her for long

enough that Heather wanted to scream. "I must admit I don't understand why you seem so jumpy. I'm afraid it has something to do with your employment, and I'd like to solve whatever problem is interfering with your peace of mind, if at all possible."

"It's not," burst from Heather's lips, and she mentally kicked herself. "That is to say, there's nothing wrong."

"Hmm. Are you sure? You're not worried about cattle rustlers, are you? We haven't had any more trouble in that regard lately."

"Oh. Good. I'm glad to hear it." She wished he wouldn't direct those deep, burning eyes of his at her in such a searching manner. His scrutiny made her want to squirm. Trying with every fiber of her being to calm down, she withdrew her hands from underneath her apron, folded them again, and put them in her lap. Exactly as a proper lady would do. Her mother would have been proud of her. She'd been trying to get Heather to sit in just such a way for years now.

"Hmm," Philippe said again. "I hesitate to call anyone a liar, Miss Mahaffey, but there definitely seems to be something wrong. Is anyone on the ranch bothering you? Any of the men who work here?"

Heather felt her eyes widen. "I beg your pardon?" She didn't know what he was talking about.

His smile looked cynical. "You must know that you're a very attractive young woman, Miss Mahaffey. You certainly wouldn't be the first to experience some measure of annoyance from rowdy young men. I know that nobody can see through the bath house windows any longer, but if any of my men bother you, I want you to tell me. Will you do that?"

"Oh." Heather guessed she understood now, although there wasn't a man working on his ranch whom Heather didn't know—and whom she couldn't lick if push came to shove. "Of course I will. Thank you for being so considerate."

He waved her thanks away. "But you say none of the men have been bothering you?"

"No. They're all friends of mine, anyway."

"I see."

Heather couldn't account for his frown. He ought to be happy that he didn't have to ride herd on his cowboys. He'd be better off worrying about himself. If Heather's sexual urges became more pronounced, she might attack him.

Merciful God, she had to stop thinking things like that.

"Then is it me? Do I make you nervous?"

Had he really asked her that? She decided she'd be better off lying. Again. "Ah, a little bit, I guess."

"Why is that? I told you once that I don't bite, and I still don't. At least not personable young women."

Heather tried to laugh, but it came out thin and strained. She scrambled madly for something intelligent to say and came up with a partial truth, which was becoming a novel experience. "I—ah, I think it's because you're so much wealthier than anyone I've ever met before." She ruined her mother's training by flipping her hand out, which a proper lady would never do. "I mean, you know, people always think rich people are different from the rest of us. Until you came to town, everybody pretty much scraped by. Now the rest of us still do. But you don't."

She was a complete and total idiot, and if Philippe St. Pierre didn't shoot her on the spot, she might just go outside and shoot herself. She quailed inside as she waited for him to say something.

"I see," is what he said.

Heather cleared her throat, but couldn't think of anything else to say, which was probably a blessing.

"I guess I can understand that, but I can't imagine why the differences in our relative wealth should make you so uncomfortable. After all, I didn't start out life as a rich man."

"You didn't?"

"Not at all. I started out with nothing. Therefore, except for my having a course in life that has garnered me rich rewards, I'm still just like everybody else in the world."

In a pig's eye. Heather remained silent.

"So I still don't understand why you should think of me as different from any of the other men in Fort Summers."

"Yes, I guess it is a pretty silly thing to do." She achieved a fairly good smile.

He looked at the fire for a moment, and Heather breathed a sigh of relief—too soon, as it turned out, because he looked at her again almost at once. "Is there anything else troubling you? Problems with your family, perhaps?"

"My family?" Heather bounced out of her chair in a panic. "Oh, no! Don't tell me something's happened to one of them?" She began wringing her hands.

"No, no, no. Sit down, please. I only offered that as a possible reason for your distress. As far as I know, your family is fine."

"Oh." She sank back into the chair, feeling like a blithering blockhead, and with her heart hammering like a woodpecker. "Thank God."

Philippe stood suddenly, and she jumped. "Miss Mahaffey, I insist on your telling me what's wrong. Something is. I can tell, and I'm sure it isn't just because I'm a rich man. There are other men of substance in Fort Summers, as you well know. And I want you to know that I'll do anything I can to assist you in any way possible."

How nice he was. Heather wished she deserved his kindness. "Thank you very much, Mr. St. Pierre. But there's truly nothing wrong. I'm only—a little nervous about cooking, you see. I, um, haven't been very handy in the kitchen before this." Which was probably the first absolute truth she'd uttered since she accepted this wretched job.

"Yes, I've heard that from Mrs. Van der Linden, but I couldn't credit her words. Your cooking is superb."

"Thank you." Heather wanted to crawl under a rug and die.

"That being the case, I wonder if you're up to doing something more ambitious."

Her heart sank. "Something more ambitious?" She didn't want to know. She couldn't ask.

"I've been considering giving a dinner party for some of my neighbors."

"Oh."

"I fear I haven't been particularly sociable since I moved to Fort Summers. The truth is that I've concentrated so hard on building my ranching operation that I haven't until now given much thought to getting to know the people in the community."

"I see." Heather tried to take comfort from the sure knowledge that D. A. Bologh could probably whip up a feast for thousands with a wave of his hand, but couldn't. D. A. Bologh gave her the creeps, and there were no two ways about it.

"Do you think you'd be up to preparing dinner for a party of. . . ." He hesitated for a moment and seemed to be thinking. Heather held her breath. "Say fifteen people or thereabouts? Sixteen, I suppose, would be better, to keep the numbers even."

"I shouldn't think that would be a problem, Mr. St. Pierre." And if it was, she'd just shoot herself.

His smile almost knocked her flat. She took another deep breath and nearly hyperventilated. This was absurd. Not only was she in a constant state of frenzy because of the lies she'd told, but she also had this terribly unladylike reaction to her employer—who thought she was a very pretty young woman. She gulped, wishing she hadn't remembered his words.

He probably hadn't meant them.

But what if he had? The other men in town seemed to think she was pretty.

Bother, if she didn't stop getting distracted, she'd never get anywhere. Philippe St. Pierre had just said something and was now looking at her quizzically, as if he expected an answer, and she had no idea what he'd said. This was terrible.

"Um, I beg your pardon, Mr. St. Pierre. I was—thinking of a menu for the party." Liar, liar. How could she tell such whoppers? She never used to be a liar.

"Ah, I see."

Was it her imagination, or did his smile warm up ever so slightly? Heather licked her lips and paid attention.

"Actually, I was asking you what you thought you might serve."

"Oh." Shoot, now what? Stall, that's what. "Um, may I get back to you on that, Mr. St. Pierre? I still have some thinking to do."

"Certainly."

He kept staring at her, and Heather felt her nerves skip wildly. He was so different from the other men she knew; she'd already discovered within herself a very improper impulse to explore his differences in depth. Perhaps by hand. If he didn't stop staring at her, her reserve might crack and she'd do it, too.

She told herself severely that just because she'd become a liar and a cheat, it didn't mean she had to become a hussy, too.

"Miss Mahaffey," he said after too many tense moments, "would you be willing to assist me with the guest list and perhaps address the invitations?"

"The—the guest list?" He was going to make a guest list and send invitations? Shoot, when her folks had people over for supper, they just invited them on the street. This, she guessed, was the difference between first class and no class. "I'll be happy to, Mr. St. Pierre." That was the truth, too, and she felt minimally better about herself for a second. Didn't last long. As soon as he smiled again, she had to fight to keep from fainting.

"Fine. That's fine. When do you suppose you'll have the menu prepared?"

Merciful heavens, he wanted to accept or reject

the menu? She was glad she lived in the West, if this is what people who lived back East had to go through in the course of their employment. "Um, I don't know. In an hour or so?"

"All right, and then perhaps you can tell me when you'd be able to prepare the feast. I don't want to rush you."

Rush her? Was he joshing her? But of course, he didn't know her evil secret. "It's not a problem, Mr. St. Pierre. I'm sure a week will be plenty of time to prepare." Then again, what did she know? Maybe dinner parties typically took months of preparation. She wished she knew more about what her job entailed.

"That quickly? I'm impressed. I thought you might have to order something special."

"Special? Er, no, I don't think so. Um, I don't go in for really fancy stuff."

"You could have fooled me." He chuckled. His laugh, unlike the mirth of D. A. Bologh, made Heather want to curl up and bask in its warmth.

She was obviously insane.

She thanked her lucky stars when Philippe dismissed her a few moments later, and she could escape to her kitchen. Except it wasn't her kitchen. D. A. Bologh still sat at the kitchen table, and he still looked wicked.

But she needed him. Heavens above, what had she done?

Philippe watched Heather leave the library and experienced a mad desire to beat her to the door, slam it, trap her, and then ravish her, totally and completely. He'd bet that it wouldn't take him too long to light the fires of passion in her—if he ever got past her tightly controlled reserve. He sensed passions inside of her, banked and ready for release.

Shaking his head hard, he told himself to stop dwelling on it. He had plans in that direction already, and he aimed to carry them out. Besides, he had a dinner party to prepare for. He snorted derisively. He wanted to socialize with Fort Summers society about as much as he wanted to return to New Orleans, which was not at all.

Nevertheless, it had occurred to him that it would be interesting—perhaps even amusing—to see how long it would take him to break down Heather Mahaffey's resistance to his charm, and he'd decided that working with her in some joint operation might do it. It generally didn't take long, primarily because he was good-looking and had lots of money. Women went for that sort of thing.

He couldn't understand why Heather didn't. Perhaps she had a beau among the rustic cowboys in his employ or the gents in town. He frowned at the thought of the lovely Heather on the arm of Sandy Porter, the town's rough-hewn blacksmith, or someone of that ilk. Not that he didn't like Sandy, who was polite and friendly. And the man was a fine blacksmith.

He cursed, furious with himself for thinking about the girl at all, much less inventing reasons to get together with her. This was most unlike him.

She was unique, however, in his experience of women. Not only was she as pretty as any of the women around whom he'd grown up in New Orleans—and the house in which his mother worked had only employed the loveliest females in town—but she seemed totally unaware of her beauty. Or, if she was aware that she was pretty, she didn't seem to value her looks a whole lot.

Her attitude, in fact, was completely out of the ordinary. Most of the women Philippe had heretofore known would have killed to possess half of Heather's natural beauty, because it would have made the chore of snagging husbands and/or protectors that much easier.

Not Heather. She didn't seem to be in the market for a husband, a protector, or anything other than a paying job.

In other words, she didn't expect the world to take care of her, but thought she should do it herself, and Philippe honored that spirit. He didn't even mind too much that she cooked in the French manner. He'd sworn that he'd never again eat anything that reminded him of his French-Cajun roots. That had been a childish vow, however, and he knew it now. Food fueled the body. What did it matter how it was prepared? At least the meals she fixed were tasty, and he shouldn't complain if they reminded him of New Orleans.

This dinner party idea was probably a good one, even if he didn't feel much like socializing. A keen observer, Philippe had figured out already that folks tended to band together here on the western frontier. People needed each other here as they didn't elsewhere. It would do him no harm, socially, politically, or financially, to be considered one of the locals, no matter how little he wanted to need his fellow human beings.

Isolation. It was all he'd ever known, and he craved it as some people craved love. Philippe didn't need love. He didn't need anything or anybody. He'd created himself, and he aimed to perpetrate his creation without assistance from anyone else in the world. If you allowed other people to matter, you were then vulnerable, and Philippe would never again be vulnerable. That was one vow he aimed to keep. He would, however, play the game society expected because it would make his life easier.

That's why he aimed to become better acquainted with Heather Mahaffey. She could be his link to the society in Fort Summers. That's really the only reason he'd asked her to assist him in preparing for the dinner party in the first place.

He felt a little better after he'd cleared up the matter in his own mind.

Yvonne St. Pierre had curled up on the gorgeous Turkish carpet in her boudoir hours before and still huddled there, her head buried in her arms, her arms folded on the seat of an expensive medallion-backed chair. She'd been alternately sobbing and moaning, wondering how much worse her life could get.

D. A. Bologh had found her son, and he now aimed to ruin Philippe's life, as he'd ruined hers. This was her real punishment. All of those preceding years had been merely a buildup to the shattering climax. She'd believed for decades that her punishment would end with her. She ought to have known better. D. A. Bologh would never let a person in his thrall off the hook so easily.

"Cheer up, my sweet, it's not all that bad."

Yvonne's head jerked up. "You," she said, her voice raw with pain.

"Who else?" D. A. grinned and twirled his mustache.

She didn't answer. What could she say? She didn't dare ask about Philippe. Not that it mattered. D. A. seemed impervious to all things, and he already knew how badly she was hurting inside. The irony was that none of her anguish showed in her flawless skin, brilliant black eyes, or lush, firm body. She took a couple of hiccuping breaths, hoping to control her tears. It always amused D. A. when she cried, and she didn't want to provide any more entertainment for him than she had to.

D. A. perched negligently on the arm of a beautifully carved medallion-backed sofa, a match to the piece upon which Yvonne had been crying. Sounding as if he were continuing a conversation they'd been engaged in for hours, he said, "This gentleman of my newfound acquaintance—the one in New Mexico Territory? The one whose last name is St. Pierre?"

Yvonne uttered an involuntary cry of protest.

D. A. laughed. "Don't fret yourself, dear heart. He's prospered amazingly. Do you know that he's a secret philanthropist?"

She didn't speak.

"He is. In fact, he supports an orphanage right here in New Orleans. I understand he feels some sort of kinship with the orphaned children, and thinks he'd have been better off to have been raised in an orphanage. He bears some sort of grudge against his mother for some reason."

Yvonne couldn't help it. A pain tore through her, and she sobbed again.

"But he's rich now. He can afford to support any number of orphanages, I'll warrant." He pretended to look bemused. "I wonder if he's already met up with one of my kin and made some kind of a deal."

"No!" She leapt to her feet and blindly attacked the man, scratching at his face with long fingernails, beating him with her fists, kicking at him with her bare feet. None of her frenzied attempts at mayhem made the least dent in his humor, of course. He merely laughed harder, clasped her wrists in an inhuman grip, and lifted her from the floor.

"Tut, tut, sweetie pie. There's no need for all of this passion. You know good and well there's nothing you can do to stop me from doing anything I want to do."

"No," she sobbed, collapsing at his feet. "No, please, no. Not Philippe."

"Nonsense. The man's already so deeply affected by our bargain that he hates you and has turned himself into a cold fish. He's sworn never to allow a woman to touch his hard heart, the fool. And all on account of you."

Beyond words, Yvonne only wept softly into her hands.

"Yes, indeed, he truly loathes you, my dear. Of course, he has no idea you did it all for him. How could he?"

No answer.

"But there's a sweet young thing working there as his cook. I think Philippe is rather taken with her, in spite of his avowed refusal to become emotionally entangled with any one female."

With streaming eyes, Yvonne looked at her tormentor. "Please don't hurt her, D. A. And please, please don't hurt him. Let them be. Abuse me if you must, but don't hurt them."

He eyed her coldly. "Why?"

"Why? Haven't you done enough damage?

Haven't you exacted enough grief from me? Why start on them? If there's a chance for them to be happy together, please don't take it away from them."

"Where's the fun in that?"

"Fun!" Yvonne was too outraged to go on. Besides, she knew no pleas of hers would touch this immovable rock of evil who'd been her undoing so many years ago.

"Unfortunately, the dear thing can't cook."

"She—she can't cook?"

"The child could burn water."

"B-but you said . . ."

"Indeed. I said she's been hired as his cook."

Yvonne brushed a hand under her eyes to wipe away tears. "I don't understand." She didn't know what she feared more: knowing or not knowing.

D. A. nodded. "Can't cook worth cow pies. The girl could probably even poison me—although I wouldn't get your hopes up if I were you. But that's all right. I'm helping her."

A horrified, strangled, "No!" crawled from Yvonne's throat.

D. A. smiled down upon her, and Yvonne knew that her sacrifice, the one she'd made thirty-three years before in the first terrifying months of her captivity in the house on Bourbon Street, had been for naught. She'd made the bargain to save her son. But she hadn't saved anybody, and now Philippe, the only person on earth who mattered to her, was going to be punished for her sins.

"Oh, but yes, sweetheart. And I think we should have us a little celebration in honor of what's sure to transpire shortly."

He slid to the seat of the sofa and lifted Yvonne

onto his lap. She protested feebly, but he only laughed and began making his devilish magic on her body. Soon she was writhing with need, hate, and passion, and D. A. thrust himself into her slick, tight passage.

"You're so very good at this, Yvonne. Everyone should be so good at their line of work."

She scratched at him with her nails even as she achieved her convulsive release.

D. A.'s laughter echoed and reechoed in the room and seemed to reverberate from the walls and floors and ceiling until Yvonne had to clap her hands to her ears.

He left her soon after that, and Yvonne did something she hadn't done in thirty-three years. She threw herself on the floor again, folded her arms on the cushion of a chair, hid her face in her arms, and prayed.

No bolt of lightning struck her, so she kept it up until the sun went down and rose again and she had to prepare for the arrival of her latest guest.

Chapter Ten

Philippe stared at Gil McGill, aghast. "Dammit, how could something like that have happened?"

Miserable, Gil shook his head. "I don't know, sir."

"Don't call me sir, dammit!" Gil flinched, and Philippe was sorry. Distracted, he ran a hand through his hair. "I'm sorry, Gil. But how in the name of all that's holy could a mile of fencing have been destroyed overnight?"

"I wish to God I knew. It happened quick, too, because I've got men riding the fences all night long. It couldn't have been more than a couple of hours between ride-bys, and that's awfully damned quick to take out a mile of fencing."

Philippe frowned and stared at the floor. What the devil was going on here? It was almost as if some malignant force was trying to drive him out of business. Or out of his mind. It wasn't bad enough that he had to consciously force improper thoughts of Heather Mahaffey out of his brain whenever he had work to do, but now his livelihood was in danger. And why? How? And who was doing it? Philippe couldn't figure it out.

Lifting his head, he again pinned Gil with his frowning gaze. "Are you sure there's no one in Fort Summers who has some kind of grudge against me?"

Gil looked startled. "Good Lord, no. Everyone respects you, as far as I know."

Philippe only stared at him for another few seconds. Then he sighed and said, "I only wish I knew what was going on. Then maybe we could figure out how to fight it."

"Er, you don't know of anyone who's mad at you, do you?"

"Not *that* mad." In spite of the circumstances, Philippe grinned. "I'm not really a bad man, you know, Gil. Only a prudent one who's quick to seize opportunities as they present themselves."

"Yeah. That's what I figured." Gil sounded almost as if he wished the problems on the ranch could be explained away by blaming them on a feud.

"Keep up the good work, Gil. I'll set men to fixing the fence tomorrow. Have you found out if any cattle have wandered off?"

"A few have. I've already sent men out to round them up."

"Thank you. I appreciate your efficiency. You probably deserve a raise in pay."

"God, no, sir!" Gil cried, startled. "I'm sure I don't deserve any such thing. After all, I'm the one who let your beeves disappear and your fences get torn down."

"That wasn't your fault. You discovered the problems as soon as any man could."

"Still and all, I wouldn't feel comfortable accepting more money from you under the circumstances."

Philippe eyed him for a moment. "You're an honorable man, Gil McGill. Until I moved West, I hadn't met very many of those."

Gil shuffled uncomfortably. "Hell, I'm no more honorable than most of the guys who live around here."

"I know." Philippe smiled. "That's what's so astonishing about this territory."

Gil returned his grin. "I reckon you might have a point there."

Philippe had a feeling had Gil had clipped off a "sir" at the end of his statement. He wondered if he'd ever get the lad to relax around him.

Good Lord, what was the matter with him? First he falls in lust with his cook, and now he was hoping to make friends with his wrangler. Maybe he was changing.

Since he'd always been a loner, he feared any changes of that nature would weaken him, and he steeled his heart. He was only moderately successful when he contemplated tomorrow's meeting with Heather to review the menu and the guest list for his party.

With a heavy sigh, he gave up struggling to make sense of anything and went to bed.

The next morning dawned clear and bright, and as windy as three hurricanes. Cowboys pulled their bandannas up over their noses even before they mounted their horses. Horses hung their heads against the blowing grit and looked miserable. The chicken house blew down, and all the chickens panicked. Gil McGill and some of his men rushed to store the chickens in the barn until they could right the chicken house once more. They did so, and reinforced it, but not one man on the place felt very optimistic that it wouldn't blow over again.

"Maybe we should set the anvil on it," suggested one man.

Gil shrugged. "Couldn't hurt, I reckon."

Heather, watching and listening to the action from the back door—while trying to hold her skirts down with her hands—shook her head. "Shoot, I wish the wind would stop blowing. Just for a little while."

"It's a devil wind, dear heart, and it won't stop for a while yet."

She turned and frowned at D. A. Bologh, who was grinning at her from his seat at the kitchen table.

"What do you know about devil winds?" she asked, not politely. She was finding it more and more difficult to be polite to the man.

"More than you'd ever imagine, Miss Heather."

She sniffed. "I'm not surprised."

D. A. laughed. She wasn't surprised by that, either.

A few minutes later, she stood in Philippe's library, cleared her throat, and referred to her list. She wished she could pronounce some of the words better. D. A. had drilled her, but she still wasn't very good with the French.

Philippe St. Pierre smiled at her from his big

leather chair behind his huge mahogany desk. He carried out the ranch business from that big desk, and he carried it out well, if Heather was any judge. He was sure more successful than most of the businessmen in Fort Summers. He seemed a little tense this morning, but Heather was too tense herself to wonder much about that.

"Go ahead, Miss Mahaffey. I'm interested to know what you'll be serving my guests."

"All right." She ran her tongue over her lower lip and wished she'd had the foresight to take a drink of water. She was dry as dust, and could hardly talk. She talked anyway. "What I suggest is that we start with something not too fancy. People in these parts aren't used to eating fancy food."

"Good idea."

She glanced up sharply from her list. He'd sounded amused, and she didn't particularly care to be laughed at. He appeared serene and obliging, and she guessed she'd imagined it. She went on. "So, all right. The soup course won't be awfully fancy. A corn chowder with a sprinkling of chives should do it." She glanced up again to see how that one had gone over. Philippe nodded, relief flooded her, and she continued.

"All right. That would be the first course, I guess." *You guess? You fool, you're supposed to be the cook!* Heather took a deep breath and said quickly, "That is to say, the corn chowder is the first course."

"Right."

He thought she was an imbecile; she knew it. Heather didn't fault him for that. She thought so, too. She took another breath and continued. "The main course would be roast beef with Yorkshire pudding."

He lifted his eyebrows. "Good. I like that. It's not—French." He waved his hand in the air in a dismissive gesture.

She peered at him hard for a moment, trying to ascertain what that comment had meant. Did it mean he liked French food, or that he didn't?

Oh, pooh, what did it matter? She couldn't cook one way or the other. After licking her lips once more, she went on. "Along with the roast beef and Yorkshire pudding, I was thinking we should serve wild asparagus spears with an oil and herb vinaigrette." Whatever that was. At least she knew what asparagus was and where it grew.

"Sounds delicious."

"Yes, and then, of course, there will be potatoes. Since folks will probably want to use the roast beef gravy on their Yorkshire pudding, I was thinking a gratin of potatoes à la Savoyarde might be appropriate. Do you think that would be all right?"

She knew, because D. A. had told her, that the last dish was potatoes sliced thin and baked in the oven with cheese and onions. Sounded pretty good to Heather, and she couldn't imagine how anybody could object, although not everyone shared her taste for onions, as she'd learned earlier. She held her breath and waited for Philippe's judgment.

"Sounds wonderful."

Heather was beginning to breathe a little more easily. "And then for dessert, I thought a nice pecan parfait. With whipped cream." Heather had never heard of anyone whipping cream until D. A. had told her good cooks did it all the time. It sounded like a terrible waste of cream to her—after all, the stuff was supposed to be used for butter and for fattening up the youngsters. Sweetening cream, whipping it up, and serving it on top of an already sweet dessert was pure decadence. But D. A. always seemed to have ample supplies of butter, and there weren't any youngsters around the ranch that needed fattening.

"Marvelous. I think you've outdone yourself, Miss Mahaffey. I can't imagine anyone not enjoying that meal."

She expelled a huge gust of breath. "Good. Thank you."

"And now do you have another moment or two to go over the guest list?"

"Um, certainly, I have plenty of time." The good Lord knew, she wasn't needed in the kitchen.

She was nervous as a cat when Philippe drew up a chair across the desk from him, although she knew she was being silly. After all, there was six feet of mahogany separating them. Even if she succumbed to her urge to fling herself into his arms, she couldn't do it. Safe from her own improper impulses, she managed to concentrate on the guest list.

"I've prepared a preliminary list. Here it is," Philippe said, handing her a sheet of paper. "See what you think."

Heather was interested to discover that Philippe's handwriting was as elegant as he was. Upright and faintly foreign-looking—although how she'd decided that, she had no idea, having no experience at all with foreigners—it was sort of spidery and quite pretty. She'd always been secretly proud of her own cursive, but his was every bit as handsome.

In her experience, the male of the species generally scrawled. Her big brother Jerry, acknowledged to be the possessor of a fine brain, had handwriting that looked as if it had been put on the paper by a drunken tarantula. Not Philippe St. Pierre. She got the impression his handwriting was only one more intensely controlled aspect of his personality. She stopped thinking about his cursive when two names leapt out at her.

"Oh, you're going to invite my parents?" She couldn't help but be pleased. She'd never considered her parents as being among the upper echelons of Fort Summers society. Not that there was an upper echelon.

"Certainly. Your father's the finest storyteller I've ever met. If things slow down and threaten to get dull, I'm sure he'll pick them right up."

She laughed spontaneously for the first time since she'd met Philippe St. Pierre. "That's Pa, all right. You won't have to worry about breaking the ice, either, because everybody already loves him."

"An admirable quality."

Heather tried to ascertain from his demeanor if he was teasing or mocking. She couldn't tell. "It is, you know. Pa is kind of a human equivalent of the Equalizer, only much better, because he doesn't hurt anyone." The Colt Equalizer had become a legend in the West shortly after its introduction. And it did, indeed, level out a man's position in society, being completely neutral as to whom it killed. "And he brings folks together. Rich, poor, in between, Pa doesn't care, which is a good thing, because he's as poor as a church mouse. He just loves people."

Philippe chuckled. "A *very* admirable quality.

Though one I fear I don't share with him."

From the way he frowned after he said it, Heather judged he hadn't meant to divulge the latter sentiment. "You don't like people?"

His smile seemed cynical and world-weary, and she guessed she shouldn't have asked. "I fear no one would mistake me for a saint or a particular benefactor of humankind, Miss Mahaffey. I suppose my talents, if any, lie elsewhere."

And that put her in *her* place quite nicely, Heather thought. She wasn't offended because she knew she'd stepped into personal territory—and she was only the cook. Or, that is to say, she was supposed to be only the cook.

"We all have our special individual skills, I reckon," she said, hoping to make him feel better. Then she took herself to task for being silly. Again. As if this rich, sophisticated man needed any help from her in feeling good about himself.

"Yes, I believe you may be right about that." Philippe rattled the list impatiently. "So you think your parents will enjoy the dinner party?"

"Oh, my, yes. My mother's always happy when she doesn't have to feed the brood. Not that she doesn't love us," Heather added quickly. "But she's been working awfully hard for a lot of years."

"Yes, I can see how an evening out might be welcome to her."

Heather couldn't account for the slightly quizzical expression on Philippe's face.

"This territory is hard on a man, but it must be hell on a woman," he continued.

The comment went a ways toward explaining his quizzical expression. "Mercy, yes." She sighed. "Ma loves Pa and the rest of us, but I know she looks forward to getting periodicals from back East and catching up with the rest of the world. It all seems so far away, you see. Of course, by the time the magazines arrive, they're six months old as a rule, but they're still fun to look at. If it weren't for the telegraph, nobody'd ever know what was going on in the rest of the world until months after it happened."

When she glanced up, Philippe's gaze was boring into her, and he looked extremely curious. Shoot, when would she learn to keep her big mouth shut? Probably never. She heaved another sigh.

"Where do your parents hail from, Miss Mahaffey? Where in Ireland, I mean."

"Dublin originally." She eyed him keenly, judged that his curiosity was unfeigned, and opened her mouth again in spite of herself. "They were poor in Ireland, too. According to Pa, everybody's poor in Ireland except the English, and it's better to be poor in America than in Ireland any day, what with the famines and oppression and all. They came to the United States in '68 and spent about a year in New York City. There weren't very many opportunities there, according to Pa, and it was dirty and crowded and smelly. That's when they decided to take advantage of the Homestead Act to secure some land, and they moved to the territory."

Philippe nodded. "I see. So now he has land of his own. That means a lot to a man."

Heather hastily scanned his face, and judged the comment had been heartfelt. So, he'd aspired to land ownership and independence, just like the rest of the mere mortals on this earth, had he? Interesting. "Yes. They never could have owned property in Ireland, according to Pa."

"I've heard the same thing from others."

"Of course, we're poor here, too. But, as Pa says, at least we're poor on our own land and nobody can take it away from us. Besides, most everybody else is poor, too." She cast a hasty glance at Philippe. "Well, most folks are poor. Not all of them."

He smiled. "Of course."

His smile had its usual effect on her, and she discovered her hands crumpling the list. She caught herself in time to keep from ruining it, and cleared her throat. "So, all right, my parents. Check." She smoothed out the paper and made a tick mark next to her mother and father's names. "And I think it's a good idea to invite the sheriff and his wife. Mr. and Mrs. Coe are very nice people, and it's good to get to know them."

She judged by his lifted eyebrow that he'd like to know why it would be good to get to know the sheriff, so she continued. "He's a rancher, too, you see, as well as the sheriff, and he gets all the bulletins and telegraph messages from other parts of the country before anyone else does. He's always the first to know any news that's likely to affect other ranchers in the area."

"That makes sense."

She noticed that his brow had furrowed slightly, and guessed the cause. "I asked Mike Mulligan if Mr. Coe had received any telegraph messages about recent problems with rustlers, and Mike said he hadn't. And Mike would know."

"You read my mind, Miss Mahaffey."

He smiled at her, and Heather felt her heart begin palpitating wildly. After licking her lips, she said, "Well, I imagined you'd be interested in that sort of news, given what's been happening around here."

"Indeed. And it's nice to know that the sheriff keeps folks informed of potential problems, even though my problem is evidently personal in nature."

"Personal?" Heather didn't like the sound of that.

Philippe gave what she expected was a very French shrug. It didn't look like a regular, old, everyday, American one to her, at any rate. "I expect it must be, since none of the other nearby ranchers are having such problems."

Forgetting all about the effect Philippe had on her in her surprise at his words, Heather gasped, "You mean somebody has it in for you? Because you're you?"

"That's what it looks like."

"Like a grudge or a feud or something?" She'd read about blood feuds, although they'd always seemed to her like a mortally stupid way of solving a problem.

"Either that, or there's a vandal in the neighborhood."

"A vandal?" She knew she ought to know what a vandal was, but she didn't remember. A vague impression of Mongol hordes tramped into her brain, but she was sure that wasn't it. Where was Geraldine when Heather needed her?

"Someone who wantonly destroys other people's property."

"Oh."

"But if it were a mere vandal, I expect he'd be picking on others besides me."

"Right. It would be less dangerous that way, I

reckon. I mean, if he spread out, folks would be less apt to catch him, because you'd be sure to set out men to watch."

"Exactly. Although," Philippe said, sounding unhappy, "so far the watchmen haven't come up with anything."

Heather shook her head. "I don't understand it. Gil told me they got your fences last time."

"Yes." Philippe seemed to shake himself out of a mood. "But that's neither here nor there. As I said, I'm glad the sheriff is privy to reports of problems that might be headed this way."

Taking her cue from him, Heather decided not to discuss his problems further. She nodded. "Oh, yes. Why, I recall that when there was an outbreak of anthrax in west Texas, Mr. Coe found out about it first and warned everybody in this area not to get suckered into buying any cheap Texas cattle."

"Is that so?"

"Yes. Some of the Texas ranchers tried to sell off their herds quick, in case the anthrax had spread to their animals. Of course, if any of the sick cattle had come here, all of the local herds would have been vulnerable. In fact, Pa tells about when there was an anthrax outbreak and the territorial government had entire herds destroyed."

"Good God, that's drastic action." Philippe's eyes opened wide, and Heather felt herself sinking in her chair.

She jerked upright instantly. "Yes, but there's no other way to stop it."

"I see."

"But Mr. Coe and his timely information prevented anybody from being duped."

"Hmm. Foisting sick cattle onto fellow ranchers

doesn't sound like a very honorable thing to do."

Heather shrugged. "It's not."

"I thought there was a so-called Code of the West, and that everybody living out here was upright and honorable."

Heather squinted at him. "You're joshing me, aren't you?"

He laughed. "Perhaps, a little. But I really am surprised to discover that people out here are as dishonest as the rest of the world."

"I don't know that they are. Out here, folks need each other so much that it doesn't pay to try to play mean tricks. But I reckon folks are apt to do almost anything when it means the difference between losing everything and salvaging something. It's not nice, but it's human."

"I expect you're right." He didn't sound as if he much approved of human nature.

Heather didn't imagine a rich man needed to. Rich folks could afford to stand on their principles a lot more easily than poor folks could. She knew it shouldn't make a difference, but it did. She'd learned from the cradle to be practical. She went back to the list.

"I think this is a fine list, Mr. St. Pierre." She frowned at it, however, dissatisfied, but not feeling free to express herself.

She was surprised when Philippe said, "What's wrong, Miss Mahaffey? Please tell me. If I didn't want your opinion, I wouldn't have asked for it." He smiled at her, and Heather steeled her nerves to withstand her reaction to him. Then she swallowed and decided he meant it.

"Well—" She took a deep breath. "Well, I think it's fine to invite Mr. and Mrs. Harvey and the Coes and my folks and the rest of these people. But this is the territory, Mr. St. Pierre. It's not like back East, where everything runs according to some kind of social code that people established decades ago and are still upholding. This is the West, where lots of things are different." Heather knew it for a fact, because she gobbled up her mother's periodicals like candy. She could hardly imagine society operating the way it did in some of those stories, but she had no reason to doubt that it did.

"For instance?" Philippe's eyebrow had gone up, and Heather swallowed again. She hated when he did that, because it always made her nervous.

But he'd asked. "For one thing, I think you should invite the schoolteacher, Miss Grimsby. I know she's a single lady and it will throw your numbers off, but she's a leading citizen. And you could invite Miss Halloran, who runs the laundry, and Mrs. Main, who's a widow lady and runs a boarding house. They all work very hard in Fort Summers, and their good opinion matters a lot. I'm sure they'd be honored to be invited."

She lifted her chin, waiting for him to scoff at her. As if a man like him would invite three single ladies to a dinner party at *his* house. Heather was sure such a thing would be unheard-of in New Orleans.

"What a good idea. Thank you for suggesting it."

She blinked at him. "You mean you'll do it?"

"Of course. Why not? They all sound like successful and productive members of Fort Summers society. Two of them are obviously fair businessmen—or businesswomen, if you prefer—and the third is responsible for the education of the town's children. They've each taken on immense responsibilities and have succeeded. Why shouldn't they be invited to a dinner party given in honor of Fort Summers's leading citizens?"

Why indeed? Heather beamed at him. "Thank you, Mr. St. Pierre. I hope this starts a precedent. It's always irked me that folks don't treat women businesspeople the same as they treat men."

"I see." His eyes were sparkling with humor, making Heather feel slightly giddy. "And how do you stand on women's suffrage, Miss Mahaffey?"

She felt her cheeks heat, and guessed she'd asked for that one. Nevertheless, she spoke the truth. "I'm all for it. Women do as much work as men, they're every bit as smart as men, no matter what people want you to think, and if they've got the responsibilities, they ought to be making the decisions." There. Let him fire her if he wanted to.

"Yours is an interesting outlook. What do you say to those people who claim women aren't emotionally stable enough to be allowed the vote."

"I say they're fools," Heather declared hotly, and then wished she hadn't when Philippe's smile broadened. "I don't know any female who isn't as sensible as any male I know."

"Is that so?"

"Yes." She didn't like his attitude. "What about you? Do you think women are stupid?"

"Far from it." He didn't sound as if he considered their lack of stupidity anything to be proud of.

"You don't sound as if you'd care to entrust women with the vote."

"I wouldn't."

"Why not?"

"In my experience, women are coy, manipulative, and dishonest, actually. I know that sounds brutal, but you asked."

Heather couldn't suppress a gasp of surprise. "Are you serious?"

"I am indeed."

"But that's absurd. Women are no more coy, manipulative, and dishonest than men are. At least not out here, they aren't. I don't know about anywhere else."

He waved her protest aside with a flick of an elegant hand. "Perhaps. I only know what I've observed."

"Well, I haven't observed anything of the kind," Heather said, miffed. "In fact, it seems to me that women are far more apt to be sensible and level-headed than men are. You don't see women sitting around in saloons, gambling their family's food money away. Or drinking themselves silly, and then shooting each other."

Philippe chuckled. "Put that way, I suppose I'd have to agree with you."

They stared at each other in silence for a moment, Heather trying to understand him. He was beyond her limited experience of humankind, though, and she couldn't do it. Impulsively, she said, "You must have had some awful experiences with women if you think they're all like that."

A flicker of something dangerous crossed his face. Heather jerked a little, startled to see it. Good heavens.

"I have," he said shortly, and didn't elaborate.

"I see." Heather paused for a moment, said, "I'm sorry," and waited.

Philippe said nothing.

Although she knew she shouldn't be probing, she

couldn't seem to hold back another question. "And I suppose most of your bad experiences were in New Orleans?"

"Most of them." His eyes had gone hard. "Not all of them, however."

"I see."

She sighed and concluded that revelations were over for the day. She was disappointed. She'd love to know everything there was to know about Philippe St. Pierre. He was a deep one, though, and incredibly reserved. He was totally different from anyone else Heather had ever met.

She didn't like it that he mistrusted women, though. "I still don't think most women are like what you said. I think you've just managed to fall in with a bad lot."

His lips twisted up at the ends, as if he found her comment funny—in a sick sort of way. "You may be right."

"I'm sure I am. Women are no more deceitful or manipulative than men are. Maybe less so, actually. Or if they are, it's because that's the only way they have of achieving their goals."

Philippe lifted that dratted eyebrow again. Heather was beginning to feel huffy. "Look at it this way, Mr. St. Pierre: If you were denied the right to vote, the right to own property, the right to your own children, for heaven's sake, if anything happened to your marriage, wouldn't *you* do anything you could to get whatever benefits you could? I mean, a man can be a mean, wife-beating drunkard, and the poor wife can't do anything about it. Unless she shoots the son of a gun, and then *she'd* be the one who'd be punished. Shoot, if a woman divorces a man because he's a low-down, gambling skunk, *he'd* be awarded custody of the children. Now, I ask you, is that fair?"

He gazed at her fully long enough for Heather to realize she'd stepped over a boundary that shouldn't have been invisible to her if she'd had any sense. She felt herself flush. "I beg your pardon." Because she couldn't help it, she added, "But don't forget Wyoming Territory. They had enough sense to give women the vote way back in '69." She sniffed and lifted her chin. "Forward-thinking, is what Wyoming is. I wish I could say the same for New Mexico Territory."

"I see."

"And anyway, women are honest. I'm sure you wouldn't see a woman rancher trying to sell bad beef to her neighbors." She was running out of steam in the face of Philippe's rigid silence.

Besides, she realized with a bitter spasm in her heart, she had no right to say such things. She was deceiving him and everybody else at the moment. That knowledge in itself negated everything she'd just said about women being as upstanding as men. Bother.

Because she was an honest girl, and because she was ashamed of herself, she muttered, "But you may be right. In fact, you probably are." She sighed heavily.

"Shall we get back to the list?" His voice was icily polite.

She glanced at him, wondering if she'd ruined herself in his eyes. Probably, and it was no more than she deserved.

They got back to the list.

Chapter Eleven

Several days later, Heather was in a dither. Any minute now, her sister Patricia and her best friend Geraldine were going to show up at Philippe St. Pierre's kitchen door to help serve at his dinner party. Mr. St. Pierre had hired them for the occasion, much to Mrs. Van der Linden's disgust.

Heather was so accustomed to the housekeeper's distaste by that time that the sour old woman didn't even faze her. She was, however, dreadfully fazed by the possibility of what Geraldine and Patricia would say about D. A. Bologh. He'd managed to keep his presence in Philippe's kitchen a secret from the rest of the household thus far, but Heather couldn't imagine how he was going to do it with two other girls popping in and out for serving dishes, platters, and so forth. She'd asked him about it, and he'd only laughed. That hadn't surprised her, but it hadn't helped her dither any, either.

He'd been in the kitchen all afternoon, doing whatever magical things he did to create his succulent meals. Heather kept watching, hoping she'd pick up a hint here or there, but he moved too fast for her.

"You might as well stop trying so hard," he told her, an ironical cast to his voice. "You'll never be able to do the things I can do."

"Maybe not, but I might be able to learn to cook something worth eating if I keep watching."

"You'd be better off reading cooking books, sweetheart."

Heather couldn't remember when he'd begun calling her *sweetheart* again, but she no longer objected. She owed him too much; she certainly shouldn't gripe if he chose to use an endearing term when speaking to her. Except that it didn't sound endearing coming from his handsome mouth. It sounded faintly contemptuous—which was no more than she deserved.

One of these days, she was going to prepare a meal on her own.

Her heart went cold at the thought. That would queer her employment in no time flat, and she knew it. And, as much as it would humiliate her to be fired, even more did she dread losing Philippe St. Pierre's esteem. For he did esteem her, at least a little bit. Heather, who hadn't ever before paid much attention to such things, had recognized the signs.

But why should serving a meal cooked by her own two hands spell her doom? If other people could learn to cook, why couldn't she? She was as smart as most people. Well, except for Geraldine, but Geraldine was smarter than anybody. It was only because Heather'd had no interest in the craft of cooking up until now that she'd avoided learning it. She'd been rebellious as well, and too much of what her mother had called a little-miss-know-it-all.

She no longer felt the least bit rebellious. And she knew good and well she didn't know it all. She knew nothing, as a matter of fact. She'd give anything to have her mother here now, teaching her how to do things in the kitchen.

Her mother might not be able to fix fancy meals like those D. A. Bologh conjured, but the meals she served were prepared with love. Heather very much feared that D. A.'s motivations were far removed from love. She didn't like to think about what the man was eventually going to require from her in payment for his services.

A knock came at the back door. Heather cast a quick glance at D. A., who winked at her. Big help that was. With a sigh of resignation, she went to the door and opened it. There stood Patricia and Geraldine, both avidly gazing around Heather to peek into the kitchen behind her.

"Where is he?" Geraldine, up on her tiptoes and squinting behind her spectacles, asked in a hissing whisper.

"Come in," Heather said irritably. "Don't strain your neck or anything."

"Geraldine told me there's some man helping you, Heather. Who is it?" Patricia hurried into the room and looked around in something very nearly resembling glee. "Where is he?"

"I don't see anybody." Geraldine sounded disappointed.

Surprised, Heather turned to look toward the stove, where she'd last seen her odd helper. He wasn't there. A quick scan of the rest of the kitchen revealed his absence in all corners.

"Um, I'm not sure where he went." Hoping to turn the conversation, she said, "Here, I have a couple of clean, starched aprons for you. I'll get the food ready to serve."

But it was already ready to serve. Somehow or other, in the second or two he'd had while Heather went to open the door, D. A. had managed to set out all the courses artistically in various platters and bowls. There was something awfully uncanny about the chef. Every time he did something like this, Heather's nerves wobbled more.

"What are we supposed to do first?" Geraldine slipped the snowy white apron on over her dress and tied a big bow in back.

"Serve the soup. According to Mrs. Van der Linden, you're supposed to hand everybody their soup plates from the right."

"Are you ready in here?" came a grumpy voice from the kitchen door.

Heather turned to find Mrs. Van der Linden standing there, hands on hips, scowling. She scowled back because she didn't want the old cow to think Heather was capable of being intimidated by her. "All ready," she said.

"Do you girls know what you're supposed to do?" Mrs. Van der Linden asked, as if she expected them to answer in the negative.

Patricia nodded. "I've been working at Mr. Gleason's chop house for quite a while, ma'am. I know how to serve food to people."

The older woman sniffed. "Get a move on, then, because the guests are being seated in the dining room right this minute."

Heather took a deep, steadying breath. This was it. She almost wished D. A. would show himself again, because she was unsure of how to carry on serving at a big dinner party. But he didn't show up, so she took charge.

"Put the soup tureen on this cart, Geraldine. Patricia, the bowls are on the sideboard. You know how to serve the chowder."

"Right. After I put two ladles full into each bowl, I sprinkle the top with the chopped chives."

"Right. Don't use more than a half spoonful or so of the chives, or they'll overwhelm the delicacy of the chowder."

Both Geraldine and Patricia gawked at her for a couple of seconds. Heather shut her eyes, took a deep, sustaining breath, opened her eyes again, and decided not to explain. If a body worked—or sat—around D. A. Bologh for any time at all, one began spouting stuff like that. She couldn't help it. "All right, get going."

The two new arrivals grinned at each other, squared their shoulders, and left the kitchen. Heather watched them, hoping nothing would go wrong.

"Don't fret, sweetie pie," came a voice at her back. She twirled around to behold D. A. Bologh leaning against the far wall of the kitchen.

"How do you do that?" she demanded, knowing she'd not get any kind of satisfactory answer.

He only laughed. "I have my ways."

Heather shook her head and wished she could start her life over again—next time she'd do it right and either learn to work in a kitchen—or have enough sense never to apply for a job as a cook.

D. A. Bologh couldn't believe his eyes.

"Yvonne!" he called. Silence answered his call, and then he couldn't believe his ears.

He made a survey of her elegant rooms, provided for her by her wealthy new protector. No Yvonne. Had she gone out? Maybe she'd gone shopping. She'd been pretty reclusive of late, but that didn't mean she *never* went out. D. A. made a search of the nearby shops she'd be likely to visit.

No Yvonne.

He went back to her house and tore through it in a fury. He didn't miss a single closet, and he looked under every stick of furniture and rug in the place.

No Yvonne.

He stood in the middle of her beautifully appointed parlor, and glared around. She'd run out on him. She'd actually managed to drum up enough courage—or desperation—to leave.

The fool. She knew what to expect by this open rebellion. She'd always been such a vain thing, he was surprised she'd found the fortitude in that pretty little body of hers.

She wouldn't get away with it. D. A. knew where she was going. She couldn't escape him.

"Bitch!" he shrieked. "I'll show you what happens when a woman double-crosses D. A. Bologh!"

It took the New Orleans Volunteer Fire Department two days to put out the fire.

* * *

The dinner party had gone splendidly. Heather's sister and friend had done an admirable job in serving up the wonderful meal. His guests had raved about the food. Even Heather's mother and father had been astonished at how delectable the fare was. Actually they'd seemed, if anything, more surprised than any of the other guests that their daughter was such a master of the culinary arts.

Philippe chuckled as he sipped at a snifter of brandy. It was late, and he was feeling satisfied and happy. His mood of contentment surprised him, as it was extremely unusual. For as far back as he could remember, he'd been dissatisfied with something, and more often than not with everything.

There must be a quality in this territory, isolated and remote as it was, that appealed to his soul, which was isolated and remote, too.

There was also something about Heather Mahaffey that made him feel good. She not only had a body he still recalled with fondness and severe attacks of libido, but he really liked the girl. She irked him sometimes, when she put forth her opinions about things—women's suffrage, for example—but it was primarily because she was always remarkably sure of herself.

He wasn't accustomed to females possessing strong opinions of their own, especially when they accompanied those opinions with examples. Like men drinking and gambling their children's milk money away. Philippe grinned, remembering. He was used to females who pretended to embrace the opinions of the men in their lives.

Not little Miss Heather, though. She was as spunky and independent as the territory itself. Odd how his territory was isolated and remote, and hers was spunky and independent—yet they were the same place.

He wondered what his life would be like with someone like Heather in it permanently. He'd never considered marriage as a viable option for his future, because he'd never met a woman he could tolerate. He'd never met one like Heather. But he didn't think marriage to the redoubtable Heather Mahaffey would be the onerous burden he'd always assumed wedlock would be. It certainly wouldn't be dull. And it would be full of good food.

Of course, if he wanted children, he'd have to get married someday. There wasn't any other socially acceptable way to get them that he was aware of. And he'd be damned if he'd bring bastards into the world. That particular family tradition ended with him. He scowled for a moment under the influence of the thought, but didn't feel like dwelling on it. There were more pleasant things to think about than his miserable past. With a grin, he wondered what Heather would do if he proposed to her.

Good God, what was he thinking?

Philippe sat up straight in his chair and frowned. He'd better watch his step or he'd be in big trouble. He sank back against the cushions and told himself to relax. There was nothing intrinsically wrong with the institution of marriage. Hell, if his mother had been married, Philippe himself might not be such an alienated creature today.

He hated thinking about his mother, because when he did, his insides got muddled. He recalled her as a beautiful woman. And even warm and tender with him on occasion. But he also recalled the screaming fits, the temper tantrums, the crying, and the men. Dozens—perhaps hundreds—of men, all taking pleasure from her and taking her away from him. He shifted in his chair, uncomfortable with the memory of himself as a lonely child who needed his mother. Philippe didn't like to think of himself as needing anything.

Except, perhaps, children. A legacy. A way to secure his worth to the world. On his own, Philippe feared he was a pitifully imperfect specimen of mankind. But if he had children who could carry on with the ranch after he died, well, then . . . he might truly believe he'd accomplished something besides rising from the mud and creating himself as a successful man.

It was strange to Philippe that he had always found himself drawn to children. He hid the weakness well, of course. He'd never let on that he had a very human desire to perpetuate himself, because it sounded so puerile a conceit, somehow. Yet here, in his own parlor, in his own house, surrounded by the trappings he'd earned by himself and by his own hard efforts, it didn't seem like a bad thing to want.

If he had children, needless to say, they wouldn't be burdened with a past like his own. No. If Philippe St. Pierre ever had children, they'd know both their father and their mother. They wouldn't have to share their mother with a thousand men. Philippe's heart hurt every time he thought about his mother—which was one reason he tried never to do so. It was also one of the reasons he supported that orphanage in New Orleans. He couldn't bear the thought of children growing up unwanted and uncared-for.

Heather was nothing at all, in any way, ever, like

his mother. Thank God. Her very difference might be what attracted him most, in fact. And that was a good thing.

He wondered what the girl, who was always nervous around him, would do if he courted her. With another grin, he decided it might be fun to find out.

By God, it couldn't hurt to try. If he could win Heather Mahaffey's favor, perhaps he could really, finally and forever, vanquish his miserable past.

The next morning, no longer under the influence of Fort Summers society, a delicious meal, and a good deal of brandy, Philippe decided to wait and see. For all he knew, Heather Mahaffey possessed ghastly imperfections that would render her an unsuitable choice for a wife. The notion of being stuck with a whining woman, for example, or one who snored, made his stomach ache. No. Philippe didn't want to make any mistakes when choosing a wife.

If he ever decided to.

He shuddered and concluded that he'd just had a narrow escape. No more drinking for him. He worked hard that day and felt much better for it afterwards.

Yvonne's heart battered against her ribs like a kettle drum, and it was all she could do to keep from peering over her shoulder every other second, searching for Bologh. She knew he'd come after her. She knew he'd find her. She only hoped she could forestall the inevitable long enough for her to warn Philippe.

"Well, ma'am," the station agent said. "There ain't no way to get there that's straight."

"No?" She wanted to scream at the man standing

before her, scratching his chin and looking stupid, that she didn't care if the way was straight or curved or went through hell itself. All she cared about was getting there.

"No, ma'am. You'll have to take this here train to Texas." He poked the schedule with a dirty fingernail. "This here one that goes to Fort Worth. Then you'll have to take another train to Albuquerque."

"To where?" Yvonne squinted at the book, trying to read it upside down. "Where did you say?"

"Albuquerque. That there's a city in the territory, ma'am. They got strange names out there. Injun, I reckon."

"Albuquerque. I see. And is that near Fort Summers?"

"No, ma'am."

Again, Yvonne suppressed the urge to scream. "Then," she said through clenched teeth, "how do I get to Fort Summers from Albuquerque?"

"I'm a-lookin' it up fer you, ain't I?" The man squinted at the book. "Hell—beg pardon, ma'am. But I don't see that there's no railroad line into the town of Fort Summers. Looks like the closest train station would be in a place called Roswell, and that's forty-five miles east of the fort."

"I'm sure I can secure some kind of transportation from Roswell to Fort Summers," Yvonne said. In truth, she knew no such thing, because she was accustomed to the civilized surroundings of New Orleans, where transportation wasn't a problem. One walked or took a hackney or a streetcar.

"I expect so, ma'am." The station agent shut the book with a thump. "So, is that what you want to do?"

"Yes." Her nerves were crawling and skipping like ants at a picnic, and this idiot stood there asking her questions she'd answered a hundred times already. Yvonne clutched her small reticule in fingers that ached from the strain and told herself it wasn't his fault she'd finally decided to break away from D. A. Bologh.

"All rightie, ma'am. Just wait a little minute, and we'll get you all fixed up."

Yvonne sincerely doubted it.

"I don't know why you're so blasted touchy today." Heather frowned at D. A. Bologh, who was throwing pots and pans around as if he were mad at them.

"I'm not touchy!" he bellowed, and slammed a skillet onto a burner.

Heather winced. "You could have fooled me."

"Anyone could fool you," D. A. said nastily. "You just try fixing a cheese soufflé in this hellhole, with all the thumping and banging going on, and see how you like it."

"Did it fall?" Heather asked curiously. D. A. had never complained about the less-than-stellar accommodations prevailing in her territorial homeland before.

He shot her a sneer over his shoulder. "Of course it didn't fall. What do you think I am, anyway?"

"I'd probably best not say."

"Ha ha. You're excessively funny today, aren't you?"

Heather sighed. "Probably not."

"You're right about *that*." D. A. stuck a wooden fork and spoon into a huge wooden bowl and tossed the salad. He'd put things in it that Heather didn't know could go into a salad. She knew about the lettuce and tomatoes, but D. A. put sliced onions and cooked beets and broken cauliflower florets and stuffed Spanish olives into his salad. God alone knew where he got such provisions. And, what's more, the salad tasted really good when he tossed everything with his very own oil-and-vinegar-and-herb concoction that he called a French dressing.

"This place is the end of the universe, and I hate it," D. A. muttered.

"Why do you stay then?" Heather wished he'd go away, actually, although that would mean the end of her employment, and abject humiliation. And no more Philippe. Her heart squeezed at the last thought.

D. A. opened the oven door and withdrew a casserole of potatoes and onions baked with herbs and milk. "I have a job to do." He sounded annoyed about it. He slammed the casserole on the counter. "Here. Potatoes. These westerners need their potatoes with everything."

"Oh." Heather liked potatoes herself. She decided to try putting a little sugar into the conversation. Maybe that would sweeten his disposition. "Thank you for doing such a wonderful job with the dinner party yesterday, Mr. Bologh. I understand from Mr. St. Pierre that everyone loved the food, and the party went very well. He called me in and spoke to me about it personally this morning."

She flushed from head to toe, remembering that conversation. Mrs. Van der Linden had been furious. But Philippe had been so very complimentary to Heather, and had thanked her so copiously for creating such a wonderful repast for his guests, that Heather almost forgot for a minute that she hadn't had anything to do with it. Which didn't last long. As soon as she returned to the kitchen and encountered a muttering, cranky D. A., reality had returned with a crash.

"Don't thank me, sweetie. You'll pay me back one of these days, believe me."

He sounded malicious, and Heather's insides scrunched up. "Er, about that, I really think it's time you told me what you want in payment, D. A. I don't like not knowing."

"You'll know soon enough." D. A. ladled out something he'd called braised endives. They looked like little cooked lettuces to Heather, and she hoped Mr. St. Pierre would like them. He probably would. D. A. knew his way around a meal; she'd give him that much.

Now she made a face at his back. "Why won't you tell me now? I'd like to prepare for it, if it's bad."

"Ha! You won't need to prepare. Trust me."

She wished she could. Unfortunately, she didn't. Although, she must admit, he hadn't gone back on his word to her so far. He'd handled cooking for several weeks now and hadn't once slipped up. Nor had he allowed anyone but Heather to see him. Even Mrs. Van der Linden almost believed Heather was doing all the work in the kitchen, and Heather knew how much the old bat hated giving credit to anyone.

D. A.'s month of service was almost up, however, and she was getting nervous about being left alone to cook. She'd been taking cookbooks to bed with her each night and reading all sorts of recipes, and she thought she might be able to whip up something very simple if push came to shove. But it would be a long time before she could create the masterpieces of culinary art that D. A. fixed every day and so easily. None of this kitchen nonsense would ever be easy for Heather; she knew it in her bones.

As she began arranging dishes on the cart upon which she took food to the dining room, she decided to broach the subject. "Um, April's almost over now, Mr. Bologh."

"Yeah? So what?"

Heather peeked at him. She didn't like him, but she'd never heard him sound this crabby before. "It occurred to me that you agreed to help me for a month. The month is over on the first of May, and I—well—I wondered—" Shoot. What she wondered was would he be willing to keep cooking for her, actually. Until she'd read more cookbooks. Say, a thousand or so.

Lord, she'd never be able to handle this on her own.

"Don't worry about it," D. A. growled. "I'll stick around for another month if you want me to. Just remember that you owe me."

"How could I forget?" Heather asked sourly.

D. A.'s laugh seemed particularly ugly today.

Philippe wasn't surprised, and he wasn't awfully amused, when Heather jumped a good three inches and gaped at him.

"You mean you want me to sit at the dining room table and eat dinner with you?"

He tilted his head to one side and observed her

through half-lowered eyelids. "Would that be such an irksome task, Miss Mahaffey?"

Heather looked around the room almost wildly. "But—but there's nobody else here. Sir."

"That's why I'm asking you to dine with me." His voice, he noticed, had taken on an edge of irritation. Damnation, why should the wench balk at dining with him? Had he grown a second head? Was he sprouting horns? Was he so evil and mean-tempered that she should have this terrible aversion to him? "Unless, of course, you have other plans." He smiled. If his smile reflected his present mood, it was wolfish, but he didn't much care. He was sick to death of Heather's attitude toward him.

"Um, no, I have no other plans."

"Good. Then please, remove that ugly apron and have a seat, Miss Mahaffey. I asked Mrs. Van der Linden to set a second place, as you can see for yourself."

"Oh, dear."

"You don't sound happy about it. Is sitting with me such a dreadful way to pass a meal?"

"It's not that, Mr. St. Pierre. It's Mrs. Van der Linden. She'll be furious that you asked her to set a place for me, of all people."

"Really?" He lifted an eyebrow and saw her swallow. "And why is that, pray?"

"Um, she doesn't like me much. Sir."

"You may toss away that sir, Miss Mahaffey, if you please."

She expelled a huge breath. "All right. Mr. St. Pierre."

He nodded. "Please sit, then, and tell me why Mrs. Van der Linden doesn't like you, if you will."

She seemed to give up the fight. Her shoulders

sagged, and she complied with his request, folding the apron neatly and laying it over the back of a chair. She sat with her accustomed grace, folded her hands, and put them demurely in her lap. Since demure was about the last adjective Philippe could think of to describe Heather Mahaffey, this behavior on her part interested and vaguely amused him.

He'd put in a hard day. More cattle had disappeared overnight, and there had been a fire in a haystack. If Gil McGill and Mike Mulligan hadn't been quick on their feet, the entire barn could have burned down. All of that, while his guests had been devouring Heather's glorious dinner.

Philippe was honestly beginning to believe that someone in Fort Summers held a grudge against him, although he couldn't imagine who it could be. Hell, he hadn't lived here long enough to make enemies.

He'd even briefly contemplated the possibility that Gil or Mike might hate him for some obscure reason, but had tucked it away. The notion was too absurd—unless one of the boys was flat crazy, and neither of them acted like a lunatic.

At any rate, the day had been difficult, he'd sweated buckets and worn himself to a frazzle, and now he wanted to relax. He felt an unaccustomed urge to do so in company, what's more, and the only company he could think of that was easily obtained and totally acceptable to him was that of Heather Mahaffey.

He was going to put her at ease in his company, starting now. He eyed her, noticing her downcast eyes and tense jaw muscles. She hadn't looked the least bit tense when she was buck naked in the bath house. He told himself to stop thinking about the bath house, or he might, by accident, let some of his lustful thoughts leak into the air in the dining room and unsettle her. If she were any more unsettled, she might just break in two. "I suppose you say grace in your family, Miss Mahaffey?"

Her head jerked up and she stared at him, wide-eyed. "Yes, we do."

"Would you care to do the honors here?" Philippe had about as much truck with prayers as he did with horseless carriages, but he didn't want to shock the natives. He'd asked Miss Grimsby, the schoolmistress, to say grace at his dinner party, thereby startling most of the men in the company. It had done Philippe's heart good to see their discomposure. He loathed tradition. Besides, the women had appreciated it—he'd thought of Heather and grinned. Fortunately, by that time, all heads were bowed, and no one noticed.

"Um, certainly. I'll be happy to say grace." She bowed her head and recited, "God is gracious, God is good. Thank you for this food. Amen."

Perfunctory, at best. Philippe snapped his napkin open and placed it in his lap. Miss Grimsby had been much more creative. She'd even thanked her Heavenly Father for Philippe, probably the first time anyone had ever done *that*. Miss Mahaffey would sooner condemn him to the pit at the moment, or he missed his guess.

"So what have you created for my delectation this evening, Miss Mahaffey?" Philippe lifted a lid and sniffed at the potatoes. "Do I detect garlic?" He liked garlic, but he hadn't encountered it much out here.

"Um, yes. Yes, there's garlic in the potatoes. And herbs. And onions." She licked her lips.

"I see. Well, it smells good enough to eat."

"I hope it is."

He glanced at her as he served a plate. "You sound doubtful."

"Oh, ah, no. It's just that I'm—always a little nervous about people liking what I cook."

He shook his head. "You need have no fears on that score, Miss Mahaffey. I've never met a better cook."

"Thank you." If her voice got any smaller, Philippe wouldn't be able to hear it at all.

"Ah, and what's this? A soufflé?"

"Um, yes. I think."

"You think?"

She stood suddenly, making Philippe blink in surprise.

"Mr. St. Pierre, I have a confession to make."

"You do?" Whatever could this sweet, innocent girl have to confess? Nothing awfully improper, surely. Unless she'd been rolling in the hay with one of the cowboys, but Philippe doubted it. She didn't seem the type somehow.

"I haven't been cooking for you."

Chapter Twelve

Philippe sat speechless for several seconds. His silence must have made Heather even more nervous than usual, because she started wringing her hands.

"It's true. A man named D. A. Bologh has been doing all the cooking. I can't cook anything worth eating. It's all him. He's the one. I only said I could cook because—because—because the wind drove me to it." She frowned. "Although, of course, it's not the wind's fault that I lied."

"I see." Good God, the girl was mad. Philippe was sorry to learn of her insanity, because he'd begun to harbor faint stirrings for her that were as alien to him as the stars and the moon. "Um, could you explain this situation a little more fully?"

She shut her eyes and a spasm of something resembling pain crossed her face. When she opened them again, she looked determined. "Yes. Yes, it's past time I explained everything to you. You see, it's—it's—it's—"

"It's?" Philippe supplied, trying to be helpful.

She heaved a huge sigh and made a gesture of despair. "Oh, it's so hard to explain."

"I can see it is."

"Maybe I should just show you."

"All right, I'm game." Completely in the dark, but fascinated as all get-out, Philippe rose and laid his napkin beside his plate. "I suppose this elegant repast won't spoil if we take a few minutes out for this. I must say you've aroused my intense curiosity."

She said, "But—oh, very well. I hope to heaven he's still there."

"Indeed." Good God. Philippe believed in magic about as much as he believed in fairies or the goodness of mankind.

He allowed Heather to lead the way. He enjoyed the view. She dressed in what Philippe had begun to think of as the frontier fashion, in simple skirts and shirtwaists, or dresses that didn't have much fluff to them. The prevailing mode in these out-of-the-way parts was simpler than fashions back East, which only made sense. It would be stupid to bind oneself into the torturous ensembles a lady in other, more refined circumstances would adopt, if one had to work like a slave all day long.

The result of such practicality was that ladies out here wore fewer petticoats and underpinnings. At least, Philippe couldn't recollect ever being as fascinated by the swaying of any hips before, as he was with Heather's. Of course, she had a stunning body. He'd only seen it in the raw once, more's the pity, but he had an excellent imagination, and he'd mentally undressed her countless times. He did so again now, thus entertaining himself as they moved down the hallway to the kitchen.

When they arrived, Heather threw open the door. "There. You can see for yourself." She stood aside and bowed her head, as if she couldn't bear to look.

Philippe stepped inside the room and saw—a kitchen. It looked as if a rather tidy person had just prepared a meal. Other than the pots and pans and kitchen equipment, the room was empty.

"It's all D. A. Bologh's doing," Heather said. She sounded miserable.

"I see. D. A. Bologh."

"Yes."

Philippe pondered this phenomenon. He didn't like the notion that Heather was crazy. He'd become—he paused, but then let himself finish. Actually, he'd become too fond of her to want to lose her to insanity. There, it had been said. He'd become fond of someone.

"Perhaps you should introduce us," he said, wondering what to do now.

"All right." She poked her head into the kitchen. "Drat. I was afraid of this."

"Oh?" He stepped aside politely to allow her to enter the room.

She threw out her arms in a gesture Philippe recognized as being typical of the woman she was—free and uninhibited. At least, she was that way everywhere except around him.

"He's never around when anyone else comes into the kitchen. He only shows up when I'm here. And he appears and disappears in the blink of an eye."

"I see."

Heather eyed him carefully for several seconds, then seemed to deflate. "No you don't."

Philippe shrugged. "Very well. I don't see." He was willing to oblige her, but he'd like to know the rules first.

"You see, it's like this. He showed up the day I was hired. I'd been looking around the kitchen, trying to figure out what to do in it, when he knocked at the back door."

Philippe tilted his head to one side. "You don't say."

"But I *do* say. And when he offered to cook for me in exchange for something, I agreed."

"In exchange for what?" Could this D. A. Bologh be the one who was causing such havoc on his ranch? Philippe frowned, which seemed to make Heather even more uneasy than she already had been.

"I don't know yet." She watched him for a couple of seconds more, then threw up her hands. "I know it sounds crazy."

"Yes, it does."

"But it's the truth."

"I see."

"You don't believe a word I've said, do you?"

"I'm not sure. I find it very difficult to believe in things I can't see with my own eyes." Philippe pondered Heather and the purported D. A. Bologh, and decided to say what was on his mind. "However, I must say that if you're telling the truth—"

"I am!"

"—then I'm inclined to be displeased, Miss Mahaffey."

She hung her head again. "You have every right to be displeased."

"Especially since there have been some ruinous goings-on at my ranch for the past several weeks."

Her head jerked up and she gasped. "Good heavens! You don't mean to say you think D. A. Bologh is behind the cattle thefts and fence cutting, do you?"

"And last night's fire."

All color faded from her face. "F-fire? In this awful wind?"

"Indeed."

"Merciful heavens." She looked as if she'd never contemplated such a possibility before, and wished he hadn't brought it up.

Philippe didn't blame her for that. If what she said was true, who better to suspect than the mysterious stranger? On the other hand, her story was fantastic, and he didn't believe a word of it, even though she both looked and sounded sincere. Which only went to further prove that her balance was off. A person who popped up to cook and vanished whenever anyone came to call? Philippe had a good imagination, but that was too much to swallow.

He pondered the matter for a moment, but came to no conclusions. "However, until you can show me this person, I fear I'm not altogether sure what to think." In truth, he thought she was a lunatic, and that was almost more depressing than thinking she'd allowed a stranger access to his property.

"I'm not surprised."

"And until we get some answers to some questions, perhaps we shouldn't discuss it further." He tried to smile at her. It was difficult to do so since, one way or another, his presumptions about her seemed to have been shattered today, and he discovered himself loath to see them go. He wanted his old semi-paragon of a Heather back. He didn't want a Heather who was insane; and he absolutely didn't want a Heather who invited strange men into his home without notifying him. With a sigh, he swept an arm out, indicating that the young woman should precede him down the hall, back to the dining room.

She went, dragging her feet slightly, and with her usually proud head drooping. She barely ate a bite of the supper she—or someone—had cooked. And that was a pity, because it was superlative, as usual.

When Heather retired to the kitchen after the ordeal was over, D. A. Bologh was sitting in his chair, and he didn't look pleased.

"You're a fool, Heather Mahaffey."

"Probably." She was too dispirited to argue.

"You'll never get him to believe in me." D. A.'s sneer was a work of diabolical art.

"Probably."

"He'll only think you're a madwoman."

"Probably."

She had to cover her eyes when, in a fit of indignation brought about, she presumed, by her refusal to fight with him, D. A. cleaned up the kitchen. It took him approximately thirty seconds, and Heather would have sworn on a stack of Bibles that a fiery whirlwind had invaded the kitchen.

On the other hand, she was probably crazy and seeing things. She was more discouraged than she'd ever been in her life when she crawled into bed that night.

* * *

Dear God, how could her son have chosen to move out here? Yvonne stared out the window of the train and her heart ached to know that her darling Philippe had run away clear to here. To get away from her and New Orleans.

This place looked like hell to her.

But no. Hell was behind her. It was certain to catch up with her eventually, but not, she prayed, until after she'd saved Philippe and that girl, whoever she was. She could die in peace then, even if her soul burned in hell for all eternity.

She didn't know why she'd been allowed to escape. She'd tried to run away before, but D. A. had always caught her.

Perhaps her prayers had been answered. She'd been through too much to believe it yet.

A knock came at the door of her sleeping compartment, and she jumped. Nervous as a hare she was, and she couldn't shake the premonition that D. A. would find her before she'd warned Philippe. The porter entered, bearing a tray. She smiled at him. Not that he could see her smile, since she was heavily veiled.

"Thank you very much, monsieur." She used her best, most cultivated purr.

"Yas'm," the porter said, and gulped.

She'd had that effect on men for almost forty years. She was used to it. She paid the man and gave him a large tip. She had plenty of money, although she expected her home was in ruins by this time. D. A. would never allow this infraction to pass by unpunished. Until he found her, he'd probably wreak his vengeance on her belongings.

With a sigh, she told herself she didn't care. Possessions were all well and good, but she'd lived long enough by this time to understand that people mattered more.

Her son mattered most of all, and she'd do everything in her power to see that D. A. Bologh didn't hurt him. Her heart ached when she recalled how pitifully weak she was against D. A.'s strength. He had all the powers of darkness behind him, and Yvonne knew from experience how potent those powers were.

The wind was shrieking like a banshee, flinging grit and dirt every which way, and Heather was feeling mighty glum when she drove the wagon to town the day following her dinner with Philippe. He must think her crazy. Although he'd trusted her enough to let her drive to town alone to pick up the month's supplies.

Still, she'd seen the way he'd watched her during supper last night. He obviously couldn't decide whether or not to have her locked up in the insane asylum in Las Vegas.

Maybe she was crazy. D. A. Bologh made no sense to her; how could she expect him to make sense to anyone else? Especially since he had never been seen by any of them. She sighed deeply.

"But that's not right," she said suddenly, aloud. "After all, *somebody's* been cooking on the ranch, and it sure as the dickens hasn't been me."

The truth of that statement didn't cheer her much. She still had no idea who D. A. was—and when she contemplated the payment he was going to exact for helping her, she went cold inside.

Could he be the one behind all the disasters at Philippe's ranch? She'd talked to Mike Mulligan about those problems before she set out with the wagon.

Mike had shaken his head. "It's the damnedest thing, Heather. We've got men all over the place, watching like hawks, but somehow somebody keeps getting in and doing things."

"I've heard about the stolen cattle, the ruined fences, and the fire." She shuddered, the idea of fire too horrible to contemplate, especially in these winds. "Has anything else happened?" She wasn't sure she wanted to know.

"Not so's you'd notice. The usual stuff. You know, a broken leg here, an injured cow there, but those things aren't weird. The other stuff is weird."

It certainly was. Because she thought she'd die if she didn't talk about Philippe, at least a little bit, she'd asked casually, "Um, do you think any of the men are dissatisfied enough with Mr. St. Pierre to do anything like that to spite him?"

Mike had goggled at her before he'd burst out, "Hell no! Damn, Heather, Mr. St. Pierre's the best boss a man could have."

Now, as she drove the team toward the small village of Fort Summers, she pondered Mike's words. She was pleased that Philippe was so well respected by his employees. She was rather annoyed, however, that she herself had done such a splendid job of getting all of her male friends to treat her like one of the boys. Mike even felt free to swear in front of her, which he'd never do in front of, say, Patricia or Geraldine. She wondered if Philippe viewed her as just one of the boys.

Not that it mattered. She'd thought the worst thing that could happen to her would be to be discovered a fraud. Now, though, Philippe thought she was a lunatic, and she couldn't decide which was worse. Of course, both problems were hers and hers alone. All of this was her fault.

Except the problems at the ranch. She puzzled over them all the way to town—in the time when she wasn't daydreaming about marrying St. Pierre.

Philippe wasn't happy when he set out for work the morning after his dinner with Heather.

On the one hand, he'd never met a more sensible, levelheaded female in his life. The fact that she was truly lovely, spirited, spunky, full of life, and had a body that kept him stirred up constantly, only added to her appeal.

On the other hand, the poor thing was obviously out of her mind.

"God, what a dilemma," he muttered as he rode out to join Gil McGill on the range. He and Gil were going to check as much fencing as they could, and discuss possible solutions to the ranch's strange series of problems. He doubted that they'd come up with anything much. They were already doing everything they could.

"A curse," he growled, thinking about the night a month or so ago when he and Gil had been discussing the same thing. "Damned if it doesn't look like a curse."

He knew that was outrageous. Although he sometimes made jokes about such things, he believed in curses even less than he believed in magic. Nevertheless, he couldn't get the notion out of his mind.

Heather was overjoyed to see Geraldine hurrying down the boardwalk when she drove the wagon into town. She pulled the wagon up, jumped down, and ran over to greet her friend.

After a spirited greeting, Geraldine burst out, "Oh, Heather! Isn't it just awful?"

Heather blinked at her. "Isn't what just awful?"

"My goodness, haven't you heard?" Geraldine slapped a hand to her bosom and stepped back, as if she couldn't believe it.

"Heard what?"

"Oh, dear." Now Geraldine looked as though she wished she'd kept her mouth shut.

Heather wasn't about to put up with that sort of thing. She gave her best friend a good shake. "What? Tell me!"

"Oh, Heather."

Heather rolled her eyes. Every now and then, she wished her friend's sensibilities weren't quite so fine. "Blast it, Geraldine Swift, what in blazes happened?"

The girl was shocked by Heather's language, as Heather knew she would be. "Heather Mahaffey, mind your tongue."

"I'll say worse than that if you don't spit it out this instant."

After tutting several times, Geraldine lowered her voice and said, "Oh, Heather, it was terrible, and it all happened on the way home from Mr. St. Pierre's dinner party. Miss Grimsby sprained her ankle, Mr. and Mrs. Coe's surrey broke down, and Miss Halloran discovered that her cat had died."

"Merciful heavens!" What an appalling series of catastrophes.

But Geraldine wasn't through with her. "Wait until you hear the rest."

"There's more?" A sinking sensation invaded

Heather's midsection. She had an uneasy feeling that all of these disasters had something to do with her, and she couldn't account for it. After all, *she* certainly hadn't done anything wrong. Unless—good God, could this be divine retribution for her having lived a lie for a month?

Nonsense. She wasn't that important.

Geraldine went on. "Mr. and Mrs. Harvey discovered that a coyote had got in their chicken coop and killed a whole bunch of birds, and—" She broke off abruptly and paled.

Heather, feeling rather pale herself, urged her on. "And?"

"And—oh, Heather, it's your parents."

Heather's heart almost stopped, and her mouth went suddenly dry. "What—what about my parents?" She was almost afraid to hear the answer.

Geraldine bowed her head. "They were held up on the way home, and your father sustained an injury."

"Held up?" Heather stared at her friend, too shocked to process this piece of information. "What do you mean, they were held up?"

Geraldine shrugged. "They were held up. Robbed. Stopped by a highwayman."

"A highwayman?" Heather realized her voice had gone squeaky and cleared her throat. But—a highwayman? Wasn't that a fancy sort of animal to suddenly appear in Fort Summers? "I've never seen or heard of a highwayman in these parts, Geraldine. Are you sure?"

"Indeed, I am sure, Heather Mahaffey. If you don't believe me, you go see your parents yourself."

"I will." Perceiving that her doubt had hurt her best friend's feelings, she laid a consoling hand on

Geraldine's arm. The wind, thus given free rein with regard to her bonnet, whipped it back until it was only hanging onto Heather's neck by its ribbons, thereby all but strangling her. She let go of her friend and retrieved her bonnet. "I'm sorry, Geraldine. I'm not doubting your word."

"Hmm."

"But—but—oh, Lord, and you say Pa was injured?"

"Shot." Geraldine had lowered her voice, and it throbbed with emotion.

Heather staggered back a step, feeling as if someone had punched her in the chest. "Shot?" she whispered, stunned.

Nodding, Geraldine said, "I believe it was a flesh wound and not serious." She rushed on. "Oh, I'm so sorry, Heather. I didn't mean to worry you. I'm sure he'll be all right. Would you like me to go with you to see?"

"Yes, please." Heather nodded. She felt numb. She felt that, somehow or other, these incidents had something to do with her. Oh, she knew she wasn't important enough for God to pay any particular attention to, but she couldn't shake the feeling anyway.

The two young women walked the half mile to Heather's parents' three-room house at the west end of town. It was an unprepossessing place, but the Mahaffeys had reared six children in those three rooms. They'd never had much in the way of physical possessions or wealth, but they'd grown up with an abundance of humor and love.

Heather found herself alternately praying and crying as she walked. As she wasn't a woman who succumbed easily to tears, she was embarrassed by this weakness. Geraldine tried to comfort her, to no avail.

Unfortunately, Heather couldn't tell even Geraldine, her best friend in the whole world, what her problem was. If she did, then Geraldine would think she was crazy, as Mr. St. Pierre did, and Heather didn't think she could stand that.

She was cheered slightly when she perceived her father, his left arm in a sling, sitting in a chair under the huge pecan tree that shaded the house. She even managed a small smile.

"Good old Pa," she said to Geraldine. "It's blowing a gale out here, and he's sitting under the pecan tree. I'll wager if you asked, he'd say he's enjoying the weather. He loves to be out of doors."

"Your father is such a nice man, Heather. You're very lucky."

The wistfulness in Geraldine's voice surprised Heather, and she turned to stare at her friend for a moment. It had never occurred to her to consider herself lucky, as compared to Geraldine, whose family was ever so much better off than her own. But the girl was right about Heather's father. He was a jolly, cheerful, *good* man, even if he was poor, and he'd made the lives of his children happy.

"Heather, me love!" he called when he caught sight of the girls. "It's about time you came to visit your old man!"

"Oh, Pa!" Weeping freely, Heather ran the last several yards to her father's chair, heedless of the wind whipping her skirts up around her knees. Geraldine followed at a more discreet pace.

"Pisht, child, what are those tears for?"

"Oh, Pa, when Geraldine told me you'd been shot—*shot*—I couldn't believe it!"

He winked at her and smiled at Geraldine. "Sure, and 'twas an adventure."

"An adventure?" Heather uttered something that sounded like a cross between a laugh and a sob. "Only you would consider being held up and shot an adventure, Pa."

"Aye, I suppose you're right, lass." He hugged her hard with his good arm. "And 'tis a good thing the villain didn't put the slug in me right arm, or he might have done me more harm. As it is, all I have to worry about is a little hide off of my left shoulder. I can still use me right hand and arm, and that's the important one." He shared his wink with both girls this time. "The right's the one I lift me glass with, don't you know."

"Oh, Pa!" Crying and laughing at once, Heather didn't notice the man who'd walked around the side of the house with her mother. What she noticed was that suddenly Geraldine, who had been smiling as she observed the touching scene between father and daughter, gasped and went as stiff as a board. Then she looked up.

And saw Philippe St. Pierre.

He was walking toward them with her mother, and he was looking straight at Heather, his direct gaze making her dizzy for a moment. She tried to hide her condition by gripping the back of her father's chair. That worked, so she attempted a smile. That worked, too, and she believed she might survive this encounter—depending on why Mr. St. Pierre was here.

If he'd come to tell her folks that she'd gone crazy and would have to be locked up in the insane asylum, Heather feared she might die here and now. And if she didn't, she'd just have to borrow a gun from one of the boys and shoot herself, because she'd never live it down.

"Heather!" her mother cried, and rushed over to hug her, then whirled on Geraldine and hugged her, too. "And Geraldine Swift. We were wondering what had become of you."

Geraldine, who evidently wasn't used to exuberant displays of emotion from her own family, flushed. "It's good to see you, Mrs. Mahaffey. I've been working at my father's hotel most days and at the chop house in the afternoons. I haven't been able to visit much."

"Well, and it's a delight to see you today, dear. And our lovely Heather." Mrs. Mahaffey hugged her daughter again. "But Geraldine, you must say how-de-do to Mr. St. Pierre, too."

Both girls did so, Heather with what she hoped was a significant smile, Geraldine with her usual shy reserve.

Thank God, thank God. Evidently Philippe hadn't spilled the beans yet, or her mother wouldn't be so happy to see her. "Oh, Ma, I had no idea what had happened until Geraldine told me. Why didn't you send one of the boys to tell me?"

"We didn't want to worry you, dear."

"I'd like to have known, though." A little bit of hurt leaked into Heather's voice. She didn't like not being in the bosom of her family.

Her mother backed away, snatched a handkerchief from her pocket, and wiped her eyes. "Oh, Heather, it was awful."

"It sounds like it. Do you have any idea who held you up?"

"No. We couldn't see his face."

Her father put in, "The lad had a bandanna pulled over his lower face, just like you read about in those novels you love so well, child. It was a queer bandanna—looked like a dish towel."

"Aye, it did," confirmed Mrs. Mahaffey

"Mercy," Heather whispered.

"But he had the lightest, bluest, wickedest eyes I've ever seen," said her mother. "And hair as black as soot."

"Aye," said Mr. Mahaffey, "and I think he had a mustache."

"How could you tell?" Heather's insides had begun to get cold.

Her father shrugged and then winced. "I don't know, but I *do* think he had a mustache."

"Oh." The highwayman sounded suspiciously like D. A. Bologh to her.

But that was stupid. Nobody could be in two places at once, and D. A. had been in the kitchen with her. Hadn't he? She couldn't remember, exactly. Heather pressed a hand to her eyes for a second and wished her life would stop being in such a turmoil.

Not that she didn't deserve it.

"Mr. St. Pierre was kind enough to ride over here as soon as he heard about your father's accident, and to ask if there was anything he could do to help us." Mrs. Mahaffey had to wipe her eyes again.

Heather was touched. "Thank you, Mr. St. Pierre." The thanks came from her heart—and for more than one act of kindness on his part. He clearly hadn't tattled on Heather, and she was as grateful for that as she was for his solicitude toward her family.

He bowed slightly. It had been so long since Heather had been the recipient of his courtly manners that she feared she might have gaped slightly.

"It was nothing, Miss Mahaffey." He nodded at Geraldine. "Miss Swift. It's a pleasure to see you today. This gives me the opportunity to thank you once again for assisting at my dinner party the other night."

"Oh—oh, thank you. I mean, it was nothing. I mean—" Geraldine, who was usually the most poised of young women, turned brick red and shut up.

Heather knew that it was only to be expected of the folks who'd lived in Fort Summers for years to visit neighbors in distress. But Philippe was a relative newcomer. The fact that he'd bothered to pay a call on her parents touched her heart. Not that her heart hadn't already been touched by Philippe. With an internal sigh, she turned to her mother.

"How's Henry?" The lad had broken his arm a month ago. Heather hadn't seen her family in that time, except during Philippe's dinner party. She missed them.

"Ach, he's gettin' right along," said her father. "He's a sturdy lad."

"Aye, he is."

Mrs. Mahaffey seemed inordinately happy, given the injuries that had lately plagued her family. Heather eyed her for a minute, wondering. Then she glanced at Philippe, who was gazing off into the distance as if he were bored by the proceedings, and she ceased wondering.

But that bored, world-weary stance was a pose. She knew it in her bones. He was here to help her family. She wasn't sure how to feel about that, either. The good Lord knew, her family needed help. Still, the notion of accepting charity galled her.

She reached into her pocket, withdrew a leather pouch, and handed it to her mother. "Here, Ma. I saved my pay. You can use it to help pay Doc Grady. I'm sure we owe him even more now that Pa's had to be all bandaged up." She stooped quickly and kissed her father.

"Ah, Heather," Mr. Mahaffey said. "You're a good daughter."

Mrs. Mahaffey sniffled. "Thank you, Heather. You *are* a good daughter."

Now she was embarrassed. "Nonsense. We're family."

That said it all, and both Heather and her parents knew it.

Chapter Thirteen

Intrigued, Philippe watched the Mahaffeys interacting. He'd never seen anything like it. They genuinely loved and cared about what happened to one another.

How odd.

Philippe's experiences had led him to believe that family members were akin to sucking parasites, forever trying to drain a body of his independence, self-respect, and spirit. Of course, Philippe had never known his father. Perhaps that might have made a . . .

But no. It wouldn't have mattered. There was no getting away from the circumstances of his birth. His mother probably didn't even know who his father was. And the fact that he'd been reared in a whorehouse by a woman who cared more for her looks than for him had made an indelible mark on him. That was his kind of family.

Not the Mahaffeys. This Irish clan actually, really and truly, loved each other. He shook his head and butted into the conversation. "Actually, Miss Mahaffey, I was here to ask your parents to allow me to pay the doctor for assisting your father."

Geraldine goggled at him.

Heather did, too, although she ceased almost at once, drew herself up as straight and tall as possible, and planted a frown on her face. Philippe experienced a weird mixture of exasperation and amusement when he realized she was going to try to refuse his offer. As if any Mahaffey could afford to refuse a good turn.

"We can take care of our own, Mr. St. Pierre, but thank you very much for the kind offer." She looked like she wanted to pop him one.

"Ach, Heather," her father muttered. "It's a stiff-necked lass you are."

"Heather, please," her mother pleaded. "Mr. St. Pierre explained it all to us already."

"Explained what all to you?" Heather demanded.

Philippe stepped in. "Unfortunately, Miss Mahaffey, it seems that my dinner party was the trigger to a series of unfortunate events, and I feel responsible for them."

"Fiddlesticks. It's not your fault there are robbers and coyotes loose. And ruts in the road. And things to trip over. And—and, well, cats die. Everything dies. Eventually." She got a perplexed look on her pretty face.

Philippe smiled. So the indomitable Heather Mahaffey believed the events of the party evening were strange, too, did she? He said, "Perhaps, but the fact remains that a good third of the people who attended the party at my house that night experienced accidents afterwards." And if they weren't directly related to the other peculiar things that had been happening on his ranch, he'd be very much surprised. Somebody had it in for him, and he was going to find out who, and put a stop to the shenanigans. In the meantime he planned to take care of anyone who got hurt because of that person—whatever the man's problem with him.

"That's still not your fault." Her brow furrowed. "It's queer, but it's not your fault."

"Nevertheless, I have visited everyone who was affected, and I insist upon paying for the repair of any damages my guests endured as well as any doctor bills incurred. I don't intend to be thwarted, Miss Mahaffey, so I hope you won't argue." He gave her a smile intended to mellow her into compliance.

She spluttered a little bit, but didn't press the matter. Philippe could tell she wasn't satisfied, in spite of his smile.

"Well . . ."

"Then it's settled." Without waiting for Heather to respond, Philippe turned to Mrs. Mahaffey. "Thank you very much, ma'am. I trust your husband and son will regain their full health soon." He bowed formally, and shook Mr. Mahaffey's hand.

"Wait a minute," Heather said suddenly. "Pa's accident might or might not have anything to do with your party and your ranch, but Henry's arm doesn't, and you can't make it." She scowled up at him.

He scowled back down at her and said in the coldest, most authoritarian voice he had in him, "The matter is settled."

"But—"

"And I refuse to hear any further arguments about it." To Mrs. Mahaffey, he said, "Thank you, ma'am. I appreciate your understanding."

"Oh, my," said Heather's mother. "It's we who thank you, Mr. St. Pierre."

"It's nothing. Truly, it's nothing."

He knew good and well it wasn't nothing to the Mahaffeys, who obviously weren't well off, but he'd be damned if he'd ever allow himself to be labeled a philanthropist. Lord, they'd be inviting him to church and to school socials if that happened. The thought made him shudder.

Heather didn't dicker with him again, but she was frowning up a storm when he turned back to her and her friend, who was still goggling. Philippe said, "If you will allow me, Miss Mahaffey, I'll help you with the supplies and drive the wagon back to the ranch. I can tie my horse to the back."

It looked for a moment as if she intended to quarrel with him. Prudence prevailed—or perhaps she was still worried about her crazy behavior of the night before and didn't want to reinforce the idea that she was a lunatic—and she accepted with fair grace. He accompanied the two young women back to Mr. Trujillo's dry goods store, leading his horse.

A crowd stood in front of the store. Philippe frowned, wondering if all those people were there to confront him for being behind the rash of incidents that had recently happened to citizens of the town. Although he'd had absolutely nothing to do with any of the injuries or accidents, he honestly wouldn't have blamed anyone for challenging him about the strange events, since they'd occurred immediately after his party guests had departed his ranch. He learned his mistake as soon as Geraldine and Heather expelled twin gasps.

"Oh, Geraldine! The stage is coming. I forgot all about this being Thursday."

"Let's wait to see who gets off," Geraldine suggested, excitement vibrating in her voice.

"Well . . ." Heather hesitated, glancing up at Philippe, and he could see the longing in her expression.

He made a sweeping gesture, giving them leave. It was the least he could do. "Certainly, ladies. Be my guest. There's no rush about the supplies."

Philippe watched the two young women for a moment, curious. Then it dawned on him why they were so fascinated by a stagecoach's arrival. It made sense that they'd be excited about the stage coming to town. This was a backwater. An outpost on the isolated American western frontier. These two seldom saw strangers. The most by way of excitement that ever happened in Fort Summers was watching the troops practice drill exercises in the desert. Pitifully small onions for two inquisitive young ladies who yearned to experience something of the world. He felt an unaccustomed tugging at his heart that worried him a little bit. He couldn't afford to let softer emotions take over.

But honestly, what circumscribed lives these two lived. If he could, he'd snatch them both up—or perhaps only Heather—and spirit her off to exotic ports. Or at least to San Francisco and New York City.

He smiled inside, considering how Heather Mahaffey would react to the big city. She'd probably leap into society with both feet, if she was anything like he supposed. Not shy and retiring, Miss Heather Mahaffey. Not at all. Oh, she might be a trifle cowed at first, but she wouldn't be for long. He'd bet on it.

They hadn't been standing amid the small throng for very long before the cloud of dust in the distance drew closer, eventually resolving into the horses pulling a dust-brown stagecoach. The crowd began to mutter as soon as the horses became discernible. As the stage drew closer, the mutterings turned to talk, then to clamor, and as soon as the horses passed the westernmost boundaries of the town, everyone began cheering.

Even Heather and her more genteel friend set up a holler. Philippe was completely disarmed. Now this, he thought, was an aspect of territorial life he hadn't imagined when he'd made up his mind to move here, this anticipation and excitement over an event that, in any civilized place, would be commonplace.

By the time the stage pulled up in front of Trujillo's store, which also served as the town's depot, Philippe could see that the horses were sweaty and exhausted. Thanks to the wind and dust, they were also the same color as the stagecoach, the driver, the driver's assistant, and, it appeared, most of the passengers.

He shook his head, confounded again by the resiliency of the human spirit. Or its refusal to face reality. Whichever prevailed in these particular human breasts, they weren't daunted much by the expectation of hardships. He discovered himself feeling much more charitable toward his fellow creatures than he generally did.

"Oh, look, Geraldine!" Heather's whisper held a

world of enthusiasm. "That poor man's never going to get his suit clean again."

Geraldine tutted, and then giggled. "Perhaps Mrs. Halloran can brush the dust out."

The gentleman in question looked as if he had once been a fairly natty specimen—perhaps a drummer or some other sort of businessman. He looked a little shaky as he heaved himself out of the stage. And, Philippe noticed, Heather was right. His suit was probably black under its coating of red-brown dust, but it would take a miracle to get it to look that way again. The newcomer nodded to the milling crowd and smiled, and Philippe shook his head in wonder. Human beings were an amazing lot. Imagine being jostled for hundreds of miles, practically smothered in dust, and being able to smile upon arrival at one's destination. Especially when one's destination was the small and unlovely town of Fort Summers, New Mexico Territory.

The next passenger, a plump woman of forty or so, uttered a shriek that at first alarmed Philippe. Then, when he saw her fall into the arms of a younger woman, and heard the younger woman cry, "Mother!" he realized there was no need to worry. Mother was here either to visit or to stay, and her daughter was happy about it. Good for them. Chalk up another point on the side of families.

Perhaps, Philippe thought, all of these familial observations were good for him. They might make him less cynical about the world and the people inhabiting it. And—*mon dieu*, he could hardly believe he was thinking about it again—marriage.

On the other hand, they might not. Philippe was

enjoying his education, whatever result or lack thereof eventuated.

The next people to step out of the stage were a young woman and her small child, whom she held by the hand. She glanced around uncertainly for a moment. Then a huge smile lit her rather plain face, the child—Philippe couldn't tell if it was a girl or a boy—shrieked, "Papa!" and the two were enveloped in a king-sized hug by Sandy, the blacksmith.

Philippe entertained two emotions at the sight. He was touched by the reunion of Sandy and his wife and child. He was also pleased to learn that Sandy was already taken, and therefore wouldn't be wooing Heather Mahaffey. He frowned, wishing he'd stop thinking such irrelevant things.

He stopped thinking altogether when the next passenger descended. He heard Heather gasp.

"Oh, my goodness, Geraldine, have you ever seen such a beautiful woman in your life?"

Geraldine shook her head. Philippe barely saw the motion out of the corner of his eye.

"No," said Geraldine, obviously in awe. "My word, where do you suppose she's come from?"

"I don't know." Heather gaped at the woman. "And I wonder who she's here to see."

"So do I."

As if she suspected something—but didn't quite know what—Heather turned to glance at Philippe.

He knew she was looking at him, but he was unable to say or do anything for a moment. He could only stare, frozen in place, as if he'd been turned into a pillar of salt, like Lot's wife.

The woman was beautiful; perhaps the most beautiful woman Philippe had ever seen in his life—and he'd seen thousands of women. She had a complexion that was as smooth and clear and soft as a baby's. It was a little lighter than Philippe's, but he knew that was only because he spent most of his life outside, in the sun. That woman wouldn't be caught dead in the sun—not without a hat and veil, she wouldn't. Her eyes were dark and rich and luminous, and they were framed by lashes that needed no help from art to be thick and luxurious. Her figure was spectacular, her hair thick, black, shiny, and coarse—but not curly. Her hair and its lack of curliness, Philippe remembered, had been a point of pride with her. It was dressed in a way that complemented the woman's other charms, which were considerable.

She was his mother. God save them all, that was his mother.

He stood stock still for only a moment, although it seemed like hours. Then, without thinking, he grabbed Heather's arm and jerked her harder than he'd meant to. He didn't apologize. "Come along, Miss Mahaffey. We need to get back to the ranch."

She stumbled before she realized he meant for her to follow him, and regained her footing. She stared up at him, startled, but still moving. "But—"

"Now." He remembered Geraldine, which afterwards surprised him a good deal. Turning to her, he said in clipped accents, "Good day to you, Miss Swift."

Geraldine, as shocked as Heather by Philippe's behavior, said, "But—"

Philippe didn't pause to explain. He couldn't. He wouldn't. "Hop in, Miss Mahaffey."

"I—"

Again, he didn't wait for her to say anything. Or

for her to hop in. He lifted her and all but threw her onto the wagon seat. More quickly than he believed possible, he tied his horse to the back of the wagon, jumped into the driver's seat, snapped the reins, and took off as if he were being pursued by demons.

Completely baffled by Philippe's strange behavior, Heather slapped a hand to her hat to keep it from flying away on the wind. She turned on the wagon seat, waved to her best friend, and called out, "I'll see you soon, Geraldine!"

Her friend, plainly as puzzled as Heather, waved back. "Bye. I hope so!"

Heather saw the beautiful woman standing in the dirt road beside the stagecoach, a hand on her hat, a large wicker suitcase beside her, staring after Philippe's wagon. All at once, Heather understood—and her heart cracked in two.

Which was ridiculous. What did it matter to her if Philippe had a relationship with that woman? What did it matter to her if that woman and Philippe were married, if it came to that?

It's not as if she, Heather Mahaffey, bumpkin, had any claim on him. Besides, she couldn't blame him if she was his wife. That woman was the most spectacularly beautiful creature Heather had ever seen. Granted, she'd lived all her life in Fort Summers, in the remote and uncivilized New Mexico Territory, but she still didn't think women could get much more lovely than that one.

But if they were married or affianced or had some other close and loving relationship, why had Philippe come here alone? And why was he now fairly running away from her?

With her heart in her throat, clogging it painfully, Heather turned to Philippe. "Who is she?" She wasn't sure she wanted to know, although she was pretty sure her heart couldn't hurt any more than it already did, no matter what Philippe's answer turned out to be.

"Who is who?" he responded curtly. Much more curtly than the occasion called for.

She pushed words past the lump in her throat once more. "That woman. Who is she?"

"What woman?"

Exasperated and in emotional chaos, Heather snapped, "For heaven's sake, don't be coy! Who was that beautiful woman? The one who got off the stage. I know you know her, or you wouldn't have taken off like a bat out of hell as soon as you saw her."

Oh, dear. She wished she hadn't said *hell*. It was so unladylike. She'd bet that woman who'd just gotten off the stagecoach never uttered words like that. Heather felt a prickle of tears behind her eyes, but she'd die before she'd cry in front of Philippe—and for so stupid a reason as a beautiful woman coming to town.

"You don't know what you're talking about."

Torn between anger and despair, Heather's temper cracked right in half. "I do, too! You're just trying to avoid answering my question! Why? Is it because you're married to her or something?" He wouldn't have been the first man to run out on a bad marriage, although if he had, he was not the man Heather had believed him to be.

"Married?" Philippe let out a bark of laughter that almost froze Heather's blood. She could tell he was mad as a hornet, but that laugh was horrible. Cold. Almost inhuman. His voice held deliberate scorn when he went on. "I'm not married to anyone, Miss Mahaffey. Marriage is for weaklings and fools."

Hmm. She guessed that told her something she hadn't known before, although it didn't warm her heart any. She couldn't seem to let the subject drop, though. As if propelled by some evil spirit, she declared, "Is that so? Is that why you're so afraid of her, then? Because you seduced and abandoned her? Because you promised you'd marry her and then took off and left her stranded?"

"For the love of God . . . No! That woman and I have absolutely nothing to do with each other."

"You're lying." Under normal circumstances, Heather would never have uttered such a blatantly uncivil thing to her employer. Or to anyone else, for that matter. She might be a hoyden at times, but she was at least polite. Usually.

"*Dammit!* I'm not lying!"

"You are, too. As soon as you saw that woman get off the stage, you grabbed me and dragged me off. We haven't even done the shopping! We have no supplies! How am I supposed to cook if there's nothing to cook?" Stupid question. She couldn't cook anyway. And D. A. Bologh always seemed to come up with something to prepare, no matter what supplies resided in the pantry. She tried to banish that thought from her mind.

"God damn it!" Philippe looked darker and more dangerous than Heather had ever seen him.

"Swearing won't help," she said self-righteously, reminding herself of Geraldine.

They'd exited the town limits, and were barreling along the beaten-down stretch of desert that passed for the road to Philippe's ranch. Because she was angry and hurting inside, Heather grumbled, "And you're going to kill the horses if you don't slow down."

"*Damn* you!"

Suddenly, Philippe pulled up on the reins—not, Heather noticed, quickly enough to hurt the horses's mouths—and drew the wagon to a stop in a swirl of dust. The dust got blown away on a gust of wind before it could choke them to death, thank goodness.

Then he grabbed her by the arms. "Stop talking about that woman! I won't talk about her with you or anyone else. You know nothing about her or me or anything else having to do with me, and you never will. Do you understand me?" He shook her.

Indignant and frightened, Heather cried, "Stop it! Stop it this instant! It's not my fault if you have a black past!"

"A black past?"

Heather, aware that Philippe was incensed in his own right, wished she hadn't said that. At least he stopped shaking her, in favor of staring at her as if she were a madwoman. "Well, maybe not a *black* past—but you and that woman have met before, and I know it. And you ran away from her."

"I didn't run away from anything!"

"You did, too, and there's no use denying it. I saw you. It was that woman. What is she to you?" Not that she had any business asking.

"Dammit, I don't want to think about that woman."

And he drew her into his arms, his lips descended on hers, and Heather's brain turned off.

In spite of Philippe's anger, his lips were soft and

sweet, and the feel of them lit fires inside her in all sorts of places unrelated to her mouth. His embrace almost crushed her at first, then loosened a little into a more tender clasp. She'd never felt anything like the sensation of being in Philippe St. Pierre's arms. She liked it. A lot.

Heather had been kissed by boys before; this was the first time she'd been kissed by a man—and Philippe's kiss thrilled her. She heard a sound, realized it had come from her throat, and didn't even care.

His lips left hers and skimmed her cheek and chin. "Dammit, Heather," he muttered, his voice rough, like crumpled velvet. "I don't want to talk about that woman."

Heather was in no fit condition to talk about anything. She felt as if she'd been fed some sort of drug that fogged her mind, turned her limbs to rubber, made her body tingle, and created perfectly shocking sensations in places too delicate to mention. Nevertheless, she was too stubborn to give up entirely. "I do."

That was a lie. At the moment, she didn't want to talk about anything at all, much less another woman and what that other woman might or might not be to Philippe. What she wanted was for Philippe to keep kissing her and to progress from there into the dark and mysterious world of lovemaking, about which Heather knew nothing.

His wonderful mouth had nibbled its way to the sensitive spot under her ear, and she sighed. This was heavenly.

Well, except for the surroundings. Not only was the wagon bench hard as a rock, but the wind was still trying to blow them both off of it.

"That woman is nothing to me," Philippe growled. "She's nothing at all."

He'd left her ear and made his way to her throat, where he was now nuzzling. She'd never realized how sensitive a person's throat was until right this minute. Actually, it seemed as if Philippe had turned some sort of switch in her, and her entire body had become sensitive. Exquisitely so.

However, she still wouldn't let the matter die, sensing somehow it was important to her life—and Philippe's. "She's not nothing. She's something."

It wasn't much, but Heather's brain wasn't working too well just then. Merciful saints in heaven, if he stopped, she thought she might die. She'd simply melt into a puddle of bubbling sensation right here in the middle of the desert. Or catch fire and burn to a crisp, and then the wind would pick up her ashes and scatter her over hundreds of miles of territorial soil.

His hand covered her breast—which was well protected beneath layers of fabric and well bolstered by whalebone—but Heather almost fainted anyway. His touch was like nothing she'd ever felt before. She thrust herself at him, and knew she should be embarrassed, but she wasn't.

When he lowered his head to allow his mouth to play where his hand had been, she gasped. This was too incredible for words. Her determination to get to the bottom of Philippe's relationship with the woman on the stage blurred around the edges.

"*This* is what I want," Philippe whispered.

At least Heather thought that's what he whispered. Her brain had turned to mush, and her thought processes had ceased operating. She said, "Hmm?"

He said, "*This*. I left all that behind. This is what I need."

Merciful heavens, was it really? Heather writhed on the wagon seat, knowing she'd never find whatever it was she needed that way, but understanding she needed something. Desperately. And whatever it was, Philippe was the only one who had it. She said, "Ahh."

Because she had an academic knowledge of such things and was a woman of great curiosity, Heather allowed her hand to drift to Philippe's thigh. His was a grand thigh, heavily muscled, corded with Herculean sinew. That's not what she was interested in, however. She let her hand travel up his leg, toward his crotch. Ah, yes. There it was.

Philippe groaned audibly, and unbuttoned the top button of her shirtwaist. Heather barely noticed.

Good heavens! The man was gigantic. Was this right? Was it proper?

No, forget the part about proper.

But were men's things really that large? How did they fit? She was in no condition to ask, but she did experiment by rubbing her palm over the bulge in his trousers to see what would happen. He groaned again, and then he growled.

Interesting. She wondered if that would keep happening, so she did it again.

He let go of her so abruptly, Heather nearly fell backwards out of the wagon. She caught the back of the seat in time to prevent that particular catastrophe, but she was too fuddled to speak. Her hand lifted of its own accord to her lips, which felt swollen and hot. She noticed that Philippe seemed to be in some kind of distress. He'd flung himself back against the bolster, and was frenziedly passing his fingers through his black, black hair. His hands were trembling as if he had a palsy.

"Merde." He sounded as if he had the croup. His voice was as hoarse as a bullfrog's.

Heather didn't know what that word meant, but she didn't think it was a polite one. She was breathing heavily herself, and in a state the likes of which she'd never been in before. Her whole body was primed for procreation, and her nerves were drawn as taut as a fiddle string. Her blood raced, her body sang and buzzed, and the pressure in her lower belly and between her legs was close to unbelievable. She squirmed again, but couldn't find her voice.

Why had he quit? Damn and blast, she wished he hadn't.

Blinking furiously in an attempt to reestablish some sort of hold with the mundane world in which she usually lived, she darted a wild glance around, and a semblance of normality began to pervade her fuddled senses.

Very well, perhaps this wasn't the best time and place to perpetrate a seduction. She was sure a bed would be more comfortable.

Good heavens, what was she thinking? Had she really sunk as low as that? Just because she'd started telling a little lie about cooking?

Little lie be damned, a voice sang in her head. *It was a great big whopper of a lie, and you know it.*

The truth did a good deal to dampen her ardor. She sat up straight and, with trembling fingers, groped around for the ribbons to her bonnet, which Philippe had pushed aside in pursuit of sensitive body parts. She cleared her throat.

Philippe had covered his face with one hand. Hearing her, he parted his fingers and peered through them at her. Heather didn't know what to do or say, so she only watched him. He sucked in about three bushels of air and let them out slowly. He did it again.

Then he said, "I beg your pardon, Miss Mahaffey."

She had to clear her throat once more before she could get her voice to work. "I, ah, think we're past the Miss Mahaffey stage, don't you?" She smiled, trying to make it a down-home, friendly smile. In truth, she felt rather like a lioness about to snag a mate. Except she had a feeling that, in this case, she had the metaphor backwards. If there was any mating going on here, it was Philippe doing the snagging.

Still, she had a good deal of pride, and she'd be hanged if she'd let him know how he'd gotten to her. "You may call me Heather, if you like." Because she wasn't sure how her offer would be received, she hurried on to say, "As friends. No strings attached." She knew good and well that many women would consider such a kiss as they'd just experienced in the light of a marriage proposal, but Heather wasn't one of their ilk.

Not only did she scorn such underhanded tactics in pursuit of husbands, but she'd have to know a good deal more about Philippe St. Pierre than she did now before she'd marry him. And, she acknowledged, with the sinking in her chest that always accompanied the thought, he'd have to know a good deal more about her, too.

Besides, while she couldn't very well ignore the fact that Philippe had succumbed to lust momentarily, she had no idea that he'd ever even consider marrying her. In fact, she rather doubted it, which made the sinking feeling in her chest develop even faster.

"Heather." He said her name softly in his deep, rich, velvety voice, and Heather had never liked her name more.

She sighed. Her name sounded so wonderful coming from his lips. His wonderful lips. She wished they were still attached to her body somewhere.

"Please call me Philippe, Heather."

Her heart fluttered. In a voice that, wonder of wonders, didn't quake or quiver, she said, "Philippe." What a lovely name he had. She said it again. "Philippe." Because her heart was full and her senses still ariot, she said, "It's a beautiful name."

He uttered a short "Hmph," which didn't do much for Heather's self-confidence. Then he leaned back against the bolster again and, with his eyes shut, breathed deeply for several moments. Heather wasn't sure what to do.

But she wasn't a woman who had ever allowed circumstances to master her. Rather, she was accustomed to taking circumstances by the scruff of the neck and bending them to suit her. Therefore, she wouldn't allow herself to sulk, fall into a daydream, or let matters remain in confusion. She drew herself up straight once more and buttoned the top button on her shirtwaist. She was a little disappointed he hadn't unbuttoned more of them. She'd be interested in his opinion of her body, actually.

"Um, Philippe, I'm not sure what that was all about."

He didn't stir anything except his head, which he twisted until it faced her. He had a sardonic smile on his face. "No?"

Offhand, she couldn't remember when he'd sounded more French, which was slightly daunting. "No."

"I should think it must be obvious."

Nettled, she said sharply, "It isn't to me."

It seemed to take an effort for him to draw himself away from the bolster, pick up the reins—God alone knew what he'd done with them when he'd grabbed her—and pick up his hat, which had fallen to the floor of the wagon. "It means I'm a man, you're a woman, and I desire you."

Oh. For some reason, while technically his explanation accounted for what had happened, Heather remained unsatisfied. "And do you always kiss women to whom you're attracted if you manage to get them alone with you somewhere?"

"No." He flicked the reins, and the horses started off, making the wagon jerk, and propelling Heather to brace herself.

She was getting a little more than merely nettled by his curt words. "Now just a little minute here, Philippe St. Pierre, I want to know what you meant by grabbing me and kissing me that way. It's because of that woman, isn't it? What is she to you?"

"Nothing!" He turned an enraged face her way. "Dammit, leave me alone about that woman. She's nothing to me. In case that little exhibition back there didn't teach you anything, let me spell it out for you, Heather. I want *you*. I desire *you*. I crave your body. I want to make love to you, to carry you to my bed and ravish you. I want to take your innocence and teach you the pleasures of the flesh. I want to lick you from one end of your luscious body to the other, and to teach you the art of love."

He sucked in another gigantic breath. Then he smiled a smile that made Heather swallow and wish she could dunk her head under the pump. "Do you need further explanation, Heather, or do you think you understand now?"

She had to lick her lips. "Um, no, I don't think I need further explanation."

"Good." The one word was hard and clipped.

Heather turned on the wagon seat and stared straight ahead of her until Philippe guided the horses into the ranch yard and pulled them to a stop. Then she climbed down out of the wagon, walked to the kitchen door, and went in. She didn't turn to see what Philippe was doing.

As soon as she got inside, she sagged against the door and whispered, "Oh, my God."

Her legs gave out, and she slid down until she was sitting on the floor.

Chapter Fourteen

"What's the matter with *you*?"

Blast! Heather looked up from where she was sprawled and saw D. A. Bologh sneering at her from his chair. His chair. Merciful heavens, when had it become his chair? She said, "Nothing." Her legs had turned to water, and she couldn't get up yet.

"I don't believe you, Heather, my sweet. You're flushed and behaving very oddly." A wicked grin spread over D. A.'s face, and he waggled a finger at her. "If I didn't know what an upright, righteous girl you are—except when you need help in the kitchen—I'd actually think you'd been doing something naughty. Probably with your esteemed employer."

Heather scowled at him. A host of grievances against him flooded into her mind. She chose to ignore his implication—which was the truth, curse it—and said in a hard voice, "Did you shoot my father the other night?"

His eyes went big, his eyebrows lifted into two incredulous arches, he splayed a hand against a place on his chest under which a heart would reside in a normal human being, and said, *"Moi?"* He sneered some more. "You'll notice I used the French form of the pronoun, since you seem to be under the influence of something extremely French at the moment."

His snicker made Heather's skin crawl. It was a struggle, but she got her legs to bend and shoved herself to her feet. She had to brace herself against the kitchen door for a minute before she trusted herself to walk.

"Yes," she said. "You. Did you shoot my father and cause a lot of other accidents after Mr. St. Pierre's dinner party?" She knew it was impossible for him to have done so, but she had to ask. She *had* to; her mother's description of their attacker had only seemed to fit one man. Bologh.

"Good heavens, Heather, when would I have had time to shoot anybody the night of the party? In case you don't recall, I was slaving away in the kitchen all night. Doing your work."

Heather stared at him hard. There was something distinctly uncanny about D. A. Bologh, and she didn't like it. Even if he had saved her job. "Do you have a twin brother?" She'd heard about entire families who had turned to crime. Look at the James brothers, for heaven's sake. She'd always chalked such behavior up to a quirk in heredity, and why shouldn't the Bologh family be prey to a similar hereditary quirk?

"I have many brothers, my sweet, but none of us

are twins—or triplets or anything else along those lines—and none of my kin are currently abroad in the territory."

That was an odd way of expressing it. Heather continued to squint at him for a minute. "How many?"

"How many what?" He sounded bored.

"Brothers. How many brothers do you have?"

"Hundreds."

Heather pursed her lips and forced herself not to say anything unladylike. "Right." She guessed she wasn't going to get a straight answer from him about brothers. Why should she? He had yet to give her a straight answer about anything. She persisted anyway. "And how do you know none of them are in the territory?"

"We all have business, sweetie. And I don't believe it has called any of my kin to hereabout."

"I see."

She saw nothing. Yet there was obviously no way she was going to get any useful information from the man. She gave up. "We didn't get the shopping done. I don't know what we can have for supper tonight."

"You never do," he said nastily. "But don't worry your pretty little head about it, my sweet. Good old D. A. will provide, as he always does."

She squinted at him. "Don't make it anything too fancy, or Mr. St. Pierre will think something funny's going on."

"Something funny *is* going on, isn't it?"

"Yes," she said through gritted teeth. "But I'd appreciate your not fixing anything fancy anyway."

He waved a hand in a careless gesture. "Don't

worry, sweetie pie. D. A. will come through. He always does."

It went against the grain, but Heather managed to choke out, "Thank you."

"You're entirely welcome."

She didn't like his smirk today even more than she usually didn't like it.

Philippe slammed his driving gloves onto the table in the foyer. He ripped his hat off and flung it at the hat rack in the hall. He took the stairs three at a time, stormed to his room, threw the door open with such fury that it crashed against the wall and dislodged plaster, went into his room, and slammed the door so hard a picture fell down and broke. He kicked the frame and glass fragments across the room. Then he went to his bed, sat down, tugged his boots off, and threw them, one at a time, against the wall. They each made a satisfying thwack as they struck.

He still felt like killing something.

Damnation, how could he have kissed Heather Mahaffey that way? He'd just grabbed her and kissed her, roughly and unmercifully. He ought to be horsewhipped. If he had another set of arms and hands, he'd horsewhip himself.

But, good God almighty, that had been his mother on the stage. His *mother*!

How in the name of holy hell had she found him? And what did she want?

Philippe knew good and well she wanted something. And she wanted it from him. Yvonne St. Pierre wasn't a woman to bestir herself, or endure rough accommodations, for the hell of it. She'd sure as the devil not have come all the way out here except to find him, although he had no idea how she'd done it. He'd believed he'd covered his traces. He'd thought no one could ever find him, unless he wanted to be found. He'd cherished the notion that he'd left his past behind, and that it would never catch up with him again.

But it had. In the form of his *mother*, for God's sake!

Damn, damn, damn, damn, damn.

Should he go back to town and confront her? Should he tell her to stay the hell out of his life? Maybe she needed money. Hell, he'd pay her to stay away. He had lots of money; he could afford it. It would go against the grain to support the woman who'd ruined his life, but he'd do it if it would keep her away for the rest of it.

Great God in heaven, what if Heather met her?

Philippe buried his head in his hands and groaned for a moment before he sat up and spat, "Dammit, what you told Heather was the truth. That woman is nothing to you. And she's not going to defile your life again."

He felt better after he'd made his goal clear to himself, although he wasn't sure how to arrange it, especially if she'd come to the territory with the intention of butting into his affairs. There must be something he could do to prevent such a catastrophe from happening.

What he'd do was ignore her. That would suit the situation admirably. He simply wouldn't allow her to affect him one way or the other.

Of course, his mother, no martyr if Philippe recalled correctly—and he did, God save him—would probably not stand idly by and allow her son to deny her. She'd probably raise a stink. Call him a bad son. That sort of thing.

But there was such a thing as fighting fire with fire, and if she tried anything of that nature, he'd repudiate her right back. It might not be the gentlemanly thing to do, but he'd never claimed to be a gentleman. And if his neighbors shunned him, so much the better. He didn't care. He hadn't ever planned to get chummy with his neighbors in the first place.

Heather would care. She was enthusiastic about family and family connections and friends and her fellow citizens of Fort Summers. She'd think he was a skunk if he refused to acknowledge his own mother. She'd probably think so even if he told her what his mother's line of work was and how she'd treated the child Philippe used to be.

She'd probably sermonize at him. She'd probably say that forgiveness is a virtue. She'd probably say that Philippe should honor his mother, no matter what she'd done when he was a child. She'd probably say that his mother must have changed or she wouldn't be here now. She'd probably say that this was his chance to reestablish the family he'd missed for so many years.

Not, of course, that he'd missed a family in *that* way. He couldn't, since he'd never had one. A man couldn't be expected to miss what he'd never had.

Aw, hell, he was haggling with himself. This was a new low in his experience.

Philippe muttered a savage "Damn." There was no easy solution to this mess. As he contemplated the latest hazard to the comfortable life he'd tried to create for himself, he hated his mother with a fury he'd not felt since he was sixteen years old.

* * *

Yvonne St. Pierre felt old, weary, and completely demoralized as she glanced around the plain, bleak, and very ugly hotel room to which she'd been shown. She managed a smile for the boy—probably the son of the proprietor—who'd carried her bag upstairs. He blinked at her and swallowed, from which she deduced that her looks hadn't deteriorated on the long trip from New Orleans to the territory.

For all the good that would do her. Yet she managed a kind thank you for the boy and handed him a coin. She was almost amused when he stammered his own thanks, tipped his hat, and fled from her presence as if she were a queen or a goddess or something. If he only knew.

Philippe still hated her. She removed her hat, tossed it onto the rickety dresser, the scarred surface of which was partially hidden by a natty doily, and sank onto the creaky bed. She wished—for about the millionth time—that she were dead.

"Oh, my," she whispered, recalling the moment when she'd spotted Philippe standing in that filthy, milling throng outside that horrible, shabby building. Her throat ached and her heart hurt.

"He's grown up so well." She smiled, feeling such a tug of longing in her heart that she was surprised her heart didn't break. But, of course, hearts didn't really break. She knew that well enough by this time.

But, oh, her little boy had become such a handsome man. Since she hadn't seen his father since before Philippe was born, Yvonne had always thought of Philippe as hers alone.

Which had been a silly thing to think. He didn't

belong to her or anyone else; he was his own man, and he'd proved it beyond question all those years ago.

She ought to have given him away at birth, she realized now. It would have been a kindness, both to Philippe and to that nice lady who'd offered to take him so long ago. That lady had yearned for a child of her own, and had been distraught when Yvonne had refused to give up her son.

If she'd had the courage to give Philippe to that woman, though, he'd probably have been better off. It was true that he might never have known his mother, but he'd have had a good life.

But Yvonne hadn't been able to bear the thought of giving away her baby when she was sixteen years old. She'd been sold into that house on Bourbon Street the prior year by her miserable excuse of an aunt and uncle, and she'd been so frightened. When she got pregnant by the man she loved, in spite of the techniques drilled into the girls of the house, she'd believed, in her innocence, that at least she'd always have her baby to love. And to love her back.

She hadn't, back then, understood the nature and perversity of human beings. At first she'd believed the father of her child would marry her. Silly Yvonne. When she finally realized he was gone for good, she felt good that she'd at least have her baby. She truly believed that she and Philippe could survive in that house as a unit and both grow up strong and loyal to each other.

"Bah!" What a fool she'd been.

And then she'd met D. A. Bologh, and her life began and ended in the same evil moment—the moment she'd bargained away her soul. Youth and beauty, she hadn't understood what they would cost her. Not back then. How could she? She'd been a child.

Yvonne sighed deeply, wondering when D. A. would find her. She knew he would. She was, in fact, surprised that she'd come this far without being discovered.

"That lovely young woman, the one Philippe dragged away from me, must be his sweetheart." Idly fingering an earring, Yvonne contemplated another sort of meeting with her son and his sweetheart. If her life had been different—if she'd been the product of a normal family—Philippe might be bringing that girl proudly to meet his mother, with love in his heart for both of them.

"He has no love, poor boy," she whispered into the empty room. "No love at all." Yvonne herself had seen to that, albeit unwittingly. "I never meant to make him hate."

Who was it who'd written that the saddest words ever spoken were, *It might have been*? Whoever it was had been, unfortunately, correct. Yvonne knew it for a fact. A bitter fact.

She got to her feet, feeling completely drained of energy, and went to the window. From there, she could see the entire town of Fort Summers—what there was of it—spread out at her feet. She shuddered, wondering why any son of hers could have found this miserable, desolate place better than life in the vicinity of his mother, even a mother such as she.

Ever since she left New Orleans, she'd been praying she'd discover the exact words to say to Philippe; that she'd hit upon the one small phrase that would soften his heart and allow her back into his life, however briefly. She'd been praying for other things as well: Philippe's safety and that of his young woman. What was her name? Heather? That was a pretty name. Soft and lovely. It suited her.

So far, her prayers had remained unanswered. She still didn't know how to approach Philippe in a manner that would make him forgive her.

Yvonne whispered, "So be it." He might well never forgive her for what she'd done all those years ago. He might well hate her for the rest of his life. She still had to warn him. She had to protect him from her youthful folly. If it killed her, she'd do it.

And she knew it probably would kill her. She didn't care a jot about her life any longer. It hadn't been worth living for years. If she knew she'd done this one thing to protect her son, she wouldn't care if she died a thousand times over.

The weeks of tension, coupled with exhaustion and total misery, finally engulfed Yvonne. With a ragged moan, she flung herself onto the bed and sobbed until she cried herself to sleep.

Two hours after Heather and Philippe had returned from town, the wind was trying to lift the roof from the house. Thunder grumbled in the west, and Heather saw sheets of lightning illuminate the mountains in the distance. She hoped it would rain, but didn't believe it would. The genius of the weather, as Charles Dickens had called it, wasn't so kind a benefactor. Especially not in Fort Summers. Fort Summers and its environs were more apt to suffer a prairie fire.

Heather told herself not to be pessimistic as she

stood in the dining room, facing Philippe. She never *used* to be pessimistic. Of course, she never used to be a liar and a fraud, either.

"Um, it's called a cassoulet de Toulouse," she said, trying very hard not to make mincemeat of the pronunciation. Because she was uneasy in Philippe's company this evening—she hadn't been able to cease thinking about that kiss for a second—she added with a nervous wave of her hand, "They're really only beans and sausages. But they're good."

Philippe had been staring at her ever since she brought the tray into the dining room. He had taken it from her hands without even bothering to lift a cover or sniff, had set the tray on the table, and was now standing at the head of the table, staring at her. She wished he'd stop. He was making her want to scream.

"I know what a cassoulet is, Heather." His voice was very low, very soft, and very gentle.

Heather swallowed. Her swallow was very hard, very loud, and very rough. "Oh." Then she said, "Of course." He knew a good deal more about food than she did; she'd known as much for a month now.

His smile came out of nowhere and almost knocked her over backwards. "You are a very clever young woman, Heather Mahaffey. With no other food around—because the master of the house had a temper fit in town and spirited you away before you'd done the marketing—you have still managed to create a wonderful supper. You're a perfect example of frontier indomitability, and I admire that quality in you."

Dear Lord, please save me. Heather swallowed

again and, in spite of the boulder lodged in her throat, whispered, "Um, I know you probably won't believe me, but I didn't do it, sir. It was D. A. Bologh." Her heart hiccuped when he suddenly frowned at her.

"Don't"—Philippe took a big breath—"call me sir. Please." He sighed heavily. "Some day, Heather, you'll have to introduce me to this person you claim has done the cooking since you've been in my employ. Until then, I hope you won't be too offended if I give you the credit for creating the masterpieces I've been eating for the past month."

Defeated—indomitable, phooey—Heather said, "Of course not." Her insides were as tumultuous as the weather outdoors.

"Please, take a seat and dine with me. I'd like to discuss something with you."

Blast. She'd hoped to escape to the kitchen. Actually, what she wanted to do was go to the bath house if the wind didn't blow her to perdition, wash up, get into her big flannel nightgown, crawl under the covers, and sleep for a thousand years or until the end of the world, whichever came first. Since that delightful option was denied her, she said, "Of course. Thank you."

"Thank *you*. In the face of your denials, I still thank you for this wonderful meal, Heather."

Right. He would. Heather sat and decided she probably had better not thank him a second time, or the cycle would begin all over again and she might lose control of her emotions and shriek. At the moment, the wind was doing her shrieking for her, so she decided that would have to do.

Philippe sat, too, and lifted the cover from the cassoulet dish. "Smells heavenly."

"Yes, it does." She only said it because it was the truth, and she'd had nothing to do with its creation, so she didn't consider it boasting. She had enough sins on her soul lately without adding boasting to the lot.

"And what do we have in this dish?" Philippe smiled one of his prize-winning smiles at her.

She wished he wouldn't do that. Every time he smiled, her guard dropped a tiny bit. Pretty soon, if he kept it up, the combination of Philippe's smiles and her own lies would probably vanquish her resolve to live a decent, honorable life, and she'd jump into his bed.

If she'd been alone, she'd have buried her head in her hands, rocked back and forth on her chair, and groaned.

Never, ever, ever had Heather Mahaffey *ever* had trouble controlling herself—not in that way. Until she met Philippe St. Pierre, she'd *never* have considered going to bed with a man until his ring was securely on her finger and Mr. Harvey or perhaps an imported priest—one had to make do in the territories—had pronounced them wed in the eyes of God and the rest of Fort Summers. Shoot, until she met Philippe, she hadn't wanted to go to bed with any man. St. Pierre, unfortunately, was different.

Geraldine had been absolutely right. A moral decline could begin with so small a thing as a lie. It picked up speed from there and soon was rushing straight downhill, taking a body's moral strength and resolve with it. Sort of like a snowball. Or an avalanche.

Since he'd asked, she said, "It's a corn pudding." Thank God D. A. hadn't given her a fancy French name for that.

"I see." Philippe leaned over and sniffed the pudding dish. "What are those green specks?"

"Green chilies. There's chopped green chilies and cheese stirred into the mixture. With some eggs, milk, and a little bit of flour. The eggs help it to puff up like that."

"Very clever. It smells wonderful."

Heather didn't hear him. She was too busy considering what she'd just explained to him about the corn pudding. For heaven's sake, was she actually beginning to understand the craft of cooking? Could such a thing be possible?

It was true she'd been taking her mother's cookbooks to bed with her at night, reading everything she could about the culinary arts, but she'd become so accustomed to thinking of herself as a failure in the kitchen that she hadn't given herself credit for having absorbed anything. She wondered if she dared . . .

The notion so frightened her that she almost couldn't complete it.

But, did she? Did she really dare to try cooking on her own? Without D. A. Bologh to help her?

"Heather? Are you awake?"

She started, realizing that Philippe had been speaking to her and she hadn't heard a word he'd said. Flushing, she said, "I beg your pardon. Philippe." She had trouble saying his name, mainly because she wasn't sure she should. After all, he was her employer, and she was perilously close to a complete fall already. "I was thinking about something."

"Obviously." His dry tone made her flinch. "Here. Please allow me to serve you some of this delicious food you've prepared. That's what I'd been trying to make you hear."

How embarrassing. Heather mentally smacked herself. "Thank you." She accepted the cassoulet and a serving of corn pudding, and waited until he'd served himself. Then she dipped her spoon into the cassoulet and tasted.

It was delicious. And it wasn't hard to make. Not at all. She'd watched D. A. All he'd done was mix some beans that had been soaking for several hours with some fried—sautéed, he'd say—onions, peppers, carrots, and cut-up, cooked sausages, and simmer them all together for a little while. He'd told her you could add chicken or rabbit or anything else you wanted in with the beans and sausages, if you felt like it and had time. And she'd read recipes for corn pudding.

She imagined she could make those two things without much trouble. All she'd have to do was pay better attention to her job. Her problem had always been that she got distracted too easily.

But that was childish, and she was no longer a child. She owed it to herself and to her employer—and to Philippe the man, who was a kind and good-hearted person, even if he didn't want people to think so—to do the job for which she was being paid, and do it well.

She'd bargained with D. A. that he'd cook for the rest of this new month. After that—good heavens, did she mean it?

Heather chewed a bite of delicious sausage and considered the matter. She thought and chewed, and chewed and thought. She swallowed.

Yes, by gum, she did mean it!

Because her decision excited her—and scared

her a lot—she gave Philippe a broad smile. "I'm glad you like this, Philippe. It's a simple meal, but it turned out pretty well."

He smiled back, obviously amused. "Yes, it certainly did."

They ate for a few minutes without trying to maintain a conversation. Heather was glad of it because her brain was spinning with the novelty of her decision. She was actually going to *cook*. It hardly seemed possible.

A soupçon of doubt wriggled its way into her heart. What if she wasn't good enough yet? What if she poisoned Philippe? She'd never forgive herself if that happened.

But why should she? Women with much less in the way of brain power than she had cooked every day and didn't poison anybody. Why shouldn't she be able to master the kitchen?

There was no good reason she could think of, and her heart lightened again.

"May I ask you a question, Heather?"

She looked up from her cassoulet, startled. She'd forgotten all about Philippe being in the same room with her, much less sharing the same meal, for a moment. "Of course." She smiled again to let him know that, while she might be somewhat distracted this evening, her state of distraction had nothing to do with him.

He cleared his throat. Heather was surprised, as it seemed a nervous gesture, and she'd never pegged him for a nervous man, or one who hesitated when it came to speaking his mind.

"I wanted to talk about what happened today, actually," he said after another moment of hesitation.

Immediately, Heather's appetite fled, and she felt her face heat. "Oh?"

Then it occurred to her that there had been more to the day than that stunning kiss. There had been the incident with her parents and the incident with—or without, actually—the woman on the stage. She told herself that he probably wasn't going to mention the kiss.

"Yes. That kiss."

Blast. She wanted to talk about the woman. The kiss was too perilous a topic to discuss, in her opinion. "Oh."

"I suppose I should apologize for it."

Heather's mood slipped another cog. She supposed he should, too, but she didn't want him to. Instead, she wanted him to kiss her again. Mercy, she was losing control of herself quickly. Since she couldn't think of anything to say, she didn't say anything.

"But I'm not going to apologize."

She remained mute, but her eyebrows lifted of their own accord. Good heavens, he must consider her no better than a strumpet. What a depressing thought.

"Indeed, I wanted to discuss something in relation to that kiss."

She swallowed and managed to squeak out another tiny, "Oh?"

"Yes. I—" He pushed his chair away from the table and stood, walked to the fireplace, and picked up the poker. A fire hadn't been lit in the house for a day or two. In spite of the wind, the weather had been warm and dry—so dry, indeed, that when people met, they were apt to experience sparks as they shook hands. Philippe stabbed at the fire-ready logs with the poker and stared into the fireplace, away from Heather. "Curse it, Heather, I've been thinking too much lately."

That didn't explain anything to Heather. She carefully laid her fork on the edge of her plate and folded her hands in her lap. She didn't want them to get away from her and do something embarrassing.

He didn't continue and, because she was becoming more and more anxious with each passing second, she said, "About what?" Then she wished she hadn't asked, because she wasn't sure she wanted to know.

"About my life."

Oh. She waited. And waited. And waited.

After what seemed like an eternity, Philippe continued: "And what I want from it."

She remained silent.

Suddenly he swirled around and glared at her. "Curse it, why aren't you saying anything?"

Feeling helpless and a little scared—he was, after all, still holding the poker—Heather lifted her shoulders a quarter of an inch and let them drop. "I—don't know what to say, Philippe." Because he didn't relax his glower, she added, "I'm sorry."

"Damn!" He turned again and replaced the poker. He huffed. "What I'm trying to say is that I've been considering a lot of things lately that I'd never considered before. Since you came to work for me, actually."

She swallowed and said, "Oh?"

"Yes." He walked back over to the table and sat.

Heather had been much more comfortable when he'd been at the fireplace. Now his gaze was boring into her, hot and dark and compelling, and it was all she could do to keep her seat and maintain her composure. She wanted to leap up and fling herself into his arms. This was awful.

"And what I've been considering is marriage."

She felt her eyes open wide. Her mouth opened and closed, doing her no good at all, since all of her words had deserted her.

"I know this surprises you, although I don't know why it should. Surely you know that I've come to value you."

"V-value me?"

He nodded. "Admire you."

He admired her? "Um, thank you." She couldn't resist asking, "Why?" If it was because of her cooking, she was going to go out to the bath house and slash her wrists.

His posture relaxed slightly, and his smile was tender. Heather felt herself beginning to melt into the embroidered cushion of the chair upon which she sat, and she braced herself. "You're a beautiful, lively young woman, Heather. Surely you know that."

Actually, she hadn't known it until he'd said it. She knew the boys she'd grown up with thought she was pretty, but prettiness had never counted for much in Heather's life. Until right this minute. "Um, I guess I'm lively, all right. Nobody's ever said they considered it much of a virtue, though."

He chuckled, sending waves of heat through her and making her wish once more for rain. She wanted to fan herself, but didn't dare let go of her hands for fear of what they'd do.

"I don't want you to make a decision right away. I want you to think about it. Will you do that?"

She blinked at him. "Th-think about what?"

He threw out his arms in a gesture that Heather had always thought of as French. "Why, marrying me, of course. I know you need to think about it. Any woman would. But I think we'd suit and, if you think we would, too, well then . . ." He shrugged. "I believe I would make a good husband for someone like you. Not, of course, for anybody, but for you, yes. Despite what I said earlier about marriage."

Heather swayed in her chair and had to unclench her hands so she could grip the table. "You—you want to marry me?" Good heavens, she'd never, in her wildest dreams, contemplated such a blissful option. Not really. Certainly, she'd entertained daydreams, but she'd never really and truly thought he'd ask her to marry him.

"I do," he said, still smiling. He plainly thought her confusion was amusing, even charming.

Heather didn't. She thought it denoted a weakness of character that had manifested itself all too often in recent weeks. She wanted to scream, "Yes!" at the top of her lungs and then go hollering it down Main Street. She wanted to grab Philippe and kiss him wildly. She wanted to run to her mother and father and cry in their arms out of sheer happiness. She wanted to yank Geraldine out of her staid life and swing her around, as they used to do when they were little children, until they both fell, laughing and panting, to the ground.

She didn't, of course. Rather, she stood on shaky legs and squeezed out, "Thank you, Philippe. I'll be happy to think about it." Then she walked, trying not to stagger under the weight of his proposal, out of the dining room, down the hall—ignoring Mrs. Van der Linden, who glared at her as usual—and into the kitchen.

Chapter Fifteen

D. A. Bologh had finished cleaning up the pots and pans, and looked as if he were merely awaiting the arrival of dishes from the table so that he could whip them clean and vanish. He squinted at Heather when she entered the kitchen with his usual sneering condescension.

Heather wasn't in any condition to resent D. A.'s attitude. Actually, she was feeling like one of those "undead" zombie things that hail from the Caribbean Islands. She and Geraldine had read about them with fascination once.

"What's wrong now?" D. A. asked in a tone that told Heather he didn't care at all. "You look like you've seen a ghost." He wrinkled his nose and eyed her more keenly. "Rather, you look like you were attacked by a herd of them. What's the matter with you, lovey? I thought you had more spirit than this."

Heather fell into rather than sat on a chair, and wished D. A. would vanish forever. "I, ah, am a little shaken."

"I can see that. Why?"

She turned her head and stared straight at him. She didn't like him. She didn't trust him. She was scared to death that whatever he expected her to give him in return for his help was going to be something she didn't want to give. Yet she had to tell someone, and D. A. was the only person available.

Her heart was doing an alarming dance that oscillated maniacally between an uproarious jig and a somber funeral march. Her nerves were strung like piano wire, alternately playing an exalted melody and a gloomy lament. Whatever was she going to do now that Philippe had proposed to her?

She'd already confessed about her job, and he hadn't believed her. She'd known for a week or more that she loved Philippe, but should she marry him? It wouldn't be right. It wouldn't be fair. He only thought he liked Heather because he didn't know the truth about her—rather, he wouldn't believe the truth about her.

Bother.

She licked her lips. "Mr. St. Pierre asked me to marry him."

The grin that spread over D. A. Bologh's face was so diabolical, Heather had to shut her eyes against it. Why did this man have such a terrible effect on her?

"He did, did he? He worked faster than I thought he would."

She opened her eyes and blinked at him, confused. "I beg your pardon?"

He waved his hand. "There's no need to beg, sweetie pie. It's unbecoming." His sneer was even more ghastly than usual.

Before Heather could think of something suitably cutting to say, the door was shoved rudely open, and D. A. Bologh vanished in a poof of—well, nothing. If Heather hadn't been staring straight at him when it happened, she wouldn't have believed it. As it was, she believed it because she'd seen it, but she couldn't account for it by any means known to her rational, sane, thinking mind. She could only gape at the chair where D. A. had been for several moments.

Mrs. Van der Linden's unpleasant voice jarred her out of her stupor. "I swear to goodness, Heather Mahaffey, if you aren't the most scatter-brained, irresponsible creature who ever drew breath, I don't know who is."

The woman was unquestionably peeved at her, and Heather wasn't sure why. She wasn't sure of anything right then. Standing—she held on to the table for a couple of seconds to make sure she wouldn't topple over—she said, "I beg your pardon?"

"You heard me." Mrs. Van der Linden tromped over to the sink and plunked the dinner dishes on the counter. "This is your job, and I don't appreciate Mr. St. Pierre making me do it. I have plenty of my own work to do without being saddled with your chores as well."

"Oh." Heather realized what had happened. She'd been so befuddled when Philippe had extended his proposal—his rather tepid proposal, if she recalled correctly—she'd forgotten all about the dinner dishes. "I'm sorry, Mrs. Van der Linden. I'll go fetch the rest of them."

"You'd better." The housekeeper gave her a good hot scowl to let her know she wasn't forgiven. "I do declare, Heather, you're a hopeless case. Hopeless!"

With a deep sigh, Heather started for the door. "I suspect you're right, Mrs. Van der Linden."

She heard the woman huff at her back, but didn't bother to turn or say anything else. She had a feeling the beast would have liked to do battle, but Heather wasn't up to it. She wasn't sure she was up to entering the dining room again for that matter, but she knew where her duty lay—even if she hadn't been doing it for a month or more.

Thank God, Philippe wasn't there. Quickly Heather retrieved the rest of the dishes, tidied up the room, and fled to the kitchen. Mrs. Van der Linden was nowhere in sight. D. A. Bologh was back—and smirking.

Heather didn't even ask how he'd accomplished his vanishing and reappearing act this time.

Philippe frowned at the book in his hand. He'd taken it down from the shelf, thinking he could while away the hours before bedtime with a read. Unfortunately, he didn't want to read. He wanted to be making wild love to Heather. His fertile imagination conjured all sorts of likely scenarios—and positions—for the consummation. He couldn't recall ever wanting a woman more, and he didn't understand her hold over him.

She wasn't the most beautiful woman in the world. She wasn't the cleverest. She wasn't the shapeliest—although Philippe hadn't seen too many shapelier.

"Dammit, man, it's glandular."

Far from satisfied with this conclusion, but perceiving no other answer to his condition, Philippe considered how she'd reacted to their dinner table conversation.

She'd seemed more astonished than pleased by his marriage proposal. He didn't understand that. Philippe wasn't a vain man, but he knew good and well that he was considered a good catch in the extremely small Fort Summers matrimonial market. Hell, he was rich and single; most communities never asked for more when contemplating husbands for their daughters. He couldn't imagine why Heather hadn't immediately leapt to her feet and accepted him.

Then again, Heather Mahaffey had never been typical. That, come to think of it, was one of the reasons Philippe admired and desired her. If she'd been a run-of-the-mill female who was champing at the bit for some poor sucker to take her off her father's hands, Philippe wouldn't have looked at her twice. Instead, he had received the distinct impression that Heather didn't give a rap about marriage, didn't much want to be taken off her father's hands and, what's more, if she ever did leave home, she'd do it on her own terms, and to hell with what the world thought.

A gust of wind rattled the windows and a blast of thunder almost deafened him. Philippe put his book down on the desk and walked to the window to stare into the darkness. Lord, the atmosphere was tumultuous out there. He wondered if, with all the thunder and lightning, there would ever be any rain. The whole Pecos Valley needed rain.

Perhaps the rain god was resting and the wind and thunder gods were sporting with each other. He shook his head, peeved by the jot of whimsy that had crept into his head. Philippe had no truck with whimsy. Whimsy—and romance—were the stuff of fools, and he was *not* a fool.

By the light of the stars and the occasional jagged bolts of lightning, he could see the line of Lombardy poplars he'd planted as a windbreak bent almost double. He hoped nothing bad would happen because of the turbulent weather. These dry electrical storms were hell. A chilly feeling crawled into his heart like the premonition of catastrophe.

Which was idiotic whimsy again.

A knock at the library door startled him. He walked over and jerked the door open. Gil McGill stood there, his hat in his hands, his hair tousled every which way, and an expression of consternation on his face. Perhaps that chilly feeling hadn't been idiotic after all.

"What's the matter?" Without waiting for Gil's reply, Philippe grabbed his own hat and started making for the front door.

Gil followed at a trot. "It's the cattle, sir. The wind's blown a fence down out by the barn, and lightning struck that old live oak. Scared the crap out of them, and they're stampeding. Right toward the Pecos."

"Damn." Philippe knew what that meant, and was surprised when his hand didn't shake when he grabbed his gunbelt from the stand next to the front door. Graveyard of the cowman's hopes, indeed, that damned river. Some of the cattle would get stuck in the quicksand, others would stumble and smother, others would fall into the water and drown, others would break their necks trying to gallop over the boulders and rocks on the banks, and still others would plunge down the steep banks and kill or cripple themselves in other ways.

Since both men knew exactly what to expect of frightened cattle, they didn't waste words on questions or explanations. Philippe was pleased to see that Gil had rounded up the rest of his men. All of them were ready to set out, and one of them had saddled Philippe's horse. Philippe pulled his bandanna over his nose, secured his hat, signaled to the men, and they took off, pounding across the prairie like an earthquake. Cracks of thunder and a screaming frenzy of a wind accompanied them. Philippe got the eerie feeling they were riding into hell.

He heard the rumble of panicked cattle before he saw the herd, and he heard the frantic shouts and whistles of the cowboys who'd been minding them before he saw any of the animals themselves. The men were even shooting into the air in an attempt to get the herd to change direction. That was a dangerous thing to do, since bullets came down nearly as fast as they went up, but this was an emergency, and Philippe didn't blame the men for trying to slow the herd or turn it in any way they could think of.

"We can split up and try to surround the herd," he shouted at Gil.

The head wrangler, a seasoned cattle man, didn't even nod. He gestured to some of the other cowboys, and they set off with him in the opposite direction to Philippe. The rest of the cowboys followed Philippe.

They all knew what they were in for. Most of these men had been dealing with cattle since they were born. But experience didn't make the job any easier. The cattle were spooked, tossing their heads, uttering short, frightened bovine cries of terror, and racing to their individual dooms like moths to a flame. Thousands of pounds of steak on the hoof paid no attention to the few feeble men and horses doing their best to alter their course. Not deep thinkers at the best of times, in a storm like this the beasts acted on blind panic.

Philippe shouted and waved his hat in the air. His horse was a well-trained cattle pony and knew what he was about, so Philippe didn't have to spend any time guiding it. Fearlessly, the horse plunged into the fray. The other cowboys' mounts did the same.

It seemed like hours had passed, and Philippe's despair had grown to mountainous proportions, when he realized the herd seemed to be gradually veering away from the direction of the river.

"They're turning!" he heard. The cry sounded as if it had come from Gil's throat, although it was difficult to tell.

He didn't dare hope, but a tiny glimmer of confidence began to burn inside him. Dust choked him. He'd be coughing the stuff up for a week, and he'd never get it out of his nose, but he didn't let up. None of the other men did, either.

In fact, they'd all heard the cry, and it had renewed their whoops and cries and whistles. A little encouragement, Philippe thought wryly, helped a good deal in circumstances like these.

He didn't need encouragement. Hell, he'd never needed it, which was a good thing, since he'd never experienced any. His own fierce determination had been enough for him. He'd be damned if he'd let anything—man, nature, god, or devil—thwart his ambitions.

Centuries passed—which were only minutes, really—before Philippe comprehended for a certainty that he and his men had won this battle. He didn't know how many cattle had been lost, and he hoped vehemently that none of his men had been hurt. By the bright flash of a lightning bolt, he saw Gil, dead white in the burst of light, waving his hat. His bandanna had come undone, and he was smiling. Smiling!

Amazing. Philippe waved back at Gil, although he wasn't sure Gil could see him. His throat felt as dry as the dust inside of it, his eyes burned from grit, he was coated from one end of his body to the other with dirt, his throat was scraped raw from shouting and sucking in dust, and he wasn't sure he'd be able to breathe freely again in this lifetime, but by God, they'd done it. He didn't care what Gil said about monetary rewards, he was going to give his men a bonus when they got the cattle settled and the fences set upright.

He was surprised to hear a horse galloping up behind him. The noise from the herd had been so terrific, he figured he'd have gone deaf too by this time. But the cattle were slowing down, thank God, and Philippe clearly heard the horseman. He turned in his saddle—and his heart went cold.

Mike Mulligan drew up beside him. He had a small body propped in front of him. The body looked too small to be one of his men, and Philippe frowned. Mike looked scared and shaken. As they all were.

Philippe barked, "What happened?" His voice sounded like dry bones chafing together.

"It's Jimmy Mahaffey, sir." Mike's voice sounded the same. "I don't know how he got out here, but he fell. Thank God I saw him, and I went and scooped him up before the cows could trample him, but he's hurt. I don't know how bad."

"Damn." Philippe abruptly turned his horse and searched wildly for Gil. His head wrangler was gone. Night had fallen long since, the lightning wasn't obliging him, and the stars only illuminated a wall of dust with about a thousand cows trotting through it. The only bright spot for Philippe at the moment was that the cattle were no longer in a panicked dash to kill themselves in the river.

"Dammit." He turned toward the other man. "Listen, Mike. Take the boy to the house. As soon as I let one of the other men know what's happened, I'll join you there. Try not to alarm Miss Mahaffey."

Heather. God. Philippe didn't even want to think about how upset she'd be that a member of her family was hurt—especially Jimmy, the tree-climber, of whom she'd seemed particularly fond.

"Right." Mike, perceiving the good sense in Philippe's command, didn't bother to say anything else, but spurred his tired horse toward the ranch house. Philippe saw that he was trying to spare Jimmy from being badly jolted, and he appreciated Mike's care.

It took several minutes for Philippe to locate another of his cowboys. He had no idea where Gil was, but he relayed the message to the cowboy, who nodded his understanding and went off in search of Gil. Philippe directed his mount toward home.

His heart was hammering when he neared the house. Lights blazed from all of the downstairs windows, and the front door had been left hanging open. The wind was whipping it back and forth like a deranged fan. Philippe scowled, wondering why that was happening. The wind should either slam the door shut or bash it against the outside wall. The blasted door shouldn't be flapping like that.

There was no time to contemplate the perversity of nature, however. As soon as he rode to the porch, he swung down from his horse, patted the animal's neck, apologized for leaving it in such a condition, and ran into the house. He slammed the misbehaving door behind him, giving it a scowl in passing.

He heard Heather before he saw her, and headed straight for the front parlor, from whence the voice had come. When he pushed the door open, he stopped in the doorway, unnerved by the spectacle before him.

Heather Mahaffey was crying. Philippe had never seen her cry. She was the only woman he'd known for more than a week whom he hadn't seen in tears at least a dozen times. She was talking softly and encouragingly to the unconscious bloody body laid out on a sheet on the sofa. Mrs. Van der Linden stood in back of the sofa, watching Heather, her expression grim and disapproving. Philippe had never seen her look anything but.

He strode to the sofa and peered down. Poor Jimmy Mahaffey had not come through his ordeal unscathed. Indeed, he looked like someone had run him through a meat grinder. Philippe hoped all the blood came from surface scratches. Surface scratches, however, couldn't account for the boy's state of unconsciousness.

"Oh, Jimmy, what were you doing out there?" Heather was asking. She'd fetched a bucket of water and a chunk of soap, and was trying to sponge the blood off of the boy's face and clean the obvious wounds. She couldn't stop crying, Philippe noticed. Glancing around, he didn't see Mike Mulligan.

"What can I do to help, Heather?" he asked softly.

She glanced up abruptly. "Oh, Philippe! I'm so glad to see you. It's Jimmy. He was hurt."

"I know."

Mrs. Van der Linden sniffed her censure. "Fool boy," she muttered.

Philippe snarled, "The boy was doing a man's job, Mrs. Van der Linden, and trying his best to save my herd."

Mrs. Van der Linden's mouth shut and thinned until she had no lips, but she didn't say anything else.

Philippe's voice softened when he spoke to Heather. "Where's Mike?"

"I sent him for Doc Grady. I hope you don't mind."

"Mind? God, no. I was going to go myself, but I guess I don't have to now."

"Thank you." Heather's voice sounded shaky.

"What about your parents? Would you like me to notify them?"

Heather hesitated for a moment, then said, "No. I don't think so. It will just worry them, and they have enough on their plates right now."

"Won't they miss him in the morning?"

She chewed on her lower lip. "Oh, dear. Yes, they will."

"I'll send someone over as soon as it's light. I'll tell them we have everything under control and they shouldn't worry."

"Thank you. If—if the worst should happen . . ." Heather had to wait a minute before she could go on. "If the worst should happen—"

"We'll deal with that if it happens," Philippe broke in.

She nodded.

"Is there anything else you need right now?"

"No." She shot him a grateful glance. "Thank you, Philippe. I'm just going to try to clean him up so the doctor can see better. He's so dreadfully dirty. I—I think most of the blood is from scratches. I hope he didn't bang his head too hard. Or—or break his neck."

He'd be dead already if he'd done that, although Philippe didn't say so in deference to Heather's overwrought sensibilities. "As soon as the men come in, I'll get someone to help you." He frowned, knowing the men would all be exhausted and filthy. They shouldn't be in an operating theater in their condition.

Damn. That left him.

Mrs. Van der Linden sniffed again. Philippe turned and glowered at her. "Mrs. Van der Linden, I'm too dirty to be of any help in here at the moment. I'm going to clean up in the bath house as quickly as possible and then return to assist Miss Mahaffey.

"In the meantime, I want you to keep Miss Mahaffey supplied with clean, warm water and anything else she needs. After the doctor arrives, we'll see what else has to be done. There's witch hazel in the cabinet in the pantry, and some quinine, liniment, and laudanum. If there are any breaks—"

Heather let out an involuntary sob.

"—Doc Grady will set them. Make sure there's plenty of clean linen available to rip into strips."

"Yes, sir," Mrs. Van der Linden said, sounding as if she didn't want to be aiding a Mahaffey.

Philippe watched her for a few long minutes, hoping his expression appeared as portentous as he felt inside. It must have, for after a little bit of that, the housekeeper huffed indignantly and waddled off to do his bidding. He laid a hand on Heather's shoulder. "I'll be back as soon as may be, Heather. Are you sure there's nothing you need before then?"

She smiled up at him, and Philippe was startled to see the trust in her eyes. Her faith in him touched him deeply; he'd not expected it. "No. Thank you, Philippe. You're very kind."

"Kind? I don't think so." He felt, in fact, immensely angry and very guilty. Although he hadn't known Jimmy was working among his men—Gil did all the hiring and had likely seen nothing wrong with employing a youngster—Philippe felt somehow that he'd failed to protect him. If he had known, he'd have sent the boy home.

It did no good to second-guess the fates, though, and Philippe wouldn't make the attempt that evening. He went upstairs to get fresh clothes, and from thence to the bath house. He didn't bother to heat the water before he bathed because he was in a hurry, and he was shivering when he finished his ablutions. He'd had to wash his hair three times to get the grit out.

His mind wandered back to the evening he'd seen Heather, in all her naked glory, bathing in this very room, and his sex stirred. Damn, he'd be glad when she accepted his proposal and he could slake his lust. Until that time, he'd just have to suffer, he reckoned. The notion held little appeal.

When he finished cleaning up and returned to the house, several of his men had come back. He greeted them, told them about Jimmy, and said he'd talk to them later. Two of them offered to help, and Philippe thanked them sincerely. He asked one of them to take care of his horse, as he hadn't had time to do so. After that was attended to, he asked Sandy, a hardy sixteen-year-old from Fort Summers who knew all the Mahaffeys, to clean himself up and be prepared to notify Mr. and Mrs. Mahaffey at first light that their son was at Philippe's ranch.

"Try not to frighten them. We'll probably have more news before then. You can give them the latest report from Doc Grady."

Sandy nodded. Philippe got the impression he knew exactly how to approach parents of injured sons, undoubtedly having had such experiences in the past. He would have grinned except he was too tired to do so.

When he returned to the parlor, Heather had stopped crying—thank God—and was absorbed in her task.

"Merciful heavens, Jimmy Mahaffey, what ever possessed you to ride into a stampede?" Heather's heart had been lurching around like a wounded sparrow ever since she saw Mike carrying the small body into the house. She hadn't known it was Jimmy until Mike had told her. If he hadn't told her, she'd only now be discovering the truth, because the poor boy had been covered from head to foot with filth, sticky with blood, and unconscious.

"I didn't mean nothing by it." The voice was small and hurt, and Heather could tell poor Jimmy was trying his best to act like a man. "It wasn't my fault."

"So he's conscious at last, is he?"

She started a little, having forgotten that Philippe had told her he'd come back. When she saw him standing there, tall, muscular, competent, and about as handsome as a man could—or should—get, she wondered how she could have forgotten him for as much as an instant. She was so happy to see him, she nearly burst into tears again. She wouldn't do that, however. Tears were for emergencies and funerals, unless one were feeble. This particular emergency was over, if Heather could help it there wouldn't be any funeral, and she was definitely not feeble.

"Yes." She smiled at Philippe. "He woke up a few minutes after you left."

"I didn't mean to take so long." Philippe didn't return her smile. He looked worried. "How's he doing?"

"He hurts all over, I expect." She made sure her tone was light. She didn't want to worry Jimmy.

"Yeah," the patient grunted. Then, when Heather took her soapy rag to another scratch, he added, "Ow! Dang it, Heather, be careful."

Finally Philippe grinned. "He sounds like he'll be all right."

"Eventually." Heather stuck her tongue out at her brother. "If you hadn't gotten hurt, I wouldn't have to be washing you off, Jimmy. You just stay still and stop complaining."

"I'm not complaining," the boy muttered.

"Could have fooled me," said his adoring sister.

Philippe came over and stood behind where she was kneeling on the floor next to the sofa. She felt him there like a warm, protective presence, and wished she could turn and ask him to hold her. If she'd accepted his proposal on the spot, she guessed she could have, but she hadn't, blast it. Trying to keep her mind on the business at hand, she said, "Philippe, I don't believe you've been formally introduced to this scamp. My brother, Jimmy. Jimmy, say how-do-you-do to Mr. St. Pierre. You're reclining on his sofa at the moment."

"Hello, Jimmy," said Philippe. "I'd shake hands, but you seem to be laid up."

"H'lo, Mr. St. Pierre." Jimmy's big blue eyes rested with fascination on the ranch owner. Heather was beginning to believe he'd pull through this ordeal without too much lasting damage. He hadn't cried once so far—which was more than his older sister could claim—and if he was more interested in Philippe and his surroundings than upset about his medical condition, she considered it a good sign.

"I'm sorry you were hurt, Jimmy," Philippe continued. He squatted next to Heather on the pretty Persian carpet covering the parlor floor. "Mind telling me what you thought you were doing in the middle of a stampede?" He grinned to let the boy know he wasn't accusing him of anything.

Heather's whole body throbbed with love for him in that instant.

Jimmy let out an exasperated sigh that made his sister smile, although she tried to hide it. "I didn't *mean* to ride into a stampede, Mr. St. Pierre. It was when that man came and said Heather was hurt and asking for me. That's why I was there. I just went. I didn't stop to worry about stampedes."

"What?" Heather hadn't meant the word to come out quite so shrilly.

"I beg your pardon, Jimmy," said Philippe, no longer grinning. "But did you say someone came to your house and said Miss Mahaffey was hurt?"

"Yeah." Jimmy's gaze flicked between Heather and Philippe. "I don't know why he come. You don't look hurt to me." He gave Heather an accusatory frown.

"I'm not hurt." She'd stopped smiling too; indeed, had seldom felt less like smiling. "Who came to the house?"

Jimmy shrugged, then winced. "I dunno. Some man. Tall, black hair, mustache, blue eyes. Ma sent me because she couldn't leave Henry and Pa."

"I see," said Philippe.

"I don't," said Heather. The person who'd come to her parents' door sounded uncannily like D. A. Bologh. But it couldn't have been. Nor could it have been D. A. who'd shot her father. She shook her head, wondering if the whole world was going mad, or only her.

"Well, I don't see, either," said Jimmy. "But he didn't give us a name. Just said you was hurt bad, was asking for your family, and took off. I sure as blazes didn't know I'd run into a stampede."

"Mind your tongue, young man." Heather spoke

the reprimand automatically. She was too busy thinking to care if Jimmy swore.

Jimmy sighed heavily, as one grievously put upon. "Well, I didn't. And it was danged hard to see in the dark, too, and there was lightning and thunder all over the place, and the wind like to knock me off my horse. It wasn't any fun, I'll tell you."

"It sounds terrible, Jimmy. Thank you for riding to my rescue."

"But you didn't need rescuing," Jimmy pointed out, obviously unhappy about having been tricked.

"But I might have, and I think you were very brave and awfully sweet to come." Heather wondered if she was merely being silly to be so touched by her little brother's worry. Probably.

"It wasn't much," muttered Jimmy, embarrassed by his sister's lapse into sentiment.

"This all sounds like part of a great big puzzle to me," said Philippe.

His tone carried a strange note, and when Heather turned to look at him, his expression was strange too. His brow was furrowed, and the lines beside his mouth were deep. "What is it, Philippe?" she asked softly.

"I don't know."

"Do you think it's—connected to everything else?"

He understood what she'd left unsaid. "I don't know." He shook his head and shoved himself to his feet. "But let's not worry about it now. Do you need any supplies?"

"I could use some more hot water and rags. I think I have enough soap here."

"Dang it, Heather, you're scrubbing me raw. I'm

already cut up. I don't need you to finish me off."

With a laugh, Philippe said, "I don't think your sister's going to do you in, Jimmy. And if she is, I'll be abetting her, because I'm going to get more hot water this minute."

Jimmy let out an aggrieved huff.

Heather said, "Thank you," in a voice she realized too late was dreamy.

When she glanced at her brother again, he was watching her through slitted eyes, as if he neither appreciated nor approved of that tone of voice when directed at Philippe St. Pierre.

Heather flushed and renewed her efforts on her brother's behalf.

Chapter Sixteen

By the time Doc Grady had come and gone; pronounced Jimmy healthy but for an alarming number of scrapes and cuts and a wrenched shoulder; prepared a very interesting sling for him to wear for two weeks; dosed the boy with a vile-tasting substance that Jimmy barely gagged down; and Philippe had carried Jimmy to a spare room upstairs, midnight had long since passed. Mrs. Van der Linden had been cajoled against her will into preparing Jimmy's room, and had then retired to her own with a sharp word from Philippe speeding her on her way.

Philippe had recruited one of his hired hands to sleep in Jimmy's room and to report if the boy experienced any strange symptoms. The hired lad wasn't much older than Jimmy, but already he was willing and able to assume the duties of an adult. Such behavior wasn't uncommon in the territory, and Heather appreciated her fellow New Mexicans a lot during that crisis.

As she stood in the hallway outside of Jimmy's room after giving her brother an unwanted good night kiss, she realized she was so tired, she was shaking. Passing a hand over her eyes, she murmured, "Thank God he'll be all right."

She felt Philippe's hand splay gently on her back, and almost succumbed to the urge to turn and throw her arms around him. "I'm glad of that. I was worried when I first saw him. So was Mike."

Heather managed a wan smile. "I imagine he was. Mike has a brother just Jimmy's age."

"He'll be fine in a few days."

"I reckon."

Knowing she had to do it sometime, and it would be wise to do so before she fell over in fatigue, Heather turned and held out a hand to Philippe. "I can't thank you enough for all of your help tonight, Philippe. You've had plenty to worry about without having to take care of my family as well, but you have been taking care of us." Tonight she was too tired to resent it. "And I can't tell you how much I appreciate your help."

He took her hand, but didn't shake it. Instead, she felt his thumb gently massage her knuckles. The caress sent sparks through her. "Taking care of you and your family is a pleasure, Heather. It's not a bother."

Her hand felt so good in his. He was so big and safe and comfortable, and she felt so small and insecure and alone.

"Heather . . ."

Her eyes drifted shut, and she didn't want to speak. She sort of wanted to cuddle up and purr, actually. "Yes?" she managed after several seconds.

"About tonight."

"Yes?" Glory, she hoped he wouldn't renew his proposal now, because she knew good and well that in her present state she wouldn't be able to dillydally or to "think" about it. Rather, she'd accept him on the spot, thereby ruining his life. Or maybe not. Her physical strength was too depleted for her brain to think the matter through.

He tugged gently on her hand, and she stumbled forward—smack up against him. Since she was there, and since she didn't care to fall over, and since she'd wanted to do it all evening anyway, she wrapped her arms around him and rested her head against his broad, hard chest. She felt *so* good there.

His lips touched her hair, and she sighed deeply, pressing her breasts against him. Oh, my, that felt good. Because she was longing for some kind of closeness, she tilted her head back and looked up at him, hoping he'd kiss her. His eyes warmed her through and through. She wouldn't have been surprised if steam had risen from her, in fact.

"Heather," he said again, his voice rough.

She sighed.

He didn't speak again. Instead, he did as she'd hoped he'd do and kissed her. Thank God. Heather melted into him as if she and he had been crafted together at the beginning of time, separated somehow by an evil fate, and had finally been reunited there, in the upstairs hallway of Philippe St. Pierre's ranch house.

Before she could dissolve into a puddle of melted flesh on the hall carpet, Philippe swept her up into his arms. Heather was awfully glad of it because her legs had begun to quiver like rubber bands. She hoped he wouldn't carry her far—for example, downstairs to her own room—but would opt for a nearby and more intimate resting place. Hang the consequences.

Fortunately for her, Philippe was of a like mind. His room was only two doors down and across the hall from where they'd stashed Jimmy. Heather was very happy when he carried her there, kicked the door open, and took her inside.

She heard him murmur, "This is wrong," and a frisson of alarm shot through her.

"No, it isn't," she whispered, frantic. If he stopped now, she'd die; she knew it. "It's not wrong at all." It was precisely what she needed, although she wasn't sure what "it" was, exactly. Something that only married people were supposed to do—that much she knew.

He carried her to the bed. "You're right. It's not wrong."

Thank heavens. Heather had been worried there for a minute. He set her tenderly on his bed. It was a high bed, a four-poster with a heavy tester. It was a lovely bed, really, and Heather liked it a lot. She sank into the feather mattress and felt like the princess in the fairy tale, only without the pea. She couldn't feel anything but blissful softness.

"You're a beautiful woman, Heather."

Oh, how sweet. "Thank you." She wondered if she was supposed to say something about his handsomeness and decided it wouldn't hurt. "You're the most handsome man I've ever seen."

His crooked grin looked a little cynical. Heather blinked, wondering if her eyes were too tired to be seeing things correctly. She guessed she wasn't when he spoke again. At the same time, he started unbuttoning his shirt. Heather listened and watched, fascinated.

"I'm handsome. I'm rich. So why do you have to think about accepting my proposal of marriage?"

He slipped his shirt off, and Heather gaped at his chest, covered with black curls. Not too many black curls; just enough. And what a chest he had. Corded with muscles, lean, spare. The man was perfect. She swallowed and said, "Um—what?" She'd forgotten his question.

Chuckling, Philippe unbuckled his belt. Mercy sakes. This was it. Or it was about to be it. She stared at him, figuring it was impolite of her but unable to resist. Since he was staring back at her, she guessed she wasn't being too awful, although she was pretty sure her mother would think so.

Lord, what a perfect way to dampen one's ardor. Heather mentally smacked herself and told herself she didn't need to think about her family right now. In fact, family was the last thing she needed to think about in this instance.

In order to get herself back into Philippe's bedroom, she slipped her robe off and let it puddle on the bed. That left her in her unrevealing flannel nightgown—she hadn't had time to dress when they'd brought Jimmy into the house—and she decided to leave it on until Philippe either took it off of her or worked around it. She had no idea how these things went forward.

Philippe nodded at the nightgown as the last button on his trousers popped open. Heather noticed that there seemed to be a huge bulge behind his fly, and she could hardly wait to see what was causing it. She was also a little frightened, but overall she was pleased to note that her anticipation far overrode her fear.

"I've seen more seductive garments on horses, Heather."

Startled, Heather glanced down at her nightgown and then up at Philippe. He was smiling at her, genuinely, and with a good deal of warmth in his expression, so she guessed she shouldn't be offended. In fact, he was probably right. With an answering grin, she said, "I'm afraid my mother would have horsewhipped me if I'd tried to wear anything less, um, flannel."

He laughed and shoved his trousers down. Heather suppressed a gasp with difficulty when his fully aroused sex thrust out at her.

Good God! Was that thing supposed to fit inside her? Impossible. At least, it looked impossible from where Heather sat. She was no longer sure this was such a good idea.

Heather guessed she was goggling because Philippe said softly, "Don't be frightened, Heather. I'll try to be very careful. The first time always hurts a little bit." He sank down onto the feather mattress next to her, and lifted an eyebrow. "It will be your first time, will it not?"

Shocked out of her trepidation by his question, she blurted indignantly, "Of *course* it will be! What kind of woman do you think I am, anyway?"

His fingers found the tie at the throat of her nightgown, and he laughed softly. "The kind of woman I want to marry." His big hands pushed the fabric aside and down her shoulders.

"Oh." That put everything in a much better light. Heather sucked in a deep breath. Merciful heavens, his hands felt good on her naked skin. Were women supposed to feel this way when men touched them?

"Oh? Is that all you can say?"

"Um, yes."

"Ah." Philippe's warm lips touched the flesh at the base of her throat, and Heather feared she'd die right there, in his bed, from sheer pleasure. "That's the word I wanted to hear."

Her thoughts were getting fuzzier by the second, but she didn't think fuzzy thoughts accounted for her not understanding his comment. "I, ah, beg your, ah, pardon?" The *pardon* ended on a gasp when his hand pushed the nightgown all the way down until it puddled around her naked hips and his mouth—his wonderful, talented, brilliant mouth—covered her left nipple. Her head fell back when his warm tongue flicked over the pebbled nub. Good heavens, that felt good.

"I wanted to hear you say yes, Heather," Philippe elucidated in a husky voice. "I wanted to hear you say yes to my proposal."

Ah. That cleared it all up. And, while she hadn't actually accepted his proposal, but rather his proposition, Heather understood. Proposal. Proposition. Whatever. This was heaven.

"After tonight, you won't be able to refuse me," Philippe went on.

Little did he know. Heather could do as she damned well pleased. She always had, much to her mother's dismay.

However, in this instance, she did believe Philippe was right. If this is what marital intimacy entailed, Heather would be very happy to be married to him. Not to anyone else. Just to Philippe.

She couldn't even imagine another man doing these things to her. Not if he expected to live, anyway. But Philippe . . . Well, Philippe was special.

She said, "Oh, my."

"Feels good, does it?"

"Oh, my, yes."

"Good." He laid her back gently and maneuvered the nightgown the rest of the way down her legs and off of her body. He tossed it aside. "I'll get you some more appropriate night-wear soon, sweet." His lips kissed a path to her other breast and murmured, "Or perhaps I won't. This is much more enticing."

Yes indeedy. It sure was. Heather arched her back, thrusting her right breast into Philippe's mouth. Fortunately, he knew what to do with it, and Heather worried that she might shriek or do something else to embarrass herself if he kept it up. What he was doing to her felt *so* good.

His lips moved from her breast, much to her displeasure. She almost uttered a protest, but didn't, which was all right, since what he did next was every bit as luxuriously thrilling as what he'd been doing. Heather hadn't realized how sensitive the flesh around her breasts was until Philippe taught her. She delighted in the lesson.

When his lips feathered down her body, she gasped and dug her fingers into his hair. She could feel him chuckle as his tongue slid around her belly button and finally dove into it. Her hips lifted involuntarily, and she uttered a small scream when his hand covered the curls at the juncture of her thighs.

Good Lord, was he supposed to be doing that? "Ahh," she moaned when his middle finger sought and found the most sensitive nub on her body, and guessed that answered her question.

"You're so beautiful, Heather. So damned beautiful." His words spread out with his breath, warm and delicious, on her lower belly.

She appreciated his assessment of her relative loveliness, but couldn't thank him at the moment. There was too much need and too much sensation rioting inside her.

Mercy, mercy, mercy, was he kissing her even lower? Heather jammed a fist into her mouth to keep from crying out when she felt his tongue take over from where his fingers had been playing. Good Lord in heaven, what was he doing to her?

Pressure, pleasure. Pleasure, pressure. The feelings became so intense that Heather discovered her body going rigid with anticipation. All at once, the dam burst, and she hurtled over the edge of pleasure and pressure into an ecstasy of carnal delight.

Thank heavens she'd already covered her mouth or she'd have roused the household with her scream of pleasure.

She had no idea how long she writhed in satisfaction, or how long Philippe had been murmuring to her when she finally came to her senses.

"Beautiful. Beautiful."

The words slithered around in her mushy brain for several seconds before she understood they came from Philippe, and that he'd been watching her. She supposed she should be embarrassed, but she wasn't.

Feeling exhausted and absolutely fulfilled, she sat up suddenly and reached for Philippe. He let her pull him up so that she could kiss him madly.

Sweet heaven above, but she loved him!

She kissed him and kissed him and kissed him, and hardly realized what was happening when he positioned himself above her and guided his enormous sex to her still-sensitive passage.

When she'd first seen it, she'd been a little alarmed because it seemed awfully big to fit down there. She had no qualms anymore.

Sure enough, when Philippe engaged her in a long, deep, thrilling kiss, and she felt him there, opening her, she didn't even think about it, but thrust her hips upward to receive him. With a groan, he plunged home.

Heather's eyes, which had been closed as she thoroughly enjoyed her first sexual experience, popped open. She found Philippe gazing tenderly down at her, an expression of concern on his handsome face.

"Did that hurt, darling?"

Darling. Oh, wasn't that sweet?

However, it did hurt. A little. Before she answered, Heather tested the sensations going on within her.

Actually, it wasn't so much pain as a feeling of fullness, of having something unusual happening to her. Which it was. She moved her hips a little, tentatively.

Philippe uttered a small grunt of pleasure, as if he couldn't help himself. "Be careful," he whispered. "I'm about to explode."

Now what, Heather wondered, did he mean by that? It sounded rather exciting. She decided it didn't hurt after all and said so. "No, Philippe. You're not hurting me."

He let out a breath of relief, as if he'd been hoping to hear her say so. Then he started moving—really moving—inside of her, and Heather got so caught up in the activity that she forgot all about the newness of it all, the possibility of pain, and the unconventionality of her, an unmarried woman, making love with an unmarried man. The pressure and pleasure started building again, shocking her, and it wasn't long before she was carried away entirely and achieved a second shattering release.

Afterwards, she decided it was a very good thing that Philippe had taken that moment to kiss her deeply, or she'd have screamed for sure, and probably scared the cows outside into another stampede. Shortly after her second amazing release, Philippe roared like a lion, bucked hard, and achieved his own.

Panting heavily, he lowered himself onto her, slid to one side—presumably so he wouldn't squish her with his weight, although Heather would have welcomed it on top of her—and held her tightly. She was glad to note that he seemed as depleted by the experience as she. Although she hadn't considered it before hand, Philippe probably had a lot of experience doing this sort of thing, and she might well have disappointed him. She didn't *think* she had, to judge by his present state.

After a moment, he lifted his hand and brushed her hair back from her damp forehead. "You're wonderful, Heather. You'll marry me now. You'll have to."

She would? She did? Hmm. Heather wasn't sure about the have-to's inherent in this situation—but she was going to marry him. He was too wonderful to let slip away. She snuggled against him. "All right, Philippe. I'd love to marry you."

He hugged her hard. "Good."

Speaking of love . . . Heather frowned into the darkness. She was happy, to be sure. And she was pleased that Philippe wanted to marry her. But he hadn't said a single, solitary word about love. Unless she'd been so engrossed she'd missed it.

But no. She was sure she'd have remembered that. She sighed heavily. It was no matter. Life in the territory was too uncertain a prospect to make it prudent for a woman to hold out for everything, she reckoned. If she lived, say, back in New York City or some other place where life wasn't so precarious, she'd probably have held out for a declaration of love. In the territory, folks had more common sense than that.

After all, what did love have to do with anything? What mattered was stability, strength, and honor. Money helped a good deal. And Philippe had all of those attributes. And, what's more, he obviously desired her. That was a good start. It was a whole lot better than many folks started with.

Heather couldn't figure out why she still felt a tiny bit bleak in her heart of hearts after she'd cleared up all of those points in her mind.

"Ha! I knew you couldn't hold out against a rich man's wiles."

Heather scowled at D. A. Bologh, who was whipping up a breakfast soufflé, replete with bacon, cheese, and mushrooms. Heather wished he'd stop using those dratted mushrooms. She was afraid Philippe would ask her where they'd come from again, and she'd have to tell him again she didn't know because D. A. Bologh did all the cooking, and he'd think she was crazy. Again.

At least she knew what a soufflé was now. When she'd first started this job, she wouldn't have known a soufflé from an outhouse. She'd read about soufflés in several cookbooks by this time; she might even be able to make one by this time if she tried hard enough, although she wouldn't try it unless forced to do so, for fear she'd bump the stove or underbeat the eggs or something and make it fall.

"That's not nice. And it isn't true, either. I don't care if he's rich or not. I'd never marry a man for his money. I think Philippe is a wonderful man. Why, just look at what he's done for the town of Fort Summers!" She spread her arms wide and felt a little silly—but it was the truth. Philippe never advertised his good acts, but he'd helped more people than anyone else in town ever had. Why, he was almost like Fort Summers's own personal Saint Nicholas.

D. A. snorted, which didn't do much to keep Heather's mood cheerful. She'd been as near to floating as she'd ever been after her night with Philippe. She'd never felt so perfectly feminine and beautiful and wanted and desired in her life. The feeling had lasted through the night, into the morning, and even a little while beyond Philippe's good morning kiss and sweet questions regarding the state of her health.

Then he'd left for work, and Heather had returned to reality with a thump. A painful thump. Muscles she hadn't realized she possessed were aching this morning.

Nevertheless, she wasn't on a honeymoon or anything, and she had work to do. Not to mention a brother in less-than-dire, but still extreme, need. Her first duty, therefore, after washing up and tidying and trying to make herself appear as if she hadn't been making delicious love to Philippe all night, was to visit Jimmy's room. He was sitting up in bed, playing cards with Mike Mulligan.

Both males had smiled at her, she'd asked about Jimmy's health, been reassured, and had told her brother she'd bring up a breakfast tray for the both of them as soon as she could.

Jimmy had looked skeptical. "Are you gonna cook it?"

Heather felt her lips pinch up and tried to relax them. "I'm regarded as a fine cook these days, Jimmy Mahaffey."

"Yeah?"

"Stop looking at me like that!" Heather cried. "You look horrible enough with all those scratches and bruises, without adding that look to the mix."

Mike had laughed. Jimmy had huffed crossly. Heather had absconded to the kitchen, her mood somewhat mangled. And now here was D. A. Bologh, killing it off.

"This isn't fair," she muttered as she flipped ham slices onto a platter for Jimmy. Her brother adored fried ham for breakfast. "I was feeling wonderful until you and Jimmy and Mike started in on me."

D. A.'s laugh sounded as mean and cynical as it ever did. "It's because you're living a lie, and you know it, sweetheart. You're going to marry the man, and he doesn't have any idea what he's getting."

Recalling the night she'd just spent in Philippe's arms, Heather said, "Yes, he does!" She slammed her hand on the table so hard, the platter jumped and a piece of ham skittered off onto the table. She picked it up in her fingers—a breach of etiquette her mother, not to mention Mrs. Van der Linden, would deplore—and slapped it irritably back where it belonged.

"Like hell," D. A. said, smirking.

"He does! I told him all about you."

D. A.'s head swiveled, one of his eyebrows lifted, and he sneered at her. "Ah, yes. I recall the night of your confession. And I suppose he believed every word of it."

Glowering, Heather muttered, "No. He didn't."

"I thought not."

"But I told him."

"You're just trying to make yourself feel better. You know he thinks you're the one who's been doing the cooking."

She sighed heavily. "I know."

D. A. slipped the soufflé into the oven, turned, leaned back against the stove—which must have been blazing hot—crossed his arms over his chest, and grinned at her. "I think it's about time for a reckoning, Heather Mahaffey, you sweet little thing, you."

She eyed him uneasily as she stuck a soft-cooked egg into a pretty porcelain egg cup. Jimmy would think that was swell, never having seen an egg cup before. "What do you mean? What kind of reckoning?"

"I think it's about time for you to pay up."

Heather's heart skidded and fell sickeningly. She swallowed. Her throat closed up on her, and she couldn't ask.

D. A. evidently didn't expect her to. "I've been

doing your job for over a month now, dearie. And quite well, too, if I do say so myself."

She nodded because it was true.

"But, as you know, we made a bargain before I started working here. And it's just about time for you to pay the piper. So to speak." His grin broadened. For the first time, Heather noticed that his teeth were kind of sharp, like the canines of a dog, although not quite so pointy. They gave him a truly evil appearance, and she wished he'd stop smiling.

D. A. tapped those pointy teeth with his forefinger. "What do you say, sweetie pie? Don't you think it's time you started paying? For services rendered, you know."

Heather's spunk returned like a cyclone. Her spine stiffened, her heart lifted, her throat loosened up, and so did her tongue. Her voice was quite vinegary when she snapped, "I have no idea what we bargained for, because you never told me, don't forget. Perhaps I'll believe the price is too high." That was good; she wished she'd considered such an option before. She sniffed disdainfully to add emphasis to her words.

D. A. didn't like that at all. His grin vanished. "You'll pay," he snarled. "You have to because you said you would."

She wagged a finger at him. "But I didn't say *what* I'd pay. It's not fair to expect a person to pay unless she knows what the price is ahead of time."

"You didn't care about the blasted price before you said yes."

She huffed, irked at having the truth used against her. "I know. And it was foolish of me to make a bargain when I didn't know what I was bargaining with." A little less sure of herself and afraid of his answer, she asked, "Um, what exactly were you expecting in return for your services, D. A.?"

He eyed her keenly for a moment, and his grin slowly returned. Heather's skin crawled when she saw it. "You."

She blinked at him. "Um, I beg your pardon?"

He pointed at her with a long, sharp finger, tipped by a long, sharp fingernail. "You heard me, Heather. You."

She pointed at her chest. "Me?"

"You."

She squinted at him. "Um, I don't think I understand."

"Oh, yes, you do. You might not have known it at the time, but you bargained your sweet little self with me when you begged me to cook for you."

Heather's hand dropped to her side. She stared at D. A., unbelieving, for a couple of seconds. Then, as the full meaning of his statement curled through her, making her insides ice up as it did so, she shook her head. "No." She sucked in air. "Oh, no. That's not fair, D. A. Bologh."

He shrugged insolently. "We aren't talking fair here, Heather my love. We're talking a bargain."

She shook her head hard. "Oh, no, we aren't! If I'd known what you wanted, I'd never have made a deal with you!"

Another shrug made her want to run him through with a cooking fork. "So what? You did make the deal."

Heather planted her fists on her hips. "That's not fair! If I'd known what you were bargaining for, I'd have told you to go right straight to perdition, and you know it!"

"A likely story, however apt." D. A.'s sneer was terrifying to behold. It was a sneer that was calculated to wither Heather's heart.

She knew it, and used her fear to embolden her, sensing that there was more at stake here than her physical body. She leaned toward D. A., allowing her rage to propel her words. "You're a lying, cheating, sneaking skunk, D. A. Bologh! You know good and well that you can't expect a person to agree to something unless you tell them what it is they're agreeing to before they agree to it!"

"Bah. You're just a sore loser."

D. A.'s scorn was tempered slightly when the two of them heard the wind, low and menacing, outside the window. A rumble of thunder reached their ears, sounding as if it came from very far away. Heather was surprised to see him cringe and glance behind him, as if searching for the source of that thunder. She used his moment of discomposure to further her point. Shaking her finger right under his nose, she said, "I'm not a sore loser! If you'd told me what you wanted in exchange for cooking for me, I'd never have agreed to it, and you know it as well as I do! I might be a stinking cook, but I'm not an idiot. And I'm not a whore! I'd rather be roasted over hot coals with the fall chili peppers than give myself to you!"

"How appropriate," D. A. said, although his sneer had faded some. Another rumble of thunder, closer this time, made him jerk his shoulders. The wind had commenced howling like a soul in torment outside the window.

Heather's brow furrowed. What was the matter with the man? He surely wasn't afraid of thunder, was he? She couldn't imagine D. A. Bologh being afraid of anything.

Through the kitchen window, she saw a flash of lightning in the distance. Strange weather they were having. Fort Summers never experienced thunder and lightning in the morning. She didn't let the oddity of New Mexico weather thwart her. This was too important.

"Don't you bandy words with me, you louse," she shouted. "You know very well that you cheated! Cheaters never prosper!" It was trite, but Heather couldn't think of anything more brilliant at the moment.

"Cheater, my hind leg!" D. A. shouted back.

A gust of wind sounded like a locomotive as it rushed past the house. An enormous crack of lightning shook the house. It was accompanied by a roar of thunder that made Heather clap her hands over her ears. "Good heavens!" She was so disconcerted by the stormy weather that she was momentarily distracted from her argument with D. A., and whirled around to see what was going on outside. Bolts of lightning and cracks of thunder were ripping through the sky like fire from a Gatling gun. Her mouth fell open, and she could only gape, hoping against hope that the cattle wouldn't stampede again. She raced to the window to see if the fences were being damaged.

"All right! All right! I give!"

D. A.'s shriek turned her around again. "What?"

A boom of thunder shook the house so hard, she nearly lost her footing. The wind threatened to tear the roof off the house.

D. A., his hands covering his head as if he feared

for his very life, screamed, "I give up! You're right! I cheated!"

The thunder and lightning ceased.

Heather's shocked gaze darted between the kitchen window and D. A. Bologh and back again. She didn't know what to make of anything.

Chapter Seventeen

Heather allowed her arms to fall to her sides. She was glancing around, nervous, wondering where the weather had got itself off to. She'd thought they were in for a tornado, at least. She tried to focus on D. A. "Um, I beg your pardon?"

D. A. looked mad enough to spit tarantulas and horned toads. Maybe a rattlesnake. "I said I give. You're right. I cheated." He whirled around and slammed his fist on the stove. Heather winced, knowing that such a jolt was bad was for the soufflé.

She cleared her throat. "Yes, I do believe you did cheat."

He whirled again and pointed that wicked-looking finger at her heart. "But you're not off the hook yet, sweetheart. Just because I waffled a little bit at first—"

Another roll of thunder, faint, in the distance,

made him jump, and he muttered, "Oh, hell." Then he heaved a huge sigh. "Very well. I cheated. It wasn't merely a little waffling."

Outside, the clouds began to part. The sun suddenly appeared and shone down brightly from above. Heather passed a hand over her eyes, wondering, for about the millionth time in recent weeks, if she'd lost her mind.

"I cheated," D. A. declared flatly. "Is that all right?" He glanced around as if waiting for somebody—not Heather—to answer him.

Heather, unsure what to do, murmured, "Well, it's not all right with me, actually."

D. A. skewered her with a glare, and she shut her mouth. "I'm not talking to *you*, of all pitiful creatures."

"Oh." She decided to await events and see what transpired. Obviously, she had no idea what was going on, although she sensed it had to do with more than mere kitchen bargains. Something universal seemed a more likely prospect, although it also seemed nuts.

Expelling another huge breath, D. A. went on, snarling a bit. "Very well, I cheated. And the boss doesn't like that. He thinks it's more fun when people know what they're getting themselves into and do it anyway and then try to wriggle out of it."

He paused and, feeling compelled, Heather said, "I see," although she saw nothing. Except the sunshine outside. Oh, dear.

"Like hell you see," D. A. said scornfully. "You don't see a damned thing."

Heather silently agreed with him.

"But you're not getting off the hook. I cooked for you for nearly two whole months. I even went so far as to forgo truffles and shallots in order to fit my magnificent meals to your shoddy provincial surroundings."

Feeling pressed to say something—after all, he *had* been of tremendous service to her—Heather said, "You did a marvelous job, D. A. Everyone thinks so. And I appreciate the part about not using truffles and shallots." She didn't bring up the mushrooms.

He rolled his eyes. "Garbage. This place would think garbage is wonderful."

"I wouldn't go *that* far," Heather said, defensive. "After all—"

"Oh, shut up."

She did so.

"But you have to pay." He turned and tapped his chin thoughtfully. "Now, let me think about this. I'm sure I can come up with an appropriate payment."

"Um, while you think, shall I serve breakfast? It's about time, and I have to take Jimmy's tray upstairs."

He waved a hand in the air as if he didn't give a rap what she did or didn't do. Heather quickly picked up the tray intended for Jimmy and Mike and carted it out of the kitchen and up the stairs. She was so glad to have escaped the kitchen, she actually contemplated running away after she'd delivered the tray. She'd never do anything so cowardly—but she thought about it.

Jimmy stared at his breakfast tray and then stared at his sister. "You didn't cook this stuff."

"I did, too!" Offended, Heather whipped the silver cover off of the dish containing the pretty egg cup, and glared at her brother. "I fixed the ham, and boiled the eggs, and even made the bread. And I made the jam, too."

"Naw. You couldn't have. The bread looks like it's got yeast in it, and it's not burned."

"I no longer burn toast, Jimmy Mahaffey." Heather knew she was being needlessly offended—after all, Jimmy's experience of her cooking skills was vast—but she was offended anyway. She'd been trying *so* hard to learn her job.

"I don't believe it." Jimmy's frown faltered when he saw the flowery egg cup. "Say, Heather, that's real pretty."

She sniffed. "Yes. Mr. St. Pierre has many pretty things."

Jimmy grinned up at her. "I'll bet the egg's hard as granite."

Heather's teeth gritted so hard, she could barely squeeze words past them. "It is not."

"Let's try it and see," Mike suggested in a mollifying tone.

Grateful to him, even though he did look as though he were trying not to laugh, Heather smiled. "Thanks, Mike. What a good idea." She turned, intending to go down to fetch Philippe's breakfast to the dining room. If the soufflé had fallen, maybe she could call it an omelet or something.

She heard the tapping of a spoon against a soft-cooked eggshell, and then heard Jimmy's happy, "Say! It *isn't* boiled hard!" And, with a swish of her skirts and a feeling of pride in her bosom, Heather left the patient and his nurse and skipped down the stairs. By gum, she was learning to cook!

Her happiness fled when she realized it might be

too late for that. With a good deal of trepidation, she reentered the kitchen. D. A. Bologh was nowhere to be seen. Reprieve! She was sure it wouldn't last long. Nevertheless, her heart was light when she slid the soufflé, as light and fluffy as a soufflé should be, onto another tray, loaded the side dishes, and carted the whole shebang to the dining room.

Philippe was there, and he hurried to take the heavy tray from her hands, set it down, and enfold her in a welcoming embrace. Heather thought life could hardly get any better.

Well, except for D. A. Bologh.

"Are you feeling all right, darling?" Philippe asked, solicitously leading her to a chair. "I don't think you should be working so hard today. I'll tell Mrs. Van der Linden—"

"No!"

Philippe blinked down at her, and Heather felt herself blush. "I mean—I'm sorry, Philippe. I didn't mean to shout at you. But please don't ask Mrs. Van der Linden to do anything for me. She already hates me."

He frowned. "She's a very bitter woman. I'm rather tired of her attitude."

Because she felt particularly vulnerable today, especially after her chat with D. A., Heather didn't agree out loud. She merely said, "Um, she's quite set in her ways," and let it go at that.

Philippe chuckled, which made the world bright again. "I suppose you're right. But I still don't want you working hard today. In fact, I insist that you take the day off."

Wasn't that nice of him? Heather knew she was suffering from an emotional overload when she felt a sniffle coming on. She swallowed it without mercy. "That's very kind of you, Philippe. If it's all right with you, I'll go to town and see my parents. I want to reassure them that Jimmy's going to be fine."

Philippe had taken a bite of soufflé, and he frowned as he chewed it. Heather watched, wondering at his frown. Good heavens, was D. A. losing his touch? "Is the soufflé all right, Philippe? There was a big, um, boom outside the kitchen. I didn't think it fell, but—"

He swallowed, took a sip of coffee, and said, "No. The soufflé is delicious. As usual." He gave her a beautiful smile, and she felt better. "I don't know about you going to town, though."

Surprised, Heather said, "But why not?" then wished she'd kept her mouth shut. They weren't married yet, after all, and she remained his employee. She supposed he could still fire her. "That is to say, I'd really like to see my folks and to tell them about Jimmy. I went up to see him this morning, and he's fine. Almost as good as new."

Another smile from Philippe, this one kind and tender, smoothed her feathers a good deal. "I'm glad of that." He ate another bite of breakfast and seemed to be thinking.

Heather had no idea why he should worry about her going to town. After all . . . Oh. Suddenly a light went on in her brain, and she understood exactly why he didn't want her to go to town: that woman. She said, "I'll only visit my folks, Philippe. And Geraldine." She considered mentioning the woman, and didn't, sensing that would be unwise.

Besides, she might just bump into her by accident, and then—but who knew? All sorts of things might happen in town.

At last Philippe shrugged. Heather presumed the influence of good food and a fulfilling night had something to do with his ultimate decision. "Very well. Would you like me to go with you?"

"You probably have lots of things to do here, so please don't take time away from the ranch to accompany me." She fiddled with a piece of toast. "Um, were there any more problems with the cattle? That was a whopper of a storm we had this morning. Short, though. I've never known a storm to last that short a time."

Philippe had been concentrating on his breakfast, but he looked at her now, puzzled. "Another storm? This morning?"

Oh, dear. Heather felt a sinking sensation in her stomach. "Um, I thought I heard thunder this morning. And a really high wind."

Philippe shook his head. "Must have been one of the men chopping wood or something. I've been outside since I got up, and there hasn't been a cloud in the sky. Even the wind's down. Thank God. We don't need the damned wind, and we've got a lot of fixing of fences to do today."

"I see. Yes, I suppose it must have been one of the men."

In a pig's eye. Heather had been through enough thunderstorms to know one when she heard one. And it was more than merely unsettling to think that she and D. A. Bologh had been privy to their own exclusive storm. The notion made her a little queasy, actually, and sent her thoughts, like vicious pointy arrows, in the direction of what D. A. might be going to exact from her in payment for his assistance. She dropped the piece of toast, her appetite having vanished.

"Are you sure you're all right, Heather? You look pale."

Philippe's big, hard hand covered hers, and his beautiful dark eyes caressed her with a gaze as soft as velvet. Heather sighed, turned her hand over in his, and squeezed gently. "I'm fine, Philippe." Because it was true, and because she loved him, she said, "I'm happier than I've ever been."

Except for one niggling problem that might possibly ruin both their lives. She didn't mention it.

He squeezed her hand back and smiled at her in his turn. "I'm glad. I'm happy too. I hadn't ever really considered marriage before I met you."

"Really?" How sweet. Maybe he did love her a tiny bit.

"Really. I hadn't believed I could ever find a woman who wouldn't drive me to insanity. Then you knocked on my door."

Heather sighed. That had been a fateful day, all right.

And he still hadn't said a word about affection. Because she had gumption and pride—perhaps foolish pride—Heather would die sooner than declare her love for him before he declared his for her. Which meant, of course, that they might go to their graves without admitting love for each other. And that seemed tolerably silly, although Heather wasn't ready to give up her dream of being adored by Philippe this early in the game.

He leaned toward her and kissed her, and Heather melted into his arms. She felt so good there. In Philippe's arms, she felt protected from the buffets of life and poverty and hard work—and D. A. Bologh.

Drat! She wished D. A. would stop intruding himself into her thoughts.

She was disappointed when Philippe pulled away with a shaky laugh. "I'd better get back to work. You're an immense distraction, Heather. I'll be glad when we're wed."

"So will I. Do you think I won't be a distraction then?"

He laughed and grabbed his hat from the back of a chair. "No. I fear you'll be a distraction to me until the day I die, but when we're married, I won't have any qualms about carting you off to bed in the middle of the day. Since you came to work here, all I've been able to do is think about it."

Heather pressed a palm to her flaming cheek. "Oh, Philippe, truly?"

"Truly." He grabbed her up from her chair, wrapped her in a crushing embrace, and kissed her hard.

She'd never known folks could kiss with their tongues as well as their lips. It was delicious to taste Philippe, to press his tongue with hers, and to abandon herself to the feelings he aroused in her. When he gently disengaged his arms from around her, she staggered slightly, befuddled. His warm chuckle filtered through her like some kind of healing balm.

"I'm glad you respond to my touch, darling. And, as you can see, I respond to yours." He guided her hand to his crotch, where she felt his sex, as rigid as an oak log, through his trousers.

Heather was slightly shocked. Did all almost-married couples do these stunningly intimate things?

The door opened behind her, Philippe drew her hand away from his leg and up to his mouth where he nuzzled it in front of God and Mrs. Van der Linden and anyone else who might happen to be watching, and Mrs. V. answered Heather's question for her.

"Well, I never!"

Heather was absolutely, positively sure that Mrs. Van der Linden had never, ever, in her whole entire life, done anything even remotely as scintillating as Heather and Philippe had just done. She cleared her throat. "Hello, Mrs. Van der Linden."

Philippe settled his hat on his head and straightened his vest, which had become cockeyed during the preceding few minutes. "Good morning, Mrs. Van der Linden. I'd like you to be the first to know that Miss Mahaffey has agreed to become my wife."

Mrs. Van der Linden said, "Well!" again. Then she tottered a few steps and fell into a chair. Heather winced for fear her bulk would break it. Fortunately, Philippe could afford to purchase sturdy furniture, and the chair creaked once and held. "I never."

Heather didn't know what to say in the face of Mrs. Van der Linden's overt horror.

Philippe did. "I'm sure you'll want to wish Heather the best of luck, and offer me your hearty congratulations." His voice was as dry as sand and as cold as ice. "And now I've got a lot of work to do. I'll see you this evening, darling." And he kissed Heather again, hard, and left her and Mrs. Van der Linden alone together in the dining room. Heather appreciated the wink he gave her before he shut the door.

The housekeeper picked up a linen napkin and fanned herself violently. She eyed Heather with perfect loathing. "I have never," she said distinctly, "been so shocked in my whole life. To come into this room, all unsuspecting, and to find the two of you doing—doing—well, I never."

That was probably true, too, but Heather didn't think it was very nice of the old hag to say so. She lifted her chin. "Is it so impossible that Mr. St. Pierre has formed an attachment to me, Mrs. Van der Linden?"

"Yes."

Heather frowned. "That's not very nice."

"It's the truth."

"Nevertheless, it's not nice." Heather thought of an even better argument against the woman's insensitivity. "Besides, who are you to disagree with Mr. St. Pierre's choice in a wife?"

Mrs. Van der Linden fanned herself more furiously still and said through gritted teeth, "Nobody, I suppose. But I must say you're the slyest thing in nature, Heather Mahaffey."

There were several things she could do, Heather thought. She could pick up a plate and crack Mrs. Van der Linden over the head with it. She could thump her with her fists the way she used to thump her brothers. She could verbally fuss and fight with the woman. She could berate her for being a mean old cow. She could say awful—but true—things about her behind her back, or even in front of her face. She could argue with her about Heather's own personal merits as a bride for Philippe St. Pierre.

She did none of those things, ultimately deciding to ignore Mrs. Van der Linden's unflattering opinion of her. In that way, Heather thought smugly, she would show the old bat that she was superior to her.

After swallowing her bile and forcing her heart to quit slamming itself against her rib cage and unclenching her fists, she said sweetly, "I'm going to see how Jimmy's doing, Mrs. Van der Linden, and then I'll be going to town. Would you like me to procure anything for you while I'm there?" She gave the housekeeper a sweet smile along with her sweet question and hoped she'd gag on them both.

Mrs. Van der Linden stood on shaky legs and gripped the back of the chair tightly. "No."

Heather was interested to note that Mrs. Van der Linden had to force the next words out of her mouth. "Thank you."

Ah. That was better. The old hag was going to have to be nice to Heather if Heather was going to be Philippe's wife. And she'd hate it. That in itself was almost enough to make her forgive Mrs. Van der Linden for her hostility during the past several weeks.

She was actually humming a merry tune as she gathered up the breakfast dishes and carried them to the kitchen. Her merriness departed as soon as she saw D. A. Bologh, sitting on his accustomed chair, looking bored and glowering at her. She sighed, put the dishes on the counter, and said, "You're back."

He said, "Obviously."

"And have you decided what my payment is to be?"

"Yes."

Oh, dear. How unfortunate. Nevertheless, Heather had known all along that this reckoning day would come eventually. She was only glad she wouldn't have to give D. A. her body. Especially after last night with Philippe, she couldn't bear the thought of another man, and particularly this man, touching her intimately. She sat, too, folded her hands in her lap, braced herself mentally, and said, "All right. What do I owe you?"

"It's more complicated than that." D. A. sneered. As usual.

Heather frowned. "What do you mean, it's more complicated than that? You cheated, remember?"

A very faint rumble of thunder sounded in the distance, and Heather's heart skittered and bumped. She wished she hadn't brought up the cheating part.

He growled, "I remember," and it looked as though he'd heard the thunder, too.

"Sorry I mentioned it." He looked so ferocious, in fact, she pushed her chair back a foot or so.

"You should be. But I have selected a suitable payment."

"All right." Heather held her breath.

"And it's still you."

She jumped up from her chair, sending it crashing over backwards. "Now, you just wait a blasted minute here, Mr. D. A. Bologh. I'm not about to—"

He held up a hand to silence her, snickering as he did so. "Don't get all het up, sweetie pie. That's not all of it."

Scowling, not trusting him, Heather picked up the chair and sat again. "What's the rest of it?"

"The difference is, I'm going to give you a chance to get away scot-free."

"Oh?" She didn't believe him. "What do you mean?"

"I mean that if you're able to do two tiny little things, you won't owe me anything."

She squinted at him, sure there was something else to this latest offer. "You mean it? You won't exact any kind of payment, at all, ever, in any way, shape, or form, for doing my job for me during the last two months? If I do these two tiny little things?"

"Right. Precisely. You're not as stupid as you look, sweetheart."

Heather didn't grab the bait. She knew better by this time. "I think I'm going to want this agreement to be put down in writing, D. A. I don't trust you."

"Too bad, sweetie. I don't put things in writing. But you can trust me on this one. I don't have much choice."

It appeared to Heather as though D. A. was resentful at not being able to simply claim her, so perhaps he was telling the truth. "Hmm."

"Better accept it, Heather. I'm not going to make the offer again. This is your last chance."

"All right. What do I have to do?"

"I'm going to give you until the eve of your wedding day to discover who I am. That's the first thing. And then you have to convince the happy bridegroom. That's the second thing." He grinned wickedly.

"I beg your pardon?"

"You not only have to figure out who I am, sweetie pie, but you have to convince your dear Philippe of the same. It's a two-part deal. If you can do it, I'll go away and you'll never be troubled by me again. If you can't you're mine."

"I don't understand."

"You do, too. You're not really thick, Heather my love, whatever else you are. You heard me. If you can figure out who I am before your marriage to Mr. St. Pierre, *and* convince Mr. St. Pierre of it, you'll be free of me forever. You have to really convince him, you understand. He can't merely pay lip service to agreeing with you because he wants to humor you even though he thinks you're crazy. If you can't do both of those, you're *mine*." He reached out one of his pointy fingers and tapped her on the chin. "I've taken rather a fancy to you, dearie."

Shuddering at his touch, Heather jerked her head back. Good gracious, she couldn't even stand to be touched by his finger; how could she tolerate doing with him what she and Philippe had done? There was no way.

As if he read her thoughts, D. A.'s grin broadened. "It won't be so bad, sweetheart. I have any number of women who can testify to my skill."

"Ew."

D. A. stood, flicked a wrist, and the breakfast dishes were sparkling clean and stacked, ready to be put away. Another flick and they were gone, stashed, Heather knew, in neat rows in the cupboards. She blinked. She'd never get used to how he did things. "That's about it for me, sweetie. While you try to figure out my name, I'm going to leave you to your own devices in the kitchen."

"You mean, you aren't going to cook for me any longer?"

"That's right." He winked. "You'll do all right. In spite of yourself, you've learned a little. You'll never be as good as I am, of course."

Heather's heart reeled and staggered for a second before it straightened itself. "I'm sure of it." Oh, dear, what was she going to do? How could she cook without D. A. to help? Or do it for her?

"Oh, and there's one more thing."

Heather's dismal reflections skidded to a halt. D. A. seemed to loom over her as she sat there, staring up at him. She wished she'd never seen him. "What?" Blast, she'd croaked the word.

"You might have noticed certain odd things have been happening around here lately. If you figure out who I am, and if you do it in time, all of those things will stop. If you don't, I fear Fort Summers is in for a long siege of similar plagues."

Forgetting all about having to function as a cook on her own, Heather jumped up again, and this time she headed for D. A. Bologh with her fists flying. He caught them easily in his hands and held her at bay, but Heather was too shocked and furious to care. "You *are* the one who hurt my father! *You're* the one who cut the fences! My brother could have *died* last night. *Philippe* could have died! *Anyone* might have died! *You're* the one who's been causing all these things! You're the one! *Damn* you, D. A. Bologh!"

He'd started laughing when she'd first erupted from her chair. He laughed harder as she started screaming at him. By the time she was through and panting, unable to hurt him because he was preventing her, he was laughing so hard, it looked as if he were having trouble controlling his hilarity.

And then he was gone and Heather was standing beside the kitchen table, holding her arms out as if he were still there and still holding onto them.

She looked frantically around the kitchen. No D. A. Bologh.

The kitchen door opened. "What on earth is going on in here? Why are you shrieking, Heather Mahaffey? You sounded like a madwoman. Is that the sort of behavior your mother taught you?"

Heather whirled on Mrs. Van der Linden, her emotions riled so high, she wasn't sure she could control them. "Don't you dare say anything about my mother, Mrs. Van der Linden."

Evidently, Heather looked as menacing as she felt, because Mrs. Van der Linden drew herself up short, blinked several times, flapped her mouth once, turned tail, and exited the kitchen. She even allowed the door to slam after her.

Heather stared at the door for several moments before the rage drained out of her, and she sank into a chair.

"Who *is* he?" she whispered to the empty room.

No answer occurred to her and, after another minute or two, she felt strong enough to visit her brother, who was cheerfully telling a friend from town all about his hazardous exploits of the night before.

Then Heather gathered her shawl and bonnet, hitched the horses to the wagon, and set out for town.

Chapter Eighteen

Philippe's mood was remarkably light, considering the damage that had been done to his herd and his ranch the night before. Not only was the wind slumbering this morning—how long the peaceful condition would last was anybody's guess—but he was happy. Philippe hadn't been happy for so long, he couldn't even remember when the last time had been. Happiness, perceived as impossible, had long ceased to be a goal with him. He'd forgotten all about happiness as a state of mind. Until this morning.

Heather. He really did like her. A lot. In fact, he'd never felt about a woman the way he felt about Heather. He had an almost intolerable itch to attach her to his side permanently, and the sooner the better, for fear she'd slip away from him somehow. How odd that he should fear her absence. Could he be suffering from love?

"God, what an abysmal thought."

Gil McGill rode up, and Philippe greeted him much more cheerfully than Gil greeted him. Gil looked, in fact, almost green.

"What's the matter, Gil? Bad news?"

Gil wiped a bandanna over his sweaty forehead. "No worse than you'd already guessed, I imagine. We lost fifty head."

Philippe nodded. It wasn't good news, but it could have been much worse if they hadn't turned the stampede. "It's not as bad as it might have been."

"Yeah. And at least none of the men were hurt."

"Except Jimmy Mahaffey, but Heather tells me he's doing well this morning."

Gil grinned at last. "And he isn't quite a man yet, I reckon."

"No, but he's a brave little guy."

"That he is. All the Mahaffeys have spunk."

Spunk. What a wonderful word to describe his adorable Heather. "Right. So, what about the fences?"

"Got men out right now, fixing them. I can't figure out what happened. They shouldn't have given out like that. It's almost like somebody's been doing some of these things on purpose, Mr. St. Pierre. Like someone's trying to put you out of business. I swear, I don't know how else these things keep happening."

"Right. The thought's occurred to me more than once." But he didn't understand it either. Unless he was much worse at judging his fellow men than he thought he was, Philippe didn't know a soul who wished him ill. Unless . . . But that was absurd. His mother couldn't manage the sort of destruction his ranch had been prey to in recent weeks. Besides, why should she? She'd never bestirred herself for him—or against him—before; why would she come all this way to destroy him? It made no sense.

One of her men friends might be behind the trouble. He shook his head, trying to dislodge the notion.

"Anything the matter, Mr. St. Pierre?"

When Philippe glanced at Gil, he looked worried. "No. Just thinking." He didn't like the notion of Heather running into Yvonne in town, though.

Of course, she might have left town by this time, since she had to know he didn't want to see her. He'd made his unwillingness to resume any kind of relationship with her abundantly clear when he'd dragged Heather by force away from her.

A sharp pain in his chest made him frown. It wasn't guilt. Couldn't possibly be. What did *he* have to feel guilty about? It must be—indigestion. Yes. That was it.

"Are you sure you're all right?" Gil asked. "You don't look so good all of a sudden."

"I'm fine," Philippe snapped. Then, repentant for having barked at Gil, he said, "A little indigestion is all."

Gil's eyebrows arched. "Heather's cooking's finally getting to you, huh? Nobody thought it'd take this long, to tell the truth. The boys have been taking bets on when you'd give up on her. She's pretty, and she's a great rider and roper, and she's true-blue and about the best pal a fellow could have, but she can't cook for beans."

Philippe turned in his saddle and eyed Gil carefully for a moment, believing at first that the boy must be making a joke. A critical survey of Gil's trustworthy face told him it wasn't a joke. "I believe you've been misinformed, Gil. I've never eaten so well in my life as I have since Miss Mahaffey—Heather—came to work for me."

Gil's astonishment appeared genuine. "Honest to God? Well, I'll be kicked. I didn't think she'd ever learn to cook. Her brother Jerry used to keep us in stitches talking about her accidents in the kitchen, and her ma all but gave up on her after she poisoned the dog."

"She poisoned a dog?"

Gil shrugged. "She didn't mean to. Hell, Heather loves dogs. And the dog didn't die. She just put the wrong ingredients into its food, and it was sick for a good long time."

"Hmm. She must have improved considerably." Philippe frowned, wondering how Heather could have come by such an undeserved reputation as a bad cook. A person couldn't be so bad a cook that her brother talked about her one day and turn into a premier chef the next. Or, at least, it didn't seem likely.

He recalled her preposterous story about another person cooking for her and shook his head again. He didn't have time to think about cooking, for God's sake.

However, as long as Gil was here, he might as well let him in on the news. "You might be interested to know that Miss Mahaffey has agreed to marry me, Gil."

"She *what*?" Gil gaped at Philippe, who didn't take it kindly.

"Yes." His voice was frigid. "Is that so surprising? I suppose I'm as good a catch as the next man."

Gil's mouth shut with a clank. "Oh, yes, sir. You're a better catch than most, if it comes to that. It's only that I didn't think Heather'd ever get herself hooked."

"No?" Philippe was accustomed to looking upon marriage from the perspective of a possible hookee, not the one doing the hooking. It was an odd concept and took some getting used to. "And why is that?"

Gil shrugged. "She's so blamed independent. She even used to tell fellows who tried to court her that she was happy being single, thank you very much—she'd say that, 'thank you very much,' all snippy like—and didn't aim to let a man drag her down."

"She said that? She didn't want a man to drag her down?" How strange. Philippe was certain Heather loved her father; how could she say a thing like that if she loved him? Unless she was even more clearheaded than he'd heretofore given her credit for being. Something else to think about.

"Yep. I think it's 'cause of her pa, don't you know. She'll never say so, but I think she's always felt sort of sorry for her ma, because Mr. Mahaffey don't keep the family as well as he might, if you know what I mean. Mr. Mahaffey's a hell of a good talker, and he's as nice as they come, but he's kind of worthless."

"I know what you mean."

"That's why she'd never let any of the boys get serious. And they all wanted to at one time or another. Even me." Gil blushed.

Philippe said, "I'm a fortunate man."

"You sure are."

Gil was shaking his head, ruminating, Philippe presumed, about the perversity of a fate that would allow Heather to accept a newcomer over a local lad, when he and Gil came upon three of his men who had been working since dawn, repairing a huge stretch of fencing that had been trampled the night before by terrified cattle.

Fences were tolerably new to the territory, and most of Philippe's range land was open. Because of the weather and the fact that the men had begun rounding up the beeves for the summer cattle drives, however, a good portion of his herd had been driven closer to the ranch, into enclosed pasture land. The cattle were easier to keep track of when they were bunched together, but they were also more prone to touchy behavior. They'd proved it again last night when they'd stampeded during the storm.

"It's looking good, men. Take time off to eat and drink something. Gil and I can take over for a while."

The men were glad to oblige. Philippe knew he was considered a good boss by those who worked for him, and he took satisfaction, not untainted by cynicism, from the knowledge. The truth was that he treated his employees as he himself would like to be treated if their situations were reversed. He also knew that, but for the grace of God—or whatever benign spirit reigned over the universe when the malevolent spirits were sleeping—their situations *might* be reversed. Philippe had a good deal of respect for the chanciness of life.

Which made him think of Heather. Which made him begin whistling without realizing it until he glanced over at Gil and found him smiling. Damn. He used to be better at hiding his emotions than this. He stopped whistling.

"Geeze, the cows did a good job on this fence," muttered Gil at one point, when he was trying to salvage fence posts and unwrap wire.

"Yeah. They didn't leave much but trash behind."

Gil shook his head as he gazed at a shattered stake. "There's blood on this one. Reckon some poor cow got her leg scratched good."

"I expect."

Philippe hoped Gil wouldn't continue to talk, because his ears had picked up something that didn't sound right to him. Fortunately, Gil decided to use his energy on the job and not on his mouth, because he didn't speak again, but began untwisting wire from fence posts.

Mon dieu, there it was. Very quietly, Philippe said, "Don't move, Gil. Be very still."

"Beg pardon?" Gil straightened and looked a question at Philippe.

The movement was enough to set the rattler off. In the split second before he shot his hand out, Philippe saw it dart its head toward Gil's leg. He could hardly believe it when he straightened, gripping the snake's body right beneath its diamond-shaped head.

Gil gaped at him, horror-stricken. "Holy cow. You just up and grabbed that thing." He stopped goggling at the snake and goggled at Philippe. "You saved my life, Mr. St. Pierre. Damned if you didn't save my life. That damned snake might have bit you."

Philippe's heart had jumped right straight to his

throat, where it seemed to be lodged too firmly to allow him to speak. He didn't answer, therefore, until he'd grabbed his knife out of its scabbard and, with one clean cut, sliced the rattler's head off. Because the fangs could still poison a man or an animal even after the snake was dead, he crushed the head under his boot heel, shuddering slightly on the inside as he did it. He respected the territory, but it was a damned hard place. Everything in it either pricked, stung, bit, or stabbed if you weren't watching out for it every minute. It kept a fellow on his toes with a vengeance.

He also felt uncomfortable with Gil's overt appreciation. Because of it, he held the snake, a good five-footer, out to Gil. "Want the skin for a souvenir? I hear snake makes good eating."

"I've heard that too, but I'd have to be awful hard up before I'd eat me a snake."

Philippe chuckled, glad for an excuse to let out some of the energy that had blocked up inside him. "Me, too." Something that might or might not be brilliant occurred to him. "Say, I'll wager Jimmy Mahaffey would like a rattlesnake skin. What do you think?"

Gil was breathing hard, a condition Philippe was glad to see. He didn't want to think he was the only one who'd been affected by what might possibly have been a deadly encounter.

"I think it's a real good idea, Mr. St. Pierre. If you don't mind, I'll skin it and take it to him. I want him to know his sis is marrying a brave man."

Gil stuck his gloved hand out, and Philippe shook it, feeling foolish. "Don't give me too much credit," he advised dryly. "It was mostly luck."

"I don't buy that for a minute. That was quick

thinking, and ever quicker acting. I never saw anybody move that fast and that straight." He took the beheaded rattler and shuddered visibly. "Lordy, I hate these things." He shook the rattles, which made a dry, rustling sound in the still air. "But at least they warn you. Guess my ears aren't as good as I thought they were."

"You were listening to wire scraping against wood at the time. That's why you didn't hear it."

"I reckon."

The two got back to work without further discussion. That's another thing Philippe had noticed about the territory. The folks in it didn't bother repeating themselves. He'd saved Gil's life. Gil was grateful. That's all that needed saying. Jimmy Mahaffey would have a superior snake skin to tack on a wall somewhere. And Heather would be proud of him.

Before Philippe knew it, he was whistling again.

Heather paid a nice visit to her folks, taking tea and bread and jam in the kitchen with them. Her father's arm was healing nicely, Henry would be up and about any day now, and Mrs. Mahaffey had even been able to pay Doc Grady.

"How'd that happen?" Heather was so surprised, she let jam drip on her skirt and had to go to the sink to rinse it out.

Her mother put a hand to her mouth. "Oh, dear, I wasn't supposed to tell you yet."

Turning, Heather peered at her mother as she blotted the splotch on her skirt. "Tell me what?"

Mrs. Mahaffey heaved a sigh. "It's nothing, dear. It's only that it sounds so strange. But he said it wasn't charity. He said he doesn't believe in giving charity. Got quite touchy about it, in fact."

"Who? What are you talking about?" Heather had a niggling notion that Philippe's name was going to crop up any second now. She couldn't imagine how he could have finagled a way to help her parents financially. Both of her parents were too proud to accept money for nothing.

"I'm such a dolt. I knew I couldn't keep it a secret." Mrs. Mahaffey's blue eyes were brighter than Heather had seen them in a long, long time. "But he made it all sound so reasonable."

Wishing the woman would spit it out, Heather nevertheless made herself sound patient when she said, "Who made what sound reasonable?"

"Mr. St. Pierre."

Aha. She'd known it. "What did he do?"

"He said that it was because of Jimmy's accident that the cattle turned during the stampede. He said that it was due to Jimmy's intervention that he didn't lose the whole herd in the Pecos."

"He said that, did he?" If he'd made that big whopper sound reasonable, he must be more of a silver-tongued rogue than Heather'd figured him to be—and she'd already figured him to be a good one.

"Yes. He sent the message via the Billings boy, the one who rode over here last night with the news."

"Sandy Billings? He gave that message to you?"

Mrs. Mahaffey nodded. "Yes. He said Mr. St. Pierre is the fairest man he knows, and the best boss; he doesn't lie—tell stretchers, is the way Sandy said it—and, therefore, it must be true."

Heather guessed there was no arguing with that kind of logic. Not that she wanted to argue. What she wanted to do was throw her arms around Philippe St. Pierre and tell him how much she loved him. She always wanted to do that, but hearing of this latest bit of benevolence—offered as if it were nothing more nor less than an everyday occurrence—intensified the feelings.

The only reason she didn't tell her mother that she and Philippe were going to marry was that she couldn't quite make herself believe it yet. She wondered if that signified a failing in her nature, or if she thought Philippe had lied to her. She suspected the former.

She left shortly after the conversation, spurred on her way with a kiss from both parents, a snarl from her brother, who was tired of being laid up, and a sack full of jams, jellies, preserves, and half of an applesauce cake. She was feeling pretty good about life, except for one rather blackish aspect of it, when she guided the wagon back through town.

The beautiful woman who'd stepped down from the stage the last time Heather'd come to town caught her attention by stepping slap in front of the wagon while Heather was daydreaming. The horses almost knocked her over before Heather, shocked, pulled them up short. Good gracious! That had been close.

She leaned out of the wagon. "I'm sorry, ma'am. I didn't see you walking across the street."

Pulling a gorgeous red silk shawl tightly to her shoulders, the woman walked out from in front of the horses and went to Heather's side. "It wasn't your fault. I wanted to meet you." She had a voice as beautiful as her shawl. It was deep and rich and velvety and contained musical overtones. Heather wished her voice was like that.

"You wanted to meet *me*?" Unbelieving, Heather pointed at her chest.

The woman nodded and said, "Yes. If you don't mind."

"Mind? Of course I don't mind." Shoot, Heather'd been wanting to learn the woman's story—and what she was to Philippe—ever since she'd first set eyes on her.

"Would you care to come up to my hotel room? I would appreciate it. I—don't like to be out of my room very much."

"Wouldn't mind at all," Heather said briskly. She clucked to the horses and drew them up alongside the boardwalk. This was all very curious. She couldn't wait to find out all about it.

Although, she thought a moment later as she followed the woman into the hotel and up the stairs, she wished she'd dressed better for the occasion. Not that she'd known ahead of time that there'd be this occasion. But that woman, and the way she was dressed, and the way she carried herself, and her beauty and elegance weren't exactly calculated to make Heather feel awfully feminine. In truth, they made her feel like a lump. Since folks had been praising Heather's looks since she was a baby, feeling lumpish was a new and unpleasant sensation to her.

But that was stupid. Looks weren't worth a hill of beans in the overall scheme of things. Heather told herself that at least fifty times before they'd made it to the woman's door.

She glanced around curiously as she entered. Whoever this person was, she'd fixed this room up as if she aimed to live in it forever.

"Please," said the woman, "take a chair. I must

introduce myself, but first I want you to know that I only want the best for you."

"Thank you." Now that, to Heather's mind, was an odd way to begin a conversation. "Likewise, I'm sure."

The woman sat in a chair facing Heather—if *sat* was the proper word. In truth, she sort of sank into it gracefully, as if she'd been taught the fine art of sitting in some kind of school. Maybe that's what girls learned in finishing school. Heather didn't know anyone who'd been to a finishing school. Since the woman seemed a little uneasy, Heather smiled at her.

"You are Miss Heather Mahaffey, aren't you?"

Heather blinked at her. "Yes, I am."

The woman nodded. "Yes, I knew it was you. You were pointed out to me."

"I was?" Heather wasn't sure she approved.

"Yes. You see, I came here to find you."

"You did?"

It was disconcerting that the woman seemed so intent upon her. Heather found herself wondering again if this person was a former lover of Philippe's, and if she had come all the way to the territory from wherever she'd originated to eliminate a rival. The notion wasn't a happy one, and Heather decided it was time she took steps. She sat up straight, lifted her chin, and said, "You know my name, but I fear I don't know yours. It is?"

And she smiled the most winning smile in her repertoire. It was her, "I'm as good as you and anyone else in the world, and you can't intimidate me" smile. She'd found it most effective when dealing with men. For some reason, men seemed to feel that, because of their gender, their intellects were superior to those of women. Heather knew good and well that was poppycock. The smile came in handy today, too.

The woman tightened her lips—not, Heather thought, in anger, but in some combination of fear and perplexity. This whole situation was extremely odd.

Rising from her chair and taking a turn about the room, the woman kneaded her hands together. "I wish I could offer you some sort of refreshment, Miss Mahaffey. This is a hotel room, however, and I can't."

"I don't need refreshment," Heather murmured. She could sure use a dose of information, though. She'd just about decided the woman hadn't come to Fort Summers to do her in; rather, she seemed to be in some kind of distress. "I would certainly like to know your name, though." She said it kindly, because she sensed the woman needed kindness.

The woman turned and sucked in a deep breath. She let it out in a whoosh and, along with it, blurted out, "My name is Yvonne St. Pierre."

"Oh." Heather went numb for a moment before she had a brilliant idea. This woman was Philippe's sister! Why, they looked so much alike, Heather was surprised she hadn't thought of it before. They must have had some sort of family spat and lost track of each other. Now, Yvonne was here to mend fences and—

"Philippe is my son."

Heather's tumbling thoughts crashed to earth and left her blank. Not only couldn't she think of a thing to say; she couldn't think at all. She could only stare.

Yvonne took note of her astonishment and produced a grim smile. "It's the truth, Miss Mahaffey. I gave birth to Philippe thirty-three years ago, in New Orleans." She paused, took another deep breath, and added, "I'm sure he's never spoken of me. He's—not very proud of his heritage."

She'd been dazed by Yvonne's astounding news, but Heather rallied at that bit of information. More or less. She exclaimed, "But you can't be his mother. You're younger than he is!"

That wasn't very polite, and she knew it as soon as the words had spilled out of her mouth. She was still too fuddled to think properly, but she tried. "That is to say, I can't believe anyone as young and beautiful as you could possibly be Philippe's mother. I mean, Mr. St. Pierre's mother. I mean, well, I call him Philippe, because we're to be married, you see, and—and—"

She jerked with alarm when Yvonne rushed to her, fell on her knees in front of her, and grabbed her hands. Her dark, gorgeous eyes were passionate, and Heather was uncomfortable to see tears standing in them.

"That's the reason," Yvonne said, in a low, intense voice. "That's the reason I came here. It will mean certain doom for me, but I had to save him. And you! I had to save you! It may already be too late, but I've made it safely this far. If I can only make you understand, perhaps together we can stop him."

The tears spilled from her eyes and coursed down her perfect cheeks. "If we can't stop him, Philippe's life will be ruined, as mine was. It's all my fault, and I can't bear it. It's one thing if a person's past comes back to haunt them, but when I realized my past was endangering my son and the woman he loves, I had to do something! I had to!"

Heather began to wonder if Philippe had left New Orleans because of his mother's—no, no. His *sister*'s insanity. Maybe this was his sister after all.

"Er, and what was it you thought you had to do?" Heather used her most soothing tone, hoping to calm the agitated woman. The good Lord knew, she didn't want her to get violent or anything.

Yvonne stood up again, and wiped her cheeks with a perfect hand. Everything about her was perfect. Heather had never seen a woman so perfectly perfect. She felt rather inadequate standing next to her, actually, although she would never let on.

"I have to stop him."

Heather sighed. "Yes, you said that before, that you have to stop him. Whom do you have to stop?" She offered another smile, this one her "I'm really trying to be encouraging here" smile.

"The man who ruined my life. He's trying to ruin Philippe's life now, and yours, and I have to stop him before he accomplishes his job." Yvonne turned abruptly and started pacing again. It hurt Heather's heart to watch her, she was in such obvious anguish.

Yvonne whirled around, making Heather start in her chair. "He's already done so much evil here!"

"He has?" Heather wished she knew what the woman was talking about.

Yvonne nodded. "I've heard. People have told me. He's caused accidents, even here in the village, and he's stampeded Philippe's cows and broken his fences and done all sorts of terrible things. He's made the devil winds blow until the whole town is going crazy."

It sounded to Heather as if Yvonne were talking about God, although she wouldn't say that, either. But who else was in charge of the weather and random accidents?

The extremely localized thunderstorm she and D. A. Bologh had experienced recently burst into Heather's brain, and she frowned. This was all terribly confusing. "Um, who is this 'he' you're talking about, Mrs. St. Pierre?"

"Mrs. St. Pierre?" Yvonne stopped her agitated striding about and gaped at Heather. Then she threw her head back and laughed.

What in thunder was the matter with the woman? Heather was not amused. After several seconds of watching Yvonne and listening to what sounded like her hysterical laughter, Heather rose from her chair. Feeling stiff, uncomfortable, and peeved, she snapped, "I fear that unless you can make sense, I must be on my way, ma'am." She didn't offer any of her practiced smiles when she said it.

Yvonne stopped laughing abruptly. She appeared startled and afraid. "Oh, no! You can't go! Not until I've told you everything."

Heather pressed her lips together for a second, then said, "I suggest you begin, then, because I have to get back to the ranch. I have meals to prepare." That almost wasn't even a lie any longer. Knowing it gave Heather a modicum of courage, and she didn't unbend an inch.

"Please," Yvonne pleaded. "You can't go yet. I have to talk to you. I'm sorry I've made no sense so far. But it's all so impossible to talk about—to understand."

Heather huffed impatiently. She knew it was impolite, but she'd never been long on patience. "Just spit it out, and we'll see if I can understand or not," she suggested, none too gently.

"Yes. Yes, I must do that," Yvonne murmured. "But please, sit."

Heather sat.

Yvonne did, too. "You see, Miss Mahaffey, when Philippe was a baby, I wasn't married. I was left in New Orleans, abandoned by Philippe's father."

Goodness, how shocking. And sad. Yet it didn't explain anything. Heather nodded to signify she understood Yvonne's plight, which had been a terrible one indeed.

"I was only sixteen years old, and I was beautiful, although beauty had never brought me anything but unhappiness."

She sounded bitter, and Heather was interested to note that what she'd believed through her life seemed to have been given a grain of confirmation. Beauty didn't mean squat in a world kept spinning by deeds.

Yvonne lowered her head and began fiddling with a pleat in her skirt. "I—took up employment in a house of ill repute."

Good gracious! Heather didn't know if she was more shocked than fascinated or the other way around. She didn't speak.

"It was the only work I could get, you see, because my heritage is mixed."

"Mixed heritage is nothing to be ashamed of. Most Americans are mixed." Heather didn't know if it was true or not, but she thought it might make Yvonne feel better.

Another harsh laugh from Yvonne's throat made Heather shrink inside.

"Thank you, Miss Mahaffey, but you don't know what you're talking about. If you don't mind my plain speaking."

"Of course not," said Heather, who did mind—very much.

"But there are different types of mixed ancestry. Some of my ancestors were African slaves, you see, and that makes all the difference to most people."

Good Lord! Heather could only gape.

"And the only employment I could procure was as a—courtesan."

"My goodness."

"Goodness didn't enter into it, I fear," Yvonne said dryly. "But that wasn't the bad part."

It wasn't? Heather couldn't imagine anything worse.

"My true downfall came when I met a man and made a bargain with him."

Heather's skin began to crawl and her heart to shrivel.

Yvonne looked her straight in the eyes. "His name was D. A. Bologh. And to him I sold my soul in return for eternal youth and beauty."

Chapter Nineteen

"Stay still," Heather hissed. "We'll never get you out of town unnoticed if you keep wriggling." She waved at Geraldine, who was sweeping the boardwalk in front of her father's store, and had just caught sight of the wagon.

"I'm trying." Yvonne's muffled voice came from underneath the horse blanket on the floor of the wagon. The woman sneezed.

"Hush! Do you want D. A. to catch us?"

"God, no. I think I'm allergic to horses."

"It's probably the dust. Hold your nose."

"I ab."

Heather's heart fell when Geraldine let out a whoop, dropped her broom, and began racing toward the wagon. "Bother. I'm afraid I'm going to have to pull up and talk to Geraldine. Try not to sneeze. Don't forget. Philippe is worth the sacrifice. We have to get to him before D. A. finds you."

"I doh."

Heather did feel pretty sorry for beautiful Yvonne, huddled there on the floor. She'd bet anything she owned, if she were ever to bet again, which she wasn't, that Philippe's mother had never endured a more uncomfortable ride in her life. And now she was going to have to suffer through Heather's conversation with Geraldine. Heather aimed to keep it short, and not merely in deference to Yvonne's comfort. She felt an irresistible compulsion to get back to the ranch and settle everything once and for all. She only hoped she, Philippe, and Yvonne would survive whatever confrontation ensued.

She and Yvonne had talked for two straight hours after Yvonne had made her startling confession. It hadn't taken much persuading on Yvonne's part to convince Heather that D. A. Bologh—and what a diabolical play on a name *that* was—was a minion of Satan.

"Diablo," said Yvonne with scorn. "He thinks he's so clever." In her faint accent—sort of like Philippe's only more French, Heather thought—Yvonne lifted scorn to an art form.

"Actually, he is pretty clever," said Heather, because she thought it was true.

"Bah!"

Nevertheless, D. A. had managed to rule Yvonne's life for more than thirty years. When Heather had pointed it out to her, she'd burst into tears, so Heather didn't rub her nose in it. Poor Yvonne had paid for her foolishness, many times over.

Now, however, the hard part was coming. They had to convince Philippe that D. A. Bologh was a demon. And Philippe didn't seem the sort who'd easily be persuaded that an otherworldly being was behind all the problems that had lately plagued his life.

Worse, perhaps—at least Yvonne thought so—would be to convince Philippe to associate with his mother again. Yvonne was skeptical, and was willing to leave Fort Summers and never see him again, as long as she accomplished her purpose. Heather, who couldn't tolerate the notion of family members being estranged from one another, was more optimistic. She knew how much Philippe didn't want to see this woman, however. Convincing him to reestablish a relationship with her was going to be hard, and she didn't try to fool herself on that score.

"Heather! Oh, Heather!" Geraldine was out of breath when she reached the wagon. Holding a hand to her thundering heart, she panted, "I heard the news. Oh, Heather, it's so exciting!"

Heather tried to be glad for her friend's presence and happiness. "H'lo, Geraldine. I don't have much time." That was rude. Heather would have been ashamed of herself if a whole bunch of people's lives weren't hanging in the balance.

"You surely have time to accept my good wishes," Geraldine said, sounding a trifle put out.

Heather pressed a hand to her head. "I'm sorry, Geraldine. I've just been in such a—a dither today." That sounded right; any woman would be in a dither if she were going to marry Philippe St. Pierre.

"Oh, Heather!" Geraldine put a hand on Heather's arm. "It's so thrilling! I'm so happy for you."

"Thank you, Geraldine." Feeling contrite, Heather decided she could spare a few minutes for her best friend.

Yvonne sneezed. The sound came, fuzzy, from the floor of the wagon.

Geraldine stepped back a pace. "What was that?"

"I, ah, sneezed," said Heather lamely. To argument her lie, she sneezed. Her sneeze didn't sound the least little bit like Yvonne's.

"That wasn't you before," Geraldine said flatly.

Feeling bedeviled and at her wits' end, Heather said, "Yes, it was."

"It couldn't have been you. Your lips didn't move."

Heather huffed. "Oh, for heaven's sake, if that's all you have to say to me, I'll be getting along now."

"Heather Mahaffey, what's the matter with you?" Geraldine looked accusingly at her. "Just because you're about to marry a rich man doesn't mean you're going to get too big for your britches, does it?"

"No. Of course not." Heather sought about in the jumble in her head for an excuse for her strange behavior, couldn't find one to save herself, and decided she'd have to make it up to Geraldine later. "Listen, Geraldine, I'm a little distracted today. I'm really sorry, but I have to get back to the ranch."

Yvonne sneezed.

Heather said grimly, "Now." She flicked the reins, clucked to the horses, and left Geraldine in a puff of dust. When she glanced over her shoulder, she saw her friend staring after the wagon in befuddlement, waving dust from her face with her hand. "Lord, she'll probably never speak to me again."

"I'll nebber breathe again."

"Sorry. I'll try to hurry, but that'll only kick up more dust."

Yvonne groaned.

It was about a half hour later, and they'd driven about two miles outside of the village limits, when Heather said, "I think it's safe now."

"Thank God."

Heather watched Yvonne throw the blanket back, and felt sorry all over again. "Shoot, you're really a mess."

Her dark eyes snapping, Yvonne frowned as she struggled up from the floor and onto the wagon seat. "You'd be a mess too, if you'd spent an hour on the floor of this ghastly thing."

"I know. I wasn't casting aspersions, just mentioning it."

"Humph." Yvonne began slapping her skirts in a futile effort to get the dust out.

Heather shook her head. "You'll never get it clean that way. You'll have to wash it. There's a wash house at the ranch where you can wash yourself and your clothes both."

"Wash my own clothes?"

Yvonne sounded as if she'd never heard such a preposterous suggestion. Heather gazed at her, surprised. "You mean you didn't have to wash your own clothes in New Orleans?"

"Of course not." Yvonne looked peeved. "I had servants to do those things for me."

"I see." Wondering if Yvonne was truly cut out for life in the territory, Heather drove in silence for several minutes. "Um, do you think you'll want to go back to New Orleans after this whole thing is over?"

With a very French-looking shrug, Yvonne said, "I don't know. Probably not. I imagine D. A. will have destroyed any remnants of my life in New Orleans by this time."

She was quiet for a minute. Heather shook her head and murmured, "I'm really sorry, Yvonne."

Another shrug and more silence. Then, in a voice that was straining to keep steady, Yvonne said, "It doesn't matter. I wouldn't be able to go back to work anyway, because if we succeed, I imagine I'll begin to look my age. If I'm allowed to live through it."

Good gracious, that's right. Heather stared at Yvonne for a few seconds, appalled by the options facing her companion. She licked her lips. "Um, maybe it won't be so bad." Feeble. Very feeble. It would, too, be so bad, and Heather knew it as well as Yvonne did. "That's silly. Of course it will be bad."

"Yes. I'm sure it will."

"But, Yvonne, listen, you won't have to worry about where to go or where to live. You can stay here. With us. At the ranch." Was that presumptuous of her? Perhaps, but if Philippe was too stubborn to help his mother after she'd sacrificed her entire life for him, then Heather wasn't sure she wanted to marry him at all.

That was stupid, too. She loved him. Of course she wanted to marry him. No matter what.

Which left her with only one option. She'd have to convince Philippe to accept his mother and to acknowledge D. A. Bologh as the devil.

What could be easier?

It was all Heather could do to keep from whimpering.

* * *

Philippe downed a shot of brandy and growled, "Where the hell is she?"

Mrs. Van der Linden looked shocked. "I'm sure I don't know, Mr. St. Pierre."

Philippe didn't care if Mrs. Van der Linden was shocked or not. He needed to see Heather. She'd been gone all damned day long, and he was getting worried. Too many strange things had been going on around here for him to be comfortable when one of his employees was late getting back from a trip.

Not, naturally, that he cared about Heather any more than he cared about any of his other employees. She was, however, the woman he'd chosen to marry, and he hadn't become tired of her yet. That's the only reason he was feeling snappish about her being late. He wasn't truly going soft; he knew better than that.

Mrs. Van der Linden sniffed and said, "She's always been an irresponsible chit, Mr. St. Pierre. You can't expect her to change just because you've gone daft and asked her to marry you."

He turned to stare at her, and from the expression on Mrs. Van der Linden's face, Philippe imagined he looked as furious as he felt. He really, really didn't like Mrs. Van der Linden. And he especially didn't like the way she was always belittling Heather.

"That is to say," Mrs. Van der Linden said hastily, "that in her younger days she was heedless. I'm sure she's changed considerably."

"Yes," he said. "She has. And since she's soon to become your mistress, I suggest you begin to speak of her with the respect she deserves."

Her face draining of color, Mrs. Van der Linden said, "Yes, sir," and escaped before Philippe could throw anything at her.

"Damned woman," he muttered, refilling his glass. He wished his heart would stop careening about in his chest. It was very uncomfortable, and it was a direct result of Heather's tardiness. He'd have to speak to her about adhering to some kind of schedule.

He strode to the mantel, picked up the big clock sitting there, and held it to his ear. It hadn't run down. That's one thing Mrs. Van der Linden was good for: winding clocks. However, if it hadn't run down, then Heather was past her time by a couple of hours at least, and Philippe was getting more and more fidgety as the seconds passed. He was on the verge of giving up any pretense of patience and haring out toward town to find her when he heard the wagon rumble into the yard.

Fearing it wasn't Heather and hoping it was, he raced out of his office, down the hall, and to the front door, getting there a scant second ahead of Mrs. Van der Linden, who turned on her heel and hurried off in the opposite direction. Philippe sped her on her way with a ferocious scowl.

His heart lightened by at least a ton when he saw Heather in the driver's seat. He squinted into the gathering dusk when he realized she'd brought a passenger with her.

That was all right with him, as long as Heather was safe. Perhaps she'd brought Geraldine Swift from town to help nurse her brother. Or maybe her sister Patricia had insisted she be allowed to come to the ranch to care for Jimmy. Or it might even be her mother, who felt a compelling need to see to her son's—

"Merde!"

Philippe stopped dead in his tracks when he recognized the woman sitting on the wagon bench with Heather. It wasn't *her* mother. It was *his* mother.

In a heartbeat, his rage returned, bringing along all of its enraged relatives. He stormed the rest of the way to the wagon.

"Hello, Philippe." Heather gave him her brightest smile. "I'm sorry I'm so late. You see, I met your—"

Her explanation ended in a screech when Philippe grabbed her around the waist and hauled her out of the wagon. She dropped the reins and the horses shuffled nervously. Yvonne gasped and clutched the wagon seat.

"Stop it!" Heather cried. "Before you go off in an apoplexy, at least let me explain!"

She began battering him on the back with her fists and wriggling so much that Philippe finally set her down—not very gently—in the dirt yard. He was so angry, he could barely see straight, much less talk. Fortunately, Heather didn't suffer from his affliction.

"What's the matter with you, Philippe St. Pierre?" she hollered, obviously mad as thunder. "I brought Yvonne to the ranch because we both have something vital to talk to you about."

Towering above her, Philippe felt akin to a black cloud hovering. She glared right back at him, though, so he clearly wasn't as intimidating as he wished he were. Because he knew he had to do it some day, he transferred his glare to his mother.

She looked frightened. Good. She deserved to be frightened.

"For heaven's sake, Philippe," Heather continued. "Stop being silly about this. Do you think I'd have done this—knowing how much you'd hate it—just for fun? This is important. You *have* to talk to us, whether you want to or not."

She was trying to keep her voice down—Philippe was pretty sure she'd like to yell at him—but some of his men had been attracted by her initial screech. Several of them had wandered out from the bunkhouse. A couple of them seemed to have been stricken dumb by his mother, who looked like she wanted to hide away somewhere and cry, and were gaping, wide-eyed, at her. He thought savagely that perhaps he should hand her to his men and let them take turns. That's what she was good at, after all.

Heather poked him in the chest with her finger, and he turned his attention back to her. She was sure furious. So was he. He was, however, having a difficult time keeping his anger at Heather cranked up to a proper pitch. He was so damned glad she was here, and safe, that it took a good deal of energy to stop himself from crushing her in a huge hug of relief and then carting her off to bed, and to hell with supper. Making love to her all night would be much more fulfilling than eating.

Through his teeth, he said, "Stop yelling, dammit. Get that woman into the house. She's making a spectacle of herself." Which was silly. Yvonne was only sitting there, trying to be invisible. Philippe was, however, in no mood to be rational. "I'm not eager to create a scene in front of my men."

"You can at least stop being hateful," Heather huffed.

"Hateful?" If she only knew. God, if she'd been with Yvonne all afternoon, maybe she already did. "Get her the hell into the house, Heather. Now."

She chuffed angrily. "Very well, but you'll have to let me go first."

He did.

"I'll probably have bruises for a week." She rubbed her upper arms and gazed sternly up at Philippe.

He didn't feel guilty. "Hurry up. I don't want my men exposed to her." He said it spitefully, as if he feared his mother carried some deadly, disgusting plague. He hoped Yvonne had heard him. As far as Philippe was concerned, his mother *was* diseased. And disgusting. And probably deadly.

"That's a horrible thing to say!" Heather cried.

"It's the truth." And Philippe turned on his heel and stormed back to the house. He didn't look to the right or to the left, and he was pretty sure his men—those who weren't gaping at his mother—were staring at him as if he'd lost his mind.

He felt as if he had. His mother. His *mother*! And *Heather* had brought her! God, he couldn't stand it.

Heather stared after Philippe for a moment, then walked over to Yvonne, who was huddled on the wagon seat, looking unhappy and ashamed. Heather didn't blame her much. Philippe had been a beast.

True, he believed he had a right to dislike his mother. And if she were to be honest with herself, Heather guessed he had cause. Yvonne had admitted to being a bad mother: selfish, self-absorbed, more concerned about herself and her beauty than her son. Nevertheless, Heather had a feeling Yvonne had done her best under unmerciful circumstances.

Heather Mahaffey wasn't one to cast stones at others for making mistakes. She'd made plenty of her own. And if she'd been in Yvonne's position, she might have done the same thing. After all, Yvonne had been alone in the world, and Philippe's father had talked a good story—according to Yvonne. It wasn't poor Yvonne's fault for believing the louse.

Heather huffed and told herself to think about it later. Right now she had to get the horses taken care of and Yvonne into the house. And, since Heather wasn't Philippe and didn't hate Yvonne's heart, liver, and gizzard, she aimed to do those two things in the proper order.

Glancing around, she noticed Gil McGill standing a few yards off, goggling from Yvonne to Heather and back again. His gaze seemed to get stuck on Yvonne for longer than it did on Heather. Heather pursed her lips and told herself she didn't care. "Gil, can you get the horses taken care of? I have to get Mrs.—er, I mean Miss—Oh, blast. I have to get this lady inside."

Gil jerked out of his trance. "Huh? Oh, yeah, sure, Heather."

"Thank you." She held up a hand for Yvonne. "Here, Yvonne. I'll help you down. Please try not to think about what Philippe said. I'm sure he didn't mean it." Those words were not only hopeless, but probably moronic as well, and she knew it. Nevertheless, she tried to make her tone of voice kind and encouraging.

Yvonne wasn't buying it. "He meant every word." She sounded very discouraged. Yet she took Heather's hand and climbed down from the wagon seat. She plainly wasn't accustomed to such rude conveyances, and she stumbled and nearly fell flat on her face. Not that she would have damaged her clothing any, since it was already filthy from having spent so much time on the floor of the wagon. She was graceful, though, and righted herself almost immediately.

"I'm so sorry to have brought all of this trouble on you, Heather," Yvonne said in a strangled voice. "You're a lovely young woman, and you don't deserve it."

"Fiddlesticks," said Heather briskly. She'd been thinking something of the sort herself, but Yvonne had enough to worry about. Besides, Heather had gotten herself into this mess all on her own. If D. A. Bologh had come to Fort Summers in a premeditated attempt to ruin the last of Yvonne's life, Heather could have resisted temptation. She hadn't, and now they had to figure a way out of the pickle she'd helped them get into.

She shoved the door open and allowed Yvonne to enter first. Gazing over the shorter woman's shoulder, Heather didn't see Philippe anywhere. He'd probably gone to his library. Heather had begun to think of the library as Philippe's throne room. He was probably sitting at his desk, looking regal and imperious. He always looked regal and imperious. When he was angry, as he was now, he also looked quite intimidating, but Heather was up to it.

Glancing at Yvonne, she changed her mind about what to do next. She'd been planning to lead Philippe's mother directly into a confrontation with him. But poor Yvonne was looking mighty bedraggled. Heather sensed that she'd feel more comfortable if she cleaned up first.

When she suggested it, however, Yvonne vetoed the notion. "No, thank you, Heather. We should get this over with."

"I suppose you're right." Heather wasn't looking forward to the confrontation.

She led the way down the hall to the office, Yvonne trailing behind, reluctant but determined. It seemed a shame to Heather that a mother should learn about her own son's life through the agency of the devil. She tried to clear her mind of the notion.

"After we get this mess taken care of, I'll give you a grand tour of the house and the ranch. It's really something. You should be proud of your son."

"I am. I'm sure he won't want me staying, though, and you mustn't try to force him to acknowledge any sort of relationship." Yvonne's voice carried a world of affliction.

The older woman's sorrow stabbed Heather's heart painfully. "Nonsense. Of course you'll stay. It's a beautiful place, and Philippe earned every scrap of it himself."

Yvonne mumbled almost inaudibly, "I'm sure of it. I certainly never helped him. He wouldn't have let me."

There was no winning this battle. Heather decided she wasn't going to tackle it at the moment. One battle at a time; that was the way to win a war. If they got through their encounter with D. A. Bologh unscathed—or at least unslain—then she'd contemplate how best to reconcile Philippe with his mother.

She knocked at the door of the office and jerked when Philippe's voice came hard and loud, "Enter."

Enter? Oh, dear. He was still mad. She smiled encouragingly at Yvonne, who wasn't fooled.

"I'm sure it will be fine," Heather said bracingly.

"No it won't. But we might be able to save his life and his life's work."

With a sigh, Heather gave up trying to instill optimism in Yvonne. Shoot, she couldn't even make herself be optimistic. She did, however, enter the office first, in case Philippe had a gun aimed at the door or something.

He didn't. Rather, he was sitting, as Heather knew he'd be, in his big leather chair, behind what looked like a sea of gleaming mahogany. He was also glaring with intense ferocity at the doorway.

Heather bridled. "You can stop frowning, Philippe. This is important."

Philippe ignored her, having caught sight of his mother. "What in the name of all that's holy are you doing here, at my home?"

"That's no way to talk to your mother, Philippe St. Pierre. I think you should—"

"Silence!"

His roar actually did silence Heather, something that had never happened to her before. She'd always been up to anything or anybody. This was different. She'd never before been faced with anyone as evidently unhappy as Philippe. She swallowed.

Yvonne put a hand on her shoulder. "Thank you,

Heather, but I don't want you to suffer for my sake." She turned and faced her son. "Philippe, I know you never wanted to see me again."

He snorted derisively.

Yvonne sucked in air. "But something has happened that requires you to listen very carefully to what I am going to tell you. You must believe me, son—"

"Son?"

Heather recoiled at the bitterness in his voice. She wanted to say something, to make him stop, but again Yvonne restrained her.

"I know you don't want to acknowledge the relationship, Philippe."

"I?" Philippe's dark eyebrows rose over his dangerously flashing eyes. "I think you have that backwards. Mother."

Heather had never heard the word *mother* sound like a curse word before this evening. She wished she'd been spared the privilege now.

Yvonne took another deep breath. "Yes, of course. You would believe that."

"Is there a reason I shouldn't?"

"No." Yvonne shook her head sadly. "You have every reason to hate me."

Philippe acknowledged her statement with a nod. Heather wanted to cry.

"But you still need to know the things I'm going to tell you."

"Then get on with it." He pushed himself back in his chair, until he was sitting in an insolently casual manner.

There still remained that huge chunk of mahogany between him and his mother. And Heather. She wanted to run to him and throw her arms around him and tell him everything would be all right if only he'd believe. But that was foolish, and she didn't.

Yvonne told Philippe her story, beginning when she herself was sixteen years old, pregnant, and having been abandoned by the man who had sworn his love for her. "That's when a person named D. A. Bologh showed up to ruin my life."

Philippe turned to Heather when Yvonne said D. A.'s name. She only nodded. Her throat was thick and aching, and she wasn't sure she could talk even if Philippe wanted her to, which she suspected he didn't.

After swallowing and clearing her throat, Yvonne continued. She told Philippe how she had bargained her soul away for the sake of youth and beauty. She threw out her hands in a gesture of despair. "It's the only way I knew, Philippe. I'm an octoroon. There's no other line of work open to people like me. You know it as well as I do."

Philippe didn't want to buy it. He still frowned. "In New Orleans. There are other places in the world to live."

Heather finally found her voice. "For a sixteen-year-old girl?" she asked indignantly. "And an octoroon?" Whatever that was. She still hadn't quite figured out the degrees of separation and which made a person what. As far as she was concerned, a person should be judged by what he did in the world, not how he looked in it.

"It's all right, Heather," Yvonne told her softly. "I have to do this."

Heather didn't like it, but she knew Yvonne was right. Because she was mad at him, she gave Philippe a good hot scowl, which he didn't acknowledge by so much as a lift of his eyebrow.

By the time Yvonne finished her story, she was in tears. Heather wasn't, but it was a struggle. Toward the end, she took Yvonne's hand to give her courage, and was rewarded by a grateful glance.

Silence loomed in the room when Yvonne's voice died out. The two women clutched each other's hands tightly.

After what seemed like several centuries, Philippe rose from his big leather chair. He pressed his palms flat on the gleaming mahogany of his desk and leaned over it until he looked like some avenging god out of mythology going to blast the earth to smithereens. Heather stood her ground with difficulty. Yvonne shrank back.

"That," said Philippe in a voice Heather had never heard from him before, "is the most asinine story I've ever heard. It's a pathetic attempt to make me take you into my life. And it won't work." He pointed at Heather. "This woman, who is worth at least a million of you, and I are going to be married as soon as may be." His eyebrows dipped suddenly. "Tomorrow. Tomorrow, we're going to town, and we're going to be united in holy matrimony. And you," he said, glowering ferociously at Yvonne, "are catching the stage. I don't care where you go. As long as you never darken my vision again. I'll give you money. That's probably why you came anyway."

Heather had been trying not to cower beneath the fury of Philippe's terrible edict. It was only when silence again reigned in the library that the full impact of his words hit her. Hard.

"Tomorrow?" Her voice squeaked.

"Mon Dieu," whispered Yvonne.

"But that means—"

Heather's explanation was cut off by a sudden intense howling of wind outside. The windows crashed open. Lightning rent the sky. Thunder boomed, shaking the house on its foundation. Yvonne screamed. Heather covered her ears. Philippe raced out from behind the desk and grabbed Heather close to his chest.

And D. A. Bologh appeared in the middle of the library floor, dressed all in red, from his hat to his shoes. He'd even grown a pointy beard.

He took in the astonished faces of those gathered there, threw back his head, and laughed.

Chapter Twenty

"This is insane," Philippe declared after he'd caught his breath. "Who the hell are you, and what are you doing in my house?"

"Ah, I do so love family reunions," D. A. said in his most sardonic voice. "They're always so touching."

Heather winced. "I haven't had time to explain it all to him, D. A. This isn't fair."

"Tut, tut, sweetie pie. I told you I'd give you until the eve of your wedding day. I reckon this is it." He shook his head in a mock show of sympathy. "It's a shame, but there it is."

"D. A., please," Yvonne pleaded. "No, don't do this. Please. Take me instead. Please!"

"I've already had you." Derision dripped from the words. "I want this fresh bit of goods for a while."

"No," whimpered Yvonne. "Not that. Please."

"Wait a damned minute," Philippe broke in, dominating the women into silence. "What in blazes is going on? Who are you?"

D. A. turned to Philippe and cast an appraising eye over him. "The name's D. A. Bologh, Mr. St. Pierre. My, you're a fine-looking man." He glanced at Yvonne. "Your son does you proud, Yvonne. You must be extremely pleased with him." He laughed again, a terrible laugh that reverberated through a room that seemed too small to contain it.

"Stop it!" Heather, still in Philippe's arms, clapped her hands over her ears.

"Get out of here," Philippe demanded. "Get out of here now, or I'll throw you out."

"My, my, aren't we fierce." D. A. smirked at Philippe. "Try it, why don't you?"

Philippe thrust Heather aside. "Gladly."

She screamed, "Philippe! No!"

Yvonne tried to stop him, but he shoved her to the floor. He reached out to grab D. A. Bologh, who didn't resist. As soon as Philippe's fingers touched D. A.'s arm, Heather saw him jerk back as if an electrical current had gone through him. He staggered backwards as if he'd been struck by lightning. She caught him before he could go down, and was horrified to feel his skin jump under her fingers.

"Stop it," she shrieked at D. A. "Stop it! We made our bargain, and this wasn't part of it. Don't hurt him. Please don't hurt him."

"D. A.," begged Yvonne. "Please don't hurt the children. They don't deserve it. I'm the one who deserves to be punished, not them."

"Honestly, you two." D. A. sneered. To Heather, he said, "We made a bargain, my pet, and it's time to pay up. Unless, of course, you've managed to convince Prince Charming here who I am."

"I haven't even had a chance to *talk* to him about it!" Heather cried.

"What a shame." D. A. sounded bored.

"I'll do it now. Please wait just another little minute, D. A." She was desperate by this time.

D. A. rolled his eyes. "I swear, my generosity will be the end of me. All right, sweetie pie—"

"Don't call her that!" Yvonne had managed to get to her feet. "You hateful wretch! Stop this!"

"Honestly, Yvonne, how you do carry on. You know better than that."

"Oh, God, please help us all," Yvonne moaned.

Philippe, still stunned, shook himself like a wet dog. When he spoke, his voice was ragged. "What in blazes is he talking about, Heather? Who is he?"

"That's the whole point, Philippe." Heather turned and grabbed him by the arms. In a voice tight with terror, she told him exactly who D. A. Bologh was. "He's the devil, Philippe. Or one of his minions. I bargained with him. He agreed to cook for me since I can't cook, and in return, I agreed to give him something. He didn't specify what, though, and when it came time to pay up, he said he was going to take me."

"What?" Philippe managed a fairly creditable roar, considering the state of his health. He tried to take a lunge at D. A., but Heather held him back. He was still weak, or she'd never have been able to do it.

She shook him as hard as she could. "Wait! Stay away from him. Don't you understand, Philippe? He's a *devil!* Your mother bargained with him when she was young and scared and poor. I bargained with him when I was—I don't know. Crazy, I guess."

D. A. snickered. "No insanity pleas in this court, sweetie. That rationalization is a hundred years away."

"What's he talking about?"

Philippe gazed down at Heather, and she was horrified to see the doubt and anger in his eyes. Lord, Lord, he wasn't going to believe her. She knew it in her heart. "Please, Philippe." She started to cry, in spite of the fact that she never, ever cried unless a family member was in peril. She loved him so much, and she'd die if she lost him. "Please, Philippe. Please pay attention to me. He's the *devil*. Can't you understand that? He's going to take me away unless you understand what's going on and believe me."

"She's telling the truth, Philippe," Yvonne put in hopelessly. "He ruined my life and yours, and now he's working on Heather. Then my ruin will be complete, don't you see? It isn't enough for him to destroy me. In order to exact perfect revenge, he needs to hurt the only person in the world I care about."

Philippe shook himself again, as if he were having trouble understanding anything anyone said. "And who's that?"

"You!"

"Don't make me laugh."

"Oh, Philippe, don't, please," begged Heather. "It's the truth."

"That's the stupidest thing I ever heard, Heather. I don't even believe in God. I'm sure as hell not going to believe this trickster is the devil."

"No!" shrieked Yvonne.

But it was too late. D. A. let out an ear-splitting bellow of evil laughter and snatched Heather away from Philippe. Philippe reached out to her, but D. A. slapped his hand away. He shouted, "Heather!" as he fell to the floor. He was crawling toward D. A. and reaching frantically to grab hold of a leg with which to hold him back, when D. A., Heather in his arms, leapt through the open window.

Philippe heard Heather scream before he fell, knocked back by D. A.'s inhumanly powerful arm.

Yvonne, sobbing as if her heart were breaking, raced to the window. At the top of her lungs, she screamed into the night sky, "Heather!"

Heather had never experienced anything like her ride through the air with D. A. Bologh. He held her tightly, but she struggled her arms free and battered at him with her fists. She was too furious to cry anymore. And she was too frightened to give up. She shrieked in his ear, "This isn't fair, D. A. Bologh!"

"You're just a sore loser." D. A. sounded smug. "You're only going to hurt yourself if you keep carrying on like that."

"Damn you!"

"Ha. Too late."

"But you're wrong! You aren't supposed to take me yet. It's not midnight. It's still the evening before my wedding day, and you're taking your reward too soon." Her heart almost stopped when she didn't hear an immediate sneering rejoinder. She'd grabbed that last bit out of thin air; she hadn't said it because she believed it.

When D. A. spoke at last, he didn't sound quite as smug. "It's midnight somewhere."

She thumped him hard. Not that anything she could do would ever hurt him. "It's not midnight *here*. And *here* is where I live. You're not being fair. You're cheating! Just like you did before."

"You're quibbling again."

"It's not quibbling! I haven't given up yet. You said I'd have until the day before my wedding, and the day hasn't ended yet."

"Balderdash."

"It isn't balderdash. I know who you are! And I haven't had a chance to persuade Philippe yet. You took me away before I could do it."

"Nonsense. The fellow will never believe in me. He said so. He doesn't even believe in God." D. A. laughed evilly. "A fellow who claims not to believe in God can't very well believe in me, can he?"

"He only said that because he—" She had been going to say that Philippe hated his mother, but she couldn't make herself do it. "Because he's mad at his mother."

"He hates her guts, my dear sweet thing. You don't have to act coy with me."

"If he does hate her, it's your fault," Heather grumbled.

D. A. chuckled. "This has been one of my best jobs so far. It's turning out exactly right."

"You're sick."

"Not sick, sweetie pie. Evil. There's a big difference, although it will become blurred in years to come."

"You're still cheating." She couldn't figure out where they were. She knew they were above the ground somewhere because she'd seen the roofs of the ranch house, bunkhouse, and outhouses as they'd sped by them. Now when she looked down she could detect the outline of a whole lot of cows. And there was one of Philippe's ranch hands, riding the fence, probably singing softly to the cattle. Anguish rose up in her when she contemplated never seeing this again. And never seeing Philippe. Sweet heaven, she *had* to get out of this!

"Cheating, ha." It wasn't very forceful, Heather was interested to note.

"You *are* cheating. It's not a new day yet. There must be hours left, and I should have this time to try to convince Philippe of who you are."

"Fudge."

In a surge of fury, she pounded him with her fists. "It's not fudge! You're a dirty, low-down, sneaky cheat, D. A. Bologh, and it's not fair!"

Suddenly D. A. screeched to halt, midair. Heather screamed and squinched her eyes up tight.

"Blast," D. A. muttered.

A huge, echoey voice that sounded to Heather as if it were being processed through some kind of very deep canyon, said, "She's right. You're cheating, Diablo." The voice didn't enter Heather's ears and end up in her brain; rather, it rolled through her entire body and lodged everywhere. It was an intensely creepy sensation.

D. A. heaved a huge sigh.

Scared to death, Heather managed to open her eyes to slits. At first she didn't see anything. When she looked down, she still saw the backs of lots of cows. It was a long way down, and she didn't look for long, but lifted her gaze and tried to discern what it was that had stopped D. A. so suddenly. That voice; she shuddered, still unable to discern any cause for D. A. to have stopped.

"No getting out of it, Diablo." Again, the voice reverberated throughout Heather's body.

"Pooh," muttered D. A. in a pouty tone.

"You're cheating," rumbled the other. Heather shuddered again.

"Oh, very well. I may have cheated a little bit. But only about the time of day." D. A. was obviously unhappy about this latest disciplinary action.

"We don't care for cheaters, Diablo," the voice spoke again, reverberating through the air and Heather like an echo.

Heather wished it wouldn't do that. The effect was awfully disconcerting.

"You've bungled this whole job badly. The boss doesn't like that."

D. A. growled and gnashed his teeth.

The voice disappeared, and Heather was left in the middle of the air, clutched in D. A. Bologh's arms, and wondering what in the world was going on. She cleared her throat. "Er, was that the boss?"

"No," D. A. snarled. "But we have to go back."

Thank God, thank God. Heather was too overcome with relief to say anything.

"But don't think you're off the hook, lovey, because you're not."

Heather had feared as much. Nevertheless, she was going to have another chance, and it was difficult to tamp down her elation.

Far from elated himself, Philippe St. Pierre dragged himself to the window, pulled himself up with arms that shook like elastic bands, and peered out into the blackness of the night. Heather was gone. Because of him. Because he'd been too damned stubborn and too damned angry to say he believed in the devil. Even though he didn't believe in the devil, he should have said he did.

It was obvious to him now, and should have been obvious before, that although D. A. Bologh was probably a wicked charlatan, he was a good one. Philippe should have said he believed. He hadn't, and Heather was gone.

He turned to see where his mother had gone and saw her huddled up on a chair, her face buried in her hands. He tried to drum up some of the resentment and fury against her that had driven him for so many years, but he was too weak. She lifted her face, white and drawn—and still impossibly young-looking—and peered at him. Philippe had never seen a human being appear so completely devastated.

She said, "It's my fault, Philippe. If I hadn't made that bargain with the devil all those years ago, you'd not have lost Heather."

Merely curious, Philippe asked, "Why did you do it?"

Yvonne held her arms out helplessly. "I perceived no other choice."

"Yes." He nodded. "I see." It made sense to him now. Life was a damned hard proposition. It was hard for men, and it was doubly so for women. And Yvonne had been right about the prospects available to people of color in the south. It was only luck that Philippe himself was light enough to pass as an interesting sort of white male. And if he'd been the slightest bit less judgmental all these years, maybe he'd have recognized the necessity of Yvonne's choice long since.

He hadn't, and now Heather was gone, and his

heart felt as if it had been ripped apart with a pitchfork. He hadn't even told her how much he loved her. He snorted, disgusted with himself. That had been his pride holding him back. What good was his precious pride now? Now that Heather was gone.

"Philippe?"

He turned, found his mother gazing at him with undisguised longing, and realized something else for the first time. Yvonne loved him. He was her son, and she loved him. She'd sold her soul to the devil so she wouldn't have to give him up. He closed his eyes for a moment, contemplating the orphanage in New Orleans he'd been supporting for so many years—during every one of which, he'd believed he'd have been better off if Yvonne had shucked him off to the nuns. What an ass he'd been.

"I'm sorry, Mother." He stood on legs that still felt as if they were supported by water rather than bone, and held out a hand to her. "I'm sorry."

She blinked at him for ten seconds before she understood. With a little cry, she jumped up from the chair and ran into his arms.

She was still sobbing on his shoulder, and he was patting her on the back and muttering soothing noises, when a great rush of wind nearly knocked him over. He and his mother staggered across the room, turned, and Philippe could hardly believe his eyes when D. A. Bologh, Heather still gripped in his clasp, hurtled through the window.

Yvonne gasped.

Philippe practically pushed his mother away in his eagerness to get to Heather, who met him halfway and crashed into him. He wrapped his arms around her, buried his face in her hair, and whispered, "You're back. God, Heather, I thought I'd lost you."

"I know. I thought so, too." Heather seemed to be trying not to cry.

"I love you, Heather. I love you so damned much. When I thought you were gone, I knew what a fool I'd been not to tell you sooner."

She pulled away from him far enough so that she could stare up into his eyes. "You love me? Really?"

D. A. muttered, "Tripe."

Philippe managed what was probably a very crooked smile. "You're the first and only woman I've ever loved."

"Oh, Philippe." She sank against him for only a second before she pulled away again. "But we're not safe yet."

"That's right," put in D. A. "Let's get on with it, shall we? I'm finding this reunion a bit sickening."

"You're a fiend, D. A. Bologh," said Yvonne, who'd recovered some of her composure.

"Trite tripe," grumbled D. A. He glanced at the watch on the mantel. "You've got a half hour, Heather, my sweet. Get at it. I want to get you away from here as soon as may be."

"You're not taking her again," declared Philippe, tightening his hold on her.

D. A. sneered magnificently. "Oh? And who's going to stop me? You, rubber legs?"

Dammit, the devil was right.

His own choice of words gave Philippe pause. He glanced down at Heather. "What was it you said earlier, Heather? About my admitting or confessing something?"

She wiped tears from her cheeks and nodded. "Yes. The bargain D. A. finally struck with me—after he'd refused to tell me his terms for so long—"

"Get on with it!" snapped D. A., stamping a cloven hoof. "There's no need to go into all of these piddling details."

"He's a devil, Philippe," Yvonne told her son softly. "I sold my soul to him so that I could keep you with me when you were born. Now he's hoping to complete the ruin of my life—and yours—by taking Heather away from you. Because you love her. He wouldn't settle for taking just anyone." Her voice reeked with bitterness. "He only takes a person's most cherished loves."

"There's no point to it otherwise," D. A. muttered.

"Ah," said Philippe.

"You see," said Heather, "I had to figure out who he was, and then I had to convince you that he is who he is. That was the deal. I met Yvonne in town, and she told me who he was." She spared a glower for D. A. "That was the easy part. I already knew him for a devil."

She sucked in a deep breath. Philippe realized she was going to say something she didn't want to say and hugged her hard. "If we win, Philippe, there's something else you need to know."

"What's that?"

"This is *so* boring" taunted D. A.

"It's your mother."

"No, Heather," Yvonne broke in. "That doesn't matter. Nothing matters but the two of you."

Philippe looked at his mother, puzzled by the expression of fear on her face.

Heather shook her head. "No, Yvonne, it is important." She tilted her head to peer up at Philippe again. "You see, if we win this battle with D. A. Bologh tonight, Yvonne will lose, too. She bargained for eternal youth and beauty, and that bargain will be canceled."

"I don't care!" cried Yvonne, wringing her hands. "Youth and beauty don't mean a thing compared to the happiness of my only son!"

Philippe could scarcely believe his ears. His eyes, however, didn't deceive him. Yvonne meant what she'd said. He couldn't force words out of his mouth.

Heather continued. "Anyway, it was Yvonne who told me who D. A. really was. I wasn't surprised, as I'd pretty much figured it out for myself by then. Yvonne and I both knew that the hard part would be convincing you."

"You both know me," Philippe murmured, feeling ashamed of himself.

"I guess." Heather shrugged. "At any rate, those were the terms of the bargain." She peered up into his face, and he saw the love in her eyes. "So, it's up to you."

He shut his eyes for a second, marveling at the possibilities in life. He'd never believed in second chances before, but he'd been given a second chance. And he wasn't about to hash it up again.

"Yes, I'm absolutely convinced D. A. Bologh is the devil. And I want him out of my house and my life and your life and my mother's life. Now."

D. A. stared at the scene before him for only a second or two before he uttered a terrible howl, sent up a ghastly screen of smoke that stank of brimstone and sulfur, rocketed around the room three times, and vanished through the window, leaving the library in ruins and the three people in it huddled together.

Silence, as deep as the night sky, descended on them as quickly as had the storm engendered by D. A.'s passing. Philippe opened his eyes slowly, afraid of what he might find—or of what he might not find. He felt Heather in his arms, but that might be an illusion.

It wasn't. When he realized she was still there and he still held her, he let out an involuntary and inarticulate cry of joy and kissed her passionately. She kissed him back just as passionately. The kiss went on for seconds that felt like hours, and Philippe's heart rose higher and higher, as if it were being transported to heaven on clouds of happiness. He couldn't recall another single time in his life when he'd felt so free, so unencumbered by the bonds of worry, responsibility, and the memories of his past. They were bonds he'd forged by himself for himself, and they snapped now as if they'd been crafted of mere twigs.

Heather finally broke the embrace. Philippe didn't want her to and tried to prevent her, but she insisted. "No, Philippe. We have to make sure Yvonne's all right."

Oh, damn. That's right. His mother. He heaved a huge sigh and, still holding Heather for fear she might slip away if he wasn't careful, he turned toward where he'd last seen Yvonne. She was still there, still sitting hunched over in a chair that was much too big for her. Her hands covered her face. Philippe studied her curiously, wondering what was going to happen now that Yvonne was no longer governed by a devil's bargain.

Heather said softly, "Yvonne? Are you all right?" She made as if to go to her, but Philippe wouldn't let her go, so she had to walk with him. He wasn't sure he wanted to see what had become of his mother. It would be a shock to see the woman look her age. Philippe didn't even know what that age was.

With what appeared to be extreme reluctance, Yvonne slowly let her hands fall into her lap, exposing her face.

Heather cried, "Why, you don't look any different at all!"

She didn't. Philippe squinted hard, but he didn't detect an iota of difference in his mother's appearance. She still looked younger than he was.

Yvonne stared incredulously at Heather and Philippe. "I don't?"

Philippe shrugged. "No. You look just the same as ever."

"Good heavens." Yvonne stood, swaying slightly, from which Philippe deduced she'd been as affected by recent events as he'd been. She tottered to the door, opened it, and went into the hall, aiming, Philippe imagined, for the mirror on the wall.

Heather peered up at him. "Do you think we should follow her?"

"I—I suppose so." It came as a huge surprise to him to learn that he cared what his poor mother was going through. He didn't feel an ounce of disdain in his heart for the poor woman who'd given up everything for the one commodity she possessed that she knew was worth something to her: beauty. And now her beauty was in jeopardy. He realized he felt an odd combination of pity and affection for his mother, and walked with Heather out into the hall.

Yvonne was there, leaning toward the mirror, and feeling her face with her hands. She glanced at Heather and Philippe out of the corner of her eye. "I—I guess it's going to happen gradually."

"It must be going to happen gradually," agreed Heather. "It sure hasn't happened yet."

Philippe felt the strangest compulsion he'd ever felt in his life. He smiled at his mother and, taking Heather with him, went up to her and drew her into his embrace. Yvonne buried her head against his shoulder and wept.

Heather, recognizing a scene of reconciliation when she saw one and, Philippe imagined, deeply touched by it, cried onto his other shoulder.

He'd never been happier in his life.

Eventually, they settled Yvonne into a bedroom upstairs and down the hall from Philippe's, right next door to the one in which Jimmy slept. Philippe didn't give a thought to proprieties or Mrs. Van der Linden when he took Heather to his own room. He'd be damned—no. He didn't think he'd better use that expression anymore—he'd not allow her to sleep away from him again, ever, if he could help it.

He felt free tonight; free from old worries and hates; free to love for the first time. He loved Heather. He loved his mother. He no longer had the least desire to punish her by proving himself. He didn't care what anyone thought of him—except Heather. He cared a great deal what she thought of him.

He took her in his arms as soon as the door closed behind them. "I love you, Heather."

"I love you, Philippe."

Very tenderly, he helped her undress. "You're so beautiful," he murmured against her softly rounded belly.

She gave a low, soft laugh that sounded like music to his ears. "Beauty's in the eye of the beholder. I'm glad you think I'm beautiful. I can't hold a candle to your mother."

He shook his head, and pressed his cheek against her warm flesh. One of these days, a child of his would be nurtured in there; his heart swelled when he thought about it. "You're the most beautiful woman in the world to me."

She sighed happily. "I'm glad."

They made slow, beautiful love. Philippe stroked Heather to fulfillment before he entered her. He wanted to make the night last. It had already been the most important night of his life; he wanted to extend it for as long as he could. He knew he'd cherish the memory forever.

Her skin was as soft as silk and as smooth as satin. Her every reaction to his touch was heaven to him. And, as much as he tried to prolong the moment, his passion carried him away, and he achieved release sooner than he wanted to, although he took Heather with him.

After he caught his breath, he whispered, "I wanted it to last longer."

"It was perfect," she said, on a long, replete sigh.

"I should have made it last longer."

She was silent for a moment. When she spoke again, he heard a distinct smile in her voice. "Well, then, I reckon we'll just have to do it until we get it right."

They did.

Chapter Twenty-one

Yvonne's appearance didn't change overnight. She talked to Heather about it a lot, fearing she'd become an old hag in no time at all. Heather didn't believe it.

"You're too beautiful ever to be an old hag. Shoot, Yvonne, you'll be beautiful when you're ninety."

Yvonne, whipping egg whites into froth for the soufflé she was preparing for breakfast—she was as accomplished a French chef as D. A. Bologh, although it took her longer to do things since she didn't have any unearthly help—frowned. "No woman is beautiful when she's ninety."

"Fiddlesticks. *You* will be." Heather, who was no slouch in the kitchen herself—wonder of wonders—opened the oven door to check on the Potatoes Lyonnaise.

Heather was right. Eventually, Yvonne began to

show her years, but she never, ever, once, looked anything but beautiful—even when she got to be ninety. By that time, she was universally acknowledged to be the most beautiful grandmother in the territory.

Philippe and Heather's first son was born in May of 1897. That spring had been kind to the territory. The winds, which always blew in the springtime, didn't rip any roofs away or tear any fences down, and the town of Fort Summers, situated next to the fort that had protected that end of the territory for decades, prospered.

Philippe's ranch prospered, too, much to the town's delight. The entire population accepted Yvonne St. Pierre as Philippe's long-lost and much-admired mother. Not even Mrs. Van der Linden's dark tales of mysterious doings at the ranch on a certain night dampened the town's enthusiasm for the St. Pierre family.

Yvonne discovered she didn't mind looking her age. She also discovered that grandchildren were perhaps the greatest blessing in a woman's life.

It was a good thing, too, since she eventually had a whole flock of them.

Heather, who'd had her doubts earlier in life, forever after that blustery spring of 1895, adored the wind.

A
GAMBLER'S
MAGIC
EMMA CRAIG